D1646596

HYMNS TO THE ANCIENT GODS

Michael Harding began studying astrology in 1979 and has been a full-time astrological consultant since 1983. A former chairman of the Astrological Association, he now chairs the Association of Professional Astrologers and is also on the councils of the Faculty of Astrological Studies and the Society for Existential Analysis.

He has run experiental workshops in England and abroad, teaches astrological techniques for the Faculty of Astrological Studies and runs a course on the existential approach to counselling for the School of Psychotherapy and Counselling at Regents College in London.

He is co-author, with Charles Harvey, of *Working with Astrology* (Arkana, 1990) and is a frequent contributor to the *Astrological Association Journal*.

CONTEMPORARY ASTROLOGY
Series Editor: Erin Sullivan

Hymns to the Ancient Gods

✷ ✷ ✷ ✷ ✷ ✷ ✷ ✷ ✷

Michael Harding

ARKANA

ARKANA

Published by the Penguin Group
Penguin Books Ltd, 27 Wrights Lane, London w8 5tz, England
Penguin Books USA Inc., 375 Hudson Street, New York, New York 10014, USA
Penguin Books Australia Ltd, Ringwood, Victoria, Australia
Penguin Books Canada Ltd, 10 Alcorn Avenue, Toronto, Ontario, Canada m4v 3b2
Penguin Books (NZ) Ltd, 182–190 Wairau Road, Auckland 10, New Zealand

Penguin Books Ltd, Registered Offices: Harmondsworth, Middlesex, England

First published 1992
1 3 5 7 9 10 8 6 4 2

Filmset in Monophoto Sabon

Printed in England by Clays Ltd, St Ives plc

This book is dedicated to
E.K.L.
with great affection

Contents

* * * * * * * * * *

Acknowledgements   viii

Introduction   1

1. Shrinking the World: Astrology and Psychotherapy   5
2. Time and Time Again: Re-thinking Synchronicity   23
3. The Selective Unconscious: Archetype, Race and Illusion   42
4. Alternative Archetypes   60
5. Interpreting the Unconscious: Astrology and the Primal Zodiac   88
6. The Cosmic Womb   112
7. Life Sentences: Symbol, Cycle and Language   135
8. The Quintessence of Creation: Sex, Language and the 5th Harmonic   166
9. A Degree of Meaning: A Case Study of Saturn and Neptune   207
10. Case Studies: Triggering Our Memories   236
11. Case Studies: Patterns in Family Charts   262
12. The House of Ill-repute   290
13. Life, the Universe and Everything   319

Appendix 1: A Brief Introduction to Midpoints   342

Appendix 2: Chart Data   347

Appendix 3: Addresses for Further Information   349

References   352

Index   359

Acknowledgements

I would like to thank Babs Kirby, Percy Seymour, Sue Tompkins and Gaila Yariv for comments and observations made during various stages of the manuscript's evolution. I would also like to thank those clients and colleagues who gave me permission to use examples of astrology at work in their own lives; thanks, too, to Steve Eddy for his contribution of the Cave Divers charts referred to in Chapter 9.

I would also like to thank Babs Kirby for permission to use extracts from her 1989 Astrological Association talk, Dr Paul Kugler for permission to quote extensively from *The Alchemy of Discourse*, and Marjorie Wallace for permission to quote from *The Silent Twins*, published by Chatto & Windus.

Many thanks to Robin Waterfield for his help with the initial structuring of this book, and particularly to Erin Sullivan for all her help, encouragement and comments during its writing and editing.

Finally, I would like to thank my wife Judith for drawing the charts, for her reserves of patience and humour, and for all the cups of tea.

Introduction

* * * * * * * * *

The mischievous might suggest that one of the reasons this book came to be written is that the letter A comes before S.

This may need some explanation.

During the 1970s I was attached to the occupational therapy department of a London hospital; part of my job involved running work-groups at the hospital's psychiatric day centre. At this time I was coming towards the end of what was to be a twelve-year analysis, and saw my future lying in some area of psychotherapy.

Someone attending the day centre – I was never quite certain who – had embellished one of the hospital's exterior walls with the signs of the zodiac in red paint, adding the message 'Our Destiny is Controlled by Unseen Forces' in a firm hand, no doubt for the benefit of any who might have missed the point. Some of the staff considered that this statement was open to interpretation under a variety of transference theories, others believed it was a reference to the hospital's Management Committee.

Those attending the day centre offered their own thoughts on the nature of exterior control from time to time, often during the Large Group meetings. These observations ranged from mundane but important issues such as how the late or early arrival of lunches completely destroyed intricate therapy timetables, to exotically paranoid visions of unseen forces at work that were breathtaking in their ingenuity.

In truth, these two polarities were often entwined. The kitchen staff were notoriously retentive of their bounty, and frequently sent over too few lunches. To compensate for this we ordered more than we needed. The kitchen staff, however, had suspected that we were doing this all along, and began sending over fewer than ever, thereby forcing us to increase the proportion of non-existent patients requiring nourishment, to ensure that those who *were* there got fed. As several of those who attended had to be routinely discouraged from communicating with non-existent people, the fact that the staff were now apparently ordering lunches for them was an irony that they generously overlooked.

It was during this period, immediately following the activities of the cosmic vandal, that I decided to do a course in stained glass.

The astrologically astute will have already spotted the similarity between the nature of my intended course and astrology. Glass is a Uranian substance; to cut it, a Uranian activity. A piece of stained glass represents an intricate series of patterns, held in place with Saturnine strips of lead, and decipherable only as a whole. As a subject, it appears under 'S'.

In the guidebook I was using to locate my class my eye first fell on 'A' – and there was Astrology.

Astrology had previously nudged itself in and out of my life on a few occasions, prior to it catching my attention that day, but I had never before taken the bait. For instance, my mother had been a keen believer in it, and had even had my own chart calculated, but I never paid it much heed. As a child I had considered that astrology was just one of the many daft and pointless activities that adults were prone to embark on. Much later on, and many years before starting to take any interest in astrology myself, I had briefly met Charles Harvey, via a friend of his who worked with me at a theatre I was then managing.

(Yes, I do have the dates; and, yes, they do.)

But it was not until I caught sight of Astrology as a subject to be studied that I gave it any thought. It was then that I decided to go along to see if it would throw any light on the message left on the hospital wall. After all, there was a chance it might be *true*.

To a large extent this book is an attempt to clarify some of what astrology has come to mean for me since that day, as well as to make at least one or two practical suggestions as to how its symbolism might be applied in specific circumstances. Writing it has been akin to stopping and taking stock of a situation during some long journey; I am well aware that the view may change further along the trail.

The German philosopher Martin Heidegger often used the image of ideas as 'paths through the forest', thus not to be read as completed or finite statements. Such an image also applies here; the way I work with astrology is to see it as a method for exploring the nature of our experience, and for providing a context in which these experiences may become more comprehensible. As experience is limitless, we shall never be able to draw a final line around it, and define it thus.

We may get closer to understanding astrology's processes along the way, but I am very aware that any attempt to describe them is going to miss as many points as they might come close to touching. In this book I am concentrating only on some very basic issues which revolve around one of today's main astrological concerns: the possible relationship between astrology and depth psychology.

In writing this book I was constantly aware that time and time again I was touching on one issue or another which needed a chapter, if not a *book* on its own; for all the obvious reasons this is not possible, and much that is clearly of great importance has been seriously short-changed.

The book itself has many roots, and quite a few go back a long way, via philosophy and psychology, to link into areas which concerned me long before I became involved in astrology at all. Some of these concerns revolve around issues of how consciousness is portrayed or described, which, by and large, have been ignored by both psychology and astrology equally. These can lead to some conclusions which may not appeal to everyone.

In learning astrology I was fortunate enough to study under Charles Harvey, and at a time when John Addey was still able to lecture for the Faculty. The approach to chart analysis that emerged from their teaching has formed the basis of much of my work, and I am greatly in debt to it, and to them. Thus there is an irony that many of the ideas put forward here are in some contradiction to the Platonic ideals that have illuminated and inspired the work of these two, considerable, astrologers.

This fact caused me some unease during the writing of several sections of the book, but to some extent such a shift of orientation was inevitable. One of the factors that generated much of the content of those chapters is that I do not believe that either the philosophy or the psychology yet exists to match the complexity and grandeur of the view that emerges as we begin to absorb the implications of astrology.

Despite its venerable age, astrology has yet to find its voice in the world. It has lain at the crossroads of so many ideas, and though it may have the potential to signpost them all, in practice it has tended to take on the language of the last traveller.

Again and again astrology is described in the words of others; laid against this discipline or that theory to see how it might measure up, somehow always to be found wanting, and reluctantly or triumphantly set aside. Currently it is being stretched out on the analyst's couch, once again to check the closeness of fit.

While this was initially seen as a most promising development, there are some growing doubts that it will ever respond to such treatment, and this may have more to do with the underlying assumptions of *psychology* than may at first be apparent. There is no doubt that astrology has an enormous amount to offer those interested in the complexities of human behaviour, but to be effective in the world astrology may have to develop more clearly its own method of analysis, and its own coherent philosophy.

This book is an attempt to take at least a few steps in that direction, wherever it ultimately may turn out to be.

27 October 1990
9:56 BST

I.

Shrinking the World:
Astrology and Psychotherapy

* * * * * * * * * *

According to the *American Journal of Psychiatry* there were some 400 different schools of psychotherapy existing at the beginning of 1989. Nothing is so diverse, or fragments so quickly, as endeavours to trap and order the human mind in an attempt to explore its workings and explain its mysteries. However the snares are laid, and whatever the bold claims for scientific objectivity, the *mind* is not a medical matter but a philosophical construction, unobservable through any instrument, accessible only to introspection.

Any school of psychology that moves one iota from examining the purely biological and chemical constructions of the physical brain has taken a massive step away from science. The insecurity felt in facing that sudden darkness is reflected in the desperate calls so many make to the claim of rationality. From the time of Freud and Jung the justification of science has been called down upon a myriad psychologies that in virtually no way whatsoever can be thought of as having a basis in the mechanical physics of our world. Concepts of consciousness, identity, morality and – above all – the unconscious cannot be explored by science; a fact borne out by the few schools that *do* adhere to cerebral mechanics and its attendant determinism, and consequently deny the existence of these central analytic concepts altogether.

A cursory glance at the literature will show us – if we *need* to be shown – that the human race is perpetually returning to analyse the origins of its existence. As astrologers, we too continually reinterpret what we experience of ourselves in the light of what we believe is going on around us. Considering that the vast majority of astrologers are quite unmoved by the demands of science, it is ironic that our attempts to understand the nature of our world have a claim on objectivity unmatched by any branch of mechanistic psychology. We believe that somehow or other the planets affect or influence us, or are a mirror of our experiences, and that these planets have *specific* meanings. These meanings are quite *independent* of us and would exist just as strongly if the whole human race were to vanish overnight.

Unlike the archetypes of depth psychology, the principles of astrology do not owe their existence to *us* but work *through* us in some manner, as they work through *all* aspects of nature, animate and inanimate. Insomuch as we do not know *how* they work, then whatever processes do take place must be considered unknown or *unconscious*. If we acknowledge this probability or question what such unconscious processes might be, we suddenly find ourselves sharing common ground, perhaps uneasily, with a significant number of psychologists.

Central to virtually all forms of introspective psychology is the concept of the unconscious. It may be personal and purely instinctual, connecting us to our animal past, or collective and numinous, forging a link with the divine. It may be psychic, genetic or morphogenetic but it is *there*, and we shall not learn about it from a dictionary. The unconscious cannot really be described by any concise definition, but only hinted at by that which it is *not*. Perhaps Freud was closest to it when he suggested that the unconscious is simply everything that is not conscious; a view substantially endorsed by Jung.

If this view is correct, the unconscious would then comprise everything we do not know, do not recognize, cannot see, will not comprehend, cannot feel and do not understand. It contains all the words, sounds, touches, feelings and emotions we have ever experienced. It stores the unspoken opposition to all our actions; it contains the truth of all our lies, evasions, denials and betrayals. It haunts us, accuses us, helps us, protects us, absolves us or drives us mad. It is something we cannot see by looking at, but only divine by where it once was. In searching for it we walk as in a children's game, constantly sensing the imminence of capricious energy just behind us; but when we turn, find everything suddenly still and holding secrets in tight hands.

We live through the unconscious and it lives through us. It connects us to the human condition, it separates us from our closest kin. It can be both an answer and an excuse and we make a terrible mistake if we think we know what it might be. Yet we have to ask, if only to remind ourselves that the concept of the unconscious has not been with us for long, and that everything we believe it might be might turn out to be nothing more than what we might believe it to be.

The concept of the unconscious emerged from the battle between religion and rationalism, and in many respects it emerged from a literal battle between two men, a preacher called Johann Gassner and Dr Anton Mesmer, the founder of what has since become known as hypnotherapy.

Before the middle of the eighteenth century, concepts of the unconscious appear as fragmentary as our attempts to define it now. The Italian philosopher Vico suggested that perceptions and beliefs could exist communally in what he described as a 'common sense'; such beliefs would be primitive and unconsidered, and shared by all. Vico also believed that certain aspects of language were held universally at a common level and were a measure of human evolution; a clear precursor of psycho-linguistics, to which we shall return later. Poets and writers, of course, had long held that inspiration came from unknown depths, as did the source of dreams. Religious philosophers described similar depths of the soul which united all humanity with God; other civilizations saw 'soul worlds' which lay behind sleep or could be contacted through ritual or drugs. But it would appear that until there came a need to define certain human experiences in quasi-rational terms rather than the religious or the romantic, such all-embracing images served humanity well enough. As rationalist concepts began to spread through Europe, the need to describe and re-define human behaviour took form in a variety of men who were exploring the boundaries of their experience from philosophical or humanitarian points of view. One of those was Anton Mesmer.

Mesmer was born in Germany on 23 May 1734. He trained as a doctor and his dissertation was on astrology and human diseases.

He used astrology extensively to treat his patients, making detailed studies of planetary cycles and the recurrences of ailments. Following reports he had read, Mesmer began to experiment with magnets and on 28 July 1774 achieved what he believed to be a profound breakthrough when a seemingly miraculous cure took place. His researches led him to believe that some form of animal magnetic power existed within all humans in the form of a 'universal fluid'. This fluid was affected by the positions of the planets and this could be the source of disease. The cure lay in manipulating the magnetic fluid through what we would now call suggestion or hypnotism.

He worked by inducing 'crises' within his patients, often causing them to have some sort of fit, after which they frequently lost their symptoms. Mesmer's patients in the main seemed to fall into the category of hysterics, and the fits or crises he induced seem very similar to the cathartic release of abreaction techniques which make use of CO_2 gas or the so-called 'truth drug', sodium pentathol. His success attracted the attention of Johann Gassner, who was an exorcist.

In many respects Mesmer was a threat to Gassner, as his concept of animal magnetism as the core of human energy, whose manipulation can bring health, clearly runs counter to the traditional religious doctrine of possession by devils. Mesmer responded to Gassner's criticisms by suggesting that the priest was – unknowingly – using the principles of animal magnetism to cure those he believed to be possessed. This not only comes very close to a therapeutic interpretation, it also ensured that Gassner challenged Mesmer to a 'duel'. The fame of both men was such that Max Joseph of Bavaria appointed a commission to oversee both men's work, and on 23 November 1775 Mesmer began to demonstrate his technique before the Imperial Court. Mesmer's results so impressed the Court that they were convinced that *his* was the correct approach to healing.

Thus the religious attitude had been overruled by one based on dynamics inherent in the human psyche, and Gassner and his church supporters fell from grace. In his masterly book *The Dis-*

covery of the Unconscious, Henri Ellenburger writes of this day as 'the fatal turning point from exorcism to dynamic psychotherapy'.[1] Mesmer's work revealed a complex web of psychic energy operating within the individual, hidden from normal view. Illnesses could be switched on or off at will, forgotten memories could be recalled, cures could be effected from the discharge of released emotions, and separate personalities could now emerge telling tales no one had heard before. The stage had been set for the arrival of the analytical therapies needed to explore systematically these new realms.

While Mesmer himself was later to fall victim to the plots and intrigues of French society, his development of therapeutic hypnotism began to reveal deeper layers to the human psyche and forced the minds of the day to rethink their concepts of consciousness. The work of Charcot, Janet, Bleur, Breuer, and Freud can be traced back *directly* to Mesmer's discoveries, as Ellenburger's *Discovery of the Unconscious* clearly demonstrates.

Thus it is not inappropriate to remind ourselves that the foundation stone of modern psychotherapy was laid by a practising astrologer.

Those astrologers who *today* work in the area of counselling or therapy have to try to reconcile current concepts of psychodynamics with their own experiences as astrologers. These therapeutic concepts invariably assume a relatively linear development of the personality. The infant comes into the world and at once the world – generally through the medium of its parents – begins to impose a variety of experiences which constellate within the child and get re-expressed in several forms during the course of life. Some schools would claim that *all* behaviour is a repetition of early experiences, without exception; others would take a more generous view. Neither case comes anywhere near to approximating the complex world-view held by astrology, and there is a real danger that the therapeutic potential of astrology is limited by an unspoken need to conform with accepted personality theories. Even attempting to reconcile such simple concepts as the four elements with Jung's four functional types reveals immediate discrepancies which can be resolved only at a cost to one or the other system.

There can also be somewhat arbitrary connections, such as equating the Ascendant with the Persona. In Jungian terms the Persona has a compensatory relationship with the Anima/Animus, which can result in it becoming a rigid 'face' with which to cope with the issues of the world. This may well be so; but there is no evidence that the Ascendant alone fulfils that function in the birth chart; our habits in responding to the demands of life come from several sources. In dealing with a presumed need to keep the world at a distance and make a 'proper impression on others' as Jung suggests,[2] we may find a number of variables within the chart that perform this task equally effectively. To link the Persona to the Ascendant so hastily can act as a brake to the unravelling of astrology's own inner dynamics.

However understandable this need to relate astrology to more acceptable models might be, it may nevertheless be more useful to suggest that we begin to turn the problem around and ask what *astrologers* would demand of such a theory. What would the unconscious look like from a purely *astrological* point of view, and how would we recognize its expression in the world?

The possible advantage of this approach is that ideas about the unconscious will emerge from our *experience* rather than a choice to adopt or adapt a particular existing model. To be told that Freud saw the libido as primarily sexual while Jung saw it as the 'life-force' is not particularly helpful, especially as we know that other schools hold still different views and some deny the libido altogether.

To trawl through such theories is certainly a useful exercise from an educational point of view, but we still come back to the issue of *Freud* saying this, *Jung* saying that and the hosts of their descendants amplifying the innumerable permutations of the initial schism. We need to discover what *astrology* might say and explore the concepts of others only when we believe that they might be obliquely and unknowingly picking up astrological information, such as in the case of Jung's theory of the archetypes. It is also important that we recognize the natural divide that exists between psychology and *psychotherapy*; to formulate or perceive an approach is by no means the same as to apply it.

The techniques or attitudes adopted by therapists and counsellors should not be confused with the *substance* of their particular school. Those holding very different theoretical models may nevertheless approach their clients in very similar ways, and the following chapters are an attempt more to evaluate some of the underlying concepts of psychotherapy rather than their methods of practical implementation. These methods can be thought of as part of 'process', and some ways of considering process from an astrological point of view will be discussed in the final chapter.

However, there is one overriding reason for suggesting that astrologers should themselves formulate what they believe to be taking place within the individual and the world, so that they can work towards creating a coherent astrological understanding of the psyche.

That reason is quite simple: conventional psychotherapy as a curative process cannot be demonstrated to work.

The concept of an analysis as a method of bringing about a *cure* through the process of verbalization is one of today's popular misconceptions. It is important to recognize that the vast majority of those in a full, formal analysis are themselves analysts-in-training and are paradoxically the least able to assess their situation objectively. Theirs is a closed loop where status and job prospects can only reinforce the intellectual conviction that attracted them to the theoretical framework in the first place. No one enters a training analysis to question the efficacy of the process or its theoretical underpinning; the cost – in all senses of the word – is too high and any overly successful querents would be out of a job. A deselection that would probably be rationalized by the training analyst through the use of resistance theories.

With the exception of status and job prospects, this situation has some strong parallels with the process of becoming a professional astrologer. While professional astrologers are happy to argue about the merits of various techniques (as do psycho-analysts), they are most unlikely to question whether or not as-trology works at all. They share with psychoanalysts a dislike of questioning whether they and their clients are participating in a shared illusion, no matter how many times this has been suggested of both professions by outside observers.

When the claims of psychoanalysis and other psychotherapies are investigated they reveal a lamentable performance. After the extensive testing of a variety of analytic and psychotherapeutic claims, including the assessment of over 7,000 patients from both private and hospital practices, Eysenck and Wilson conclude, 'The figures fail to support the hypothesis that psychotherapy facilitates recovery from neurotic disorder.' Eysenck himself is harsher still with Freud: 'his place is not, as he claims, with Copernicus and Darwin, but with Hans Andersen and the Brothers Grimm, tellers of fairy tales'.[3]

However harsh this may sound – and the criticism could be applied equally to any one of psychotherapy's founders – we have to recognize that the originators of introspective psychotherapy actually asked for their ideas to be submitted to precisely such an objective analysis. Virtually *all* the therapies which emerged from psychoanalysis were developed to *cure ordinary neurotics of their symptoms*. They were developed for the *treatment* of depression, anxiety, obsessions, phobias, frigidity, impotence, hysteria, com-pulsions and a host of similar conditions. Freud said this was the case, Jung said this was the case, virtually all of their disciples throughout the middle of this century said this was the case, a very few are *still* saying this is the case. But as a cure for neurosis orthodox psychotherapy is *still* not working, and it is dem-onstrably not working.

It is worth noting that, following the publication of such critical findings, the American Institute of Psychoanalysis conducted its own research in an endeavour to counter the charges levelled against it. The findings of their own survey were so poor that they were never published.[4]

There can be little doubt that each of the 400 therapies mentioned at the beginning of this chapter came into being because their originators believed that all the rest were substantially ineffective and that only their new approach would work. It hasn't and it doesn't. Psychotherapy, on the whole, *still* does not work, and there is not the slightest indication that its medically orientated, psycho-diagnostical approach ever will.

The concept of 'curing' people and 'making them better' by applying a 'treatment' based on a variety of theories which claim an objective reality which they have singularly failed to demonstrate is perhaps not the best approach for astrologers to emulate.

At this point we must recognize that many people *do* report clear benefits from undertaking some form of therapy and that others enter analysis for very complex reasons. We cannot easily quantify a subsequent shift of awareness, cannot graph out a sense of purpose regained, or plot precisely how indefinable inner connections can become established as a source of creativity. We must also recognize that this shift of emphasis away from 'cure' and 'treatment' towards 'exploration' and 'growth' is comparatively modern, and to some extent came about following the publication of Eysenck and Wilson's researches.

Since the early 1970s there has been an upsurge of interest in the Humanistic schools of therapy, which are less goal-orientated (in the traditional sense) and are concerned more with exploring the potential of the human being than with ascribing diagnostic labels. Their emphasis is generally to facilitate growth and change within the individual and to encourage a greater sensitivity towards life, both inner and outer. While such an approach towards wholeness and integration has a natural affinity with much of astrology, we must not forget that much of Humanistic therapy emerged as a reaction to the failure or shortcomings of traditional psychotherapy, and for the most part it has yet to develop a coherent philosophy of its own.

The philosophical factor is extremely important, as it marks the historical divide between those therapists who viewed the person in mechanistic terms, and those whose approach was essentially spiritual. Only those existential schools that emerged from

Freudianism via Ludwig Binswanger's *Daseinanalysis* do not explore the psyche primarily from the perspective of seeking a cure, because their model is *philosophical* rather than medical, and there is a total rejection of viewing the human being in terms of *any* psycho-dynamic theory. Much of Humanistic psychology has been touched by such phenomenological or existential thought, and it has also surfaced in the work of some current psychoanalysts.

It is almost impossible to read the work of a small minority of 'traditional' Freudian analysts – who have returned, perhaps via Jaques Lacan, to the analysis of the unconscious rather than ego-defences – and not be left with the impression that it is not *therapy* which is being described, but a mystical process of infinite subtlety and wonder. Such encounters with the unseen dimensions of existence – wherever they occur – may ultimately prove more genuinely therapeutic than the processes and theories which engendered their initial experience.

As far as other schools are concerned, it is certainly true that Jung adopted a quasi-philosophical approach to certain aspects of the psyche, and wrote extensively about neurosis in a mystical manner which dramatically downplayed the emphasis on treatment and cure. His espousal of the alchemical process as a symbol of individuation is a clear example of this, or as clear as Jung ever gets when writing of these matters. Nevertheless, it is also obvious from his later writings that he is still using the medical model and his disciples go to some lengths to describe Jungian analytical psychology as a modern science, choosing that actual expression as a book title.[5]

Despite their dependence on the medical model, there is no doubt that for a very long time psychotherapists have recognized that the reality of introspective psychotherapy has fallen far short of early expectations. The fact that certain supposed 'cures' were not taking place was already emerging in Freud's time. Initially it was felt that this was due to a lack of the 'proper techniques' being applied or, as far as America was concerned, it was seen as the result of cutting down on the total analytic time. Neither suggestion was ever really convincing and we currently face a situation where *post facto* rationalizations have moved the therapeutic goalposts so often to catch the drift of the prevailing winds that the majority of players now concentrate more on observing the game than bothering too much about where the ball goes. True, the minutiae of its motion are earnestly recorded in learned journals, but few are unsporting enough to point out that this is more for the benefit of the crowds than the players.

Even those psychotherapists whose views have been fundamentally at odds with the mainstream therapeutic procedures have had to confront psychotherapy's failure. During 1965–8 R. D. Laing, David Cooper, Aaron Esterson and others set up a therapeutic community, Kingsley Hall, which allowed its members to live together and work through their psychotic or schizophrenic episodes. This was an approach to healing that emerged out of Laing and Cooper's rejection of the often brutal physical treatment of mental disturbances in large state hospitals. A former resident at Kingsley Hall describes that the community was:

a link in the chain of counter-culture centres. Experimental drama groups, social scientists of the New Left, classes from the Antiuniversity of London, leaders of the commune movement and *avant-garde* poets, artists, musicians, dancers and photographers have met at Kingsley Hall with the residents.

The Founder members of the project ... hoped to fulfil in the community their seed-idea that lost souls may be cured by going mad among people who see madness as a chance to die and be reborn.[6]

Overall, it cannot be said that the project was a lasting success, though whether one would choose to celebrate one's rebirth in the company of a performing dance troupe, a gathering of *avant-garde* poets and an assortment of hirsute rejects from the London School of Economics is another matter.

In one of his last interviews Laing revealed an attitude towards mental suffering that was almost diametrically opposite to the 'working-through' approach he had previously facilitated: he counselled that if you *are* suffering, try and forget it.

The best way to keep depressed is to keep thinking about it. Forget it if you can. If you can't forget it then, all right, we'll have to go into it . . . I have developed the therapeutic idea that it is not necessarily a good idea . . . to adopt the policy that I'm not going to walk out of this state of affairs [depression] until I discover how I got into it . . . It does not necessarily help you to get out of it, to find out how you got into it. It might be useful, but it often isn't.[7]

During the course of the interview Laing recounted how he and a depressed patient told each other jokes, to the apparent benefit of his patient's mental state. This is remarkably similar to the well-meaning but simplistic lay advice to those so afflicted, that they should try and 'do something to get their mind off it' or even 'try to pull themselves together'.

Laing was obviously aware that simplistic homilies are, of themselves, of little use, and we now recognize that the mental condition he initially chose to focus on, schizophrenia, may well have such a strong genetic component to its aetiology as to make the 'living-through/working-through' approach quite pointless. Nevertheless we have to recognize that both the conventional and the unconventional approaches to understanding mental states have not lived up to *their own* expectations. Many experiments similar to Kingsley Hall have been tried in various countries, yet it has to be reported that neither the conservative nor the radical attitude has so far offered a systematic technique for providing a genuinely curative psychotherapy for schizophrenics, or for anyone else.

What probably keeps everyone so convinced that this goal is ultimately attainable, despite all the negative findings, contradictory theories and some downright nonsense, is that, without a doubt, *something very important is going on.* Something is taking place during the process of psychotherapy which is not part of normal experience and has defied any clear explanation as to its nature. There is no doubt that to enter into analysis is to step into another world.

The problem with this other world is that it continually folds back on itself, its undertow hauls in all that it has cast on to the shore. Nothing is available for permanent inspection, there is only the rattle of the stones being pulled to and fro, neither here, neither there, always in the process of shifting places with their identical equivalents.

It is a recursive ocean and we float in it, aware of our feelings and emotions being constantly redrawn in the light of our own recollections. Recollections that are in turn redefined by our own discoveries which are dependent on how we perceive what we recall with perceptions continuously attenuated by our own re-assessment of how we perceive all we recollect. It is a Mediter-ranean world, the tide moves neither in nor out, but the shoreline is permanently alive with our disturbance.

In it we slide backwards and forwards through time, carried by the ebb and flow of associations, slipping from the cerebral to the somatic, from intense emotion into sterile silence. Parents, friends, lovers and a host of unbidden acquaintances circle around us, forming a holding pattern of all possible relationships caught in the matrix of two people, the analyst and the client. It is a situation only in part understandable, and then only by those who have actually experienced it, and it is one capable of being viewed from an infinity of perspectives. It can provide the substance for count-less theorems but the proof of none. It is a self-evident process for those who believe that each self seeks the same evidence, but a religion, a delusion or a bought friendship for those who do not. Despite the concerted attentions of intellectuals, scientists, philoso-phers, mystics, artists, the sane, the mad and the undecided for well over half a century, there is no one who could now pick up a pen and write down for us exactly what it *is*.

Whatever astrology might have to offer, whatever possible clarification or confusion it could bring, it is against *this* back-ground that astrological practice is to be judged. We have to ask ourselves if our own attempts to explore the unconscious would fare better or worse than all that has gone before.

The vast majority of today's psychotherapists are most unlikely to suggest that what they 'do' can effect a 'cure' within an in-dividual, even if they can – and do – argue most vociferously about the most effective way it *might* be carried out if it ever *could* be done. What *is* on offer is a very wide variety of methods for exploring the dynamics of an individual's life and bringing to the surface those issues that might underpin the presenting problems. They have arrived at this position, however, not as the result of the *achievements* of psychotherapy's past, but of its *failure*. They are not in this position of semi-stalemate from choice. The majority would probably much rather be somewhere else, perhaps in a world whose inhabitants behaved in the manner described by the founders of modern psychotherapy.

What psychotherapy *does* have to offer the counselling astrologer is its very considerable expertise in understanding *process*. That is 'what goes on in people' and 'what goes on *between* people' – client and therapist included. Here, psychotherapy's record of clinical observations is impressive indeed. There is a vast catalogue of all the nuances of projection, transference, denial, displacement, conversion and what have you. There is an enormous literature on the ramifications of that essentially simple act of therapy – two people talking to each other – that offers profound insights into the mechanism of our behaviour and the intricate pathways our inner needs follow on their journeys to the surface of our lives. It is a guidebook of human behaviour and a literature of discoveries that counselling astrologers ignore at their clients' peril.

The strength of this catalogue of observed behavioural characteristics is that it accurately delineates so many of the processes of 'being human' and the manner in which humans go about their lives. Its failures are that it effectively says nothing about what 'being human' actually might mean and offers virtually no insights into what we should do about it. The intricate network of its surface-awareness rests on an almost total absence of any philosophical base. Indeed, for many psychotherapists the word 'philosophy' is met with puzzled bemusement, as if an old, battered Olivetti portable had been discovered lurking inside their word processor.

'Being human' is not a psychological condition, much less a psychiatric one: it is an existential state and it cannot be cured.

No matter how many neuroses, hang-ups or quirks we may have, the central issue of our life – *being alive* – can only be truly explored from a philosophical perspective. Any neurosis which emerges from the issue of our 'being in the world' is unlikely to be exorcized by a therapist who has not considered the implications of that state, and consequently just wishes to remove it.

It is at this point that astrology has much to offer the psychotherapist.

This is not so much for astrology's capacity to map some of the dynamics of the psyche – this comes more fully into its own as an adjunct to our understanding of *process* – it is more for initially providing a coherent framework in which to explore the *condition* of being human, the nature of 'what is going on' and 'what is being experienced', in a manner which allows for some approximation of objectivity. While fully recognizing the uniqueness of the individual, it offers the possibility for investigating what this 'nature' may be in a way that it was once hoped the unconscious, similarly probed, might reveal its own interior meaning.

Despite the imperfections of both psychological theories and astrological understanding, there are compelling reasons for bringing both disciplines closer together, though there are many who may assume that this has already been done, and that a coherent 'psychological astrology' already exists. In reality this is far from being true, however widely that term has been used.

Psychological Astrology

It does not seem possible to say exactly when the move towards 'psychological' astrology actually began, or what initially prompted this departure from tradition. Charles Carter's encyclopedia on the subject was first printed in 1924, though this is more concerned with character traits and medical conditions than with exploring specific psychological theories. In 1929 the Swiss astrologer Ernst Kraft urged that astrological symbolism be reportrayed in terms of the psychology of the modern age.[8] In this way he hoped that the practice of astrology might benefit from the advances then being made in the depth psychologies, as well as being made more accessible to those already interested in these growing disciplines.

During this same period Dane Rudyhar was beginning to bring the works of Jung to the attention of astrologers and allying both to varieties of spiritual philosophies. In Germany Witte and the Ebertins, in particular, proceeded with the approach of correlating psychological or psychosomatic issues with their astrological counterparts, and during the war years many astrologers in Europe and America were bringing together astrology with psychological and spiritual ideas. To some extent this blend appears to have supplanted some of the more esoteric attitudes previously linked to the practice of astrology. By 1950 there were clear attempts by Jungians themselves to lay claim to the planets, no doubt as a reflection of Jung's own interest in the subject.

In 1950 the Jungian journal *Spring* carried an article by Hector Hoppins on the psychology of the birth chart.[9] The author was not particularly enthusiastic about his subject; astrology was described as being 'a luxury rather than a necessity' and he doubted whether 'it can ever be a very useful tool, except in rare cases'. Nevertheless, he attempted to wed Jung's concept of the four functions to the four quadrants of the birth chart, and backed up his argument with the diurnal position of Mars in the charts of some prominent personalities, including Mussolini and Freud.

Despite his reservations about astrology's usefulness, Hoppins felt that Mars's diurnal position gave strong indications of the presumed inferior/superior functions in the two men's personalities. This research would have been more convincing if the charts he had used had been accurately cast for the correct times. In fact they were sufficiently inaccurate to render his observations meaningless.

A single failure such as this, however, is hardly the end of the matter but it did underline the growing need felt by some to connect astrology to some system which could then 'explain' it. While it is perfectly natural that a convinced Jungian should seek to explain a phenomenon that was new to him in Jungian terms, we should be wary of following suit by attempting to tack astrology on to some existing personality theory without first being certain that the theory in question is correct.

As we have seen, we have to recognize that there are no schools of depth psychology which can offer an objectively correct assessment of the human psyche, and the fact that many of their initial goals are almost certainly unreachable makes it unwise to use them as vehicles for the benefit of achieving current astrological respectability. Furthermore, as the issue of 'being human' is primarily a philosophical one, quite inaccessible to the science that allegedly underpins the major schools of analytic theory, the search may well be misdirected from the outset. The language of astrology, by its very nature, may be better suited to investigating the realms of what we call the unconscious than those tools which have emerged from a medically orientated psycho-diagnostical system.

What depth psychology *does* have to offer are a variety of theories about the development of the personality, and mechanisms for exploring and describing human interactions. These are vital areas about which astrology is virtually devoid of both theory and observation. Considering that *all* the schools of depth psychology are, in effect, theories about personality development, and gain their authority almost solely from their ability to substantiate – in their own eyes at any rate – the position they adopt, astrology is left somewhat out on a limb.

Until astrologers develop a coherent theory about the development of the personality, which can be explained in terms of astrological processes and backed up with convincing case material, then the term 'psychological astrology' will remain something of a misnomer. What we have managed to achieve so far, interesting though it may be, is woefully inadequate for the task that we seem to have set ourselves.

If we examine the attempts that we have made so far to reconcile astrology with the observations and theories of psychologists, then it would appear that the term 'psychological astrology' is applied almost exclusively to varieties of Jungian archetypal theories, and their development by others.

There could be no quarrel with this approach were it possible to demonstrate convincingly that these theories were *correct*. Indeed, were this the case then the path we have already begun to take would be the only sensible track. But it is *not* the case. Whatever we may learn from Jung – and there is much that we may want to consider – his theories have not been universally substantiated and there is a real risk that, in embracing his position, we may take on board much more than we realize.

By adopting the currency of Jung's language we buy our way into a system of thought which has implications which are not always immediately recognized by astrologers, and which contain attitudes that are not necessarily in astrology's best interests.

What *does* make Jung so immediately attractive to astrologers are almost certainly his concepts of synchronicity and archetype. These seem to share immediate affinities with astrology, but closer inspection suggests this may not really be the case. There are aspects to both of these concepts which may well run counter to some very basic astrological considerations, and this possibility has often been ignored.

In the following chapters we shall explore in some detail the substance of these two powerful ideas, as well as examining some of their less obvious implications.

2.

Time and Time Again:
Re-thinking Synchronicity

* * * * * * * * *

Many astrologers relate astrology to depth psychology via the work of Carl Jung. This is probably because so many psychologically orientated astrologers consider themselves Jungians, and even those who do not will frequently use Jungian imagery when trying to convey some aspect of astrology to someone who knows nothing of the subject. There is no doubt that Jung's language lends itself to this process of translation, and much of what he wrote has been absorbed into the public arena, albeit at a somewhat superficial level. Nevertheless, the psychological foundations that Jung lays down, even if imperfectly understood, may be seen as convenient stepping-stones for astrologers to use when taking their ideas to a wider audience. There can be a danger, however, in relying too much on another language to suit astrology's purposes, for it is very unlikely that this bridge was ever built for the traffic it is sometimes made to carry.

Linking Jung's name to astrology in the way that is so often done at once raises the question of whether or not he believed in or even used astrology himself; an issue that surfaces regularly in astrological circles. The consensus seems to be that he *did* believe in it and this assumed fact is often used to give astrology some external authority. It is as if astrologers are hoping to sneak in to some exclusive gathering by claiming they came with the man in front. All research indicates, however, that the man in front had his own invitation and our names are most definitely not on it. To avoid further social embarrassment it would be a good idea to go over what Jung has actually written on the subject.

There are many individual references to astrology in his complete works, though in the vast majority of cases this is because

23

the word *astrology* appears in a sentence such as 'astrology and alchemy are both examples of . . .'. Thus Jung's own assumptions of what astrology might be are being used to support an argument that he is putting forward; astrology itself is not specifically being commented upon.

In other cases Jung *does* comment directly on either the planets, the zodiac or the subject of astrology as a whole. He also reports the statistical results of experiments he conducted over the years with the charts of married couples. These results are then returned to on a number of occasions and portrayed in a way which is used solely to back up his own concepts of synchronicity, which, as we shall see, is itself used to explain the workings of the archetypes. The actual astrological implications are ignored, at least on a conscious level. All in all, the amount Jung specifically wrote on astrology is *not* extensive and it can all be read in a few hours. Before looking at what this writing reveals, we should first remind ourselves of what he wrote on *synchronicity*, for his views on this theory are integral to our understanding of what happens next.

Jung's Theory of Synchronicity

During the course of his life, Jung sought to develop a theory which could explain events which occurred together in time – often with dramatic consequences – but could not be related by any known causal mechanism. In fact, he came to reject completely the idea of 'cause' and espoused a non-causal, or *acausal*, connecting principle which he named 'synchronicity'.

Not surprisingly, Jung's views on synchronicity shift slightly during the course of its development, and we meet the subject in a number of different guises. Sometimes it is viewed from the point of the mystic and the symbolist, sometimes – as when Wolfgang Pauli is quoted – from the perspective of the physicist complete with diagrams relating to the laws of energy conservation within the space/time continuum. It is in the latter case that it moves a little towards being a *theory*, although, despite it often being referred to as 'Jung's theory of synchronicity', it is never developed beyond an initial outline idea. No testable hypothesis is ever proposed and it remains completely within a conceptual framework. Indeed, 'the idea of synchronicity with its inherent quality of meaning produces a picture of the world so irrepresentable as to be completely baffling'.[1]

At one level, the concept of synchronicity was arrived at to fill a gap. It is 'an intellectually necessary principle',[2] running in some way counter to the everyday rules of causality and used to define events which cannot be explained by known laws. The obvious question of whether the concept of synchronicity is the *only* principle which might account for any observed anomalies is not addressed. This omission is made even more glaring when we remind ourselves that the principles of astrology would fit the bill very nicely, but these are never alluded to even when the subject itself is discussed!

Synchronicity, as presented by Jung, is a principle that exists outside of ordinary space and time. It transcends all physical boundaries and is unconstrained by all the known laws of physics. Its motivating energy is claimed to originate in the unconscious and its purpose is to impart *meaning* to the moment. There are points in Jung's writings when he is clearly adopting a more universal, less individualistic attitude towards the function of synchronicity, but he returns again and again to his main premise: synchronistic events create individual *meaning*.

This meaning is generated by the archetypes within the unconscious at the same time as being expressed as an event in the world. When the significance of the event is recognized and its latent unconscious energy made conscious, 'its synchronistic manifestation ceases'.[3] Furthermore, 'meaning arises not from causality but from freedom, i.e., from acausality'.[4] A synchronistic event is meaningful by definition, while 'pure causality is only meaningful when used for the creation and function of an efficient instrument or machine . . . a self-running process that operates entirely by its own causality, i.e., by absolute necessity, is meaningless'.[5] A good example of a self-running process which operates entirely by its own causality is the Solar system.

If these 'meaningful coincidences in time' were proved to be operating according to some clear physical principle, such as the laws which govern planetary motion, then they would cease to be synchronistic. 'Owing to their peculiar nature . . . they [events] will hardly ever be prevailed upon to lay aside the chance character that makes them so questionable. If they did this, they would no longer be what they are – acausal, undetermined, meaningful.'[6] This, too, is a very important distinction; the collective unconscious expresses itself through synchronistic phenomena, not through the laws of Kepler and Newton. Anything operating with the precision of mechanistic science is not operating with the energy latent in the collective. Furthermore, the process of synchronicity seems to exist to bring something to the attention of an *individual*, in his or her own specific context, emanating from their own internal psychic needs at that moment.

The psychologist Marie-Louise von Franz takes up this theme and re-states the principle of synchronicity as 'a meaningful coincidence of an external event with an inner motive from dreams, fantasies or thoughts. It must concern two or more elements which cannot for an observer be connected causally, but only by their meaning.'[7] As astrology can be demonstrated to work with earthquakes, plants, chemical processes and a host of mundane events, which presumably neither dream, think nor fantasize, astrologers have to recognize the possibility of external or underlying principles at work which have nothing specifically to do with human life. But if this *is* the case, then however they operate, it will not be synchronistically.

Someone may be sitting in a library feeling compelled by their unconscious to understand a particular problem, and getting nowhere. Quite suddenly, a book falls from a stack and lies open at a particular page. On picking it up the student recognizes at once that it contains precisely the information that is being sought, but all the other readers see nothing more than someone picking up a fallen volume. The *meaning* is not universal, but related solely to the individual whose unconscious somehow precipitated the incident. Events such as these could certainly fall in with Jung's theory, though if one noted which midpoints, for instance, were being triggered off in the student's chart at the moment of realization, one might begin to suspect that even here synchronicity leaves much unanswered and unrecognized.

While synchronicity, for Jung, may have been an intellectually necessary principle, the reasoning used to justify its veracity sometimes lacked intellectual elegance. Space, Time and Causality are portrayed as the triad of classical physics,[8] to which is now added Synchronicity. Jung seems to be aware that Time cannot really be treated as a single unit any more than Space can, but chooses to ignore this irritating fact as it destroys the symbolism he is about to adopt. He is eager to get to the quarternity by adding Synchronicity. To validate this new cruciform physics he quotes an alchemical sage, Maria the Jewess – 'Out of the Third comes the One as the Fourth' – and tells us that 'this cryptic observation confirms what I have said above, that in principle new points of view are not as a rule discovered in territory that is already known, but in out-of-the-way places that may even be avoided because of their bad name'.[9]

Actually, this cryptic observation – the quote Jung used is given in full – confirms only that Jung is capable of anticipating Von Danikan's simplicities if it's all in a good cause. Much more interesting is Jung's assumption that synchronicity is to be more readily discovered in areas which lack academic respectability, such as astrology. He is clearly getting together a good excuse should he be stopped in the wrong part of town.

Jung and Astrology

To Jung, astrology is just one expression of the principle of synchronicity at work: 'astrology would be an example of synchronicity on a grand scale, if only there were enough thoroughly tested findings to support it'.[10] But the astrological images themselves have no validity apart from their role within the collective: 'these [astrological] influences are nothing but the unconscious, introspective perceptions of the activity of the collective unconscious

... projected on to the heavens'.[11] Thus astrology is, in Jung's eyes, a handmaiden of his acausal theory operating from its base in the collective. It has no objective reality and, like all symbols, no inherent meaning when taken out of its psychic context. For Jung, astrology is not related to the actual planets spinning in their mechanistic orbits; to him the planets are the mirrors of the many projections of our unconscious, and whatever power they might have is sourced there. This would have to mean that since the time of the Babylonians, and since its even more ancient Hindu beginnings, astrologers have been projecting much the same things in the same direction, their totally different cultures, ages and attitudes notwithstanding. This would be a bold assumption indeed, and one suggestive of a racial and cultural similarity that Jung categorically rejects elsewhere, as we shall see in the following chapter. Astrologers, however, would see the whole matter very differently.

Astrological symbols may *exist* within the unconscious but they are not confined to it, nor do they originate there. The symbols and energies of astrology are not *contained* within the psyche, but in some way permeate it as they permeate everything. Individuals or collectives may well project their specific astrological issues on to the heavens – or anywhere else for that matter – but for the astrologer the *sources* of the energy symbolized by the astrological icons do not lie within the unconscious, collective or otherwise. This difference should not be underestimated, for it reminds us that while the archetypes of Jung and the principles of astrology share some common psychic imagery, they are not interchangeable. Like twin figures looming out of the darkness, their differences become more noticeable with every step of their approach.

Before looking at the result of Jung's astrological experiments, and their implications, we must try to discover how much Jung actually *knew* about the actual practice of astrology.

From his published work, the answer has to be 'not very much'. He clearly had little regard for astrologers and there is no clear indication that he even understood how astrologers viewed the zodiac. 'Even today, people who still believe in astrology fall almost without exception for the old superstitious assumption of the influence of the stars. And yet anyone who can calculate a horoscope should know that since the days of Hipparchus the spring point has been fixed at 0° Aries, and that the zodiac on which every horoscope is based is therefore quite arbitrary.'[12]

He repeats this assertion elsewhere: 'Because of the precession of the equinoxes ... if there are any astrological diagnoses of character that are in fact correct this is not due to the influence of the stars but to our own hypothetical time qualities.'[13] In other words, astrology cannot have an objective reality because the astrologers have failed to notice precession, thus if there is anything of interest it is due to synchronicity.

Similarly: 'At the same time the zodiacal qualifications of the houses, which play a large part in the horoscope, created a complication in that the astrological zodiac, although agreeing with the calendar, does not coincide with the actual constellations.'[14]

Jung is obviously commenting here on the fact that there is a discrepancy between the starting point of the zodiac used by western astrologers – known as the Tropical zodiac – and the fixed constellations, known as the Sidereal zodiac. This discrepancy increases at about 1° every seventy-two years, with the result that the zodiac's starting point – known as the Vernal point – moves backwards against the fixed stars. The astrological ages – the Piscean Age, the Aquarian Age and so forth – are said to start when the Vernal point changes signs, which is approximately every 2,160 years.

In his monograph on the image of the Fish and Christianity, Jung speculated that there was a connection between Christianity's growth and the Vernal point moving into Pisces. Although he wrote much on this subject, there is nothing that indicates that he has explored the implications of the shifting, Tropical zodiac that western astrologers use, or that he even understands that they *did* use it. Neither is there any indication that he understood the Eastern use of various *ayanamsas* – the Hindu word for the discrepancies between the Tropical zodiac and various fixed stars said to mark the 'real' starting points of the several Sidereal zodiacs.

In short, he obliquely criticizes astrologers in exactly the same manner as that of most contemporary scientists, assuming that each one is in total ignorance of precession. In Jung's case, however, this 'argument' does more than just reveal that he has failed to grasp Lesson One; we begin to see how astrology *must* be demonstrated to operate non-scientifically, to contain basic errors of mathematics or logic. In that way any meaningful correlations astrology comes up with can *only* be explained by synchronicity. We have a right to ask why this might be so.

Jung might be accused of many things, but this could not include a lack of scholarship or dedicated research. The scope of his learning is staggering and his ability to track down the derivations of symbols to their first appearances in the earliest languages is similarly remarkable. Why, then, could he somehow fail to absorb an elementary textbook on astrology? Why is the subject, almost from the first, defined by Jung in *his* terms and not in the language used by practising astrologers through the ages? Jung approaches the subject as if hardly anything had ever been written on it beyond a few phrases on the meaning of planets or the signs of the zodiac.

There is no real discussion on the rights and wrongs of the astrological perspective, and no attempt to explore its abundant writings. It is not as if the subject was held up to the light of his scrutiny, only to be finally rejected after dissection and argument. It was never even examined. It is almost as if astrology never fully existed in the first place, as if it was a ruined language that Jung picked up one day, dusted down and filled with a new litany that turned out, surprisingly, to praise the collective unconscious.

Unlike alchemy, which *is* explored in relation to its past, unlike the *I Ching* which is similarly placed in *its* historical context and allowed *its* traditional role, astrology's place in the development of human thought is virtually unmentioned by Jung. In fact, astrological tradition is actually presented as having *harmed* our understanding of the human situation: 'As we know, some of the old gods became, via astrology, nothing more than descriptive attributes (martial, jovial, saturnine, erotic, logical, lunatic and so on).'[15] This travesty of its position, in which the canon of astrology is reduced to a series of banal adjectives, is even harder to understand given the fact that Jung's work was conducted during an extremely fruitful period of astrological growth – particularly so in Europe – and much medical research was being done by astrologers who were also doctors or psychologists. This deliberate shunning of astrology is nowhere more clearly demonstrated than in the index to Jung's *Collected Works*. For instance, there are well over 700 index lines referring to the symbol of Mercury in its exclusively alchemical context and just nine lines in reference to astrology. On inspection, virtually all of the latter references prove to have very little astrological substance and would more correctly be numbered with the main body.

There is simply no indication in his published writings that Jung took any real interest in or had any real knowledge of the depth of the subject, either in its historic or its contemporary role. What he took to be astrology was to a large part his own assumptions of it, and when he *did* come across a glimpse of the real stuff it was hi-jacked and driven quietly away to Bollingen to be buried among the stones. I believe that part of the reason why this is so emerges when we examine the simple astrological experiment that he carried out. It is this experiment we should now look at.

Jung's Astrological Experiment

Briefly, the experiment consisted of matching the charts of 400 couples to see if classical conjunctions took place between combinations of the Sun, the Moon, Venus, Mars and the Ascendant/Descendent axis, within an 8° orb. The charts arrived in several batches and were processed as they came in.

As Jung gives no details of how the test was carried out, what the statistical methodology was and – most importantly – no actual data, no one can make any comment as to its accuracy or otherwise. But this is not the point; what is important here is what Jung himself describes as going on, as it is here that his views about astrology are expressed at their clearest.

A sentence much quoted by astrologers is: 'Astrology is in the process of becoming a science.'[16] But the actual context of that has to be taken into account. It continues with: 'But as there are large areas of uncertainty, I decided some time ago to make a test to find out how far an accepted astrological tradition would stand up to statistical investigation.' In other words, it is not *Jung's* opinion that astrology is about to become a science, he is aware that this might be the case and so uses the tried and trusted method of statistics to see if these beliefs are justified. In other words, he is setting out to *prove* whether or not astrology can be justified, and he employs mathematicians to help him. There is a need to underline what Jung has written here, even if it does seem like stressing the obvious, for despite the clear expression of his need to 'make a test to see how far an accepted astrological tradition would stand up to statistical investigation', he was later to categorically deny that he did anything of the sort.

His initial results are very encouraging (for astrology), and before long Jung is speculating as to whether proton radiation might be an actual *causal* factor in the results.[17] Such a phenomenon, if it took place, would invalidate synchronicity from playing a part, which would have very serious implications for Jung's psychology.

As Jung has already stated that astrological correlations are an expression of the psyche's projections on to the heavens, and if astrology is now a *causal* phenomena, then synchronicity is out of the picture and *something else is going on*, something that does not operate from the collective unconscious but has a causal relationship with the psyche. We would have to admit that it would help Jung's case a lot if astrology as an incipient science was swiftly nipped in the bud.

The charts were analysed in batches and the results totalled. The initial exceptional results were quickly cut down when some basic mathematical errors were discovered, the nature of which, like the initial calculations, Jung also fails to reveal. In one (small) batch Jung finds some striking lunar conjunction contacts between marriage partners and then states that these results can only be explained by 'intentional or unintentional fraud, or else precisely such a meaningful coincidence, that is synchronicity'.[18] This really is pushing it a little. The word for apparent significance in small batches of data is *chance*. Virtually *all* research data, astrological or non-astrological, will show random clustering of – at first glance – seemingly important information that vanishes when further data is added. Jung's insistence that it could only be explained by synchronicity has just a hint of desperation about it. But there is more.

Jung continues:

Although I was obliged to express doubt, earlier, about the mantic [intuitive] nature of astrology, I am now forced as a result of my astrological experiment to recognize it again. The chance arrangement of the marriage horoscopes, which were simply piled on top of one another as they came in from the most diverse sources, and the equally fortuitous way in which they divided into three unequal batches, suited the sanguine expectations of the research workers and produced an overall picture that could scarcely have been improved upon from the standpoint of the astrological hypothesis.[19]

It would seem that 'chance' can be blamed for the arrival of letters, which made the early results look so good, but cannot be considered as a factor in the ensuing analysis of their contents – that can only be due to synchronicity! This is a neat variation of his 'astrologers overlook precession so mathematics is out and intuition is in' argument which we looked at earlier, although it is somewhat less convincing. Jung's next stage, however, is even more interesting.

He returned to the subject again later in life, and his account of what took place during the experiment is a little baffling to anyone who places the two versions next to each other. In his second version he writes that he never intended to experiment to prove anything, 'nothing could have been further from my mind'.[20] Yet he had previously written to Professor Fierz, who had assisted with the statistical analysis: 'May I at least conjecture that it [the results] argues *for* rather than *against* the traditions since Ptolemy.'[21] To press for the astrological case one moment while denying doing anything of the kind the next clearly indicates that something must have happened during the interval. It is a rare person who has the time and money to employ researchers to set up, by hand, the charts of 400 couples, analyse the results, publish a report which includes nearly seven pages of research statistics – and all to prove nothing. At this point one might just hear the sound of a hobby-horse being swiftly back-pedalled through the streets of Kustnach.

Despite the fact that the whole experiment was not done to prove anything, Jung is convinced it proved synchronicity: 'Naturally I do not think that this experiment or any other report on happenings of this kind proves anything; it merely points to something that science can no longer overlook – namely, that its truths are in essence statistical and are therefore not absolute.'[22] The concept that the laws of science are not absolute, but gain their strength from the fact that they generally work – i.e. a statistical probability – was not a new idea even in Jung's time and owes absolutely nothing to his experiment, which is wholly inadequate for the complexity of that particular problem.

However, this task completed, Jung could feel free to write that 'Synchronicity is a modern differentiation of the obsolete concept of correspondence, sympathy, and harmony. It is not based on philosophical assumptions, but on empirical experience and experimentation.'[23] The concept of correspondence is of course astrological, and thus according to Jung could never be proven as all that could ever be proven from tests designed to prove them is that they cannot be proven which of course proves synchronicity. That is, if you were actually trying to *prove* anything, which of course he was not.

In fact, Jung is as wrong as his logic is tortuous. Astrological phenomena *cannot* be 'explained' by synchronicity, for it is a much too limited concept. It is described as working in a random and sporadic manner, inaccessible to any real observation. This is quite the reverse of astrology's practice and assumptions, and the theory is tied almost exclusively into a specific approach towards the nature and workings of the unconscious. In fact, in its described form it is effectively made redundant, and by the very beast Jung thought he'd slain: astrological research.

The Gauquelins and Peter Roberts

The most powerful argument that Jung's concept of synchronicity *cannot* be applied in the way described emerges from a consideration of the harmonic analysis of the Gauquelin data, although clear evidence for this has been there from the start. At the 1987 Astrological Association Conference Professor Peter Roberts brought this fact to the attention of astrologers, following his re-examination of major Gauquelin studies.[24]

As most astrologers will know from the Gauquelin data, the most powerful placement of Mars in the charts of athletes is just above the horizon. 10° above the horizon, in fact. This same point is also the most powerful position for Saturn in the charts of scientists, Jupiter in the charts of politicians and the Moon in the charts of writers. In other words, it appears as if birth tends to be triggered when the key 'character-trait' planet reaches 10° above the horizon, whether this planet is the Moon, Mars, Jupiter or Saturn. But this *cannot* be described as a synchronistic event because we are not recording the actual moment when the planet climbed above the horizon but the moment when *its light* was visible at that point. As the light from Saturn can take up to 1 hour and 20 minutes to get to Earth, the 'real' Saturn would have aligned with the horizon 1 hour and 20 minutes *earlier. That* would have been the moment when the event *actually* took place. (See Figure 2.1)

As that key horizon degree remains the same whether the planet is the Moon – whose light reaches Earth within a fraction of a second – or whether the planet is Saturn, whose light takes between 1 hour 12 minutes and 1 hour 20 minutes to reach us, depending on the Earth/Saturn distance, we are clearly seeing a phenomenon at work which is dependent on the speed of light. A phenomenon which so obviously falls within the accepted laws of space/time physics *cannot*, in Jung's own words, be a synchronistic

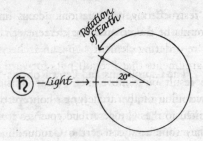

Figure 2.1 At a specific moment in time the difference between Saturn's real and perceived position relative to the horizon can be some 20°. For harmonic analysis to reveal that the key Gauquelin degrees are so *consistent* suggests that it is the planet's *perceived* position – not the *real* position – that indicates the effect. Thus the effect operates at the speed of light and not synchronistically. In the diagram we see that the observer on Earth has moved some 20° during the time it takes the light from Saturn to reach our planet. When we perceive Saturn as being on the horizon it is, in *actuality*, now some 20° above it. For a fuller analysis of the implication of the Gauquelins' findings, see Peter Roberts's *The Message of Astrology*, Aquarian Press, 1990.

event: 'as the time-factor is indispensable to the concept of causality, one cannot speak of causality in a case where the time-factor is eliminated'.[25] Far from being eliminated, the time factor is *central* to the success of the Gauquelin data. If it were not the case, we would not get this precise 10° relationship with the horizon.

This means that any astrological observation which is dependent in its interpretation on the relationship between planets and angles – and this of course includes every house system imaginable – is based on positions obtained by *including* the time-factor of the planets' distance from earth – it thus *cannot* be described as synchronistic in Jung's own terminology.

In his book *Jung, Synchronicity and Human Destiny*, Ira Progoff attempts a re-definition of synchronicity as a phenomenon which occurs as a direct result of an archetype's capacity to 'reach across the causally unrelated lines of causation and draw them together in a striking and significant event'.[26] He argues that this process results in a 'restructuring of situations across time and beyond causality in terms of the re-ordering element at the depth of the psyche'. The 're-ordering element' being an archetype.

While the arguments that Progoff puts forward to back up this view are the result of a more methodical consideration of the apparent functioning of the archetypes, he nevertheless comes to the same conclusion as Jung. Archetypes give *meaning* to the events that they somehow conspire to produce in the world and 'the manner in which this meaningful restructuring takes place is elusive, primarily because it cannot be brought about by deliberate purpose'.

The Jungian concept of archetypes will be examined more closely in the following chapter, but so far we can see that the concept of synchronicity cannot be correctly applied to describe anything which is deliberately created or experienced at will, or results from the application of known causal systems.

Astrology would have to fall into this category as, at one level, it is the application of a self-regulatory system, finitely explicable through the medium of celestial mechanics, applied to human experience and affairs.

It is quite possible to sit down and quite deliberately experience astrology at work in everyday surroundings. Group meditations which take place at moments of planetary angularity reveal a striking similarity of eidetic imagery, which graphically reflects the experience of the relevant planetary principle. The experiment is particularly potent when carried out with groups who are unaware of which planet is about to become angular.

In these circumstances the group is asked to relax and focus on the images which begin to appear during a few minutes of meditation. When the meditation is completed no communication is permitted until each participant has finished writing down his or her own experiences. When confronting a number of surprised faces, each registering the recognition that what one person is now reading out is remarkably similar, in symbol or language, to what they have written down before them, it is impossible to avoid the awareness that, somehow, something has been 'done' to a roomful of people. Astrology has been made to 'take place' quite deliberately and almost in the manner of a clinical experiment.

Similarly the 'Kolisko' experiments, first carried out in the 1920s and subsequently replicated by Kollerstrom and Drummond,[27] demonstrate a very clear astrological effect on the precipitation rate of various metals, which cannot realistically be thought of as having an unconscious to work meaningfulness for them in the world. These experiments clearly show that the rate at which dissolved metals are absorbed by filter paper varies directly according to both planetary conjunctions and diurnal position. These relationships cannot in any way be thought of as synchronistic; there is no energy moving from unconscious to conscious, no human participation and no 'meaning' awaiting perception. But something is definitely going on; it is not synchronistic but has its own time sequence and its own parallel symbolism.

Whatever this 'something' is, it does not just lie hidden deep within the collective unconscious, but is in part connected to the precise geometry of the planets, following their finitely predictable rules as they pace out their wide ellipses. I believe that at some level Jung recognized this, saw how its implications could only question the foundation of his own work, and recoiled.

There is some anecdotal evidence that in later years Jung actively returned to astrology and began to rethink his ideas on synchronicity, but in his own writings there is no indication of this. Quite the reverse; six years before his death he wrote in a letter: 'It is especially not understood what an excellent joke was made with the use of astrological statistics; people have even thought that I wanted to prove something in favour of astrology; it is hardly worthwhile to deal with all this pack of nonsense.'[28] Until we have something in Jung's own hand, this might have to be his last word on the subject.

The Role of Synchrony

For the moment, what is important for us as astrologers is to recognize that the 'synchronicity' described by Jung is very different from the *synchrony* described by astrologers. Synchrony is the relationship between what astrologers see as the living flux of time into which we are born and whose dynamics we seem to absorb and express, and everything that has gone before. It describes the resonance which the present maintains with the past, the relationship we have with our *inherited* experience of time and all that has taken place within it.

Synchronous events happen together because they are resonating to the same astrological patterns, and to some extent have the same history. This would suggest that we do not in fact 'take on the moment' when we are born; we are born when we 'match' the moment of our birth, and thus bring that moment into being.

This idea will be explored in much greater detail in Chapters 4 and 5, but to see it in operation now requires only a simple example. Ask any redhead.

For once tradition and science seem to agree: redheaded people are more likely to be born with Mars near the Ascendant than anywhere else in the chart. The work of the American astrologers Judith Hill and Jacalyn Thompson[29] confirms earlier observations made by John Addey – and of course those of the ancients, who came to similar conclusions without the use of computers. An angular Mars is a clear symbol of a possible redhead. Obviously, there is the requirement of a genetic disposition for red hair, as if some triggering mechanism is at work which seeks out only babies with the appropriate genetic structure.

As far as its hair is concerned, the baby is *not* 'taking on the moment'. Its predisposition towards red hair might go back to our earliest history. Every ancestor of its own sex might have had red hair, an event replicated every generation for thousands of years, like a stone skipping back through time to the unknown moment when some new genetic structure first came into being. Every one of those receding moments is as much keyed into the meaning of the angular Mars as the one we observe now. They are inextricably connected throughout the ages towards its first expression on the material plane.

The case of an angular Mars and redheads is quoted solely because astrologers now have hard proof that this relationship *does* exist, but there are innumerable other examples from astrology's tradition which may at some point *also* be more formally verified. Do Aquarians have blue eyes? Does Taurus rising tend to correlate with a stocky physique? Do prominent Leo features suggest a mane of blonde hair? Are Geminis thinner than average? The list is as long as the combined observations of our history. Are astrologers really suggesting that the infant miraculously restructures its genetic code at the moment of birth just to fit in with a Jungian view of astrology? The baby is not 'taking on the moment' – all of these factors will have pre-dated that moment by centuries, at the very least. What is more, they will be centuries of highly complex genetic relationships which *now*, at the moment of birth, coincide with external symbols which astrologers imply in some way 'cause' the correlation to happen. We seem to be moving in two frames of time simultaneously, as 'present time' and 'past time' coincide and interact. What is certainly clear is that the baby holds its own history within itself, and its life also expresses *that* experience at the physical level, if not beyond.

This observation does not just hold true in the area of our genetic inheritance. Everyone who has ever undergone a deep analysis will know that very early memories – of sounds, sensations and occasionally also visual images – can come back from experiences absorbed *prior* to birth. Many therapists from the time of Otto Rank have stressed the need to explore the moments surrounding birth, and others such as the late Joyce Martin in England and Stanislav Grof in the USA have worked extensively with psychedelics to explore the sensations of inter-uterine life.

In Chapter 6 we shall consider some of Grof's findings and what they might suggest for astrologers, but even without his specific observations the fact that we are alive and aware in the months prior to birth, and capable of powerful emotional response that can stay with us for life, is a fact astrologers have to acknowledge, whatever it subsequently forces us to confront.

It is unlikely that the issues this situation raises can be dealt with by the somewhat discredited prenatal epoch chart, nor are attempts to take the birth chart and in some manner turn it backwards to a hypothetical moment of conception particularly impressive. Charts for the *real* moment of conception – if they were ever obtainable – would certainly be most interesting to explore, but it would be equally wrong to assume they held the final clue. Such a chart would be another step in the same process that spirals back into the past, a similar example of the interaction between the *moment* and its own history.

It would seem that the message we are getting here is that we are not keyed in to one static moment but to a *succession* of moments that might at first appear as a scattering of disjointed occurrences, but are in reality different phases of familiar cycles. We seem to contain a whole series of different rhythms which began at different times, whose starting points might be hundreds, thousands, or even millions of years in the past.

Whatever their age, they continue to tick out within us, each one unravelling a separate pattern at a different speed. The current astrological attitude presents each instant as separate from the history of its own dynamic process, and the sequence of life as a stroboscopic discontinuity frozen at the moment of birth.

If synchrony is the plane of time which joins all things existing in the Now, then the history of the events so brought together can be viewed on the axis of time running backwards from the present to the past: the diachronic axis. It is only by ignoring the diachronic axis of time, seeing the moment divorced from its own beginnings, that we become seduced by the concept of synchronicity. What we are more properly perceiving is the interweaving of images in time, each harmonized to its initial beginning, each moving in and out of phase with the other, coexisting momentarily in the synchronous plane, sharing in the process of creation.

3

The Selective Unconscious:
Archetype, Race and Illusion

* * * * * * * * * *

As we have seen, synchronicity can be properly used only to explain certain functions unique to Jung's cosmological theories. The concept itself emerged from his observations of the dynamics of the collective, and the part he believed played by archetypal energies in the manifestation of meaning. Thus events may be created by the shifting of energy from unconscious to conscious, and these occurrences may express or symbolize archetypal concerns.

It has been suggested that whatever the validity of these ideas might be for explaining the workings of the individual psyche, synchronicity cannot be used to explain the workings of astrology. We face similar problems with Jung's theory of archetypes.

At first sight the concept of the archetype as some sort of underlying pattern for human behaviour is both simple and attractive, but closer inspection suggests that it is an extremely complex idea and one which can pose as many questions as it might answer, particularly for astrologers.

Jungian Archetypes

Jung's concept of an archetype emerged from his reading of both Christian and Platonic texts as well as his re-working of the Freudian theories of racial memory-traces. At this level they are at their most naïve: 'archetypes are simply the forms which the instincts assume'.[1] Such a statement would then imply that instincts are deeper or more reduced than archetypes, and elsewhere Jung suggests that the archetype is the 'instinct's perception of itself'.[2] But they are *not* instinctual in the sense that the biologist might claim non-learned patterns of behaviour are embedded genetically, even if elsewhere Jung *does* suggest that archetypes are 'inherited with the brain structure';[3] a quasi-Freudian idea which, as we shall see later in this chapter, he put to some extremely dubious use.

Jung describes *instincts* as being 'typical modes of action, and wherever we meet with uniform and regularly recurring modes of action we are dealing with instinct, no matter whether it is associated with a conscious motive or not'.[4] *Archetypes* are defined almost identically as 'typical modes of apprehension, and whenever we meet with uniform and regularly recurring modes of apprehension then we are dealing with an archetype, no matter whether its mythological character is recognized or not'.[5]

Perhaps part of this similarity is because, as well as focusing around instinctual needs, archetypes can also 'arise spontaneously, at any time at any place, and without any outside influence . . . There are present in every psyche forms which are unconscious but nevertheless active – living dispositions, ideas in the Platonic sense, that preform and continually influence our thoughts, feelings and actions.'[6] In practice Jung does not really adopt the Platonic concept of the external unfolding Divine Idea, but instead, and quite rightly, he explores the internal dynamics of the human psyche from the point of view of a psychologist. It is here that his ideas of the archetypes are at their most complex.

To begin with Jung suggests that deep within the human psyche the archetypes underpin common human experiences and imagery. The image of the Mother, of the Father, of the Child, of the Self are all archetypal in that the totality of all possible expressions of their experience is held within the appropriate centre – the relevant archetype – a core that is being added to by the process of our psychic evolution. The archetype contains all that has happened to the human race in those specific areas as well as holding a model of all future development: 'the archetype as an image of instinct is a spiritual goal towards which the whole nature of man strives'.[7] In this respect its relationship to Time is hard to assess as it emerges from a finite past but contains an infinite future which is always some way 'ahead' of human evolution and perhaps even capable of being accessed by a suitably advanced individual, although in practice it is something we will tend to be pulled *back* to rather than lean towards.

'Primordial image', 'mythological motif', 'collective representations' and 'psychologems'[8] are all ways in which Jung has chosen to re-express the core concept of the archetype's function. As such, the archetype can be thought of as a 'hypothetical construct, an unconscious regulator, which controls the activity of *archetypal forms* in creating *archetypal themes* (*motifs*) from the raw materials of sensation and perception'.[9] In this way, all themes common to humanity's experience have their centre in an archetype, whose images are expressed in dreams, myths, legends and the actions of those particularly attuned to the appropriate source, or unwittingly possessed by it.

At this overall, general level Jung's observations find immediate resonance; there *are* common themes to the human race, even in tribes and races with widely disparate cultures, from urban sophisticates with their filofaxed lives to the technologically primitive jungle hunters. Again and again the major rituals and processes of human life are mirrored in the most unlikely places, and are instantly recognizable across thousands of years through the surviving writings of our ancestors. It is only when we start to examine the function of the archetype in detail that we begin to see some of the problems inherent in Jung's theory.

To correspond with clinically observed human behaviour it is necessary to 'sub-divide' the archetypes from the start. The archetype of the Mother, for instance, splits first into its 'good' and 'bad' components while at other levels it may fuse with yet more differing images of women. We have the Good Mother, the Wise Old Woman (*Magna Mater*), the Bad Mother (the ugly Witch with her phallic nose and broomstick), the Shiva-like Destroying Mother, the Virgin, the Princess, the Temptress, the Priestess; each an archetype of its own, though capable of being combined in complexes such as the Virgin/Whore duality. There is also the Anima, that individual amalgam of the conscious and unconscious

Male experience of women collectively, which is yet another archetype in its own right. This list is by no means complete and capable of being repeated for the divergent aspects of Man or Child – or any other major archetypes of the collective unconscious. It is at this point that we probably start to feel some confusion, for not only do all such major components of our ordinary circumstances have archetypes which open to reveal an array of disparate and individual sub-archetypes, so does every profound human *experience*.

Death is an archetype. Birth is an archetype, so is sexual union, marriage, the Oedipus complex, sibling rivalry, the coming of age, the loss of a parent, the search for God, leaving home, the need to create, becoming a parent, losing a child, the quest for identity; all of these are archetypal human experiences with their own 'power centre'. Furthermore, Dr Jolande Jacobi, a pupil of Jung, writes that:

> In the world of archetypes we can accordingly establish a hierarchical order. We designate as 'primary' those archetypes which are not susceptible of further reduction, which represent, as it were, the 'first parents'; we term the next in line, their 'children', 'secondary', their 'grandchildren' 'tertiary' etc., until we arrive at those highly diversified archetypes which stand closest to the familiar domains of consciousness and hence possess the least richness of meaning and numinosity or energy charge. Such a hierarchical chain might, for example, be formed by those archetypes which manifest the basic traits of the entire human family, of the feminine sex alone, of the white race, of Europeans, of Nordics, of the British, of the citizens of London, of the Brown family, etc. For it is incontestable that side by side with the archetypes which belong to the entire human race of the European, an inhabitant of London will embody others that are typical only of the dweller in London. The latter, however, must be regarded as variations of the former. The basic structure is laid down, but its individual spatiotemporal concretizations are imprinted by the time and environment constellation in which they appear.[10]

If the Browns are the 'spatiotemporal concretizations' of their personal archetype then the Joneses will indubitably want one of their own, even if it means ordering it specially from Zürich. If their offspring intermarry and have children then a new family archetype is brought into being with its attendant archetypes of family life and sibling rivalries lurking in the background. No doubt if the Joneses' grandmother used to rule the roost by feigning an imminent coronary to get her own way, but the Browns' father dealt with all issues by thumping the nearest relative, then the ghosts of their respective archetypes will continue to linger on until some psychic reconciliation in the new Brown/Jones Archetype of Domestic Bliss is achieved. Behind all this, of course, is not just the weight of the mortgage and the poll tax, but the vast reservoir of social, sexual, familial, racial, local, national and international archetypes all competing for a slice of the psychic action. Behind *them* come the massed ranks of Good Mothers, Bad Mothers, Moderately Useless Mothers, Great Whores, Little Virgins, Temptresses, Witches, Wise Old Men, Eternal Youths, Tricksters, the odd *Senex* and the man from across the road who has finally come to return the mower; each and all eager for immediate constellation at number 44 Acacia Avenue.

While there is much to suggest that there are times when family life *feels* like this, and there can be little doubt that behind each new generation there is a dark choir of unspoken voices, heard only in moments of extreme desperation telling tales of the dead that are instantly denied by the living, we nevertheless have to question how effective the Jungian concept of archetypal hierarchies really is in exploring such complex areas of life.

If an archetype can so quickly subdivide, if it becomes overlaid with first one, then another different and separate archetype, or if they can nest like Russian dolls, each a separate container, from which meaning after meaning can be extracted like a conjurer pulling at an endless stream of coloured ribbons, then we are really no clearer about what might be going on than when we started. Added to this array we must recognize all those which can occur when yet more archetypes *evolve*. Just as the match of Brown and Jones brought a new family archetype into being – and of course this must also then be claimed for every coupling since the dawn of time – so can many other facets of life come together to constellate yet more archetypes. If every Brown and Jones can do it then so will every shift and change within the social fabric of each and every society generate yet more archetypes. Every new invention which creates a new social stratum or occupation, every new disease which creates a further class of victims, every emerging movement which holds up a new ideal to honour, will simultaneously activate the genesis of an original archetype within the collective.

The overkill of possibilities is staggering, and using the model provided by Dr Jacobi it is hard not to think of the collective unconscious as harbouring, more than anything else, sad remnants of abandoned archetypes; a massive scrap-heap of families lost without issue, of cities, towns and countries erased from time, of legions gone into the mists and ships that sailed but never docked. Each oblique effort of evolution that ended in sterility or decay has a matching archetype that lies there now with the dinosaurs, the Romans and the unfading image of the old man across the street who died, and no one ever knew.

Seen in this light, however much we may sense the power of Jung's concept or connect at an emotional level to the essence of his ideas, his *theory* of archetypes as a method of both exploring and explaining the dynamics of the psyche leaves much to be desired. The moment we leave the domain of the most fundamental of their number we are effectively lost. While we stay within the boundaries of those we recognize most clearly, they are by definition the most general and serve us least well for exploring the intricacies of the individual case. If virtually *anything* can be thought of as archetypal in one way or another – and it can – then there is nothing particular or specific about the whole theory of archetypes. In the terminology of Karl Popper it is quite 'unfalsifiable', it can neither be proved nor disproved and exists only for itself in its own land. If practically anything can be claimed as evidence of archetypal activity then one thing is as good as another. As the theory is diluted to cover every conceivable eventuality so it loses its power and originality. We are then left only with the *idea* of the archetype, of there being an unconscious matrix for each human experience to which we all unwittingly respond, an idea amply pursued by Rupert Sheldrake with his concept of morphogenetic fields, as we shall see in the following chapter. Astrology, of course, is a further alternative.

It is certainly true that Jung does not map the psyche with archetypes alone; constellations of symbols and complexes are also used, though invariably these come down to reflecting the underlying structure of archetypal patterns, and thus to some extent become enmeshed in the complexities that Dr Jacobi's model has outlined.

Jung's conception of archetype is inextricably bound up with his theory of the collective unconscious; these two ideas are quite indivisible. They are not, however, unique to Jung.

While he is generally credited with the 'discovery' of the collective unconscious this is a little like crediting English explorers with the 'discovery' of Africa: one or two people *did* know about its existence beforehand. In fact the idea of some form of collective or archetypal unconscious is of course very old. It exists in many and varied forms, at the very least from Plato onwards, and forms the core of many visionary pictures of the world, from the philosophical to the animistic. The shamanistic rites in many countries, for example, generally involve contact with power figures, which are seen as a form of archetype that can also spill over into the human psyche, perhaps to cause illness or mischief if the spirit has been insulted. Anthropological literature is filled with examples of such concepts of collective energies hiding just out of human sight and records innumerable legends and beliefs referring to a core, archetypal Ur-figure who dwells in the spirit world and whose characteristics and qualities underlie each earthly manifestation of its image.

The Freudian Collective

If we decide to begin our research in relatively modern times then the prime originator of the collective unconscious is Freud. The concept of an unconscious existing at a deeper level than the personal, individual unconscious, one filled with dark and powerful images of primitive experiences, is central to the whole course of orthodox psychoanalysis. Freud's life-work is founded upon it and without it his basic theories would fall apart. The main difference between Freud's concept of a collective unconscious and Jung's expansion of that theme is in the fact that Freud saw this process as being exclusively genetic, and primarily – though not exclusively – focused around issues of sexual guilt. Freud's collective unconscious was racial in origin, in which the accumulated experience of generation after generation was piled one upon the other like sloughed skin, stretching back to a mythological past in which the guilt experienced by the killing of the primal father still haunts the sons of today. This guilt forms the basis of totemic or sacrificial religions and its memory-traces fuel the Oedipal conflict in today's infants.

I must admit I have behaved for a long time as though the memory-traces of the experiences of our ancestors, independent of direct communication and the influence of education ... were an established fact ... My position, no doubt, is made more difficult by the present attitude of biological science, which refuses to hear of the inheritance of acquired characteristics by succeeding generations. I must, however, in all modesty, confess that I cannot do without this factor in biological evolution.

If we assume the survival of memory-traces in the archaic heritage, we have bridged the gulf between individual and group psychology: we can deal with peoples as we do with the individual neurotic.[11]

A person's id contains 'not only what he may have experienced himself but also things that were innately present in him at his birth, elements with a phylogenetic origin – an archaic heritage'.[12]

Freud saw the human being as being genetically keyed in to his ancestral experiences – the male pronoun is used deliberately; Freud was unashamedly patriarchal as he based his psychology in part on the analysis of the male role in evolution, a process not overly sympathetic to the rights or feelings of the feminine.

It was Freud's view that each generation endowed its offspring with some of its own experience, through the mechanism of genetics. In extreme cases, this could mean that groups could actually create a tribal or social neurosis if 'un-treated' psychic phenomena were passed to succeeding generations. This could result in some form of group psychosis which might be cathartically expressed, and, thus purged, rid the group of symptoms. Freud first put these ideas forward in 1893,[13] and they remained with him for the remainder of his life, many of them forming the basis of his major theoretical works *Totem and Taboo* and *Moses and Monotheism*, and Jung would have been exposed to them from the start.

These racial trace-memories would be stored in the id in the form of instinctual behaviour patterns demanding expression, constantly knocking at the doors of consciousness – almost certainly to be rejected and repressed. But Freud's concept of the id is not the simple storehouse of desires that many writers would have us believe, it is a rich and complex land in which a fundamental dimension of human experience is missing – *time*.

There is nothing in the id that corresponds to the idea of time; there is no recognition of the passage of time, and – a thing that is most remarkable and awaits consideration in philosophical thought – no alteration in its mental processes is produced by the passage of time. Wishful impulses, which have never passed beyond the id, but impressions, too, which have sunk into the id by repression, are virtually immortal; after the passage of decades they behave as if they have just occurred. They can only be recognized as belonging to the past, can only lose their importance, be deprived of their cathexis of energy, when they have been made conscious by the work of analysis.[14]

Thus in his concept of the id Freud is very aware that he is again confronting something which does not conform to the niceties of science. The unconscious is a source of psychic energy existing in its own frame of reference, not bound by anything conventionally causal (which must have been most annoying for such a determined determinist), and which constantly seeks expression in the 'real' world.

You are forgiven if you feel that something sounds familiar here. Any sensation of familiarity may increase when we consider what *Jung* has written about *his* concept: 'The contents of the collective unconscious are, as I have pointed out, the results of the psychic functioning of our whole ancestry; in their totality they compose a natural world-image, the condensation of millions of years of human experience.'[15] As *who* pointed out?

It is Freud's view that the psyche of the individual can be invaded by experiences of the remote past: 'All that we find in the prehistory of neuroses is that the child catches hold of this phylogenetic experience where his own experience fails ... he replaces occurrences in his own life by occurrences in the life of his ancestors.'[16]

These statements are not included to suggest that Jung has pinched Freud's ideas – there are many clear and quite irreconcilable differences between the two men's respective views, and they later branch out – with Jung's use of archetypes – in quite different directions. It does, however, underline some basic similarities that Jung did not always acknowledge, not least of all that the idea of the collective started out as racial – as a psychic equivalent of the genetic pool. Jung's later use of the archetypes as psychic factors does away with any need for him to confront the issue that faced Freud, namely that there is no scientific evidence for the transmission of experience via genes. Indeed, it is a Lamarckian heresy.* Jung, nevertheless, made much use of the idea of genetic inheritance and the concept of separate racial archetypes. These seem in some way to run parallel to those used in his purely psychic model. Regrettably, much of this began to emerge under the aegis of the Nazi party.

Archetypes and Race

In 1933 Jung became Vice-President of the International Society for Psychotherapy, a Nazi-backed organization run under the

---

* Jean-Baptiste de Lamarck was a French anatomist whose work influenced Charles Darwin. Lamarck held that learned behaviour could be passed on from parent to child. Though the idea is currently discredited it has not been absolutely disproved and continues to surface in a variety of forms.

auspices of Goering's cousin, Dr U. H. Goering. He also became President of the Supernational Psychotherapy Association, a similarly sponsored group designed to give some credibility to Nazism abroad. This it singularly failed to achieve.

Jung has always maintained that his active involvement with these organizations – which existed to promote 'Germanic' psychotherapy – was to assist the plight of German Jews, who could not, of course, practise in Nazi Germany. Even if we accept Jung completely at his word, that the sole purpose of his participation in these Nazi groups was to do whatever he could for his fellows, we have to ask ourselves if this aim was best served by the tone of his writings during that period.

In 1934 Jung published an address in *Zentralblatt fur Psychotherapie*[17] which still deserves our inspection. It is an important document, not just because it shows us an aspect of Jung not always recognized, but because we can quite clearly see how archetypal theories are actually being put into practice. The prejudices and assumptions of the day are being woven into a complex tapestry, which is then used to cover some glaring architectural blemishes. It is a passage all astrologers should read, perhaps while substituting 'Jew' with 'Libra', or 'women' with 'Cancer' (or whatever): our own generalities can sweep as wildly as any of Jung's:

The Jews have this peculiarity with women; being physically weaker, they have to aim at the chinks in the armour of their adversary, and thanks to this technique which has been forced on them through the centuries, the Jews themselves are best protected where others are most vulnerable ... Because, again of their civilization, more than twice as ancient as ours, they are vastly more conscious than we are of human weaknesses, of the shadow side of things, and hence in this respect much less vulnerable than we are. Thanks to their experience of an old culture, they are able, while fully conscious of their frailties, to live on friendly and tolerant terms with them, whereas we are too 'young' not to have illusions about ourselves. Moreover, we have been entrusted by fate with the task of creating a civilization – and indeed we have need of it – and for this 'illusions' in the form of one-sided ideals, convictions, plans etc.

are indispensable. As a member of a race with a 3,000-year-old civilization, the Jew, like the cultured Chinese, has a wider area of psychological consciousness than we. Consequently it is *in general* less dangerous for the Jew to put a negative value on his unconscious. The 'Aryan' unconscious, on the other hand, contains explosive forces and seeds of a future yet to be born, and these may not be devalued as nursery romanticism without psychic danger. The still youthful Germanic people are fully capable of creating new cultural forms that still lie dormant in the darkness of the unconscious of every individual – seeds bursting with energy and capable of mighty expansion. The Jew, who is something of a nomad, has never created a cultural form of his own and as far as we can see never will, since all his instincts and talents require a more or less civilized nation to act as host for their development.

The Jewish race as a whole – at least this is my experience – possesses an unconscious which can be compared to the 'Aryan' only with reserve. Creative individuals apart, the average Jew is far too conscious and differentiated to go about pregnant with the tensions of the unborn future. The 'Aryan' unconscious has a higher potential than the Jewish; that is both the advantage and disadvantage of a youthfulness not yet fully weaned from barbarism. In my opinion, it has been a grave error in medical psychology up to now to apply Jewish categories – which are not even binding on all Jews – indiscriminately to Germanic and Slavic Christendom. Because of this the most precious secret of the German people – their creative and intuitive depth of soul – has been explained as a morass of banal infantilism, while my own warning voice for decades has been suspected as anti-Semitism. This suspicion emanated from Freud.

Let us be quite clear what Jung is saying here. It is his contention that racial identity can be quite clearly demarcated by the unconscious, that the Jewish unconscious is less vulnerable to being damaged by Freud's sexual theories by virtue of its age, and that the 'Aryan' unconscious is destined to fulfil the historic mission of creating a new civilization and that this is a 'precious secret' that must be protected from being damaged by Jewish psychology. Finally, Jung protests that he is wrongly accused of anti-Semitism for holding these views and blames all this on to Freud.

While it is certainly true that Jung has written of Hitler as a psychotic, as a madman, of the German experience as a mass psychosis, this was after the event. His prior warnings of the blonde 'Wotan' archetype that he believed lay slumbering in the German psyche form no part of his writings for the International Psychotherapy Association. Furthermore, he actually lays part of the blame for the Nazi phenomenon on the Jews themselves: Jews have 'a specific need to reduce everything to its material beginnings'[18] and thus 'the psychotherapist with a Jewish background awakens in the German psyche not those wistful and whimsical residues from the time of David, but the barbarian of yesterday'.[19] For this second statement to have authority it would demand that a significant proportion of the German population had undergone psychoanalysis to the same ill effect, which seems most unlikely. In the midst of an essay on Eastern mysticism Jung comments on introversion and then writes that 'Freud identifies it with an auto-erotic, narcissistic attitude of mind. He shares his negative position with the National Socialist philosophy, which accuses introversion of being an offence against community feeling.'[20] This strange, non-contextual link (which is also of highly questionable accuracy) again demonstrates Jung's desire to couple Freud's name to the assumed underlying motives of Nazi philosophy. First Jung claims that it is Freud's negative psychology that is in part to blame for stirring up the demons in the German psyche, now his theories are described as legitimizing a supposed Nazi attitude towards the relationship of the individual and the State.

In all of this a number of issues are coming across quite clearly. There is Jung's troubled relationship with Freud surfacing yet again, but – more importantly – we recognize how Jung's own assumption of the psyche's nature is effortlessly blended into an analysis of the current political scene. The particular world-view that archetypal theory can create allows us to make some quite sweeping assumptions about whole groups of people – indeed, it might even *demand* it to sustain its own credibility. After all, if there were to be no evidence of group similarity, there could be no real credence given to concepts of social archetypes.

After the war, Jung was to write that 'The pseudo-scientific race-theories with which it was all dolled up did not make the extermination of the Jews any more acceptable.'[21] While this begs the obvious question as to what *would* make their extermination acceptable, his own part in providing pseudo-*psychological* race-theories is not dwelt upon.

Jung is by no means alone in ignoring embarrassing political facts. A Jungian therapist writing in 1950 about her experience of psychotherapy in the Third Reich comments: 'Students were exposed equally to the views of Jung, Freud and Adler ... gradually an increasing number made up their minds to follow Jung's method.'[22] This may have had something to do with the fact that the works of Jews like Freud and Adler were stripped from the shelves and burned long before the war started. As Freud's own doctor reports, Goebbels lit the torch himself with the words: 'Against the soul-destroying over-estimation of the sex life – and on behalf of the nobility of the human soul – I offer to the flames the writings of one Sigmund Freud.'[23] Not the greatest incentive for further study or objective evaluation.

The Supernational Psychotherapy Association existed to justify why so-called 'Germanic' and 'non-Jewish' psychotherapies were to prevail over Freud and Adler. For Jung to preside for six years over this organization while his former colleagues' and collaborators' work was destroyed – and some former colleagues along with it – calls for a far greater explanation than was ever forthcoming.

We have also to recognize that the theme of psychic miscegenation has always been close to Jung's heart. In a 'warning' to American colleagues he tells them: 'Racial infection is a most serious mental and moral problem where the primitive outnumbers the white man. I am quite convinced that some American peculiarities can be traced back directly to the coloured man, while others result from a compensating defence against his laxity.' This 'infection' is such that, according to Jung, the psyche of the white man is in some way invaded by that of the African, even to the extent of actually affecting physical appearance, something that is plain enough to Jung: 'Thus I can discern the white man clearly enough through his slightly Negroid mannerisms.'[24]

Again:

What is more contagious than to live side by side with a rather primitive people? Go to Africa and see what happens. When it is so obvious that you stumble over it, you call it going black ... It is much easier for us Europeans to be a trifle immoral, or at least a bit lax, because we do not have to maintain the moral standard against the heavy downward pull of primitive life. The inferior man has a tremendous pull because he fascinates the inferior layers of his own psyche.[25]

This infection by the primitive can, of course, be observed just as well in other countries, though not to the same degree and not in this form. In Africa, for example, the white man is a diminishing minority and must therefore protect himself from the Negro by observing the most rigorous social forms, otherwise he risks 'going black'. If he succumbs to the primitive influence he is lost.[26]

It is easy enough to pursue this point, which is, incidentally, the psychological justification for apartheid. Jung's writings are littered with condescending and ultra-conservative views that float like garbage on some of the deepest waters any psychologist has explored. Again, we may be seeing in all of this how an attempt to rationalize the prevailing social climate had become fatally ensnared by itself, constantly reinforcing a single outlook. The darkness that might have lain within became simplistically projected.

Jung was clearly worried that something black might 'infect' him, or even take him over. This fear seems to achieve paranoid proportions from time to time, and we know from his autobiography that he found his actual visit to Africa profoundly disturbing. Jung's personal identification of Africans with everything that he perceives as primitive in the human psyche reveals a fear of the instinctual side of the human race that Freud, more than anyone else, was trying to bring towards the light. This, indeed, could mask an actual fear of Freud himself, whose theories, as we have seen, he holds in part responsible for unleashing the holocaust.

Whether this suggestion is right or not, there is no doubt that Jung made some peculiar inner connection with the 'primitive' dream world and the world of the African: 'When a man is in the wilderness, the darkness brings dreams . . . It has always been so. I have not been led by any kind of wisdom; I have been led by dreams, like any primitive. I am ashamed to say so, but I am as primitive as any nigger, because I do not know.'[27] His dreams were clearly opening up something he could never fully confront, which was often conveniently projected elsewhere.

Jung's use of the word 'infection' may give us a clue as to what might have been going on in his mind. When he and Freud sailed to America to lecture on psychoanalysis at Clark University their ship arrived in New York harbour. As they passed the Statue of Liberty, Freud turned to Jung and said sardonically, 'They don't realize that we're bringing them the plague.'[28]

Whatever the reasons, Jung's continual blaming of other races, other tribes and other cultures for the ills of white Europeans deserves far greater inspection than it has hitherto received, for it reveals ways in which the concepts of archetypes can so easily be used for suspect purposes. This is *not* to condemn an approach just because it might be misused – this would be both facile and futile – but to underline how the social assumptions of the time may have been legitimized though their elevation to archetypal principle.

More importantly, we may have witnessed in the preceding paragraphs the manner in which Jung's *beliefs* have miraculously been turned into *facts*, facts which are then reinforced through social observations made through the mind-set which invented them in the first place. The concept of archetype may have something to commend it; however, in the form described by Jung, it has not been demonstrated as an objective reality any more than Freud's 'fact' of the libido. In Jung's case, it would also appear that a fundamental discrepancy in this theory has actually become incorporated within it.

According to Jung, virtually all human experience is an expression of underlying archetypal energies, which to some extent dictate our fate, though the archetypes themselves are relatively benign and 'equal'. Jung saw it as our task as humans to try to utilize and integrate archetypal energies within ourselves in as conscious a way as possible.

At appropriate moments, we may identify with the Hero, the Mother, the Wise Man, the Fool and so on; in some way absorbing their respective experiences and ideally becoming more whole as a result. The Mother is not a 'better' or 'worse' archetype than the Fool. There are only better or worse ways of experiencing the energies these archetypes contain, and better or worse ways of living them out.

It would seem, however, that the archetypes underlying the black races of the world (and to a lesser extent the Semitic races) are intrinsically *inferior*, fit only to be shunned and left in their psychic ghettos. *White* archetypes, however, do seem to be destined for better things. This is, of course, most convenient for those ruled by these alleged white archetypes, and very suggestive of the possibility that much of what Jung ascribes to the workings of archetypes may be better explained by an analysis of social and class forces, and how we react within them.

No doubt Jungians would suggest that social forces are themselves the manifestations of innumerable archetypes, but this does not address the real issue of how archetypes come to be classified, and who does the classifying. As we have seen, virtually *anything* can be called an archetype, and simply re-defining the situation in such a way does not confront the inferior/superior issue the Jungians themselves have raised. If we accept Jolande Jacobi's model of an infinity of hierarchically structured archetypes, which could also be seen as a straightforward projection of existing class and social structures, then the system itself begins to look even more suspect.

By making an archetype out of ordinary racial prejudice and slipping it in unnoticed, so to speak, to justify a prevailing social attitude, reveals just how conveniently flexible the edifice really is. We may just as well invent archetypes to justify any one of our innumerable prejudices or dislikes; and why stop there? No doubt some future court will hear a plea of mitigation in which the accused claims he was possessed by the archetype of Not Paying Income Tax, or fell victim to the Great Pickpocket in the Sky.

Prejudices stem from complex psychic processes, and would seem to revolve around how we deal – or do *not* deal – with that which appears different from *us*. Some possible underlying astrological parallels of this process will be suggested in Chapter 9, but even without exploring much further we can see that it is not enough here just to suggest that Jung's racial views only reflected the beliefs of his time, and can be discarded as embarrassing anachronisms. The *whole* of the model presented could be seen as the representation of a specific type of social order – the classic Victorian hierarchy – which Jung apparently hoped to maintain by the popularizing of his views.

If we accept the Jungian ideas as described, then the infinite complexity from which social and racial identities would seem to emerge can be conveniently ignored in favour of – at best – rather smug generalities, which are of dubious accuracy, and refer to virtually every corner of our lives. Astrologers already come perilously close to this attitude without any outside help, as will be examined in the final chapter. On the other hand, if we were to believe that the concept of archetype might be better expressed in non-Jungian forms, then we should examine whether these are any more helpful to our understanding of astrology. Some of these alternative approaches will be discussed in the following chapter.

4.

Alternative Archetypes

✩ ✩ ✩ ✩ ✩ ✩ ✩ ✩ ✩

If we consider the idea of archetype at its most basic, as being an energy or form which lies behind observable phenomena and imparts certain qualities to them, then we are faced with a number of possible theories as to how this process might take place. While the theories themselves may take us down quite different avenues they leave us with the same philosophical problem, that in expressing or acting out some pre-existing archetype we are to some extent 'being' something other than ourself. Thus the concept of a pre-existing archetype may go some way to solve theoretical problems on one level, only to create more immediate issues on another. A possible solution to this apparent impasse will be suggested at the end of this chapter, but first we should look more closely at some of the main theories of form or archetype and examine their relevance to astrology.

The Platonic Ideal

The philosopher A. E. Whitehead once remarked that all philosophy was but a footnote to Plato. With this in mind we must recognize that any attempt to summarize Plato's philosophy is bound to fall short of the mark, but we shall attempt to explore at least some of its implications for astrologers.

Plato saw the world as something like a shadow or reflection of what he conceived to be the real, underlying principles of the universe. Behind our experience of time lay a timeless state of Forms and Ideas, all of which were dimly visible in our own, imperfect world. Behind each tangible object, even something as lowly as a table, there lay the Idea of 'tableness' to which all tables resonated. Moral values such as Goodness and Truth similarly lay behind or *informed* their earthly equivalents. Most important-ly, Plato shared with Pythagoras the belief that numbers were just as powerful ideas as any traditional virtue, and were con-stantly being expressed within the nature of the material world.

While it is obvious that the theories of both Jung and Rupert Sheldrake (whose work will be explored in a moment) owe some-thing to neo-Platonic ideas, the concept of number would appear to be more uniquely related to astrology than to any other coherent cosmological system. Astrologers use numbers to describe the shape and nature of the zodiac and the manifesting qualities of the aspects – and much else besides. This approach reached its peak – in the West, at least – with the work of John Addey, Charles Harvey and David Hamblin.

Here the use of number and archetype are almost synonymous; a number is seen as containing or expressing a specific idea which is then manifested in the world again and again. In other words, the event is in some way a reflection of an underlying numerical 'truth'. While numbers can certainly be said to represent 'ideas' – and in Plato's cosmology they are exclusively used in this way – the question has to be put as to whether this really is the same as suggesting that they are the embodiment of a divine, unalterable Truth, or more properly some form of process.

It is important to recognize that we do not necessarily have to accept specific interpretations of number theory to make use of the concept of number. If a number has a meaning then this meaning can obviously be viewed from a range of perspectives; some of these give us quite a different view of what might be going on.

The mathematics of Boole and De Morgan challenged the Pla-tonic concept of the objective 'truth' of numbers. Philosophers now argued that mathematics itself knows nothing of objective truth, and indeed *cannot* do so. The only truth that mathematics can reveal is relative to its own internal construction. Different math-ematics can all be true and can operate side by side, taking their separate directions to differing ends. Provided that their method of operation contained no error of logic or process, such differing results can be equally valid. This major philosophical shift had a profound effect on the development of mathematical and geometric theories.

Previously, elegance of proof within an equation counted for much. With Boolean mathematics came the tyranny of the rigorous proof, with no other consideration taken into account, and led the development of new forms of mathematical process to facilitate growing logistical demands.

The concept of numbers embodying a universal, unvarying Truth, and permeating the universe with that Truth, had been a mainstay of much of Western philosophy, but this now changed radically with the ideas of logistical mathematicians, and particularly with the work of philosophers such as Gottlob Frege.[1]

Frege introduced the idea that numbers are more properly a philosophical or mathematical *concept*, pointing out for instance that nothing can *be* the square root of -1, yet such a function might become necessary within a specific hypothesis. For Frege number was not anything *of itself* but a constituent of a specific situation, in some manner contributing to it. For example, we may claim there are five oranges on one table and three oranges on another table; neither 'fiveness' nor 'threeness' is a component of 'oranges', but they do contribute to the nature of a specific situation, altering it in a manner similar to the addition or subtraction of another object within that situation.

In other words, number can be seen almost as a physical property of that which we observe, and not something which lies behind it. To use Frege's example, there is nothing about *gold* which is connected to the number four, unless we count its letters. At that point *four* becomes part of our concept of gold, it becomes an attribute of one of its aspects – the letters that create its name and bring it into being within our consciousness.

Here number is being used as some form of *object* – or an extension of an object – rather than as the property of an underlying *idea* which informs the object. Thus in one situation we may say five *is* the number of oranges, in another situation three *is* the number of oranges, as if five or three were physical facts which could be connected or disconnected to that which we observe. The nature of the numerical 'object' shifts, but not the concept of 'a number of oranges'. It is as if we sometimes append 'five' to the concept of 'a number of oranges' while at other times we append 'three' to that concept.

One might similarly define a large group of trees as 'a forest', 'a large wood' or '10,000 trees'; all are quite proper alternatives to describing what we may be observing.

In the example of the 'number as object' proposed by Frege, we see some similarities in the way number may be used within astrology in a manner which does not specifically tie it into Platonic philosophy; a system fraught with implications not always recognized or admitted by its proponents, as will be discussed at the end of this chapter.

We could declare here that number defined the *current state* of that of which it was a constituent part. We could suggest that number does not resonate to a primary Idea or archetype, lying behind or beyond that which it participates in, bringing that Idea or archetype into the world, it is *inherent within the process of the thing itself.*

In other words, number is a way of being, a shifting process of possibilities contained within the working of the cosmos. An angular relationship between two planets can express a 'seven' quality, a 'five' quality, or whatever, just as an individual can express any innate instinct or feeling; all are inherently possible. Put crudely, number would seem to be the way things 'work'.

As two planets move through their complete cycle from conjunction to conjunction, so their energies shift with the dynamics of their geometry. They display their range of possibilities as they move and relate, producing variants of 'being' which can be described with a shared numerological language, a language contained *within the situation of their being*, not reflecting a hypothetical truth beyond it. Looked at from the point of view of harmonics, we have a potent image of how such an interplay of planetary cycles can create pattern and rhythm by their very nature.

When a large number of harmonic tones are put or played

together, as in the case of all the planetary cycles being summed, their interacting wave-forms will tend to produce specific patterns which emerge out of the interplay of their individual frequencies. We have often experienced this for ourselves when lying awake at night listening to the sounds of a city.

From an amalgam of discordant and completely disconnected noises emerges a coherent pulse, a pattern of sound which seems to be planned and repetitive, but in fact achieves its regularity solely from the interplay of individual harmonics; there is no one behind it orchestrating everything on our behalf. During the last war this effect was regularly experienced when large waves of bombers flying overhead would sound as if their engine pitch was rising and falling in complex harmonies. Again, the combined wave-forms generated by each engine emphasized some notes and eradicated others, and a coherent pattern emerged which would be repeated again and again just so long as each component part of the combined wave-form remained constant. Such patterns, known also as *standing waves*, could appear to suggest that profound underlying principles are at work, but in fact emerge spontaneously from very simple and quite mechanical rules.

Many astrologers carrying out research work have commented on the apparent fact of there being certain clearly repeating astrological effects which last for a while, and then 'go away'. It may be that some form of standing wave is being created within the solar system which correlates with the observed phenomena and then evaporates as, perhaps, a slow-moving planet finally disrupts the resonance by moving out of orb.

Some of the philosophical implications of Plato's concept of Number and Form will be discussed at the end of the chapter, but we should now turn to a very modern way of exploring numbers in action: chaos.

The Archetypes of Chaos

Since the 1970s groups of mathematicians have become so fascinated by the qualities of certain sets of numbers to produce such coherent results out of apparent disorder that a whole new science has emerged – the science of chaos. It is a paradoxical title, for its results are anything *other* than chaotic. While many of these patterns are immensely beautiful, their true significance lies in the fact that they are demonstrating a coherent order in the underlying mathematical process, a process that would otherwise take place out of view, so to speak. Most strikingly, such patterns reveal sub-patterns which reveal sub-patterns and so on which continue to *maintain the exact mathematical relationships* in decreasing proportion, and are presumed to do so for infinity.

At the heart of their researches is the concept of what is known as *recursion*.

'Recursion' is a mathematical term employed when the answer of one formula is modified by another formula and then re-used by the first formula, a process which is repeated in an endless loop. If the modifying formula remains the same, then the answers produced by the first formula will become virtually identical after only a few loops have been completed. Then, quite without warning, after hundreds, thousands or even millions of such identical recursions, the number appears to go berserk.

A computer programmed to calculate such a formula and then plot on the screen, in dots and colours, the *exact point* at which the order suddenly breaks down can start to produce intricate patterns. These patterns reveal that what at first was thought to be an example of bizarre, random behaviour is in fact a highly ordered structure. Figure 4.1 illustrates a typical example, generated on the author's computer.

Some mathematicians postulate the idea that there is a hypothetical 'attractor' involved. That is, patterns may form which almost give the impression that events are being 'attracted' to some particular point in space or time. By evoking the idea of an attractor, the old idea of archetype or formative principle is re-emerging once again, this time inside the silicon chip.

If this were to be the case, these attractors would not mark relatively fixed and well-defined ideas such as those described by Jung or Plato, but far more abstract principles, often defined by

Figure 4.1 A classic Mandelbrot set generated on an ordinary PC computer. This shows the intricate patterns that apparently random behaviour can generate. If a small section of one of the 'tendrils' were to be enlarged we would see that it also sprouted similar tendrils; this is presumed to go on for infinity.

irrational or imaginary numbers. The recurring themes of chaos theory are more likely to define aspects of periodicity or recurrence, or point to underlying patterns in the shift from order to disorder, such as when societies or individuals may break free or break down from past restrictions.

However it is phrased, it does seem that even in apparent chaos, where numbers appear to break down, there is a unifying principle at work and its power is so great that everything ultimately bends to its will. Many mathematicians are taking the findings of chaos theory very seriously indeed and re-examining all forms of natural and human activities which were previously thought to be essentially random. The weather, movement in water, the shape of natural phenomena, stock market prices, in fact *anything* which demonstrates aperiodic fluctuations might in truth turn out to be harbouring an inner mathematical purpose.

More importantly, there appear to be emerging concepts of something like a fractional dimension – a fractal – where simple patterns can re-work themselves to infinity in all directions. Here all connection with the concept of archetype breaks down completely. What is being suggested by scientists is not so much an underlying, informing principle, but a vision of life exploding out of itself, acting out a process with wild abandon. As it has been postulated that the basic dynamics of the Solar system allow for chaotic manifestation, there is the real possibility that the astrologers of the future will need to explore the mathematics of chaos with considerable attention.

Morphogenetic Fields

One of the most recent theories which proposes something similar to the nature of archetype is that of Rupert Sheldrake. Sheldrake has advanced the concept of the *morphogenetic field* and suggests that this field has played a vital part in our evolution. A controversial biologist, Sheldrake postulates that it is possible for the universe to be imprinted with events and characteristics so that something like an infinite series of patterns is created, each with its own morphogenetic field. The effect of this field, Sheldrake argues, is to reinforce genetic patterns or ways of doing things by a process of sympathetic resonance.

For example, if I do something that has never been done before it is hard to achieve precisely *because* it has never been done before. Once I have achieved the task I have impressed a new pattern, or morphogenetic field, on to the universe which is a kind of record or blueprint of the activity. When *someone else* tries the same task, he or she somehow 'tunes in' to the blueprint of the original event and is actually assisted in repeating it. Thus behaviour patterns and evolutionary directions tend to be self-reinforcing, but at the same time have the potential to alter their direction.

Sheldrake's ideas are presented in his book *The Presence of the Past*,[2] and are backed up with some convincing evidence and the results of actual experimentation. As Sheldrake's theory demands in part that events will tend to cluster together in time, their relevance is considerable for astrologers, who might want to suggest that there could be *another* reason why this happens!

Whatever the cause, it is important to recognize that Sheldrake's concept of morphogenetic fields is not Jung's theory of archetypes in modern dress. We are not witnessing ideas about psychic energy re-presented in the language of physics, with fields and resonance replacing more mystical notions. Sheldrake is presenting something quite different. He is suggesting that the first time something happens it leaves its mark upon the universe, and that subsequent similar or identical events in some way resonate to that initial imprint.

The similarities are more with Freud and with astrology, in that Sheldrake is suggesting that *specific events* are embedded within some form of collective. More importantly, he suggests that each event is unique: I am the way that I am because I resonate to the morphogenetic field that I have created by existing. It is as if the field in some way maintains my separate identity because I continue to resonate to it, and not to some other field. Obviously, Sheldrake claims that we will resonate to many different fields in the course of life, but we have one that is unique to us and in some way it reinforces our separate identity.

Thus the picture Sheldrake's work presents focuses equally on the difference and separateness of events and individuals; quite the reverse of classic archetypal theory which seeks to explain *similarities* in terms of external agents. It could well be that we may need to reconsider how we view events which demonstrate remarkable likenesses; are they *really* just resonating to something separate from their own nature, or are we all individuals resonating to ourself, as Sheldrake suggests?

Electronic Archetypes

While Sheldrake's concept of a morphogenetic field already goes far beyond conventional ideas about archetypes, there is yet one more possible avenue that we can explore – but only with a computer.

For a number of years programmers and designers have been exploring a computer database concept called Hypertext. Hypertext is an information retrieval and exploration system that goes way beyond any conventional method of filing information, although it is rooted in something we have all done.

If we wish to research 'Astrology' we can go to a card-index which may list 'Babylonian', 'Greek' and 'Modern' under the 'Astrology' classification. We may decide to choose 'Modern', and find under that category 'Psychological', 'Mundane' and 'Technical'. If we choose 'Psychological' we will find the works of Liz Greene, Steven Arroyo and many others. If we are unfamiliar with their work we may need to look elsewhere under 'Jung' for additional information as to their underlying theories. Under 'Jung' we may come across a reference to 'Plato', and may need to find further information on him elsewhere, and so on. Thus we may end up reading about Pythagorean number theory, or about the Greek language, when we actually started out to inquire about modern astrology.

The Hypertext system takes this concept to its ultimate. It

presumes a database which will hold *all* possible information on its files. Not just every reference book and every word ever written down in any medium, but every film, play or visual image; anything, in fact, which is capable of being recorded electronically will be stored. This Aladdin's cave of information can then be searched.

We may, for instance, be watching a film on our Hypertext screen when a rather interesting animal creeps into shot. We will freeze the picture and point to the animal. Instantly a nature documentary on that animal is located and starts to play for us. The film may turn out not to be particularly interesting, but we find its theme music appealing, and at once we get biographical notes about its composer and watch a concert of that particular work – and so on, and so on, through a vast electronic maze with our computer recording each step of the journey so that we can return instantly to any point.

But this is just the beginning. Hypertext can be programmed to look not for *subjects*, but for *themes*.

For instance, many stories have the following plot: Boy meets Girl and they fall in love but are separated by Cruel Misfortune. After many years of wandering lonely, but faithfully, through all sorts of highly implausible situations, they find each other again and are blissfully happy. The Hypertext system would allow us to define such a theme and locate *all* works of fiction which depicted it. We could similarly locate, from stored biography and newspapers, all *real* occurrences of such a scenario – most useful for anyone seeking cause for litigation.

Our next step could be to define that theme more abstractly. It could be depicted as some form of graph or wave. For instance, it could be shown as a line which starts half-way up a scale (happiness), sinks to an abyss for some time (abject misery) and then rises to the heights (bliss). Our Hypertext system could locate *music* which followed a similar pattern, or *paintings* which treat colours in such a way, or *commodity prices*. Any stored data could be analysed in terms of its inherent wave-forms, and be located instantly.

Astrologers would of course insist on a Hypertext with a built-in ephemeris, so that all data which is in any way time-based can be analysed to see if the patterns it contains relate to planetary cycles.

Using such a system, we could locate the underlying astrological nature of all suitable data. If we found a specific theme which repeated in life, fiction, nature and music, we could no doubt call it an archetype. At that point we might also wish to question if this fits the initial concept of archetype at all.

Is our electronic archetype *really* underlying everything it has trawled from its memory banks, or have *we* created the connection by skilful programming? Would another culture admit to the same similarities, or do they exist only in the way we choose to phrase or perceive them?

It could be possible that the whole concept of archetype is just one attempt to make sense of how we conceive of patterns repeating, by presupposing that there is a specific form which underlies all similar occurrences. Just as we have seen how Jung created synchronicity to fill a need, so might he and others have formalized that concept of archetype which astrology has now effortlessly adopted.

Archetype and Astrology

Dr Richard Tarnas is one who presents the neo-Platonic view that 'at the heart of the astrological perspective is the claim that the planets are fundamentally associated with specific archetypes, and that the planetary patterns in the heavens are reflected in corresponding archetypal patterns in human affairs. By archetypes I am referring on one level to Jung's modern psychological conception.'[3]

In fact there would appear to be no real evidence from the past that astrologers have ever claimed that archetypes lie at the heart of astrology, and Tarnas is clearly using this concept differently from Jung. As we have already seen, Jung rejected the view that the planetary patterns are reflected in human affairs, preferring to see astrology as simply a projection of our unconscious, with no external validity of its own. Rather than admitting to the archetypal sources of Plato, much of Western astrology seems to have emerged from a quasi-divinational approach in which the Gods were assumed to talk *directly* to mortals, or to speak to them through symbols. Evidence for ancient belief in this direct, verbal communication comes from Princeton psychologist Julian Jaynes in his magnificently-titled *The Origins of Consciousness in the Breakdown of the Bicameral Mind*.[4]

It is beyond the scope of this book to explore Jaynes's theory, but in essence he proposed that up till about 3,000 years ago the two halves of the human brain operated differently from their observed functions today. Using much contemporary Greek literary source material, Jaynes suggests that the different functions of the brain were once so separate that they were actually experienced by the ancients as *separate voices*, which were then attributed to those of the Gods. Jaynes concludes that much of what we call schizophrenia is a genetic remnant of this phenomenon.

Despite his remarkable assertions, Jaynes is no Von Daniken, and marshals much evidence to his cause. The issue here is not whether he is right or wrong, but the fact that the ancient Greeks believed in direct contact with *Gods*, not archetypes, and that there is abundant evidence that the ancients believed this direct contact actually took place in everyday life. To dismiss the stated *experiences* of the ancients does them no service, nor does it help us understand their perspective or their philosophy.

In demonstrating his belief that the astrological energies are effectively the same as Jung's archetypes, Richard Tarnas carried out an extensive case study of individuals with strong Sun or Moon contacts with Uranus. Tarnas associates Uranus with the Promethean legend and demonstrates convincingly that those with such Uranus contacts fulfil a 'Promethean' function within society: they bring something of the cosmic fire to the world, via invention or discovery. Furthermore, Tarnas amply demonstrates that in many cases transiting Uranus was a major factor during the times when such discoveries and inventions took place.

In short, Tarnas's project was thorough and well researched; he confirmed what astrologers often claim to be the case, but rarely take the trouble to demonstrate. There can be little doubt that such Uranian aspects as he described *do* correlate with a specific approach towards life, and one that we could justifiably call Promethean. Moreover, key phases in those lives *do* correlate to the transiting Uranus. In other words, those with similar patterns *do* seem to act out a strikingly similar theme, though obviously modulated by circumstances unique to each life. Finally, a transit of Uranus does seem to trigger its own latent energies. But are we in reality witnessing the expression of an archetype? Is this real evidence that there is something like a blueprint, or an organizing pattern which Uranian aspects have manifested in the lives of those so touched? There is another possible explanation: things repeat.

If there are similar charts with similar patterns, then these should manifest in similar ways precisely because of their similarity. It will make no difference whether the charts are of those born weeks, months, decades or centuries apart, neither will geographic location alter this. If a similar arrangement of energies go in, we should expect a similar result to come out. This is what we see happening, and this would appear to be what Richard Tarnas's excellent research has revealed. Interestingly, neither his work nor his findings are diminished if we remove the concept of archetype from them entirely.

From an astrological perspective, we need only examine a few planetary relationships in the sample provided by Tarnas, those in which the personal points are contacted by Uranus. If the energies or drives suggested by the planets are similar in nature, we would also expect them to be similar in outcome. It is as if a group of chemists have all been given the same basic chemicals and left to their own devices. We should not be surprised if they finish the day having created similar compounds, and it would be most unlikely that we would feel a need to invent an archetype to explain why this had happened.

Astrologers, constantly working with the reality of symbols, can easily overlook the fact that psychologists do not have the advantage of this array of descriptive energies laid out for their use. For psychologists, patterns which cannot be accounted for by pathology have always to be explained by some other mechanism; for some this has been through genetics, for others through the concept of archetypes.

Recognizing that patterns can constantly re-create themselves *anew* out of their instinctual, component parts is to recognize that the idea of an essentially static archetypal force lying 'behind' the event is redundant. We have already seen that Jung himself believed archetypes to be formed from instincts; we can now see that precisely this mechanism may underlie the creation of certain types of common experiences. This also may underline further the idea suggested earlier that Jung marginalized astrology precisely because of this implication.

As we can see, there is an irony in the fact that the very repetition of astrological effects created the need within psychology for a concept of archetype to be developed in the first place, to account for those observed similarities. Without such a concept of archetype, we can not only see the astrology more clearly, we are in closer contact with our own lives. What takes place within us is *us*, and is unique to us. The themes which *do* occur within an individual's chart are expressed *within* the integrity of that individual's life, not constellated from energies outside of it. If the pattern repeats elsewhere, then the theme will repeat, created *anew* within another being. In recognizing within the lives of our clients their unique re-statement of familiar language, we recognize the authenticity of their experience, and the fact that they are experiencing, not an archetype of something else, but themselves.

It is not enough to point to a similarity of theme to demonstrate the reality of archetypes – however striking an example might be – as the existential analyst Medard Boss makes clear:

Jung thought he had to assume archetypal structures in every subject's psyche to account for the independent occurrence of the same phenomena here and there, now and in the past. He even believed that he had 'proved' the existence of such archetypes by, e.g., the observation that one of his patients dreamed of an apparition which corresponded perfectly to the 'primitive' and 'archaic' image of a 'pneumatic' divine being, in spite of the fact that the patient could not read Greek and was not familiar with mythological problems. Far from being the proof for the existence of anything within a subject, these phenomena simply gave evidence of the fact that it pleased the Divine to show Itself to the archaic individuals of past ages in the same fashion as It may appear to dreamers in the twentieth century.[5]

Medard Boss's observation is of the greatest importance. Concepts of archetypes – energies which are *external* to us, though they have in some manner been formed by human processes and instinct over the aeons – are here being used to deny the reality of what was actually being experienced. In the well-known example cited, Jung is effectively saying that the man in question did *not* experience a visitation from the Divine. He just experienced an archetype. No doubt if he suddenly fell in love with someone he would have been diagnosed as being 'anima possessed', just as the somewhat acerbic and distressingly powerful quality – distressing to men, that is – which some women express can be dismissed as their 'animus problem'.

This is a highly reductionist attitude and it permeates the Jungian world in a way not always recognized. It is in essence no different whatsoever from Freud's preoccupation with sexual trauma as the cause of all ills, and misfixated libido or ungratified urges as supplying the 'true' motive of every act. Both approaches conspire to deny the reality of experience by applying a theory to 'explain' it and make it safe. But the theories proposed have lamentably failed to demonstrate their authenticity. Indeed, as we have seen from the example above, the attempt to which Medard Boss refers – Jung's claim that similar experiences must indicate a common third source, the archetype – is capable of a dramatically different interpretation.

If something happens again and again, in all corners of the world and at all times in history, this is not proof that the observed or experienced phenomenon stems from the intrusion of an external archetype. It is not proof that there is an imagined energy separate from the thing itself, lying behind the thing itself or representing or symbolizing the thing itself: it *is* the thing itself. That is how the thing expresses itself. That is how the thing *is*.

At a simple level, we may observe a number of clocks all telling us the same time. They are telling us the same time because they are essentially similar within their own 'being', so to speak. They are all unique and quite unconnected, but they have essential similarities (as do humans on both psychic and genetic levels) and these similarities dictate the way the clocks behave. We would be quite wrong in assuming that they were all acting out some hidden archetype; they are patently not.

It could similarly be suggested that in England, and in other countries with a monarchy, the King and Queen in some way act out a parental archetype for the populace, that they constellate it in the collective psyche. Those who would suggest this would no doubt point to the fact that during times of crisis the population in some way turns to the monarch for guidance, or at least for example, as has been clearly evident during the last two world wars. There is, however, another way of looking at this: things repeat.

All of us, as children, will naturally have turned to our parents in times of stress and crisis; this is what children do – it is part of the biological pattern of survival-behaviour that we share with all mammals, and hardly demands any close psychic scrutiny or deep theorizing to understand. As such stressful events are by their nature traumatic, they will leave some echo of themselves within us *all*. That is, to some extent, we all carry within us the pattern of turning to authority figures at times of stress because we've *all done it*. When as adults we experience some collective trauma in the form of an international crisis, we will tend to respond similarly, by looking to authority for help or guidance. Not because the authority constellates some imaginary archetype, but because the residues of childhood experience which we hold within us, from our quite separate encounters with life, will push us towards reacting to such obvious symbols in the same manner.

From an astrological point of view, having similar planetary patterns should predispose individuals towards similar activities or experiences. Not because such experiences might constellate an external archetype, but because the planetary patterns symbolize each individual's separate drive towards a specific goal; a goal which others happen to share.

For example, at one level a Moon/Pluto aspect might correlate with a powerful, 'devouring' mother experience. The aspect may even describe the actual mother with some accuracy, and might be one of the symbolic factors why those with such aspects were born to such women. The idea, however, that there should be an archetype of this is quite another matter, and it is one not really needed to explain the nature of the common experience.

Indeed, the Jungian concept of archetype can so easily distance us from the immediacy of our sensations, and detracts from the complex nature of that which we *do* experience, frequently relegating it to something other than what actually took place. It invades our sense of the world, for instance by suggesting – as Jung himself has done – that problems lie with parental archetypes rather than in our stated experience of the parents themselves. Such approaches would seem to contribute very little to an understanding of the nature of our own development, and risk alienating us from the reality of our own history.

Paradoxically, it would seem that astrology itself creates the illusion of archetype, as we shall see in a moment, but it is our peculiarly Western orientation which allows the idea to flourish. Such states of perception stem in part from neo-Platonic philosophy – one of the major sources for Jung's archetype theory which have been absorbed into Western thinking.

By no means all Western philosophies share Plato's view of form and idea – some are quite opposed to it. If we examine their views on such concepts as an underlying truth or reality we may see some further implications of archetypal theory not always considered by astrologers.

The idea of a pre-existing form, one which lies behind events and experiences, may be more the result of what our personal philosophy *expects* the world to be like than how it might actually be. To go further here we may need to inquire what some philosophies actually expect of the world.

Archetype and Philosophy

From a phenomenological point of view, neo-Platonism makes an erroneous division between a world of pure 'ideas' and the humdrum reality of the world in which we all live. Indeed, all theories which postulate an 'above' which moulds a 'below' risk continuing what many would see as a specious dichotomy. In such subject/object splits – which hardly exist at all in Eastern philosophies – a distorted picture of human existence is created, an existence which alienates the *observable* aspects of human behaviour from their *unobservable*, interior, spiritual or 'higher' components. Such 'higher' components are often relegated to an external source, effectively suggesting that an individual is somehow expressing something other than what that individual *is*; a philosophical stance that many would claim was fatally flawed.

As with the concept of archetype, the removal of the essence or centrality of a thing to some point *outside* or *beyond* the thing is ultimately dehumanizing. For all the richness and breadth of Platonic thought, the ideal world of Plato is a bleak prospect indeed. Regimented, hierarchical and stripped of human individuality, it offers a vista of a world where people become the embodiment of the roles they play. Philosopher, guardian, or citizen, each manifesting the essence of something other than themselves, acting habitually in accord with some described plan.

In this ideal, 'rational' world they are denied both choice and freedom, and ultimately cease to be *themselves*; in fact, they would actually cease to *be* in any existential sense. Those who disagree, according to Plato, are most unlikely to exist in a physical sense either. He makes it clear that those who rebel, who do not conform to the city state or deny the validity of the Platonic vision, are ultimately to be killed.

History shows us time and time again that such is invariably the fate of those who fail to live up to an ideal imposed upon them, particularly when the ideal is claimed to personify the truth and thus to justify any action. It is remarkable, and frequently commented upon, that the very 'truths' which are claimed to be self-evident or universal can simply never be demonstrated.

Immanuel Kant claimed that the 'scandal of philosophy' was that it had never succeeded in demonstrating the reality of such universal truths (God or No God included), despite the frequent assumptions that it (or they) exist (or don't exist, if you're running on the atheist ticket). Considering that astrology so often claims to represent just such a Truth, or expound the cause of an underlying Reason, it is worthwhile considering for a moment how nebulous such an archetypal concept actually is.

Kant's Critique of Reason

Within weeks of the discovery of Uranus – the planet most associated with abstract thought – the philosopher Immanuel Kant published his appropriately titled *Critique of Pure Reason*. The book marked a watershed in the history of philosophy and was an attempt to confront two quite different philosophical schools which laid contradictory claims on whether or not Truth existed and was knowable.

The cause of Truth was represented by Leibniz, as the main Rationalist of his time, who declared that such a Truth was knowable through Reason, though perhaps ultimately only to God's Reason. Leibniz was a Platonist who saw the world as the creation of archetype-like forms called Monads. These were seen as being predestined by God to unfold their inner purpose via humanity, and according to rational, inevitable rules created by God. Indeed, even God would be circumscribed by the demands of the Ultimate Reason to act in accordance to that Reason; God's Reason would demand that no other course was possible.

Empiricists question the whole premise of this approach, often criticizing it as fanciful mysticism masquerading as philosophy.

David Hume in particular pointed out that all our experiences – inner and outer – come to us via the senses. All that we see of the world is similarly processed by how we are, as are the conclusions that we come to. Thus, to Hume, we are given to inventing Reasons and Truths behind the events we observe, not because such events *are* destined to be linked by the demands of a controlling Reason or Purpose, but because *we* have linked them so, by a 'reasoning' that is at the beck and call of all human frailties. In modern terms, Hume was suggesting that we were projecting our personal experience on to that which we observed, and claiming it to be an objective Truth.

Kant could recognize the compelling logic of Hume's argument; indeed he felt it irrefutable, but recoiled from its ultimate assessment of humanity. In Hume's world there could be no God, no Truth, no Good; in fact none of the eternal philosophical verities could survive the moral winter of the Empiricist's domain.

But it was not a simple question of choosing to embrace Rationalism. In Kant's mind that path, too, led to aberrant, fatalistic possibilities. For one thing it suggested that we could know what lay beyond the totality of our experience; to Kant this was an obvious contradiction. More importantly, the Rationalists of Hume's day had failed to challenge the implications of Hume's work: that events have no cause in any meaningful sense, and that no profound Truths could lie behind the world we observe.

Kant's master-work confronted the implications of both Rationalism and Empiricism – and laid some of the foundation stones of modern existentialism – by rising to take up that challenge.

Kant formulated a philosophy which fully recognized the limitations and inadequacies of our ability to grasp Truth by making an attempt to categorize different aspects of our experience. We can justly claim to know the truth of – and the cause of – worldly phenomena, but we cannot ever know the truth of what lies *behind* such experience. We may perceive the activities of 'things in the world', but we shall never know the 'thing in itself', as Kant named the hidden, noumenal aspect of phenomena.

In this way Kant removed the bleak implications of Hume's

philosophy, but at a cost. Concepts of God, Truth and so forth are similarly barred to Reason, and their ultimate veracity can never be demonstrated by argument. Kant by no means rejects them as *concepts* – quite the reverse – but he denies that they could ever be objects of *knowledge*. They remain for him valid and powerful ideas, created by our highest faculties, which can orientate and focus our life, but they are not demonstrable and knowable in the way the Rationalists had claimed.

The relevance of Kant's work for astrologers is twofold: it cautions us against the common claim that the astrological experience is an objective truth – it isn't – and it offers us a challenge in exactly the same manner that Hume's Empiricism challenged Kant. If astrology ever demonstrates an objective knowledge of that which lies *behind* the phenomena of this world, then what is possibly the greatest single work of modern philosophy will need a considerable amount of rewriting.

The important word, of course, is *if*.

Heidegger's Phenomenology

Phenomenology is that aspect of philosophy which inquires as to how things which are exterior to us are actually experienced *by us*. It differs from *ontology*, which explores how we experience *our own being* by suggesting that we can only know for certain how we experience *something else*. That is, 'we do not know objects, nor do we know ourselves the subjects . . . we only know the phenomena which are the transitory and contingent products of the two "unknowns"'.[6]

In this respect phenomenology explores the barrier between ourself and the world. It offers an approach as to how we interpret what is 'coming in to us', and it argues that we should not impose pre-existing ideas upon that experience. The experience itself should reveal itself to us; we should be prepared to recognize the truth of it on its own terms.

In *Existence and Being* the philosopher Martin Heidegger argued that Truth does not exist in some place *other* than within the thing or the experience the Truth pertains to. Truth does not correspond to something else, nor does it mirror something else, nor is it a pale imitation of some external idea; it is contained within the nature and experience of Being.

In this sense Truth can be thought of as something which shines forth like a light or a revelation from within the nature of this experience of being. Heidegger further designates the essential nature of Being as 'being-in-the-world' to emphasize that there literally 'is' nowhere else to 'be'; Truth emanates from the state of Being, and from nowhere else. As with archetypes, the Platonic concept of Ideas would seem to distance us from the central nature of our being, without materially adding to our inner understanding of its meaning.

Similarly, the concept of 'rationality', central to the philosophy of Plato, may also not be the guide that many hoped it might become. Plato claimed that men, but not women, had a Rational function. This gave them the capacity to use reason and logic in a manner quite devoid of emotion or feeling. Ultimately only those decisions made 'rationally' could be called True. The more rational, the more True; hence the Platonic concept of a hierarchy of Truth, of one 'truth' being 'greater' than another. The individual's *experience* of the Truth was not to be a deciding factor; the arbiter of Truth lay beyond the personal realm.

There is no doubt that we may see things differently when in different frames of mind, and that some approaches to a problem are more useful than others as a result, but this is not what Plato had in mind. It is, of course, a conjecture that we have a Rational function in the manner suggested by Plato; it is also debatable as to whether Truth can be structured vertically – or in any other direction.

Heidegger and others would prefer the idea that we encounter the world differently in different moods; that our varying states of 'being-in-the-world' present us with the truth of differing experiences. They would go on to suggest that an attempt to quantify or structure Truth, as it applies to our awareness of existence, is quite inappropriate to an understanding of Being. The claim that one Truth is 'greater' than another has some very serious implications – some of which will be explored in the final chapter – as does the implicit assumption that there is an unvarying Self to perceive such a Truth.

The idea of treating the Self as a substance is another Platonic legacy. For Plato the 'true' Self is immortal. It behaves like a physical object, moving from incarnation to incarnation on a specific spiritual journey. Yet what we claim as being 'ourself' often shifts dramatically during the course of life, and would appear to be determined more by a sense of inner experience or awareness – in other words, it is something capable of being constantly re-drawn in the light of sensation – rather than as a fixed, unchanging entity.

By the very nature of its implications, astrology further contributes to the idea that the Self is not a static phenomenon to which things 'happen', though in practice astrologers tend to go no further than suggesting 'unfolding evolution', 'inner expansion' and so forth. In doing so they would appear to vacillate between a perception of the Self as a primal 'thing' in the manner of Plato, and the Self as a changing entity not necessarily anchored to the past. Neither position, however, seems to consider the idea of Self in a relation to Being, and hence capable of being 'created' by the act of its existence.

The approach to astrology that we have explored so far – which favours synchrony over synchronicity – constantly underlines the manner in which we may have to begin to rethink the nature of the birth chart. We have seen that it may no longer be possible to consider that we 'are' a single moment, a single map, and thus destined to become a single entity, the pale reflection of an 'ideal' Other. Instead we see that moments of importance, moments when we interact with life, beginning before we are born, can 'add' to the sum of our chart in the manner that we have experienced them, and contribute to what we may perceive as being 'ourself'. Thus, that which we identify as being 'us' may have very little to do with pre-existing conditions implicit in the Platonic or Christian concept of an individual Soul.

Archetype and Self

The view of astrology presented so far parallels a more dynamic view of Being. Just as we might describe the present as being the current state of the past, and view the collective unconscious as the expression of moment-by-moment transits to innumerable past events, so we may also see that the Self might move in and out of phase with its own history, and consequently become re-evaluated in the light of its current dynamic.

At different times in life, sometimes at different moments quite close together, we may ally the 'self' to a variety of memories, attitudes or sensations. At other times we may renounce them, hardly believing that we could ever have identified with particular recollections, however 'true' they were believed to be at the time. This is particularly evident in the course of analysis, when enormous issues can revolve around specific aspects of the psyche – which are passionately identified with – only to be discarded as 'false' when an insight or an abreaction shifts our perspective. Similarly the use of even mild hypnosis in the majority of subjects will reveal differing sides and selves, which may be open to a wide variety of interpretation.

Implicit in this view of astrology is that the 'self' of the birth chart in some way connects up to events and individuals which pre-existed the individual, but to whom that individual resonates via contacts in the zodiac. As Freud pointed out, events which happened to our ancestors may be subsequently internalized by their descendants, and become an actual part of their own experience and identity. Astrology would take this possibility further by suggesting that we can also incorporate other non-tangible moments such as ideas, or blend in to ourselves the birth moments of cities, inventions, battles, novels, countries; any happening, in fact, which has left its mark on those degrees our own chart activates can become a part of 'us', and at some point become identified with our own experience.

Even without getting into the complexities of reincarnation we can see that we have the potential to identify the Self with events which were initially external to it, but have now become incorporated within it by virtue of a shared symbolic affinity. Through this interchange we have the potential to link up with all things, though we are probably biased or shifted by the instinctual nature of our birth chart towards specific areas of awareness and recognition.

It could even be possible that in this way we may identify strongly with (literal) aspects of specific individuals, and the mark that they have left on the zodiac. As it is almost the definition of an aspect to bring together disparate images we may get another perspective here of why it is that seemingly incongruous events or characteristics become repeated *together*. For instance, the seventeenth-century philosopher Giambattista Vico saw everything in terms of language and rhythm and cycle – and was terrified of thunderstorms. James Joyce saw life in terms of language, rhythm and cycle – and was *also* frightened of thunderstorms – and lived close to Vico Road, Dublin.

We can similarly examine the lives of famous men and women and note such interesting connections between their own experiences and the experiences of those in whose path they followed. Frequently they will themselves comment on such similarities, or note that certain events or discoveries happen to them at the same *time* as in the lives with which they in some manner identify. Such observations will force us to question again that which we consider to be 'self' and that which we reject as 'non self'.

Existentialist philosophers use concepts of 'authentic' and 'inauthentic' to describe actions or states of being which are in keeping with, or go against, what is perceived as the true nature of the Self, and they may offer us a clue as to how best we may proceed from here. First, though, it may be necessary to recognize that 'authenticity' can be quite different from the encounter group's colloquial exhortation to 'be yourself'. Nobody would deny for a moment that a two-year-old throwing its vegetables on the floor and demanding chocolate instead is doing anything other than 'being itself'. Yet this cannot remotely be thought of as 'authentic behaviour'; indeed, it could hardly be *less* authentic.

The two-year-old is acting instinctively, and without insight, awareness or consideration of its Self, and is doing so in a manner which would be termed psychopathic in an adult. There may well be, somewhere within the infant, a sense that its true needs are not being met, and its parents' choice of food may symbolize this to some extent. The subsequent trajectory of the cabbage, however, does not describe an authentic response, at least not in the philosophical sense of the term!

It would seem that our capacity for authenticity derives directly from such inauthentic beginnings, and lies in part in our ability to recognize such habit-bound, instinctual responses to life, and transcend the everyday 'self'. This everyday 'self' is all too often anchored into, and in some ways created *by*, the patterns of ordinary life, or has emerged as a result of what has been done *to* us, rather than from what we *are*. Many philosophers, such as Heidegger, would suggest that awareness of the 'true self' is possible only when we confront such major issues as death, dread and joy; only at such moments do we become aware of the enormity of Being, and of the nature of the Self, by pushing ourselves to the limits of experience.

Even if this is an unduly dramatic pronouncement, we nevertheless see that the process of 'being' is not necessarily to be viewed as a linear phenomenon, like the Soul 'thing' of Plato moving from incarnation to incarnation, and being the arbiter of reality in an 'unreal' world. The Self described by modern existentialists is capable of radical redefinition by a perception of the nature of Being; and Truth is inexorably tied into the nature of the *moment of experience*, rather than conforming to hypothesized, pre-existing criteria.

In working with the birth chart we will tend to use such expressions as 'self', 'ego', 'life-goal', 'purpose' and so on when interpreting the more focused energies of Sun, Mars, Ascendant and Midheaven. Most astrologers, however, will use these terms in a somewhat generalized manner for, as we have seen, there is *no* coherent astrological theory of personality from which to derive specific associations. Indeed, experience strongly suggests that *iden-*

tity can lie virtually anywhere within the chart, even if specific drives or responses may be more readily perceived.

As has been often pointed out, we may identify with different parts of our chart at different times, and our affinities may sometimes fluctuate rapidly. In fact the more we address the idea of Self in relation to what we perceive of the birth chart, the more we are forced to recognize that the Self may not be one particular 'thing', and instead be more of a state of perception which is by no means as fixed a substance as either Platonic Forms or Christian souls might suggest.

It may be important to recognize that in accepting the idea that there is an unchanging 'True Self', which seems to exist at least partially *outside* of the centre of our experience, we not only ignore the very real paradox such a situation presents (if the True Self is somewhere else, then what are *we* doing here?), we also see how the concept of form and archetype may contribute to creating a very considerable dualistic illusion; an illusion which astrology itself could actually dispel.

While we do not need the concept of an underlying archetype to explain why individuals born hundreds of years apart might have very similar experiences, or even appear to share images and dreams, we do seem to be irresistibly drawn to the idea of collective or shared experiences of some kind. Sometimes examples of such extreme similarity occur that we can think of no other explanation than a common source. This indeed may well be the case, but it may have nothing to do with archetype and everything to do with astrology.

In fact, if we pursue some of the implications of astrology's symbolism, they can provide a perspective from which we can obtain quite dizzying glimpses of the interplay of personality and events. Much of this may have to do with how we may view the nature of symbolic expression, and we may find some much-needed clarity if we first re-examine how symbols are believed to operate within the psyche. In pursuing such ideas we may arrive at what could be termed an astrological topography of the unconscious.

5.

Interpreting the Unconscious: Astrology and the Primal Zodiac

✫ ✫ ✫ ✫ ✫ ✫ ✫ ✫ ✫ ✫

In stating that the concept of archetype is not necessary for the explanation of shared or common experiences we must also recognize that astrology has always assumed the existence of some form of shared process in which we all participate – the birth chart. At a very basic level the signs of the zodiac and the cycles of the planets are clear examples of principles at work in all creation. Very little, however, has been done to pursue the implications of whether these principles work *in* us or *through* us, or how such a shift of perspective might alter the manner in which we perceive the nature of astrology.

In this chapter we shall start to explore how different approaches towards viewing collective or shared experiences can be brought together with the suggestion made earlier: that astrology works *synchronously* rather than *synchronistically*, and that we are in some form of constant resonance to patterns which pre-date our birth. In doing so we shall see that one of Freud's original ideas – that of archaic memory – gives us powerful clues as to *why* the concept of archetype may have emerged, and why it is so powerful. We may also come to recognize that the manner in which Freud saw the development of the human race, individually and collectively, bears a striking similarity to the way astrologers perceive the nature of our world.

To begin our exploration of this similarity we will need to look more closely at the manner in which Jung and Freud saw the nature of the *symbol*. Not surprisingly, their respective attitudes towards its possible function reflected some of their greatest differences.

A Clash of Symbols

It has often been suggested that Jung's break with Freud came about because the Swiss psychologist was not able to accept Freud's theory of libidinal determinism, but this is not really correct. Jung was *never* convinced by Freud's libido theory right from the start. We can see in the very first letter Jung wrote to Freud after their initial meeting[1] that, while he recognized at once Freud's contribution to understanding the underlying role of sexuality in cases of neurosis, a completely pan-sexual psychology was another matter altogether. In his autobiography, *Memories, Dreams and Reflections*, he tells us: 'I see man's drives, for example, as various manifestations of energetic processes and thus forces analogous to heat, light etc. Just as it would not occur to modern physicists to derive all forces from, say, heat alone, so the psychologist should beware of lumping all instincts under the concept of sexuality.'[2]

In fact the search for a single energy source is precisely what modern physicists *are* looking for, but it is most unlikely that they are doing this for Freudian reasons. Nevertheless, we do need to consider Jung's claims for multiple energy sources carefully, as they have obvious parallels within astrology. The real split between the two men, however, was over the issue of how libido – or any other energy – manifested itself in *symbols*. It was, after all, the publication of Jung's book which is now known as *Symbols of Transformation* that marked the parting of the ways.

The manner in which the two men viewed symbols is of the utmost importance to our understanding of their respective positions. As both points of view have much to offer the astrological perspective, it is important that we are quite clear as to their respective arguments. While *Symbols of Transformation* also strongly attacks the whole libidinal theory, it would be an error to confuse this attack with Jung's own concepts on the possible nature of symbols themselves. Even if Jung had been a passionate believer in infantile sexuality, his views on the symbolic expression of the unconscious would still have taken a dramatically different direction, and these views would have inevitably alienated him from Freud.

For the sake of clarity we should remove the specific issue of sexuality from the argument. In doing so we discover that, contrary to expectation, the way in which Freud perceived the unconscious operating might actually be more in line with our current assumptions about astrological processes than with Jung's concept of the workings of archetypes. To understand this more fully we need only examine how the two men viewed dreams, as here we can see their attitudes towards symbols at their clearest.

Jung saw in dreams the unconscious express itself through collective images. Certain archetypes, myths and universal patterns could appear in a guise understandable to the dreamer, telling a story that could be interpreted. If there was confusion or misunderstanding, this was the fault of the dreamer, not the dream. 'To me a dream is a part of nature, which harbours no intentions to deceive, but to express something as best it can . . . but we may deceive ourselves because our eyes are shortsighted.'[3] The dream tells a story that may be *interpreted*, it gives us a message about our inner state that the unconscious wishes us to know.

The dream is a little hidden door in the innermost and most secret recesses of the psyche, opening into that cosmic night which was psyche long before there was any ego consciousness, and will remain psyche no matter how far our ego consciousness may extend . . . in dreams we put on the likeness of that more universal, truer and more eternal man dwelling in the darkness of the primordial night . . . Out of these all-uniting depths arises the dream, be it never so infantile, never so grotesque, never so immoral.[4]

In *Archetypes of the Collective Unconscious* Jung describes one such dream, belonging to a theologian. The man had dreamed that he wished to go to a lake that was in the middle of a dense wood, but that something prevented him. This time, however, he was able to reach the lake and, as he watched, a wind passed over the water causing it to ripple. The man woke up very afraid.

Jung interpreted this dream as being a reference to the pool of Bethesda. The breath of God – the pneuma – gives the pool curative powers. The dream would seem to suggest that the theologian was resisting (by his fearful reaction) some form of direct spiritual experience, preferring dogma and academic religion instead. In fact, Jung reports that the man was most reluctant to accept his interpretation.

In many respects this is typical of the way in which Jung worked with dreams. He interprets their *manifest* content. That is, he takes the 'story' of the dream as a generalized statement about the individual, which is assumed to be true, and relates this directly back to the dreamer. The other levels of the dream, its *latent* content, are not really explored beyond a few immediate associations.

It is, in a generalized sense, true to say that traditional Jungians tend to interpret dreams while Freudians analyse them. Those Freudians who actively work with dreams will request their analysands to free-associate on all aspects of the dream; its story, its images, and all the images that come up during this exploratory process. Not surprisingly, this can be an excessively long exercise which does not always bear results proportionate to the time expended. The Jungian approach (which, of course, many other schools also adopt) has the advantage of going quickly to an indisputably important part of the dream, and concentrating on that. Using this method, the symbols of the dream are then interpreted and the dreamer confronted with their message.

These symbols, whether in dreams or in waking life, are seen by Jungians as emanating from primary sources of energy such as archetypes, and focus around a particular image or idea. The symbol might be quite literal, like a mandala object that could indicate that the process of integration was at work, or more abstract in that a scene might depict the archetype of marriage by a sequence of events rather than with a single icon. In either case the analyst would tend to concentrate on the core idea expressed and its relevance for the dreamer at that time; other images would be subsumed to the portrayed archetype.

The alternative approach would go beyond the literal, manifest content of the dream by a process of free-association towards creating a much fuller understanding of the total, latent message contained in each component part. In working with each dream image it is possible for the analysand to come to recognize that many different parts of the unconscious, and many different shades of its development at differing times, are all seeking their own expression in the dream. Behind the basic story of the dream there are a multiplicity of legends. All the images described are themselves created out of a mosaic of associated fragments. Different time-frames, different perspectives and different attitudes all coexist as one *Gestalt*. It is not a random collection; all are relevant to the purpose of the dream, all attend its call.

However trivial or seemingly ridiculous specific associative aspects of a dream might seem, they play a part because they refer to one aspect or another of the dreamer's psychic life. They may not be the most important part of the dream, but they cannot be removed. The dream has to be seen as a totality, as representing a statement that has emerged from a myriad component parts. The dream itself can be thought of as a symbol of the dreamer, of the underlying psychic tensions and the various strata of the dreamer's inner life.

Viewed in this light, we could call the dream a *complex symbol*. That is, it is not something which just *contains* symbols; it *is* one. It is a category of symbol made up of other symbols which can be understood only in their totality; we cannot extract one from the other. We shall return to this idea in Chapter 6 and explore its importance in the practice of astrology.

What we experience of the dream during its analysis is like something floating in the sea, rolling gently in the swell, gradually revealing more of itself, while much we thought familiar slides quietly out of sight. As in life, we may wake up one morning to realize with some surprise that we no longer recognize the person we once believed ourselves to be. The interests and attitudes we felt with such a certainty only a few years previously are no longer there, and have been quietly exchanged. Some Mercurial hand has dazzled us, plucked something from within and silently rearranged the unseen elements of the interior psychic puzzle while we slept.

If we read the many dream examples given by both Freud and Jung in their respective *Collected Works*, we shall see again and again how Jung accentuated the significance of an archetypal image while Freud dwelt on the latent material emerging from free-association. It is important to recognize that there is much more implied here than just a difference in technique.

For Jung, the psychic events described in the dream or experienced in the process of life happen because they are a reflection, in some way, of powerful archetypal energies. They express themselves in our lives because that is what he believed archetypes 'do'. For him, life *was* an expression of archetypal energies and that's why it is the way it is. We may theorize as much as we like, but the workings of the unconscious are quite unpredictable and, as we have seen in Chapter 2, Jung believed that the way it operated is quite impervious to rational investigation.

For Freud, things were very different. Or, rather, he hoped that one day they would be, for a number of his original ideas – which he clung to all his life – have either been quietly ignored by his disciples because of their fantastic implications or have rarely found among his followers those sufficiently sympathetic or gifted to develop them. Among these ideas was his concept of archaic memory.

Freud and Archaic Memory

While Jung viewed the unconscious as essentially a mysterious process operating by its own self-regulatory mechanisms, Freud was obsessively attached to the idea of cyclical phenomena repeating themselves and the belief that the unconscious – as well as the ego – might become knowable through the language it used to express itself.

While Jung extended the concept of the symbol towards the numinous depths of archetypal principles, way out of the reach of ordinary understanding, to becoming a universal principle in a vast cosmic process, Freud saw the symbol as being intrinsically bound up in the life of the individual. It was thus essentially *personal* and evolved through all the psycho-sexual stages of life, drawing to itself a myriad associations on its journey through the psyche, and thus capable of being expressed in a multiplicity of guises in both dreams and waking life. As we have seen, Freud believed that the natural language of the unconscious was *language*, but, much more importantly, he also believed that we are biologically rooted in the history of our evolution: in other words, we can actually experience the emotions and actions of our ancestors.

It was *this*, as much as anything else, that Jung was unable to tolerate and rejected so forcibly in *Symbols of Transformation*.

The original theory of the libido is intrinsically one of a total process of evolution expressing itself in the life of the individual. For Jung it was quite impossible to conceive of regressing further back than the womb. Regression, for him, could lead only as far as the mother; 'she is the gateway to the unconscious, into the realm of the Mother'.[5] The break with Freud comes at *this* point; psychic energy *cannot* have the biological roots that Freud ascribed to it; it must move from the earthly image to its relevant archetype. In disconnecting from the possibility of the psyche having a genetic basis – however scientifically improbable this might be – Jung veers away from the whole cyclical model of human evolution that Freud was groping towards.

This model, when examined, is strikingly similar to the one implicitly used by many astrologers.

It was Freud's contention that the development of the human race had its parallel in the psychic development of the individual, (see Figure 5.1). The great ages and traumas of human evolution, such as the Ice Age, correspond to anxiety and apprehension in the individual case of neurosis, and are also visible in the normal child's reactions to the changing 'landscape' of its early years. The child learning to crawl, to stand upright and walk, directly mirrors the shift from ape to human. Furthermore, the sequence of history repeats in the sequence of libidinal development. All major events in history, such as learning language, forming tribes, setting up chieftains, shifting from nomad to village life, all have their psychic correspondences within the individual.

Our Collective History	Our Individual History
Origin of life	Maturation of sex cells
Origin of individual single-life cell	Release of sexual cells
Beginning of sexual propagation	Fertilization
Beginning of marine life	Embryo in uterus
Move from ocean to land	Birth
Development of true sexual organs	Awareness of sexual feelings
The Ice Age	Latency period

Figure 5.1 Parallels between collective and individual processes, according to Freud and Ferenczi.

As the human race has progressed and developed, so do each of its members echo that evolutionary pattern today, every one following the identical sequence. The patterns and experience of previous 'lives' continue to haunt us; our predisposition to certain forms of neurosis or phobias are dictated by what happened centuries ago, now surfacing as archaic memories which are triggered by events in the current lifetime. While Freud recognized that his inadequate knowledge of the human psyche and its evolution prohibited an exact match, he worked with Sandor Ferenczi in an attempt to establish just such a fit. Ideally, all that was acted out over tens of millions of years is repeated again in each flickering lifetime, mark for mark, blow for blow, transit for transit.

The Freudian parallel between the individual and its evolutionary past is like that of an astrological direction; not a day for a year, or a month for a day, but a Life for its Past.

Furthermore, Freud clearly states, as we have seen in Chapter 2, that everything which has happened to us in our history is somehow embedded within us. The actions of our ancestors are continuously accessible. If an infant's own experience fails him, he 'replaces occurrences in his own life by occurrences in the life of his ancestors'. In other words, he continues to resonate directly to past events, by embodying them once again in a new incarnation.

If Freud is right then these feelings, events, sensations and occurrences are not *symbolic* in nature, they are not expressions of external psychic powers or mythical beasts: they are *real*. Each actually happened, at a certain time, on a certain day, in a certain place.

If we had charts for them we could plot their current reflection in each and every one of us, exactly as we now relate to ourselves the charts of those countries, towns and events of which we *do* have a knowledge.

Astrology is based on *precisely* this kind of cyclical repetition; of instances unfolding through the processes of time, coming into being as the key moments of their history are triggered by subsequent transits, activating their latent energy in the present. Such an astrological approach would appear to be quite in accord with Freud's original ideas on the development of the psyche. In Freudian terms, as we evolve further, so we add to the genetic store of experiences that our descendants will inherit and to which they might respond, adding another layer – or another chart – to the collective storehouse. At such moments we may wonder, improperly, how Freud might have reacted to that idea.

Freud and Astrology

During the early part of his creative life Freud was extensively influenced by some of the ideas of Wilhelm Fliess.[6] Fliess was a surgeon who believed that there were a complex series of patterns, related to numbers, which regulated our emotional, physical and intellectual states, and which began with the moment of our birth.

This theory went far beyond the concept of bio-rhythms, to which it subsequently gave birth, and included complex numerical possibilities stemming from the harmonics of certain prime numbers. Long after parting company with Fliess, Freud continued to speculate that the individual developed along certain psycho-biological wave-forms that were inherent in human evolution.

Fliess himself suspected that in such wave-forms there was a 'deeper connection between astronomical relationships and the creations of organisms'.[7]

Tying astronomical cycles directly to the birth moment *is* astrology, however delicately the faint-hearted may try to phrase it – and Freud was not ashamed to recognize this fact. When Fliess sent him the results of research into the relationship between the states of bodily organs and planetary or lunar cycles, Freud saw the immediate connection. In his letter to Fliess on 9 October 1896, Freud wrote: 'You know that I do not laugh at fantasies such as those about historical periods. There is something to these ideas; it is the symbolic presentiment of unknown realities with which they have in common . . . one can not escape from acknowledging heavenly influences. I bow before you as honorary astrologer.'[8]

Exactly *what* experiments had been carried out by Fliess will never be known: some time after 1904, according to a letter to Fliess's widow, Freud destroyed the entire correspondence of his former friend and colleague, for reasons which have never been satisfactorily explained.

Despite this loss, we can see in the early work of Freud an attitude towards developmental psychology that is remarkably similar to the astrological paradigm, with its interlocking cycles and interdependence, possibly geared to the actual movements of the planets. How far Freud allowed himself to speculate in this direction cannot, of course, ever be known. We do know that he considered our relationship to the Sun as being of primary importance, the Sun being a key factor in so many biological and reproductive cycles, and his early research with Fliess into the psychological significance of the female twenty-eight-day rhythm could not have failed to point towards a lunar component.

The main issue is not so much whether Freud ever believed in astrology (if he ever did, it was fleeting and not maintained beyond the Fliess years), it is more how we should now re-evaluate what else he believed in, and see what this might contribute to our understanding of astrology and its processes.

Freud's Concept of Instinct

Freud believed that we all have a number of instinctual drives – sex, aggression, love, hunger and so on – which seek their expression in the world and, if thwarted in specific ways, can contribute to the creation of a neurosis. Freud saw the prime energy of the human psyche as the *libido*, a hypothetical life-force which effectively underpins *all* our behaviour by somehow 'attaching' itself to the manifestations of our various drives. Thus we can see that, contrary to popular opinion, the libido is not synonymous with sexuality, although in practice it is closely allied to sexual expression.

Freud believed that the libido actually stuck – or was 'cathected' – to those experiences which were found pleasurable and to the inner image of those people with whom we formed relationships. As the infant goes through the various developmental stages, oral, anal, phallic and Oedipal, so does its libido 'stick' to the emotional and physical experiences it undergoes. Ideally, as it grows up, it will, through the processes of life, transfer part of its libido up the chain towards full adult sexual expression. But sometimes this does not happen.

If there are traumas around specific childhood issues it is possible for an excessive amount of libido to become 'stuck' around a particular situation, leaving little over for other areas of life. Thus the individual is constantly pulled back to infantile ways of behaving and has little drive available for adult sexual expression. Similarly, if adult sexual expression is blocked in some way, the individual may regress to earlier forms of sexual behaviour to seek satisfaction. Freudians would argue that, for instance, over-eating is a regression to the oral stage of libidinal development, while such common sexual offences as indecent exposure are regressions to the pleasures of childhood sex-play, chosen because they are less threatening than forming an adult relationship.

While Freud went on to develop concepts of the libido which are more complex and subtle than this brief outline suggests, his basic theories continue to demand a finite supply of this hypothetical energy in each one of us, and that it is 'used up' in the various stages and process of psychic life. It is this rigid 'libidinal determinism' that causes so many psychotherapists to baulk, rather than the issue of Freud's views on sexuality *per se*.

Whatever we might feel about these ideas, Freud has at least attempted to meet the issue of 'energy' and 'psychic forces' head on; he has constructed a coherent theory about them and sought practical ways in which to apply it. Many of those who reject his ideas, for whatever reason, have to content themselves with vague notions of energies which are frequently never really defined, or are described in such generalized ways as to be effectively meaningless.

Some schools, such as Jungians and the more mystical psychologies, see a necessity in bringing our inner energies into some sort of harmony or balance. The idea is, possibly, to achieve some sort of synthesis or fusion. Others would see this approach as leading to something akin to psychic death, demanding instead that we maintain an inner creative tension of opposing drives, seeking not to reconcile them, but to use them. Yet others describe instinctual drives towards Meaning or Self-fulfilment or Being.

In all the various cases these assumed instincts and energies – which are primary to the hypothesized workings of the psyche – are presumed to function in an almost physical manner. Yet, apart from sexuality with its undeniable hormonal function, there is no tangible evidence for them whatsoever on any practical level. Furthermore, we can choose our arguments from one camp or another to completely negate even a *theoretical* basis for just about any drive or instinct that we may choose to feel vindictive towards.

It is very important to recognize that a body of knowledge with no concrete evidence for its central assumptions – the existence and function of human psychic energy – *and* no sustainable theoretical arguments either, is not exactly in a strong position to argue its corner against astrology, whose basic 'energy theory' of human nature has been constantly demonstrated, via the Gauquelins and others, to an impressive degree.

At this point we can suggest that the planets themselves can be seen as symbolizing instinctual drives, and that these drives operate within us all. In some way the planetary drives attach or connect us to experiences and sensations appropriate to their own nature, and we participate in their symbolic expression. Just as Freud's concept of instinct demanded that the events and experiences which emerged from their expression *stay within us all* as archaic memories, so we can suggest that the emergence of planetary energy as event, action or sensation is similarly shared through the collective.

The Instincts of the Planets

If we were to describe the Sun, Moon and all the planets as instincts we could also describe the zodiac itself as an *overall process* from which these instincts emerge – the 'instinct' of the cosmos perhaps – and one which modifies the orientation or direction of the basic planetary drives and focuses them in one general direction rather than another.

The practice of astrology would seem to suggest that the Ascendant, Midheaven and Lunar Nodes seem to amplify or fine tune the personal orientation in life, tying an event or an individual to a specific direction. The houses of the diurnal circle similarly orientate the underlying dynamics towards particular areas of life, and in doing so together make the panoply of the birth chart highly personal, locking it into specific relationships with other, similar moments.

The next dynamic within the chart is provided by the aspect patterns. These identify the temporary relationship of one body to another and describe the nature of their current interaction. Those who subscribe to the ideas on harmonics put forward by John Addey would see that there are essentially just *two* factors under-lying all these possible equations. On the one hand we have the nature, principle or instinct of the planets, and on the other we have the *number* which divides the complete 360° cycle of all their possible relationships, and describes the precise phase or state of their current dynamic.

Number can be seen to operate in the neo-Platonic manner favoured by John Addey or it might be seen as representing an aspect of the 'thing itself' – as already outlined on page 63. Thus the nature of number would underlie all possible aspects between all possible planets, all planetary relationships to the Ascendant and Midheaven (in other words, the houses) and, most importantly, the instinctive nature of the zodiac itself.

In this way number would appear to be the primary process of astrology, working through and with the energies that we ascribe to the planets and other chart factors. Number gives us a possible meaning for aspects, the zodiac and the houses. It underlies all astrological processes; in short, it shows us *how* the energies of things 'work'.

Specific spiritual or metaphysical beliefs concerning the ultimate nature of any underlying principles are very much an individual concern. Here we are concerned with *how* particular images may emerge within the collective, and what they may represent.

To this end we shall stay with the concept of describing the planets as instinctual drives and processes, recognizing of course that these are not instincts or processes shared only by humans, but open to each form of life to live out at appropriate levels. Furthermore, they are primarily encapsulated within time, accessible to objects like ships and cities and non-tangibles such as ideas and dreams. In doing this we are following the tradition laid down by both Freud and Jung and innumerable others since. In defining something as a primary instinct we are not obliged to reduce it further or speculate how it got there, though it may ultimately benefit from such an endeavour.

If we view the planets as instinctual drives, and pursue this approach by suggesting that the manifestations of their expressions stay within the collective, and are at some level accessible to us all, then we would be drawn towards suggesting that we might want to depict this process as an interlocking series of charts, going back to the earliest times.

Perhaps it *is* like this.

The Charts Within Us

If we consider the relationship between individuals and the collective, we see how astrology describes the manner in which whole categories of people fall under the sway of one country or area. These are of course primary collective experiences. National charts exist and there is a presumed connection between those charts and their citizens. Similarly the foundation of a new dynasty, the evolution of a parliamentary system, the coming into power of a government or a dictatorship, will have some reflection in the life of those who live in its shadow.

The astrology of towns and cities has been pursued for centuries, and is in some disrepute only because of a history of extravagant claims for the accuracy of one chart or another. If history furnished us with irrefutable evidence that the charter for such and such a town was signed at a specific time on a specific date, no astrologer would question the validity of the resulting map for synastry with its inhabitants or for conjecturing its future prospects.

Thus the individual is by astrological tradition bound to a country, a region, a town and a family. To what extent the astrology of the country will impinge upon the life of one of its citizens will depend almost solely upon the nature of the country, the nature of its map. One with a stable economy and an established parliamentary system will obviously weather the storms of the outer planet transits more successfully than another lacking those advantages. Inflation, to most current western nationals, rarely causes more than concern; in pre-war Germany it devastated the country like a plague. It was as if the 1918 chart of the Weimar Republic was embedded in the psyche of each and every German; perhaps it *was*, as we shall see later.

Each time we admit that there is *another* chart that needs consulting alongside the birth chart, be it for the country or the town of residence, we recognize once again that something is coming into the life of individuals that *pre-dates* their nativity and to which they will, in some manner, also respond – perhaps overwhelmingly so, has birth taken place prior to a major war involving their homeland. Thus we must again recognize that the simple concept of the individual expressing the *moment* of the birth chart is a wholly inadequate one to deal with the many other factors which are also present and reach expression through the course of life.

As we have seen in Chapter 2, the Jungian concept of synchronicity – of an event being in some way 'created' in the 'real world' as energy moves from the unconscious into consciousness and endows the external phenomena with meaning – cannot be used to describe the workings of astrology. The birth chart cannot be interpreted as being solely a map of how the real-time movements of the planets conferred their meanings upon the infant. Far too much of that which will be crucial in the life of an infant pre-existed at the moment of its birth for this fact to be ignored.

A whole town is equally imprinted with what is taking place in the heavens, moment by moment. The town, however, was built *before* its charter was signed and sealed, and built with bricks that previously were sand and clay, which were each formed at certain instants and brought together with a myriad other materials, each of which was transmuted in its own unique manner at a particular time. The site for the town was probably once a village, before that a scattering of huts, before that a forest felled in a certain season.

The physical structure of the town dwelt in today is an almost infinite collection of moments occurring at a particular place and stretching back to the very first impressions of Time. They lie layer upon layer, each an off-set of the same fundamental cycles concentrated in a place now inhabited by people who contain within themselves the genetic, emotional and spiritual legacy of evolution; the astrological straticulations of all their ancestors now similarly configured at a particular location.

Viewed in this way, we must soon recognize that our own birth chart is not enough to explain what may be going on. It never has been, and for centuries astrologers have set up new charts for themselves to see in their patterns a reflection of the changing seasons of their lives.

We select for ourselves special moments: the date of our first job, the time we began an important project, the moment when we bought a car or purchased a house or decided to have children. We may also overlay these major events with the more trivial circumstances of life and note the times when household goods are bought, decisions are made, holidays are taken and phone calls made. If we do this we will rapidly notice that these charts are as alive and active as our own natal map, responding to transits and lunations and moment by moment observations. But these are *not* true alternative maps. We have depicted these moments as separate from ourselves solely to simplify their observation in much the same way as we draw out separate harmonic charts to simplify the location of relevant aspects.

In reality such apparently separate maps are the active experience of transits and part and parcel of ourselves, inextricably involved with the shape and texture of our lives and lying layer upon layer on all previous events. They reflect occasions when we confronted life, consciously or unconsciously, and took decisions which directly affected us. In interacting with the moment we accept it and absorb it and in some way make it permanent. The slow cycles of the heavens are grounded by us all and given meaning by the simple acts of being human.

Our birth chart should be more properly seen as a circle which is being continuously overlaid with the occurrences of life. The moment when we bought this or did that is not an alternative arrangement of planets to be examined in isolation but a dynamic transit moment now made an integral part of our lives. Our birth chart has been expanded and amplified and *quantitatively altered* by a particular experience.

Such an experience remains alive within us. The degrees touched as it came into being would appear to vibrate indefinitely with the memory of the event, fixing that particular expression of energy in time. This would be the zodiacal equivalent of 'planetary memory' referred to above, and probably underpins the traditional degree meanings collectively. In the individual chart such specific degrees may point to areas of particular sensitivity, which may well reflect repressed or contained experiences; examples of this possibility will be given in Chapter 9.

This seems to be so not just for the events in which we partake, but also in our relationships. The charts of parents and siblings are likewise part of ourselves and will respond to their future transits *in our life* as well – sometimes when we are no longer connected to that person. Such synastry is not to be relegated to the past, the unconscious is not rendered inert by the passing of time or a change in geography. It is working through us continuously. Our personal history involves others and this amalgam of experience also shifts and responds to the transiting planets.

If something important happens to a close partner it happens in some way to us *at the same time*. It is impossible to live or work closely with someone and not notice this. If our current concepts of synastry do not reflect what we actually *see* happening in these moment-by-moment situations then such current concepts of working with the birth chart are incomplete. This partial picture almost certainly stems from thinking of the birth chart as a static moment of time to which the individual is somehow permanently and unvaryingly attached, as if we were all to be forever identified with the grim photograph in our passport. All the evidence so far suggests that such an indelible association is simply not the case. The birth chart is more likely to be the individual's *impression* of the world at the moment of birth; an impression that is incomplete and overlaid with 'what is going on'. In other words, it is as if the psyche absorbs the message of the planets, internalizes the meaning of their symbolic structures and simultaneously activates their principles for the first time, reacting to the world with this new knowledge, *identifying with it* and believing in that moment that 'this is how it is, this is how I am'.

If particular inter-uterine experiences have been very strong, as we shall see from Stanislav Grof's examples given in the following chapter, then this would suggest that previously activated and internalized planetary energies would create a predisposition at the moment of birth towards repeating or reinforcing very early impressions of 'how things are'; a form of response that depth psychology suggests actually does take place. The process is *not* static and receptive but dynamic and responsive. Moreover, it is possible that the infant impresses *itself* on to the world as well, and from that moment the world begins to respond to the design that emerged from this primal interaction with the cosmos.

Far from there being an infinite number of separate charts created by each act of birth or moment of human endeavour since the beginning of time, we begin to move towards an image of a single 'chart' shared universally by all things. A chart on which is imprinted every human and non-human experience, every event and every moment which in some way was brought into being.

We could visualize that on this collective chart is described the psychic history of our planet. It is marked with the imprint of our totality and begins with the signature of Earth's own growth process through volcanoes, earthquakes and the slow tread of tectonic plates to the emergence of life and all the creations of the human mind. In this immense circle is their display and their recollection, inscribed by astrology in the degrees of the zodiac that identify all phenomena, and which we continuously respond to and renew.

It is a chart to which we are all somehow connected, able to draw on, add to, alter and respond to. It is an image of an infinite synastry with our total history; a timeless, unconscious pool that contains the fundamental matrix of all our genetic and psychic strivings. It is defined and divided only by the harmonics of the signs and planets, each one its own reservoir of all experience that resonates with its specific principle and on which we draw at every moment of life, minutely shifting the sum of their meaning with every act we make.

This is not the blind evolution of contemporary socio-biology, a remorseless uncoiling of genes towards a randomly selected future, but an interactive relationship capable of conscious direction. Such a collective zodiac, on which we originally might draw all our initial energies and to which our subsequent expression of their principles ultimately returns, presents a psychic equivalent to the genetic pool in which we might create our collective and individual destinies.

If this were to be the case, then the astrological perspective can provide for both the theoretical demands and the empirical observations of Freud, Jung, Sheldrake and others.

The Primal Zodiac

As we have seen, the work of Freud – and to some extent that of Jung – demands some form of 'timeless' unconscious in which apparently shared material is stored, and that the experiences of succeeding generations appear to be passed on, as if genetically, even if the idea of this taking place at a straightforward physical level is currently discredited.

Individuals expressing similar themes in quite different circumstances may do so because they are activating a common, unconscious experience, rather than an hypothesized archetypal energy. The survivors of a disaster, for instance, may individually re-live or act out that shared experience for years after the incident. Whatever the similarity of expression, the disaster itself could not be described as being an archetype that they were all subsequently expressing. At another level, we have seen from Richard Tarnas's work on Uranus aspects and their subsequent transits that major themes can emerge within otherwise disparate individuals, and that these can be described as the expression of basic planetary drives or instincts rather than through the use of archetypal theory.

Such possibilities point again to the idea that, at the moment of birth, the infant takes on the *history* of the chart endowed to it by the cosmos. It is as if the individual birth map is a reflection of a primal zodiac, which is alive with the residue of all that has ever happened and is continually modified by the processes of life.

Whatever personal issues, whatever parental conflicts, whatever individual psychic circumstances the chart suggests, there is also within it the unfolding dynamics of its inherited processes; part genetic, part familial and part social; all filtered through the simple act of being human. As the child evolves and activates those inherited processes, symbolized by both the signs and planets and the degrees they occupy, so this in turn is fed back into the primal

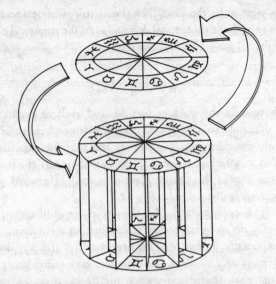

Figure 5.2 The zodiac can be thought of as holding our collective history. Patterns in the birth chart may resonate to key moments in the past, and what takes place in the present within the life of an individual or society feeds back into the collective process again. As the degrees (and the signs) of the zodiac are themselves defined by their relationship to the precessing Vernal point, such degrees should remain constant.

zodiac. Each personal achievement has a collective counterpart as it returns to the common source; each thing we do finitely shifts the sum of all things, thus we evolve interactively.

Figure 5.2 is an attempt to illustrate this process. The individual chart – the moment of 'now' – contains everything that has gone before it, and becomes fixed at the moment of birth or at the start of a distinct process. Subsequent transits trigger both it and all that it contains; the collective and personal issues are intermixed and mutually involved. As a country's chart factors are transited, so all those who resonate to that part of the chart – such as the inhabitants of that particular country – will respond to a greater or lesser degree: they have that chart within them also, and resonate to it by virtue of the co-ordinates of their birth.

Each event of life subtly alters the complexion of the birth chart and simultaneously feeds back this change into the primal zodiac, fractionally transmuting our experience of the past. As the past changes, so will future possibilities. The individual and the collective interact in the process of evolution, their joint efforts constantly re-drawing the boundaries of its potential. We are seemingly locked into a feedback loop with the universe: what we do may affect it; as we modify our own destiny so we cannot help but affect all that is around us. These changes may emerge slowly through the slow tread of time, though occasionally they may come with a dizzying suddenness that overturns a stable balance or reverses an established trend.

Thus implicit in the image of a primal zodiac to which we all have recourse, and to which the sum total of our experiences and endeavours is bequeathed, is the possibility that apparent randomness can precipitate a chaos-like event – such as was explained in the previous chapter – that might completely reverse a trend of history or the familiar expression of a particular aspect.

If we are to adopt the idea of such a primal zodiac then it will be necessary to stop thinking of Time as it is conventionally portrayed by astrology – as a series of discrete moments to be analysed in isolation as separate charts – but instead seeing it as a flowing sequence of events that merge into each other: time as a *continuum*. The meaning of each instance remains within the zodiac, to be picked up again and again as it is touched by future transits, to be in turn modified or reinforced by the nature of the later occurrences.

As we suggested earlier, we may set a chart for a particular moment, be it marriage, buying a house, taking an important decision, and subsequently note how major transits to that chart tend to manifest in our life. They do this because the chart is not separate from us, it is *part* of us and remains part of us for as long as the process it symbolizes plays a role in our life. Such a chart is, in fact, a depiction of how the energy of the moment has become fixed or locked within us because consciously or unconsciously we *acted it out*. In identifying with it at some level we have incorporated it into our psyche: the points that it has touched in our chart are now quantitatively altered, it has left its mark in our memory.

Embedded Moments

The memories we have of such events can be thought of as being held or embedded within us at a personal and a collective level. They may come back to us in many forms, returning as sensations, feelings and vivid, pictorial images. Often they will revolve around the major highs and lows of our early life, circling moments whose emotional significance is unquestionable. Many memories are disjointed and fragmentary, or are connected with particular sounds or smells which momentarily seem to collapse time, to make the past immediate for the duration of its recollection; again, their importance and painful or pleasurable content is immediately apparent. Others are more complex to understand, for while they may have a striking vividness, they seem to have no real content and point us in no particular direction. Indeed, we may even ask *why* such apparently trivial recollections can be so firmly lodged within us when so many, seemingly more important, episodes are blurred or lost.

The truth is often that these supposedly innocuous images are in some ways a cover for something else, with a content that is hidden or screened from our view. In many respects they should be treated more as a dream than a recollection, but a dream that is absolutely and directly rooted in what was then our immediate experience.

These *screen memories*, as Freud called them, often focus on a traumatic issue, but discreetly cover it at the same time. They are recalled with such vividness because they so aptly and *directly* symbolize that which is being experienced by the child, and survive within us as conscious memories precisely *because* their latent, traumatic content remains unrecognized. It is as if the shock or pain of the moment is being *fixed* within a memory, but accessible through the symbolic clues that life has suddenly presented in such graphic form, uniquely mirroring the child's internal state.

The memory is so clear because there is such enormous psychic energy invested in its depiction. The traumatic moment is being locked away by the child, hidden within a clear, pictorial representation of its expression.

As with an astrological chart, it describes symbolically what may be going on, but in a manner that requires some active analysis to bring it to light. And as with the dream, the chart and the memories it contains can be described as being complex symbols in the manner described earlier. Each one focuses or holds the totality of the experience it describes, but requires to be linked by association to earlier ideas, sensations, and charts.

From the astrological perspective, we would see the traumatic moment as an *event chart* which has become embedded within the psyche, accessible only through its symbolic content. This would suggest that the specific issues which have been brought out by a particular transit are in some way locked in to the natal planets and midpoints which were being transited. Experience suggests that this is indeed the case, as we shall see in Chapter 10.

Thus the idea of a primal zodiac can give us an image of the interactive nature of life, incorporating the highly personal experiences which contribute to the formation of our individual identity, and the forces and events which shape our collective destiny.

In it we have the astrological parallel to the concept of the collective unconscious, as an archaic reservoir of memories and events depicted with the astrological symbols of their formation. On a personal and collective level it is constantly alive and in flux, as these moments are responding to current planetary transits.

How we might resonate to specific issues, and the part we may play in bringing to manifestation some of the material held within such a primal zodiac, would depend not just on the patterns we have in our natal chart, but on the *moments* that we may subsequently lock into as our life progresses. Indeed, some of these interactions may take place well *before* our birth, as we shall see in a moment.

6.

The Cosmic Womb

* * * * * * * * *

If we adopt the idea of a shared, collective zodiac that in some way acts as the repository of all our experiences, from which we draw our instinctual responses, and which in turn responds to and is modified by the nature of each individual impression left upon it by the manifestations of life, then we have gone some way towards bringing together both the underlying thoughts and the clinical observations of a number of depth psychologies.

As astrologers we must also recognize that certain charts, those of countries, moments of invention, powerful eclipses or famous individuals, interact with us also, no matter how poor their synastry with our own birth map or how far removed in time or circumstances they are from our own. One way or another we see how such moments live on within us and express themselves inexorably in our lives through transits to charts *other* than our own.

If we come to see that perhaps these charts *are* part of our own, are indeed part of our *unconscious*, then the phenomenon which we actually have observed time and time again becomes more comprehensible. If we view the planets and the zodiac as a map of the total collective experience of all things as well as a picture of the individual psyche as a *reflection* of all things, then we might begin to see how individuals can resonate with the past as well as the present. In this way synastry could be seen to operate *diachronously* as well as synchronously; to take account of the past, of the cyclical history of an event or person, as well as what is happening in the world *now*.

If we think that moments of time become partially fixed in the collective as the direct result of the response of *life* to what is taking place with the planets, then we begin to see how we might be continually interacting with specific areas of past experience, made collective by the impression left on the primal zodiac. Astrology points to the fact that moments of time do not die forgotten, but continually re-express themselves in one form or another. If this turns out to be the case then we have to incorporate this into our concept of the astrological process.

In some cases these past events may influence us all by the nature of what is constellated around the initial moment, and emerge precisely in our lives when specific degrees or patterns are stimulated. Indeed, we might even suggest that the self-reinforcing quality of what might be taking place is in part responsible for specific manifestations of events unique to certain aspect patterns, and relative to who or what is doing the experiencing. A child may be born at the moment the Moon conjuncts Saturn, a pattern often associated with a fearful or cautious response towards life. Saturn is not *about* fearfulness, that is what *we* do with its principles; at an instinctual level, however, the baby has to draw on the stored residue of Moon/Saturn experiences in the collective; it has none, or very few, of its own to go on. The result might simply be to adopt the pre-existing pattern-response of fear contained in the primal zodiac, and repeat it. Only through the processes of its own life does it begin to grow into and modify the Moon/Saturn contact to show its many other, far more creative sides.

As we have seen, the conventional view of astrological 'effects', that the baby is synchronistically absorbing the nature of the moment and then subsequently living it out in its own life, would have to assume that such fear *was* the initial cosmic experience – can we genuinely accept that the Solar System is fearful? It is *humans* that are fearful, it is *human* fear that is being expressed.

Most births *are* fearful and frightening. For virtually every person birth is a most devastating experience; the whole known world literally bursts open and is destroyed. It is the Atlantis myth, the safe island of a golden age, surrounded by water, suddenly gone in an instant, and with it humanity's innocence. If each birth chart had to describe exactly what was going on, then every birth chart should be a graphic portrayal of terror and violence. They are not. Indeed, it is actually very rare to come upon a chart which even begins to describe the enormity of the birth experience, even if there might occasionally be some peripheral observations to be made.

The average birth chart is *not* the map of an event which might be the most singularly terrifying one experienced by an individual in the whole course of life. Yet it took place, of that there can be no doubt.

If the individual birth chart almost invariably fails to describe the enormity of the one thing that *certainly* took place we shall have to see what else might be going on. It would seem possible that the intensity of feeling is portrayed not so much by any individual characteristic of the specific chart, but by the infant drawing on the powerful forces of the collective planets; in other words, also picking up on the experiences of others.

It is easy to suggest here that there is a natural archetype of birth, that there is a specific pattern of birth. There may well be something of that nature at a genetic level, something that triggers hormones and tells the body what to do, but on an emotional/experiential level we get clear images of the outer planets at work which suggest that we are perhaps plugging in to the 'birth component' of their combined spectrum of possibilities. To look at it in this way also avoids the deterministic dogmas of certain psychotherapies which demand that the birth experience is the central formative component of the personality, from which virtually all other major reactions follow.

At first glance there may be much to support such a claim, but, as with the 'archetype' concept, there is also much that is omitted, not least of which is the *way* in which actual recollections of birth are recalled and the disparate manner in which fragments of primal moments later reappear in life. So much of astrology is, in effect, the astrology of birth – indeed, *all* conventional 'psychological' astrology proceeds slowly from the primacy of that moment. Even the psychoanalyst Otto Rank, who developed the concept of the 'birth trauma', recognized the significance of the natal chart here: 'One might even describe astrology as the first doctrine of the birth trauma. The entire fate of man is determined by what occurs (in heaven) at the moment of his birth.'[1] As this moment is so important it is perhaps worthwhile at this point to regress.

The Birth Trauma

Regression to early experiences, including the moment of birth, is quite a common experience in a variety of therapies; many exist almost solely to achieve this end, generally using modified bio-energetic techniques or mild hypnosis and 'acting-out'. It is usual for participants in these therapies to experience an altered sense of body-awareness, to have strong physical sensations somewhat akin to contractions, to suffer temporary breathing problems, to encounter powerful feelings of panic or survival issues, and finally have the need to scream or cry.

The total effect can be temporarily overwhelming, and the body is often flooded with new energy. As part of a process of working on the self it can be very useful in releasing blocked emotions which can later be explored more coherently in therapy, although there are schools that consider the experience as complete within itself.

One psychiatrist, Stanislav Grof, took a very different approach towards exploring the earliest moments of life. He came to the conclusion that the psyche contains what he termed CoEx patterns: patterns of behaviour, complete with images and memories that might seem quite disconnected but in reality are intimately linked, and frequently involve powerful perinatal memories as one of their components. The CoEx (COndensed EXperiences) patterns of many of his patients also reveal startling astrological energies of which Grof was obviously quite unaware at the time. The clarity with which he was able to locate these CoEx complexes stems directly from the fact that his patients were regressed under the influence of LSD.

A common LSD experience is similar to watching an incredibly fast tapestry of events spread out against an almost timeless background. Images from the unconscious blur together with highly distorted versions of the immediate environment, provoking a seamless stream of pictures that spin vividly across the surface of awareness while the centre seems to move with infinite slowness.

All sounds, sensations, colours, textures, smells and feelings are vastly increased and completely interchangeable; sensitivity seems limitless, boundaries dissolve. It is a multi-dimensional free-association on the nature of the psyche, constantly exploding with an outpouring of memories and fragmented images which blend effortlessly with the shifting vision of the immediate environment. Quite without warning one of these images can overwhelm the consciousness, inducing intensely powerful feelings and at the same time opening a doorway to the source of its experience. This has been described as akin to going on a psychic roller-coaster.

The slow, placid river which has been sparkling with light suddenly reveals a dark undertow, pulling the subject's awareness towards an emotional maelstrom. The experience can be one of almost being sucked out of life, out of everything recognized as safe and familiar. It comes with devastating speed, pulling the mind back through an opening in time towards dimly remembered reaches. It is a highly focused experience, physical and emotional, half-recognized, both wanted and feared and laced with forgotten terrors. There is nothing for the mind to do but let go.

Everything changes. All memories and sensations connected with repressed experience flow back in a vivid replay of everything that has ever been denied. Chains of events can assemble themselves out of seemingly random bursts of emotion, inexorably linking together the clear lineage of trauma.

For Stanislav Grof these are the CoEx events, the sudden releasing of affect that has crystallized around some primal moment, subsequently to become buried under layers of symbolic affinities. Grof suggests that what binds these images together are the emotional similarities that underlie whatever incongruity their surface juxtaposition might display; under LSD they open to reveal their true connections. Time and time again it seems to commence with birth.

LSD in Analysis

If we accept the hypotheses that the infant locks into the energies of the outer planets during the process of birth, because it is genetically programmed to use these energies, and that in doing so it inevitably 'absorbs' those experiences which all others have previously impressed upon the primal zodiac, we can see some startling evidence for their activation in Grof's observations.

For reasons that are, at the present time, not quite clear, alcoholics and drug addicts seem to have the easier access to the perinatal realm of the unconscious than individuals with ... a considerable obsessive-compulsive component in their clinical symptomatology.[2]

Grof and others have long identified early womb experiences as the precursor of ecstatic religious states and the sense of 'oneness' that Freud terms *oceanic*. The fact that people with Neptune problems find it easy to go back there while the Plutonic compulsive-obsessives have a marked reluctance to return to the source of primal battles should come as no surprise!

The clarity of the symbols is quite unmistakable, and comes through even more clearly when Grof considers the process of clients who are temporarily locked in to one of several possible negative states that he has identified. He describes one pattern, one clear CoEx matrix which revolves around the issue of the infant starting to move out of the womb, becoming aware of the shifting nature of his world and recalling the fear that was felt at the time, together with the need to return to that primary eternity when nothing changed and all was peaceful. If the LSD wears off during this process the patient can be left with the residual feelings until the next session. Until then,

the subject feels that everything is closing in on him. Suicidal cravings are not uncommon in this situation; it usually has the form of a wish to fall asleep or be unconscious, forget everything and never wake up again. Persons in this state of mind have fantasies about taking an overdose of sleeping pills or narcotics, drinking themselves to death, inhaling gas, drowning in deep water, or walking into the snow and freezing . . . Quite common are feelings of exhaustion and fatigue, drowsiness and somnolence, and the tendency to spend the entire day in bed in a darkened room.[3]

Another state, a CoEx matrix characterized by the inclusion of the actual process of emerging from the birth canal, can be experienced in its residual form by subjects feeling themselves to be

time-bombs ready to explode at any minute. They oscillate between destructive and self-destructive impulses and are afraid of hurting other people or themselves. Typical is . . . a strong tendency to provoke violent conflicts. The world is perceived as a dangerous and unpredictable place, where one has to be constantly on guard and prepared to fight and struggle for survival . . . Individuals in this state contemplate bloody and violent suicides, such as throwing oneself under a train, jumping from a window or cliff, hara-kiri or shooting oneself . . . A characteristic manifestation in the sexual area is excessive augmentation of the libidinal drive, for which even repeated orgasms do not bring satisfactory relief.[4]

The two types of birth experience are strikingly different and the first obviously refers to Neptune, the second to Pluto. The third, the Uranian component of birth, emerges on cue when the infant is finally free of the birth canal, when the umbilical cord is cut – a factor that Grof suggests may underlie later castration anxieties in both sexes:

Suffering and agony culminate in an experience of total annihilation on all levels – physical, emotional, ethical and transcendental. The individual experiences final biological destruction, emotional defeat, intellectual debacle and uttermost moral humiliation . . . He feels that he is an absolute failure in life from any imaginable point of view; his entire world seems to be collapsing, and he is losing all previous meaningful reference points. The experience is usually referred to as *ego death*. After the subject has experienced the very depth of total annihilation and has hit 'cosmic bottom', he is struck by visions of blinding white or golden light.[5]

It is typical of powerful Uranian transits that everything reliable is stripped away in an instant. Even feelings and beliefs can be temporarily lost and the ensuing fragmentation of identity, which Grof here calls 'ego death', is perilously close to evaporation. The overwhelming existential demands of Uranus for total clarity, absolute truth and divine perfection cast an unbearable light on ordinary human muddle. Its illumination of our confusions, failures and emotional uncertainties can engender a sense of utter futility and meaninglessness. The hostile world we are then suddenly plunged into can mirror the delivery room of our birth. Illuminated with a painfully bright light, we confront the fact that everything we have ever experienced has been torn away, that we are powerless and alone, seemingly discarded in an alien land-scape.

While the example given is that of a negative separation experience, it is *this* phase of the birth process that ties in most closely with the actual birth chart, the moment of first breath and separation. Hence its connection with personal identity, self-worth and the instinctual assessment of 'how things are', 'how the world is', ultimately, 'how I am', as at that moment the totality of the cosmos is drawn inwards and utilized for the comprehension of our existence.

It is possible that the infant, both in the womb and during the birth process, also tunes in to its *mother's* astrology. It is not uncommon for there to be recollections of experiencing the mother's fear at some event, or of feeling that the mother is poisoning the foetus through using alcohol or drugs. Such strong feelings leave their astrological impression, probably working through the outer planets, and not only in the infant. The mother can also experience the release of powerful outer-planet energies at birth even if no transits are apparent.

While it would be facile to suggest that the release of powerful Plutonic energy by the *infant* is the 'cause' of any subsequent postnatal depression in the mother, there are some very clear symbolic connections. The utter 'deadness' typical of the depressive experience is a direct parallel of feelings that have returned to their own womb, leaving the consciousness in winter, hiding its rage under the earth. Another facet of Pluto is also in clear sight.

Dr Desmond Kelley reports[6] that current research indicates a marked increase in obsessional neurosis in women who have just given birth; another finding which makes full sense only in the light of astrology.

Subsequent Pluto transits can also bring us back to such early experiences, but they tend to mirror the more bloody and brutal issues of fighting out of the birth canal, and we can see in them some striking correlations with other Plutonic themes, namely the connection with life and death and basic bodily processes.

The powerful contractions of birth will invariably result in the evacuation of the bowels and bladder unless prior enemas and diuretics or catheters are used, as is *now* the common practice. The Latin phrase *inter faeces et urinus nascimur* – we are born among faeces and urine – pithily describes the reality of childbirth for the vast majority of the world. Thus an infant going through the Plutonic phase of the birth – fighting its way out of the underworld – comes into immediate physical contact with the most basic of Pluto-ruled substances: the finality of matter. It is a face-to-face confrontation with waste material from which all life has been extracted and which is now fit only for decay.

Grof describes LSD experiences of this stage of birth which include hallucinations of being in sewage systems, of seeing putrefying flesh and of encountering Aztec gods – particularly Tlacoltentl, the Devourer of Filth. Very remarkably, Grof then points out a symbol which frequently emerges and for which there is no clear reason; it is *not* part of the process of childbirth, although its connection with Pluto is so obvious it needs no comment:

It is the encounter with consuming fire ... The fire seems to destroy everything that is rotten and corrupt in the individual and prepares him for the renewing and rejuvenating experience of re-birth ...[7]

The images that Grof has identified as recurring parts of the total process of birth and inter-uterine life are powerful examples of astrological symbolism in action; indeed, they would seem to be fully comprehensible *only* when their astrological significance is also considered. His concept of CoEx matrixes is similarly impressive and has much to offer us, as it suggests a way in which different aspects of planetary manifestation actually link up to primal moments, creating a cohesive unity with other major phases and experiences of life.

It is well worth considering the implications of Grof's work, in that it will help us to use astrology both more creatively and more accurately. We have seen how one experience can liberate or express a number of quite different and seemingly disparate energies, which in the birth chart may be symbolized by planets that are in *no* formal aspect relationship. As these energies clearly *are* being expressed together, it would suggest that they *must* be in a dynamic arrangement within the chart. The tendency to limit astrological aspects to those that have been in our currency since Ptolemy's time reflects an attitude peculiar to astrology. No other profession that claims, in part, to concern itself with the workings of the psyche would actually *boast* of such lamentable progress.

Those astrologers who *do* concern themselves with counselling-orientated astrology will have to confront the limitations of astrology directly, and begin to examine the different ways of relating planetary energies, such as those explored more fully in later chapters. It might also be important to consider once more astrology's genetic implications.

We have seen that certain specifically physical characteristics can correlate with astrology only if the genetic code 'co-operates' with the cosmos in some manner. The powerful energies released during the process of birth may nudge this process on a bit; much of the elaborate neural network within the infant's brain begins to form only *after* its birth. It is within the realm of possibility that this infinitely complex network with its chemical connectors is capable of being subtly modified by our experience of birth.

What we can also learn from Grof's approach is to pay much more attention to the symbolism of the specific components of an overall scene as well as the *sequence* in which it is described. Grof's research clearly shows us different energies coming in, one after the other, and in Chapter 10 we shall see further examples of using such sequential imagery in other circumstances. What we should do now is to move from the visceral beginnings of life to their cerebral assimilation: how does our *mind* begin to cope with all this raw experience?

The Psychology of Language

The symbolic linking process that Grof describes is itself part of a chain that has preoccupied psychologists for over a century. Their search has been for the manner in which we order and arrange our experiences, and the part played in this by memory. One of the most interesting of recent developments comes from the work of the psychoanalyst Jacques Lacan. It is not the intention here to outline his highly idiosyncratic theories (which often run counter to both established analytic *and* linguistic concepts), but to give an image of how language might operate within the unconscious, and in doing so, how it might actually order or structure the way in which the unconscious works.

Jacques Lacan, whose chart features on page 173, revitalized the French analytic scene in the years after the war, although in the process he created a profound schism within the French group partly as a result of his insistence in returning to basic Freudian concepts.

In the course of his life, Freud's creative thinking shifted from the analysis of the unconscious towards the analysis of the ego and its defences. It was a movement that was rapidly accelerated by others after his death and today virtually all psychoanalysis is ego analysis; indeed, some psychoanalysts no longer even explore their clients' dreams at all.

Lacan strove to recall Freud's initial preoccupation with the fundamental processes of the unconscious, particularly his fascination with the nature of *language*. Freud believed that an understanding of the role of language in the symbolic processes might hold a clue as to how the unconscious actually *worked*. He believed that there was a direct parallel between the everyday rules of grammar and the structure of dreams. Dreams appear chaotic and fragmented because there is an actual breakdown in the ordinary grammatic logic that the dreamer would use during the waking hours.[8] The subtle modifiers and some of the rules of speech are missing, thus the dream images become disjointed and the clarity of the symbolic flow is lost.

Freud's analysis of his own dreams is extensively commented upon by himself and others in the literature of psychoanalysis and needs no further observations here; suffice it to say that he believed that no dream was ever completely analysed and fully understood. Using free-association, it is possible to explore every word and each part of every image in the dream – which obviously involves further side-tracking to pursue each important association that subsequently emerges. In Freud's own case his actual dream might take four or five lines to describe, but his associations and conclusions might fill the best part of a chapter. It was Lacan's contention that this density of material suggested that the basic 'knowledge' and process of the unconscious was essentially language-orientated and he pursued it through the disciplines of linguistics and semiotics.

The application of semiotics to psychoanalytic theory was, and still is, a controversial area, due not least of all to Lacan's own highly original way of adapting semiotic and structuralist theory but also to the fact that in the process Lacan radically altered many of the practical processes of psychoanalytic procedures. In fact he was ultimately expelled from the French Institute of Psychoanalysis, formed his own group and then subsequently abandoned it before his death in 1981.

While it is impossible here to explore Lacan's approach to psychoanalysis – and many would say that because of its density and complexity it is impossible to explore it *anywhere* – some of his basic ideas may offer astrologers a very original view of our own language.

The Secret Life of the Word

Stripped of its academic jargon, all words can be thought of as splitting into two parts. One part is expressed by the *sound* of the word (and thus is of course different in every language), the other is the current *meaning* of the word to which the sound refers. This *meaning* (which is not fixed, but socially flexible) is to some extent ultimately different for all of us and evolves out of our own associations with the actual object or situation that the *sound* brings to mind. These meanings or associations in some way lie alongside what the words mean or imply for society as a whole. We might see this process in action more clearly if we first consider it from a purely personal point of view.

For instance, we all know that a dog is an animal that barks and has four legs and a tail. It is extremely unlikely, however, that each person who has just read the word 'dog' had a mental image or sensation that was identical. For some, a 'dog' is a fierce guard dog, to be feared and avoided, for others it is a lovable pet to be hugged and pampered, for a third group it might be just another animal. For those who have strong reactions to the sound of the word 'dog' there is almost certainly a chain of associations going back a long way. Perhaps those who view a dog as being fierce were frightened or attacked by one as a child. If something like this were the case then there is far more here than just a negative feeling towards 'dog'.

If the process were to be analysed we might discover, for instance, that such an attack took place when the child was with his mother on the way to nursery school. Thus there is part of 'dog' which *also* means 'going to school'. *School* might elsewhere be identified with a particularly unpleasant teacher who shouted a lot. Thus 'dog' might *also* signify, in part, 'a shouting, bullying, authority figure'. The fear that the child felt at the attack (which is of course also now part of 'dog') might be a repressed *anger* at its mother for failing to prevent the incident.

So 'dog' now has other connotations with whatever negative images of 'mother' have been built up elsewhere. In such a way the sound of the word 'dog' might evoke traces of fear, memories of being bullied by authority – or wishful desires of *doing* the bullying if it is heard at a time when the hearer is in a hostile mood himself. It might also contain an anger at the mother for being a failure in allowing the child to be abandoned and unprotected, and thus connect up with other 'bad mother' images which might well contain 'devouring' or other aggressive images. The recollection of having to go to school may associate with any unwelcome task that has to be faced, and finally it may contain the basic inner conflict between fear and aggression.

Here we see what we may 'do' with language, but not what it 'does' to us.

Language is not something that we all invent for ourselves, it is something we assimilate as we learn to speak its individual, component words (and some would argue that language may well assimilate *us* in that process). In either case it comes to us with its own rules and structures, which we unrecognizingly adopt. These structures are primarily *social*, and language introduces us to the complexity and contradictions of the world into which we are born. It overpowers us with its own demands, to which we append our own needs and desires, fitting them, as it were, into the patterns and meanings that we have received.

It could be that as we learn and recognize the sound of a word, so its interior (or ulterior) meaning is repressed within us. Thus the rules of society become embedded within us as we learn the manner in which they are expressed, and become what we would call *unconscious*. The unconscious, then, as Lacan would claim, is actually structured like a language and is thus ultimately amenable only to some form of linguistic analysis.

For some individuals the demands of socially introjected desires might overwhelm their own, more fragile connections. In such cases their articulation has to be radically re-structured to avoid fatal collisions within the psyche.

The language of certain schizophrenics, often referred to as 'word salad', can be seen as an attempt to use language to circumvent unspeakable desires. It is speech that is partially grammatical and internally consistent, even if often incoherent to others. A story is being told with an aspect of language not admitted to by us all, perhaps too far removed from our own experiences to be comprehensible. In such cases language might be too dangerous to be left to its own devices, and a psychic condition emerges which is notoriously impenetrable to the most basic tool of analysis – the spoken word.

Free Speech

Freud's discovery and utilization of 'free-association' as the cornerstone of the analytic treatment laid the foundations for such ideas. To free-associate is simply to let the mind drift, and to comment aloud on whatever image, thought or feeling surfaces, without resisting or denying them. It is so difficult to do that it has been claimed that anyone able to free-associate without blocking is 100 per cent cured of everything! In the process of free-associating, innocent words may become traps as a deeper and possibly more frightening level of their history calls up its emotional component. With experience we can come to recognize that certain words, or clusters of words, consistently overlay areas of anxiety or cause us to veer off in specific directions. Freud saw these as 'nodal points' – the intersections of different streams of experience – to which we might also be alerted through seemingly inexplicable slips of the tongue.

The connection between the mouth, the mind and the nervous system is strong, consistent and has been extensively commented upon. Freud once remarked that anyone trying to lie to him verbally would betray his real feelings with his fingers. Involuntarily they would flicker a nervous denial of what had just been said. It is almost as if the words themselves are alive, as if they want to escape to tell their own story. Which is what they try to do when we start to free-associate.

In this paradoxical state we believe we are speaking almost randomly, going in no direction, but actually we are tending to step around events; avoiding the painful and embarrassing. In evading these hidden realities it is almost as if we are simultaneously being pulled in a specific direction towards the source of our problems. We return to the same impasse again and again until we learn to take the true path, however painful or difficult the journey. At some level we co-operate with our inner language, and it beckons us on, leading us to its roots in the unconscious.

As we have seen, we can broadly think of individual words as having their own history or 'unconscious' in the specific sensations and experiences which associate with them. These are not just memories appended to sounds like multiple footnotes; the *process* is vitally important as well, as Freud was the first to note.

In a classic case study of infant behaviour he observed a young child playing with a cotton-reel. The reel was on a string and the child would throw the reel under a bed and then pull it out again; a game that was accompanied by cries of 'Gone!' as the reel disappeared and 'Here!' when it was pulled back. The game was repeated so many times, and with such emotional intensity, that Freud knew it must be fulfilling a vital function.

He came to recognize that the child was using the game to come to terms with separation anxiety; the cotton-reel was the parents who came and went. In doing so the child was also reversing the reality of the situation; no longer was he the helpless infant having to suffer abandonment at the hands of his parents, *he* was doing the abandoning by throwing the reel under the bed and gaining power over his parents by pulling it out again. For this particular child the words *gone* and *here* must have assumed momentous proportions as the issues of power and separation were wrestled with. Freud saw in this simple game how language and symbolic behaviour can be used as part of the 'civilizing' process the human race goes through in coming to terms with the stark realities of the external world and our infantile rage against the thwarting of our early desires.

Much of Lacan's theories about language make many specifically Freudian assumptions about the nature of instinctual behaviour, which many find erroneous, or utilize such linguistic complexities that they have probably never been fully understood by anyone else. Nevertheless there is much evidence from the more conventional use of structural linguistics that humans have an instinctive understanding of the rules of language. This so-called 'deep-structure' allows language to be learned in much the same way as walking and other physical skills are acquired; it is a natural process because there is a human predisposition towards it.

Language can be seen as something human beings are instinctively equipped to 'do'. Our culture could be seen to proceed from inbuilt linguistic mechanisms as our physical world was initially created by the ability to utilize the unique fivefold (quintile) structure of our hands, as we shall explore in some detail over the next two chapters. While researchers continue to argue about *how* language, learning processes and physical skills might be connected, it is not a problem faced by astrologers. We have Mercury.

Mercury and the Unconscious

All traditions tell us that Mercury rules the Mind. Considering that Mind, like Soul, is a highly complex and sophisticated concept, possibly one of the most advanced and enduring creations of human philosophy, we should perhaps think twice about entrusting it all to the very symbol also associated with lies, knavery and the immature follies of youth. Rather than attempting to encompass the complexity of one symbol, it might be better first to consider its primary relationship with communication.

If Mercury rules both language and the processes of thought, together with basic communication skills as an adjunct to its rulership of the nervous system, then our understanding of Freud demands that Mercury should be intimately connected to the Unconscious.

It is.

In fact astrology is the only coherent body of knowledge that would automatically knot these disparate threads of human experience into the same cord. Mercury the psychopomp, the Homeric guider of souls, shifting effortlessly between the realms of the dead and the world of the living, is both the god of language and the messenger of its hidden meaning. If our personal unconscious, our idiosyncratic history, *is* in part created as we assimilate language, then the manner in which our Mercury is mapped might say something about how our unconscious is experienced.

If we were to look at everything from the perspective of Mercury we might begin to get a glimpse of how we relate to our unconscious, and what its natural language might be; in other words, what 'processes' might have been primary in constructing its outlines. A strong contact with Neptune, for instance, would then mean far more than the bald 'highly imaginative but confused' so beloved of the cook books. If Neptune dominates the aspects to Mercury then does this say something about a foetus absorbing sensations through the amniotic fluid?

The undifferentiated experience of floating in the womb is a primary Neptune symbol. There *are* no boundaries, there *are* no extremes. Nourishment and oxygen pulse through the body in waves. A powerful identification with this state may predispose us to absorbing *all* our later experiences in a similar way. We may then prefer the medium of dreams, *need* the effect of drugs to replicate the underwater world of our early life, or have an abhorrence of blunt, highly focused input, which might be perceived as crassly insensitive or even physically painful.

This predisposition to the nebulous by virtue of our passive and receptive inter-uterine experiences has, of course, been pointed out by many psychologists from Freud onwards. But what we might be seeing here is not just an astrological variant of psychological determinism; what is taking place is just one expression of Neptune. It is Neptune at its most liquid and literal – we float and absorb, and in doing so begin to activate a powerful planetary principle, which might well re-emerge later in its religious form. However, the Christian claim – for example – that 'we are all one in the body of Christ' can only be fully appreciated when we see how astrology links the first experience of the principle to the physical situation of its initial assimilation.

In science, too, the pervasive residue of Neptune has shown itself for centuries in cosmological theories. Even today the concept of a universal 'ether' which in some mysterious manner spreads out and encompasses all of space is by no means finished with. If not used directly, it has been a growth medium for the development of ideas of gravitation and energy fields, and is frequently used as verbal shorthand for an unknown factor until the mechanism under examination has been fully revealed.

If this early identification with Neptune as the medium by which everything reaches us were to be the case, then as we began to learn to speak, began to create our own inner meaning of language, it would be to Neptune that we would naturally turn. Water would be the medium by which we explained what we had learned. We would instinctively refer back to the state we trusted, to those sensations with which we were the most familiar. Our language would then be laid down upon the sea, to rise and fall with the tides, never to mean quite the same thing twice, never able to separate itself from the totality of life, and inexplicably draining away into the sand if there is any attempt to circumscribe it with the Saturnine demands of reality.

Perhaps it is because so much of our inter-uterine life is spent in the Neptune state that there is a level at which it is the natural medium of the unconscious 'assimilation' process in all of us. After all, we literally grew in water, absorbed all our nutrients in liquid form and experienced the totality of our first known universe as being exclusively fluid.

This Neptunian aspect of our unconscious is our subtlest sense, acutely sensitive to the slightest emanations which seem to leak into our unconscious from the outside world, and to which we so often respond without knowing. Through Neptune we absorb ideas, fashions and attitudes that slide under the barricades of ego and intellect and gracefully reassemble themselves within the psyche without us even realizing they were there. It is only when we find ourselves humming a particularly schmaltzy song that we recognize such an invasion has taken place!

This profound sensitivity to atmosphere hints at a primitive side to Neptune which is rarely commented upon; our sense of smell. This is a peculiarly Neptunian function and potentially the most acute of all our senses, but has long been allowed to lapse under the guise of civilization. Human babies still bond to the breast by smell, we still use it to check the suitability of food or the possibility of fire, but otherwise the vast repertory of social and survival issues that revolve around smell in the animal world are now lost to us. The nearest we get is the occasional uneasy feeling that tells us danger may be in the air, a perception we too often distrust or seek to diminish by how we now define it. In describing such perceptions thus we have perhaps relegated our primary ability to an illegitimate 'sixth sense'.

The primacy of the Neptunian experience ensures that at least a part of all our later sensory experiences incorporates it. Its profound consequence as the central way of 'knowing' about ourselves is reflected in the importance we attach to its manifestations within us. Dreams and visions seem to be the universal vehicles for the deepest revelation of the self. This method of illuminating our inner language has the most profound and enduring meaning, one that links together the greatest complexities of the soul and ultimately defeats the dualism created, in part, by a blinding awareness of being *separate*. The sensation of being separate is the one that so abruptly and so literally breaks through the waters and beaches us in the world.

The opposite to the oceanic state is the Uranian separation. It is the sense of uniqueness, of being differentiated and perhaps even alienated and *cut off*. It may be like the reality of cold air after the soothing comfort of a warm bath, or the sterile delivery room with its noise, light and *strangeness*. The sense of freezing, of chill and coldness in an emotional winter, are strong Uranian experiences in later life – what might they echo?

In a strongly Uranian person we have an individual using language in a highly intellectual manner, fragmentary and disjointed – invariably *detached* and often seemingly disconnected from the body in some way. Often the speech is delivered (!) very quickly in sudden bursts and frequently with *actual breathing problems*, as if there is a constriction in the throat or the solar plexus is suddenly not working properly and must be compensated for in some way by sudden 'cries'. There can be a marked reluctance to trust others or to take the common path, as if the individual is returning again and again to the issue of separation from others and distrust of the familiar. A familiar that might be perceived as harbouring yet another shock under its guise of stability and security.

It is a frame of reference that constantly refers back to the severing of the umbilical cord. It seems to be continually pre-occupied with sensations of being 'original' and 'unique', and mentally rationalizes the immediacy of the present, as if constantly coming to terms with the impact of the moment.

The Mercury/Pluto contact might indicate an identification with our most primitive emotional source: the language of creative force and energy. Seen as a complement of birth, we may better understand why those with such contacts often volunteer so little. Reluctant to speak, they need to have their words *dragged out of them*. Often feeling actually diminished should they express an opinion, as if something has literally been taken away from them, they hold on to their past like a guilty secret. They do not want to let go of their language, as if they want to nurse and hold on to what they have produced. The standard Sakoian and Acker defini-tion for this conjunction tells us that Mercury/Pluto types need to 'get to the bottom of things' and that they 'understand the forces that generate fundamental changes in the environment'. How true!

The contact with Pluto creates a language that roots back to a time of enormous environmental upheavals. Nothing comes easy, things have to be *forced* and *pressed*; the issue is invariably one of *power*. We fight our way out or we are dominated and suffocated. We may be drawn compulsively towards acting out authority issues with others, until something finally gives. Something that has been held in for a long time suddenly comes pouring out, nothing can stop it.

To talk of such Mercury/Pluto aspects *is* to talk of birth. A language that emerges out of such issues can hardly forget the intensity of its initiation. It lies in the shadow of its own beginning and can never treat itself easily or lightly, can never forget what has been done to it. All subsequent recollections would be carried along in the same underground stream and become in some way touched by the life-or-death struggle at the very brink of creation.

If we choose to accept the idea that our awareness of the outer planets stems from our earliest experiences, that the cosmos is working its way in from the outside, so to speak, and infiltrating our unconscious long before the moment of birth, then we must again recognize that there is much that pre-dates the birth chart. Owing to the slowness of the outer planets' motion during the months of inter-uterine life, their position at birth may be almost identical to their positions during the previous months. While this is not always the case, it might suggest one reason *why* the outer planets are so powerful; it is not just the depth and substance of their message but the fact that their channels are held open for so long. The actual moment of birth itself may better symbolize how already absorbed energies are *subsequently* expressed.

To use the birth chart in a way that might provide a more comprehensive sense of what has been going on *before* birth obviously calls for a reassessment of how we choose to analyse chart factors. As far as images of unconscious processes are concerned, the aspects of Mercury – in particular – to the outer planets would seem to be of prime importance, for the reasons already outlined. These Mercury to Uranus/Neptune/Pluto aspects might form something like a neural network that keys the subsequent assimilation of language into the sensations that have been experienced before and during birth. To examine the texture of their connections more effectively calls for more discriminating techniques than to focus on the one or two major aspects that usually occur in the average chart.

In *Working with Astrology*[9] these major techniques of astrological analysis are explained for those new to the dynamic approach to chart interpretation, and a brief introduction to the use of midpoints is given here in Appendix 1, page 342. The recommended use of midpoints and harmonics will show up very clearly how Mercury, for instance, is keyed into the outer planets in many more ways than traditional methods allow. Its bias towards one or other of the outer planets may thus be instantly visible, and the appropriate assessment made.

Before pursuing how these judgements might be arrived at,

which will form part of Chapter 8, we should return to the main themes of the previous chapter: that we inherit much of our chart and that we are also continuously responding to charts other than our own, as if they too are in some way embedded in us and sensitive to transits.

In this way we seem to be born with much of our history already inside us, which in some sense can be thought of as archetypal but in fact is both more complex and far more discriminating than Jung's utilization of this theme. We can think of planetary energies as seemingly inscribed in *specific ways* on what could be thought of as a primal or universal zodiac to which we all have access, and that much of what happens to us is in fact an interaction with this primal or unconscious circle of animals on which is scattered the sum of our collective experience.

This collective experience can be expressed for us in reasonably clear astrological terms. In viewing the energies of the transiting planets as catalysts of the unconscious we can bring together very different human – and *non*-human – phenomena into a single moment. This moment then becomes observable through its internal geometry, which will continue to resonate within the collective zodiac indefinitely.

The analysis of this process is the main function of astrology. Whatever we can learn from the intricacies with which its symbols link together gives us the flow of its inner language, a language that the placement of Mercury so often dictates. So common is this observation that it is somewhat of a cliché to speak of astrology as being a language of itself: it may be more pertinent to ask if *language* is more properly an expression of astrology.

7.

Life Sentences:
Symbol, Cycle and Language

✳ ✳ ✳ ✳ ✳ ✳ ✳ ✳ ✳

When we consider an astrological symbol we start with a core meaning and allow this basic image to spread out, to diffuse and reach the edges of its possibilities. We treat the symbol as a spider's web of linked affinities, each strand leading further away from the essence, but inextricably joined to it through an unbreakable network of associations. The clearer we understand the symbol, and the more we have lived it, the further we can pursue the paths it takes. As long as we maintain an inner understanding of its principle we can follow the permutations of its possibilities for as far as we are prepared to travel, no matter how they twist or turn along the way.

We can think of an astrological symbol as a principle, as an instinct or as a source of energy that permeates our experience, colouring everything that it touches, or we may see it more traditionally as a clear chain of connections rigidly following the hierarchical order of its ancient rulerships; a message that moves from king to commoner, down to the serf, the slave and the beasts of the field, finally running to ground with the ants and the flowers.

Either way we shall get a sense that there is a coherent inner purpose being expressed. We are experiencing not a random collection of images and events, scattered with complete disregard to meaning, but a clearly defined sequence of principles spreading out in the world, resonating in each new occurrence. The planetary instincts move from that which we can clearly define and describe to expressions only deducible through inner sensation, to be hinted at or pointed towards, or gently called into being.

What starts out as a clear directive becomes camouflaged with the circumstances of its journey; we may need to hunt for it carefully, to pull away at the accumulation of events, tease out the thread that runs though disparate occurrences. When we find it, we recognize it at once. We know again that we are facing something that is quite unambiguous; a clear principle, a pure energy. It is a discovery we may make intellectually, emotionally or viscerally, but it is unmistakable. We know at once where it belongs, and from whence it has come, however it is covered or disguised.

As the planets move through signs and houses, as they pick up aspects and contacts, so the expressions of their principles are modulated and changed by the harmonics of their encounters. Complex symbols are created which hold an interior latticework of meaning, which may materialize as events or feelings, but are never completely one or the other. They are more an intricate series of possibilities, always embracing the essence of their significators, but capable of infinite expression.

We notice the nature of such complex symbols more readily when they materialize as *events*; here we have something tangible, something we can walk round and recognize. In such concrete events we can so often see more clearly how the various strands of planetary energy are interwoven through the fabric of life, gently pulling into being happenings which in some way re-state the planetary dialogue in human terms.

Sometimes the voices are clear and unambiguous; there can be no mistaking that the Gods have spoken. At others, it is hard to feel that the cosmos has done anything other than find a pale echo of its original purpose, and, as if angry at the substitute of their original intent, wreak cruel revenge on the symbolic victim.

Flight 103, the Pan Am jetliner called *Maid of the Seas*, was destroyed over Lockerbie, its name resonating to the previous Virgo/Pisces eclipse triggered at the moment of its fall. Was a factor in its demise that the Astro*Carto*Graphy of the previous Ingress Sun/Uranus conjunction fell exactly on that of the Sun/Uranus conjunction of the world's first powered flight – which was the *Maid of the Seas* flight path? (See Figure 7.16.)

It seems as if the only way we can make sense of such senseless events is if the astrological language from the past continues to

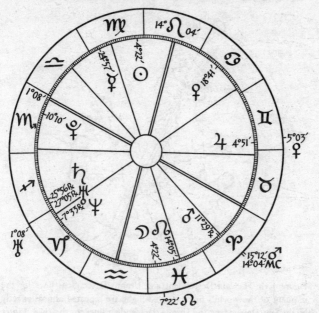

Figure 7.1a The eclipse Full Moon for 27 August 1988 at 4 VI 22, set for Lockerbie. Note that this is almost exactly square to Jupiter on the degree of Flight. Venus transited this 8th house point on the day of the Lockerbie crash. Note that the MC for the crash was at 14 AR 04 – exactly trine the Full Moon MC – and see also that Uranus was sextile the Full Moon Ascendant, to the minute. At an Astrological Association seminar in London, Dennis Elwell has also pointed out the main features of this eclipse, and the significance of the name *Maid of the Seas*. At 8.26 p.m. on 9 January 1989 this 'Flight' eclipse chart again received close transits with the Kegworth air crash. Then the Node was at 5 PI 40, the Ascendant 5 VI 31, the Sun at 19 CP 34, the Moon at 16 AQ 42 and Venus 28 SG 52. When the report on the Kegworth crash was published on 18 October 1990, Saturn itself had reached 19 CP 14 and Pluto 16 SC 48.

live. If in some way we pick it up and repeat it, so we make ourselves vulnerable to the consequences of its historical dynamics. As with the birth chart, every moment takes on the continuing process of evolution, depicted astrologically as the present's constant transit to the past. Today's planets are endlessly triggering

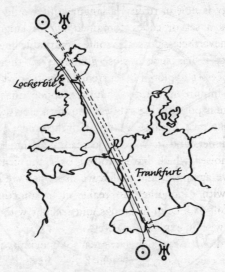

Figure 7.1b The Sun/Descendent and Uranus/Descendent lines for the moment of the world's first powered flight are repeated almost exactly by the Sun/Descendent and Uranus/Descendent lines for the 1988 Winter Solstice (dotted lines). Both sets of lines are very close to Pan Am's 103 flight path from Frankfurt. In fact, the Astro*Carto*Graphy of the world's first powered flight picks out a number of places which have subsequently become the location of major air disasters.

the residue of archaic events, constantly re-activating all that has gone before.

In attempting to confront the complexity of astrological symbols, of their capacity to locate themselves in every facet of our lives, we will often speak of astrology as the *language* of their expression, a language like any other that must be learned with years of practice.

It is a fact that one of the main difficulties in explaining astrological ideas to non-astrologers is that they have no conception of this 'language' themselves. Everything sounds gibberish, as if it is being made up on the spur of the moment to fit the facts, or is quaint medieval nonsense, like witches and cauldrons and enigmatic incantations found in mouldering volumes.

Astrology is *not*, in reality, a language (it would be viewed by linguists as a set of codes contained *within* language), but its operation nevertheless possesses some remarkable linguistic properties. In fact it has such a close similarity to those verbal and mental processes explored by current linguistic psychologists that we need to inquire more fully what these connections might be.

Language is possibly the subtlest and most elusive characteristic of the human race. Because we 'do' it all the time we automatically think we understand it. We all too readily assume it to be just a series of noises which have evolved over the centuries, whose meaning we agree on, and which we use when we wish to communicate with each other. In reality it is something far more complex, full of hidden meanings and fraught with problems for those who wish to explore its secrets.

The words we use, which may seem so innocuous and uncomplicated in a dictionary, and which we have so unthinkingly absorbed, are in actuality full of emotional and social implications. Rather than *our* using a few well-chosen words, language may in many cases describe and define *us*, almost as if we were its product. This is similar to the way in which we might be partially defined by class, colour, race, culture or religion; what we assume without thinking may sometimes assume us.

Philosophers such as Wittgenstein consider that *all* philosophical problems are essentially linguistic, and defined by the nature of the language we use. We know only what language allows us to know. After all, if we do not have a word for something, how can we ever know what it is, or know that we do not know it? What is un-definable cannot be defined.

To such linguistic philosophers, concepts beyond language are essentially meaningless, and attempts to plug the gaps are intellectually fraudulent. If we ascribe something to a god, something way beyond our knowledge or experience which has divine attributes, so that we can then worship it, this is a simple confusion of terms. The god defined in human terms by human language *is* human; it can't be anything else. Everything about it emerged from human experience and is redolent of human assumptions and human dialogue. There is nothing divine or miraculous; everything ultimately reduces to the condition of the human, and to the dynamics of the language that defines it. If there *is* anything else, anything out of our verbal reach, of that we must remain silent. Indeed, we literally have no choice; like the caveman, we can only grunt and point at the dark.

There are, of course, those who do not completely accept all of this. Philosophers in non-linguistic corners of the field have voiced the suggestion that linguists have, in effect, carefully defined the rug before pulling it out from under the feet of everyone else. An argument, of course, that many non-astrologers have used when hearing the jargon-filled *post-facto* explanations of their birth charts: those who own the language of a situation own most of the rest of it as well.

Whatever language may or may not *ultimately* define, it certainly goes a long way towards describing and defining the bounds of our horizon; more importantly, it also may well define much more than we realize, and this needs to be confronted. We saw in Chapter 6 that Freud believed language to be the natural medium of the unconscious, and that the French psychoanalyst Jacques Lacan more recently declared, 'the unconscious is structured like a language'. As we grow up and acquire our vocabulary, so we begin to assimilate the unspoken components of words *and* assign to them our own personal sensations and associations. It is this record of our individual history, embedded in language, that may comprise our personal unconscious. If we subsequently enter analysis we will explore this unconscious through its own medium: words.

It is important to recognize that we describe not only *things* in terms of language, but also our feelings and our emotions. These, too, are verbal and part of our personal language. Those early feelings which are designated 'pre-verbal' by analysts can only be approached obliquely and have to become 're-connected' to language before we can describe them. There is abundant clinical evidence that this is so.

Very often extremely powerful emotions are completely unrecognized simply because we have never put a word to them. Once we give them a word and connect them to language, they come alive and we express the feeling, often with great amazement that we have never done so before.

Currently, many feminist authors report on how their observations of women's roles within society are having a profound effect on individual women. They receive letters which say how the writer never realized exactly how she felt until she read of another woman's experience. Once another woman had given her the words she immediately recognized them, and could then articulate her own voice. Feelings which were of great importance had remained unexpressed, not because they were repressed by inhibition or fear, but simply because they had never been connected to language before, and thus could never be brought into life.

Words are not just units of informational currency, they are vivid with life and have their own purpose, their own internal dynamics. When we start to explore language we begin to see that individual words can become translucent. We can learn to see through them to every stage of their evolution. As they progress and alter over the centuries so they pick up shades of meaning, fresh shifts and nuances, associations, thoughts, feelings; even myths and fantasies. Dreams, implications, half-spoken imaginations; all of these lie under the surface of our speech, and coalesce in language.

The ancients saw language as magic, quite literally as *spelling*; that is what the word originally meant; as the Gospels were the *good spell*. Mercury dazzles and beguiles us, we are seduced by our ego into thinking he is our servant, that he gives expression to what we believe, but all the time we miss the obvious, lulled by his conjuror's voice. Moment by moment, he is bringing our unconscious into being, stringing the sequence of our life together like beads on a chain. Under the guise of expressing the present, he is telling of the past.

This potential for deception is in the Mercurial nature of language; our basic astrology points towards the truth of this. Language encircles our experience like colours fuse the surface of a bubble. The swirling patterns signal their designs to us, while surreptitiously they mask the boundary between inner and outer, between conscious and unconscious. It is a brilliance that cannot be separated from the reality of the bubble, cannot be removed or extracted or examined in isolation. It is an integral component of the shape and function of the sphere, playing its part in containing whatever might lie within. It communicates the dynamics of its own motion while defining the boundaries which guard a hidden land. In doing so, it defies us to reach for those truths that be may circumscribed by its existence.

The Roots of Language

The search for the 'beginning' of language is one which, from a purely academic or historical perspective, is doomed to failure. By definition there can be no written or spoken records and, contrary to some misconceptions, there are *no* 'primitive' languages being spoken now which might act as hypothetical models for the birth of verbal communication.

All languages are extremely complex in construction, and involve an understanding of the society from which they emerge. Technologically primitive societies have languages which are as intricate as their Western European counterparts, and attempts to utilize the lack of a specific technology as a gauge of 'civilization' does not always reflect well on those making such assessments. Thus we are left with an almost open-ended choice in speculating how language may have evolved.

There are essentially three current theories, known colloquially as the *bow-wow* theory, the *yo-heave-ho* theory and the *oral-gesture* theory. The *bow-wow* theory suggests that language emerged out of attempts to imitate natural sounds, which we *still* have a strong tendency to do. Parents use baby-words such as *chuff-chuff* to refer to steam engines, a certain type of First World War shell was known as a *whiz-bang*, cars *zoom* along, doors *bang*, corks *pop*, paper *rustles*, a type of amplifier is called a *waa-waa*; all so named because the word mimics the noise.

The *yo-heave-ho* theory proposes that language emerged out of the need to co-ordinate efforts, by making grunts or similar noises, so that a tribe could learn to operate together and thus maximize its evolutionary potential.

The *oral-gesture* theory sees language as having developed through the interaction of sound and gesture. The grunts, grimaces and arm-waving behaviour seen so often in primates may have eventually given way purely to sound. This particular idea may have some appeal for astrologers. Again, from our knowledge of Mercury, we would expect there to be a direct link between speech and gesture. This can be seen most easily in young children learning to write, where the tongue carefully traces around the mouth each letter being penned in the copy-book. From the evolutionary point of view speech has to supersede gesture, as gesture by itself is ultimately unable to convey more than the most basic statements. Anyone who doubts this should try miming something like 'I believe that my aunt in Australia, who owns a flower shop and hates dogs, is a follower of Krishnamurti.'

All three theories have their adherents, and all can offer some slight supporting evidence. Ultimately all are equally unprovable, and are almost certainly destined to remain so for the reasons given.

With this in mind, we should perhaps consider a *fourth* alternative, one which we begin to discover when we start to learn the symbolic 'language' of astrology. Before approaching this, we need to review some current ideas about the nature of language and how it is perceived to operate.

The Language of Psychoanalysis

Freud was the first of the modern thinkers to consider the function and dynamics of language from a psychological perspective. For him, the assimilation of language paralleled the development of the ego – the sense of individual identity. It is relevant to recall that Freud never used the word *ego*, he used the German *Ich*: 'I'. Thus he was placing consciousness firmly around a sense of self-identity, which he also saw as being connected to the individual experience of the physical body.

The learning of language, of the ability to communicate what the self is experiencing, has the function of separating the individual from undifferentiated feelings and impulses which then become part of a personal unconscious. This unconscious, having been created through linguistic processes, retains a linguistic framework and expresses itself through language.

In the previous chapter we saw how ideas and associations might collect around individual words during the process of life, and how each individual word thus expresses not just its dictionary meaning, but also our private (and indeed often quite unconscious) inner meanings. Language thus becomes a channel for a deep internal dialogue, whose true content might initially be quite unknown to us. Indeed, some analysts would suggest that the true meaning of the language we use is invariably unknown to us, and that our lives are spent perpetually acting out its unconscious content.

Once we start to explore how this process of associations might develop, we are forced to recognize that it does not stop with individual words, but with individual *sounds*. In a classic piece of self-analysis Freud demonstrated how his associations around the names of towns and painters led him to repress certain thoughts on death and sexuality. Freud's original account of this[1] is quite lengthy; what follows is an abbreviated version, which nevertheless demonstrates his observations clearly enough.

Freud had attempted to recall the name of the painter *Signorelli*, whose work he had seen, but could only come up with the names of *Botticelli* and *Boltraffio*.

Upon association, certain facts came back to him. He recalled having a conversation with regard to the inhabitants of *Bosnia* and *Herzegovina*. This conversation touched on two very loaded subjects, sex and death. In the first instance Freud recalled having to tell a patient there was no hope for him. The man had replied, 'Herr, what can I say?'

In the second conversation Freud remembered an anecdote

about a patient who valued sexual experiences above all others and had said, 'Herr, if that ceases, life no longer has any charms.' In both cases the use of the word *Herr* (sir) connected by *sound* to Herzegovina and by *association* to Bosnia, being the town where one of the events took place.

Freud's next association grew out of his recollection of the man who valued sex to extreme. He recalled that he had a patient who had committed suicide on discovering he had an incurable sexual condition. This news had come to him while he had been holidaying in *Trafio*. Thus the issues of sex and death now linked three places: Herzegovina, Bosnia and Trafio. If sex and death are to be repressed, then the names of the places which allude to these issues must similarly be held in check, for they are likewise strongly charged with a forbidden meaning.

It is almost axiomatic that material which we seek to keep hidden will strive to surface, perhaps initially mixing in with more acceptable associations. This is precisely what happened.

When Freud had tried to recall the name of the painter Signorelli the word instantly split into two halves. *Signor* and *elli*. The *Signor* part was repressed because *signor* means the same as *Herr* and thus associates to death and sexuality, but *elli* was allowed to remain and surfaced as one half of the (incorrectly recalled) Bott*celli*. The first syllable, *Bo*, comes from *Bo*snia, which also surfaces in the name of the second incorrect painter, *Bo*ltraffio. Bol*traffio* also incorporates the town of *Trafio*, where Freud was staying when he heard of his patient's suicide, thus linking both themes. It is an interesting aside that Bosnia and Herzegovina used to constitute a separate republic together, thus they were once joined in reality as they were in Freud's unconscious.

It is also striking that issues of art and sexuality and disease – all Mars/Neptune issues – are simultaneously repressed in the chart of a man who had Saturn on the Mars/Neptune midpoint! The implications of this type of correlation will be examined more closely in Chapter 11.

We can see from such an example how words can become powerfully charged with emotions that we may not initially acknowledge, and which are reflections of how our own specific astrological make-up has interacted with the continual process of transiting planets. Even without exploring such complexities as the linguistic analysis of free association we can recognize the power of specific words, particularly those that may emerge in a counselling situation.

Even in a relatively mild conversational exchange we can recognize that certain words hold powerful latent images. We become aware of how they dip and bob as they cross the current of emotions, like a boat traversing choppy water. People can readily cry, or laugh or explode with anger upon reaching a particular sequence of sounds, a particular word or expression. Some cannot bring themselves even to utter a certain name or discuss a situation; activating language would bring too much to the surface.

Psychoanalysts such as Jacques Lacan would suggest that it is almost axiomatic that the names of our parents contain within them the history of our most basic childhood conflicts; for their names encompass some of our earliest memories, to which we refer again and again. In *Language and Myth* Ernst Cassirer believes that the biblical text 'Where two or three are gathered in my name, there I am in the midst of them' was meant to be taken literally.[2] That is, the pronunciation of the name of God actually evoked his presence, that the *name* contained the spirit, not as a symbol, but in actuality. Cassirer also reminds us that in some societies names are changed so that the past can be wiped away, or there can be a great fear that to mention the name of a departed person will actually summon them back to life; their spirit, too, bides within their name as a real entity. In India, for instance, a child is never named after a living relative lest this be seen as wishing the older person dead.

Lacan was concerned with all that may be contained within a name or a word. His approach would be to explore the 'dialogue' that is taking place out of sight of our everyday life, a discourse based on the language of our inner truth, accessible only through an understanding of how its grammar and syntax have come into being, and of the secret meaning of its sounds.

What emerges so strongly from Freud's discovery, and has been taken up by linguistic analysts up to and including Lacan, is the significance of the role of *phonemes*: the individual sound components of each word. If the unconscious was not in some way filing each 'sound section' under a separate heading then the phenomena simply would not work as described; yet we see it happening again and again.

Freud once commented that children treat words like things, that they expect words which sound similar to have much the same meaning. In a case study, Milton Sirota[3] described the phobia of a two-year-old boy who, on learning the meaning of the word 'urine', had developed a fear of using the lavatory, a feat which he had just mastered.

At the time of the phobia the boy's mother was heavily pregnant and the issue of where babies come from had been raised on several occasions. On analysis, it was revealed that the aggression and anxiety which the forthcoming birth had evoked in the little boy had become connected to the *sound* of the word 'urine', which the boy had understood also to mean *you're in*: that is, *you may fall into the lavatory* and also *you're in the womb*. The boy had previously confused 'sun' and 'son' and wondered if children were also supposed to be up in the sky.

The phobia resulted in part from his wanting to be back inside his mother, like the forthcoming baby that was about to usurp his role, and the denial of his rage at this coming event, which threatened to 'swallow him up'. Thus the word 'urine' was linked by association to the lavatory and by *sound* to his fantasies of the forthcoming birth, and the feelings that surrounded it.

Innumerable jokes and anecdotes revolve around the confusions such word-play can precipitate, which seems to suggest that we treat the sound of a word very differently from its meaning. Modern linguistic theories would regard the *sound* of a word as being quite arbitrary. After all, if we consider all the languages of the world, there are innumerable different sounds used to describe the same object, and no evident pattern links them. However, as we shall see, this may not be the whole story.

Jung's Research of Language

There are very powerful clues as to the manner in which we treat the complex relationship of sound and meaning to be found in the early writings of Carl Jung. In Volume 2 of his *Collected Works* – generally in pristine condition on the library shelf, because it's the one no one ever reads – we find the results of all his word-association tests. They contain some quite remarkable discoveries.

During his years at the Burgholzli psychiatric hospital Jung carried out extensive research into the manner in which his patients reacted to the stimulus of individual words. These tests were quite straightforward; Jung would use a word and request an association upon it, and both the associated word and the time taken to formulate it would be recorded. Not surprisingly, he found that those words which might be linked to anxiety-producing situations often took longer to respond to; upon occasion the anxiety was so great that no word could be associated at all. Equally unsurprisingly, from our modern perspective, was that the associated words might offer considerable insight into an individual's emotional life. What *does*, however, hold very considerable interest are two specific findings which emerged from the overall project.

Jung discovered that when an individual was tested during a time of mental alertness, the results of the test were conspicuously different from those of a similar test carried out when the individual was tired. More importantly, the results of the two tests indicate a marked difference in *how* the word was responded to, and this seemed to hold good as a general rule.[4]

Tested during a time of alertness, the patient tended to respond to the *meaning* of the word. That is, 'knife' might elicit the response 'fork', 'table' might associate with 'chair'. For the most part the relationship between the stimulus and the response words were reasonably coherent and understandable. Even in those cases where an apparently nonsensical reply was received, later discussion could reveal that, for the individual concerned, the association had *meaning* and was logically linked. Things were very different when the subject was tired or distracted, and dramatically different when exhausted. During periods of tiredness, when mental capacity decreases, the word associations revolved around the *sound* of the word. That is, 'table' might evoke 'able', 'knife' could be followed by 'life' and so on. The implications are quite unambiguous: when the individual is fully conscious *meaning* predominates, when exhausted or inattentive *sound* predominates. In other words, the *conscious* mind attempts to follow the logic of meaning, the *unconscious* mind pursues patterns of sound. It might be that these two distinct approaches relate in some way to the manner in which the left and the right hemispheres of the brain process information.

Jung's next discovery was even more remarkable. He noted how same-sex members within a family tended to come out with similar, or even identical words as a response to the stimulus word.[5] This would suggest that there are patterns of language linked in some way to different psychic expressions within the family, and that similar patterns of behaviour expressed themselves, literally, in similar language. There is obviously considerable scope here for further research.

We saw in the example of Freud's dream how his unconscious had attached psychic significance to the phonemes in a number of place names, and how these became jumbled up by seemingly attaching themselves to the similar sounding components of the names of painters. Jungian psychologist Paul Kugler pursues this point, and believes that archetypes reveal themselves in language in both its meaning *and* its sound. Going back to another example from Freud, in which Freud analysed the significance of a flower which, in a woman's dream, appeared to liken *violet* with *violate*, Kugler explores what he believes are archetypal ideas being expressed.[6]

Taking the flower, a carnation, as an example, Kugler points out that its sound-component 'carn' leads us to *carnal* and *carnage*, thus linking – at a sound-associative level – the flower to sexuality and the shedding of blood. The obvious image which links these two themes is the loss of virginity; and indeed *deflower* means precisely this. Kugler suggests that, at an archetypal level, the image of *being deflowered* is in some way impressed into the various relevant words through its phonetic structure and their associated expressions.

This particular association was also commented on by the Hungarian philologist and psychoanalyst Theodore Thass-Thienemann.[7] Thass-Thienemann also quotes the dream of the patient whose carnation bled on to her dress, causing her to wake up with palpitations. He comments:

Analysis cannot be satisfied by the simple verbal reference *deflower* or *de-floration*. One would like to know what lies behind this verbal formulation; especially, why does the carnation start bleeding? The girl knew nothing of Latin, she was unaware that *carnis* means 'flesh'. She did not even think of *in-carnation*, 'becoming flesh', and had no idea of how the word *in-carnation* could have anything to do with her 'carnation'. One may say in this case that . . . an old scar starts bleeding, an old forgotten meaning . . . became alive again in her dream.

Thass-Thienemann continues by informing us of other startling linguistic associations between blood and flowers. The Latin *menstrui fluores* is the root of 'flowers' and 'flow', and refers specifically to menstruation. Until the last century in England the expression 'having her flowers' was a common euphemism for a woman's period. With a diagram (Figure 7.2), Kugler[8] demonstrates how the various associations of *carnation* can string together.

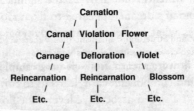

Figure 7.2 Paul Kugler's illustration of how metaphors and sound-associations can link up within language, joining ideas and themes together.

Thus we can explore the word from the perspective of its literal meaning (a flower) and list all different categories of flowers and parts of flowers, or we can start to explore what is hidden in its phonetic construction and develop these strands for as far as we might be able to pursue them, either through their historical development or in their current variation.*

Once we depart from the more familiar process of simple association (flower, carnation, rose, lily, etc.) we find ourselves in something like a dream world, where associations start to pull in concepts or images we had no idea were lurking just out of sight, revealing connections we had not (consciously) suspected. There is, however, one important element missing: astrology.

Language and Astrology

If we believe that the different planets rule or affiliate with specific objects, sensations and situations, then we must assume that something of a similar nature takes place in the way their energy links the diversity of their associations. That is, there must be an *astrological* component to language, one which links *astrological* themes together in the manner that Kugler believes archetypes may underlie language.

The big difference between the Jungian approach to the idea of archetypes and the astrological model is that, while both share the idea of 'themes', astrological principles are very precise, involved in the creation of quite specific occurrences and capable of being located in a variety of circumstances.

For example, Saturn is intimately connected to the element

---

* In both Formalist and Structuralist linguistic theory there are claims that inherent patterns in language create repeating themes within human society. For instance, Lévi-Strauss suggests that 'mythemes' exist within language to explain similarities in the myths and legends of various cultures. Such 'mythemes' encapsulate the inherent tensions within language, ensuring that there is a similarity of expression without the necessity of an underlying archetype. Aspects of the Jungian/non-Jungian argument are presented with great clarity by Paul Kugler in *The Alchemy of Discourse*, referred to elsewhere in this book.

lead. Its energy or principle is clearly and unambiguously being expressed in metallic form, just as the Moon is equally present in silver. However, while the Moon may be many things, many things may not be the Moon. Mercury may be identified with the *puer aeternus* and Saturn with *senex*, but neither Mercury nor Saturn *is* that particular archetype. As we have seen, Jungian archetypes have evolved out of astrological principles or instincts operating in the world, and are more akin to what we have described as complex symbols: the dramatization of specific astrological charts.

If language conforms to, or in some manner expresses Jungian archetypes, as Kugler believes it does, then this would suggest that it is astrology, in fact, that operates at a deeper level, playing a part in the creation of language. We may need to start with a word, such as *book*.

First, we have to recognize that there is no such thing as a book.

There is *this* book, the book you are reading, and there are all your other books. There are also libraries full of books, stacked row upon row upon row. But there is no such thing as *a book*.

A book is an abstract concept that exists only in dictionaries and definitions; it has no life of its own. A *book* is a word we use to describe the object you are holding; a word, like all words, that we understand and make use of to impart the meaning that we connect to it. It is a meaning that changes with time and associations.

Once, a *book* meant a heavy, sacred object of vellum pages covered in intricate, illuminated designs, bound in pigskin and clamped between wooden boards. As centuries passed and printing took over so a *book* came to mean a leather-bound sheaf of papers that were often interspersed with hand-pressed etchings, each protected with a soft flimsy of tracing paper. Today a *book* probably means a paperback, or any one of a dozen similar hardback formats in their gaudily illustrated dust-jackets. If we want to conjure up the image of the weighty, leather-bound volume we are likely to say instead *family Bible*, *official ledger* or *ship's log*.

But whatever word we use it remains unformed and intangible, it describes the object but is *not* the object, encompassing all its variations but owned exclusively by none of them; it is the sound that surrounds the thing.

In this way *each word* can be thought of as something like its own complex symbol, that it is a focus of astrological energy, possibly even emerging from a specific moment – after all, there must have been a *first* usage for every word. Perhaps the activation of that moment, through the word, in some way plays a part in bringing events into being.

The astrologer will see direct correlations (in *meaning*) between certain words and certain planets: Lead, Heavy, Wall, Age, Duty, Bone and so on are all 'Saturn' words while Love, Artist, Justice, Peace and Throat are all 'Venus' words. We would expect to see a Venus/Saturn contact in the chart of someone who loved out of a sense of duty or who specialized in painting murals. But how do we think this relationship between word and planet might come about?

If language were to be nothing more than a highly sophisticated method of descriptive expression then there is little we would need to consider in all of this. Astrologers could say, in effect, that planets 'cause' something to happen and that words just describe the event so caused. Thus language would be a 'second-order' effect; there would be no intrinsic relationship between the planet and the word, just a descriptive affinity. But language is *not* just a method of descriptive expression. All the evidence of analytically orientated linguists points to the fact that, in some way or another, language is *alive*, that its descriptive powers are only *part* of its function and that it is directly related to the functioning of the personal unconscious – and perhaps beyond, into the collective. In some way it is a medium for psychic power and 'makes things happen'. For this to take place demands a powerful relationship with the principles of astrology; and to explore this possibility a little further will require that we learn four words used by linguists.

In Chapter 2 it was suggested that Time can be thought of as *synchronous*, that is spreading out all around, as if it were a flat plane moving through space connecting up all events which occur at the same moment, and also as *diachronous*. Diachronous time being the 'history' of this linear development, that territory which lies beneath the surface of the present like water under a slick of oil.

In fact, both *synchronic* and *diachronic* are linguistic terms used in the exploration of language. One can study language as it is being used, without any reference to the past. Noting how one word means the same as another, or translating one language into another, or following the sequential structure of language are all expressions of the *synchronous* plane. Looking at the *history* of language, of discovering how words and phrases have changed their meaning, and coming to see language as an expression of that which has gone before, is an example of working in the *diachronous* plane. All study of languages is on one or other of these planes.

Closely allied to the synchronic mode is the term *metonymy*. Words in a metonymic relationship are those which are sequentially linked to produce a coherent meaning, such as a phrase or sentence. Again, the image of a linear or surface form comes to mind in which information builds up in a reasonable, logical manner, generally according to known rules.

The opposite of this would be *metaphor*. Words in a metaphorical relationship are those which operate more by association, in which the same term is described in another manner, or is analogous to it or associates to it by sound. Metaphor connects with the diachronic axis and includes those words which associate by their historical or symbolic connections.

From the point of view of the birth chart, statements such as 'Saturn is square to Venus, Mars is in Aries, Mercury is quintile Jupiter' and so on are all descriptions on the synchronic plane. When we begin to *interpret* the chart, and note that Mercury can mean 'child', or 'messenger', or in its quintile form with Jupiter can describe a verbose style of talking, we have shifted to using metaphor and the diachronic axis.

In Kugler's re-assessment of Jung's word-association experiments, he points out that the results of those patients who were alert corresponded to the metonymic mode, being predominantly 'logical' and sequentially linked, while those patients who were tired or distracted associated primarily with sound on the metaphoric scale. Kugler then suggests that the ego is essentially connected with the meaning/metonymic/synchronic axis while the unconscious correlates with the poetic/metaphoric/diachronic mode.'

This is a valuable observation, and it may be tempting to suggest analogies with the Solar and Lunar principles. However, it may not always be helpful to view some planets as 'conscious' and others as 'unconscious'. As with metonym and metaphor, the process of life continually intermixes these realms with infinite complexity.

Living Language

We saw earlier how Freud's analysis of his own experiences revealed the part each phoneme played in the psychic process he unravelled. Specific meanings seemed to cluster around each part of the word, as Thass-Thienemann and Kugler have also observed, even though such fragments of a word are often meaningless in themselves. In many respects phonemes are almost abstract sounds, like the components of a chant, with which we somehow identify moments of our experience. This process may take place consciously or unconsciously, but there is a demonstrable tendency for the unconscious to associate together specific sound patterns, as Jung and his co-researchers first observed. It is here that we may get a clue as to the possible manner in which such fragmentary components may operate together.

Chants are used because they are believed to contain far more than just the sense of their collective syllables; they are constructed to resonate to specific ideas. Their vibration is believed to tune into something beyond normal experience, to sensitize the individual to certain states of awareness or to alter consciousness in a manner that will allow receptivity to specific ideas. Each chant is believed to have a special function; humming any old string of words simply won't do! Perhaps language may work in a similar way, that some part of it may resonate directly to the planet with which it has an affinity.

In chanting, the metonymic joining of word upon word on the synchronic plane appears to liberate associations on the diachronic, metaphorical axis which connects directly to those energies believed to be called into being during the chanting process. The chant resonance along the surface wavelength calls up its dormant counterpart, the source of its real energies, from the depths beneath.

This is not to suggest that what might be happening here with astrology is some simplistic one-to-one relationship; that the word *anger* 'means' Mars or that *love* 'means' Venus, or some such naïve correlation. Language is the summation of millions of years of evolution and contains within itself the enormous complexity of its heritage. What is being suggested is that there is perhaps a constituent of a word or phrase that does in some way resonate to an appropriate planetary energy, perhaps because that is how language actually began to come into being; as an attempt to verbalize sensations that originated in the inner experience of the planetary principles.

The idea that language may have emerged from our inner experience of astrology is touched on indirectly by the philosopher Ernst Cassirer, in considering the relationship between language and mythology. Cassirer underscores their essentially symbolic – metaphoric – relationship by commenting that 'Even though it were possible to resolve all mythical consciousness to a basic astral mythology – what the mythical consciousness derives from the contemplation of the stars, what it sees in them directly, would still be radically different from the view they present to empirical observation or in the way they figure in theoretical speculation and scientific "explanations" of natural phenomena.'[10]

As we have observed earlier, *how* language evolved is almost certainly destined to remain a mystery for ever, but that it may have emerged from a desire to communicate a variety of instinctual, astrologically motivated sensations – our 'astral mythology' – may not be particularly far-fetched. If it *did* come into being in this way, then our understanding of modern analytic linguistics would demand that astrology is embedded in all that has proceeded from it.

How deep this actually may be is something experienced by all students of astrology. There comes a point in the process of learning astrology when we become aware that we might in fact be *re-learning* it.

The contacts between word and symbol that begin to open up within us once we start to assume the language of its expression are powerful evidence that we are re-connecting to something that is real and alive. As with the experience of depth psychology, in bringing something back again to our language, we also bring it back into our life. Again, the learning of a language on the synchronic plane calls upon a deep reservoir of symbolic expressions diachronically.

Such observations can only reinforce the idea that there may also be a constituent part of language which carries an astrological message in the same way that our earliest memories and sensations still remain within the boundaries of our words.

For instance, among the words and expressions that we would associate with Jupiter are 'philosopher', 'stout', 'religious leader', and 'the preserver'. Inherent in the names of the philosophers Socrates and Sophocles is the root *so-*, from the Greek adjectival form[11] *sos*, meaning 'safe, sound, whole' and originating from the word meaning 'stout'. It also forms part of the word *soter* meaning 'saviour' and 'preserver', and *sostra* is the word for 'thanks offered for saving one's life' and is also associated with physicians, whose glyph for 'prescription' originates in the symbol for Jupiter. Thus Socrates, Sophocles (and all the sophists) carry within their names the sound from which so many other Jupiter words have sprung. There is an underlying link which philologists unaware of astrology are most unlikely to spot, a form of planetary language running alongside the phonetic lineage.

If this were to be the case then such constituent parts would presumably continue to resonate to those astrological energies which it originally attempted to articulate. In this way language would act as something like a *carrier wave* for archaic astrological effects, and would in some small part respond to appropriate planetary relationships as they formed and re-formed in the sky.

This would also suggest that the concept of 'speaking the will of the heavens' would be less metaphorical than we might initially assume it to be; our language may indeed express some analogous resonance.

Such a carrier wave – resonating to the underlying planetary symbolism – would vibrate in all words and phrases which held the appropriate symbolic affinities, thus in some way drawing together those verbal images which, at a deep level, were already astrologically related. On top of such collective meanings would come our own individual associations, similarly linked together by our idiosyncratic use of language, keyed in to the transit-moment when we first experienced or became aware of the phenomena in question.

It would be important to recognize that at least *two* quite distinct processes are taking place here. First, words may become linked because of their assumed underlying symbolism, such as the principle of Saturn within both 'wall' and 'lead'. Here, there is presumed to be something like a shared essence within both words, that they are both symbolic of Saturn, that they are both 'really' connected to it by virtue of their essential nature. This is unlikely to be the case when we come to our own, more *personal* associations.

If we associate a particular town with a particular feeling, such as we have just seen Freud do, this linking is taking place within *us*. The town is not necessarily being associated *symbolically*; that is, there is no pre-existing, underlying affinity linking town to feeling, *we* make the connection. Here, the word *signifies* rather than *symbolizes* our inner sensations; it becomes part of our personal world. If it is *then* symbolic of anything, it is symbolic of *us* and the manner in which we experience and articulate our existence.

Thus all events and sensations may become impressed into our language in exactly the same way as events might impress themselves upon us and upon our chart; there to be held as the residue of those transits with which they correlate. As suggested in the previous chapters, our chart is infinitely modified by all the experiences of our life, and this modification must inevitably extend to the shifts in our inner associations with language, and of its formative effect upon the processes of our unconscious, in a manner similar to the Freud example outlined above.

There is real evidence that something like this actually takes place.

Russian physicists Avamenko and Nikolaiva have proposed a wave theory of the universe[12] which has received significant support with the results emerging from experiments designed to explore linguistic processes.

Soviet experiments, conducted under Balubovaya, attempted to explore the nature of a translator's work. The translator has to understand the meaning of a phrase, search for its foreign equivalent, and communicate that meaning aloud; obviously some very complex mental processes are taking place at an extremely high speed. The question Balubovaya attempted to answer was: precisely *what* processes might these be?

Up to that point, one conventional view of the possible tasks being performed by the mind during such an activity – which, of course, is typical of the way we would also have to locate the meaning of a symbol or explain the substance of an association – would be to assume that the brain is something like a computer hunting through an enormous database. That is, each time the brain seeks a new word, it has to hunt through everything, or a significant part of the whole base, until it finds what it wants, and then extracts it.

Running a series of tests, which were given both visually and aurally, and comparing the results to previously established word-association tests, it became apparent that such a model was impossible, for the translations were discovered to take place *instantaneously*. It was therefore proposed that '*every sensory signal affects all material stored in the memory and, as a result, only the appropriate response is activated. This model is analogous to acoustical resonance; when a sound wave reaches a piano, the only string which responds by vibrating has physical parameters which exactly correspond to the parameters of the sound. Therefore, the results ... support the hypothesis of wave coding of psychological processes.'[13]*

This is a most remarkable statement. It suggests that the underlying *meaning* of language responds to resonant similarities which *cross the barrier* of specific individual languages instantly. If such experiments continue to be replicated then we would be confident in asserting that language is, in part, a resonant-dependent process which responds to an underlying image, principle or symbol. In England, Dr Percy Seymour[14] has long held that the phenomenon of resonance may in due course be found to underlie astrological effects, and his own theories would seem to be in a general accord with the views of Avamenko and Nikolaiva. However, exploring the permutations of resonance theory is beyond the scope of this book.

What we *can* return to is the assertion that language may operate by resonance. We can suggest that both the collective meaning and the individual understanding of each word lie in some way behind or underneath it as a collective, and that there is some hard evidence that it 'communicates' via sympathetic vibration. Anything that resonates to the symbolism inherent in the word-structure brings it into manifestation. For astrologers this would imply that the shifting re-arrangement of planetary symbolism similarly activates linguistic expression on a moment-by-moment basis. Thus the name *Maid of the Seas* resonates to an inner amalgam of Virgo and Pisces, forever sensitive to the interplay that takes place within these signs, and ultimately affected by its expression.

Seeing language as a kind of 'carrier-wave' of information in this way may also challenge some conventional concepts of symbolism. One thing may become linked to another not just because it is in some way *symbolic* of it, by being similar to it in shape or size, or by having a similar 'feel' to it, but because it comes to be represented by the same *signifier*.

In respect to language, a signifier is the sound of the word to which we attach one or many meanings – meanings which are known as the *signified*. Thus a word may come to *signify* many things; that is, it may hold or lock together quite disparate ideas or associations, perhaps in the manner described by Freud that we have already discussed.

Unlike the symbol, however, which we would suggest links material together because of some assumed underlying process or essence, the *signifier* has no such essential or symbolic connection with anything it signifies; it just stands in place of all to which it refers.

It may well be that these two processes operate simultaneously within astrology, with both symbols and signifiers linking the material in their own manner. We might see that certain circumstances in life are clearly symbolic of specific planetary energies, as tradition demands, but also recognize that the idea of embedding our own personal experience within the zodiac would make such degrees *signify* that which they hold rather than *symbolize* them. Such an approach may well offer a further way of exploring the nature of the birth chart, and the manner in which we interpret it.

The Language of Resonance

If we now start to put together some of the ideas we have explored so far, we can begin to see what help they may offer to our understanding of astrology, or what new light they may throw on to its possible workings.

To start with, we have suggested that *all* events leave their impression upon a primal zodiac. Through the course of evolution this zodiac has become imprinted with the record of everything which has taken place; a cosmic repository for an infinity of charts. These charts *could* be looked at individually, as if disconnected from the rest of the world, but are in fact within us and, if appropriate to our genetic, geographic or familial circumstances, will continue to operate in our lives until their process is completed.

Thus the historical issues, events and circumstances which such imprinted charts represent continue to resonate with the moment-by-moment transits of the planets, creating within us a collective tide of unconscious material kept permanently alive by the current geometry of the Solar System. This can offer a further way of re-examining the concept of the collective unconscious, an unconscious which is continually being modulated by the shifting relationship between the present and the past. Such an image might suggest that what we call 'present' may be more accurately thought of as the current experience of past events, and that 'present' may actually refer to the timeless state reported by mystics.

We are also suggesting that the process of embedding a sequence of events within a zodiac, which are subsequently activated by transits, also takes place within each individual life. The moment-by-moment awareness of ourself and others, when expressed through feelings or events, can become embedded within our own birth charts, both defining how we actually *experience* our own chart and laying down sequences of memories which subsequent transits can activate. To some extent this may correlate with the *content*, but not the structure, of the personal unconscious.

Along with those transits which operate in our lives by stimulating both collective and personal issues, there is also the possibility that we may interact with our collective and personal histories through the process of language. What we may think of as astrological 'effects' may come to us from many directions. Transits may activate specific issues which could be described in terms of individual charts, were we to have the necessary data to erect them, but also there is within the fabric of language the astrological residue of our earliest experiences, which remains sensitive to the current state of the cosmos. This sensitivity to the hidden or unconscious levels of language is heightened by the evident linguistic nature of the personal unconscious.

The large, cyclic processes of human evolution have left their impression on us at a genetic level, as suggested by Freud and Ferenczi, and vestiges of these events continue within all of us. Genetic similarities, such as those within close family members, would tend to reflect a similarity of astrological purpose, perhaps even amplifying any resonance by virtue of their close proximity. What has hitherto been observed as fragmented or individualistic archetypes may in fact be discrete astrological themes seeking expression. Thus we may contain within us a vastly complex series of astrological dynamics, which are capable of finding individual expression in only a few of us, requiring perhaps specific genetic, geographic or temporal circumstances for their manifestation.

Particular aspect structures within the individual birth chart may give some indication of the type of processes to which the native is open but, just as we all contain innumerable genes which have not found, and will not find, expression in our life or appearance, much of our chart will be essentially unlived. In many respects it can be thought of as not actually belonging to us at all, and more something that we unconsciously participate in. This is not to say that planetary energy is ever *absent* from our lives. As will be suggested in the following chapter, we may well use the energy of all possible planetary patterns all the time. Rather, while we may utilize superficial aspects of specific symbol patterns in our own life, the actual 'message' of a particular aspect formation is not directed at *us*, but is part of a process which may have begun hundreds of years ago and might not come into conscious play for decades. Much of what happens to us comes from being caught on the wheel of other events.

In coming into the world we represent a particular strand of evolution, and participate in its expression. What we may view as 'fate' may well be those aspects of our planetary energies over which we have little or no control; the unwinding of those patterns within us which pull our country into economic depression, our continent into war or our race into epidemic – and us along with it. We will similarly benefit from those abundances of life which likewise have no personal relationship with us, and to which we have contributed nothing.

Insomuch as large areas of our lives may be the peripheral expression of cycles with which we have no real affinity, we have – as astrologers – to confront the issue which many philosophers are prepared to acknowledge; that much of our life is essentially meaningless. To be born with a particular genetic structure, or in a particular location, to embody a specific planetary combination, may refer very little – if at all – to the vast majority of our life, and yet may be the path on which an illness or a disaster stalks us to the death. Astrologers are often very ready to call upon all sorts of high-flown metaphysics to 'explain' such apparently arbitrary acts on the part of the fates, and it is realistic to question whether this might be an avoidance of some cold truth.

Implicit in many such 'spiritual' rationalizations is a blind disregard for the individual human experience, preferring instead a somewhat anodyne mysticism in which all unpleasant possibilities are removed. This attitude also implies such an impressive understanding of the ultimate nature of the cosmic purpose that one could be forgiven if it was initially distrusted. Some of the implications of this attitude for the counselling astrologer will be explored in the last chapter.

Finally, we have suggested that while everything arises out of the dynamics of the primal zodiac, everything ultimately returns to it. What we create out of the relationship between ourselves and the universe modifies in some way the appropriate symbols of energy and the degrees they occupy. Thus the process of evolution and the slow patterns of human nature are subtly altered by each succeeding generation, occasionally dramatically. The function of 'recursion', the ability of something to change abruptly within a continuous feedback, is a mathematical icon of our potential for transcendence.

Much of human history may read as if we remain, for the most part, following in grooves cut deeper and deeper by succeeding generations, endlessly repeating the mistakes of its parents. The image of the primal zodiac offers a clue why this might be so, and what might actually be going on. In recognizing the suggestion that real, *concrete* processes may be taking place, we may be able to take steps towards confronting what these might be and relate them to specific astrological themes.

The archetypes and mythologies otherwise presented seem destined to remain permanently elusive, and may be shadows of a more real astrology that still needs bringing into the light. So far, depth psychology has little to offer us by way of philosophical or spiritual encouragement, however impressive the range of its clinical observations. It generally sees the individual as little more than a mirror of early environment, frequently absurd and disconnected from any psychic significance. The approaches towards using astrology that have been explored so far suggest that there could be a *real* interactive process taking place, one in which we all participate to some small extent, and from which we all ultimately benefit. The philosophical implications of this are considerable.

In the following chapters we shall examine ways in which these processes may be explored in greater detail, and what practical use can be made of the ideas discussed so far.

8.

The Quintessence of Creation:
Sex, Language and the 5th Harmonic

☆ ☆ ☆ ☆ ☆ ☆ ☆ ☆ ☆

In exploring possible astrological correlations with human psychology we can apply our knowledge directly in two ways. We can note the *significators* of mental or physical factors or we can claim that there exists a *cyclical relationship* between planet and personality.

A traditional *significator* would be the Moon placement for early emotions, a Mercury/Neptune aspect for idealistic thinking, Saturn in the 4th house for the grandmother who wielded influence during the nursery years, or JU = SO/MO for an enthusiastic, outgoing personality. Here significators would be used to describe known aspects of the personality or, by reversing the process, to conjecture something of its internal dynamics and offer possible interpretations of their outcome. The latter approach is obviously the procedure of the vast majority of astrological consultations.

A *cyclical process* would be the claim that we move from being signified by the Moon in infancy to falling under the rule of Saturn in old age. We might also claim that within this general schema there are more specific cyclical processes common to all of us, such as the seven-year rhythm of hard aspects made by Saturn to its natal position, or the shifts which take place as the outer planets change signs. If we wish, we can extend this further by suggesting that we may all resonate to the basic underlying planetary energy of the times, or postulate alternative dynamics such as how the Uranian energy which is identified with during late adolescence tends to give way slowly to the claims of Saturn as maturity emerges.

While there can be many valuable contributions made to an overall understanding of the personality by an astute astrologer interpreting the chart's significators, very little can be said about the possible process of an individual's psychic development from the birth chart, and the various cyclic theories have virtually nothing whatsoever to add towards a theory of personality development.

If we come back to the traditional rulers of infancy, the Moon and Mercury, and are prepared to look at them in a new light, we may see one possible avenue to explore. From an astrological perspective, both these bodies are associated with childhood although, as we have seen, the connections are somewhat generalized and often superficial. So it is interesting to find that, from a mythical point of view, these two principles actually come from the same source.

The Egyptian god Thoth was a *male* Lunar deity, patron of all things intellectual and the inventor of writing. Thoth was scribe to the gods and also charged with the weighing of the human soul. In this ceremony, the heart of the deceased was weighed against a single feather. If it passed the test it was declared not virtuous or pure, but 'true of *voice*'.

Thoth's purely intellectual skills were often represented separately by the figure of a baboon, the Baboon of Thoth. It is only this aspect of the deity that re-emerged in Greece via Hermes and in Roman mythology through Mercury. Thus the energy we designate 'Mercury' has a primary Lunar source from its Egyptian ancestry as well as the sexual/Plutonic aspects it assimilated from the Greeks, reinforcing part of its linguistic connection to the unconscious.

It is as if the ancient myth has attempted to reconcile some of the confusions around the Moon and Mercury, and during its development through the centuries it partially assimilated other aspects of early life, intuitively associated with the early years. Thus Mercury has its feeling components, its linguistic skills and its sexuality. In fact it was precisely this intricate interweaving of infantile concerns which so drew Freud to the Thoth mythology, and to his ownership of a Thoth Baboon, which at times sat on his desk and stared wisely.

Other planets can be equally contradictory. As is well known, the traditional view of Saturn relegates it to rulership of the last phase of life, but it is in fact intimately connected with the early emergence of the individual. We can point out that it is believed that babies have no sense of time (Saturn), that this is developed only through life experience, and that the elderly frequently report time seeming to move with increasing speed, perhaps as the Saturn principle becomes more and more incorporated. But what we have here is only a poetic image of a very generalized idea. This also appears to contradict strongly an established analytic observation of very young children which touches on another aspect of Saturn, that of its possible role in the formation of the ego.

Very considerable observational and analytic work suggests that the child's sense of self, of ego, comes about partly through language, as we have seen (a Saturn/Mercury function), but also through identifying with the boundaries of its own body. The physical surface covering of the skin becomes a metaphor of the child's psychic boundaries, and thus an extension of its ego-protective mechanisms. It is no coincidence that one synonym of 'skin' is *hide*; the surface of our body is a powerful symbol of our boundary with the world, and a highly-reactive barrier against that which we fear.

Even looked at in this superficial way, we clearly have a Saturn issue of 'boundaries' at a time when Saturn is supposed to be mainly absent. If we were to explore this in some depth we might discover that Saturn would in some way circumscribe the primary Lunar/Mercurial realm and thus be intimately connected to the earliest years as, for instance, the Hubers claim. Theories of psychological astrology which identify Saturn only with specific psychic functions in the post-verbal years would miss the complexities of its possible manifestation throughout the whole course of life.

At this point we have again to recognize that much of astrology seems almost designed not to admit the complexities of issues such as these, and if this is not in some way remedied then it will have little to offer a depth psychologist. As we noted in the first chapter, if astrology cannot come up with correlations for phenomena that we *know* have taken place then there is something wrong with our understanding of astrology. We shall have to revise the manner in which we use astrology or devise new methods for locating how the significators that we know about are actually interacting.

The childhood Moon that we have looked at extends through *all* our life, not just our early years. It is involved with virtually *all* our activities, not just overtly emotional issues or mothering concerns. In so much as the Moon reflects our emotional responses it must connect to *all* matters which engage our emotions, and *all* things that we do to achieve a sense of emotional well-being, however intellectual or academic such pursuits might initially appear.

The Moon reflects itself in our home, in the patterns of our life, in much of our visceral enjoyments, and in all that we do to achieve emotional security, often including our area of work. It controls the liquid nature of our body, is involved in the balance of *psyche* and *soma*, and spreads out to encompass our possible relationships with mass groups and public feelings. Oh, yes, and mother.

Only a few words have so far linked the Moon, Mercury and Saturn to the process whereby the Solar self emerges out of the cradle of its emotional beginnings, and already our astrology begins to feel the strain. For we have to recognize that, almost certainly, *all the planets are interacting with all the other planets all the time*. We are not witnessing a process which works only in those people who happen to have the appropriate planets in the agreed arrangement. It happens to all of us, however our charts are laid out, whatever aspects we have, and however we get on with them.

All the evidence of depth psychology points to the fact that the various phases and stages through which we go are reasonably similar, even if they are open to a variety of interpretations. We must not confuse this similarity of process with the disparity of its ultimate expression. The aspects in our birth chart say virtually nothing about the process of psychic development, but give considerable clues as to the direction and uniqueness of its ultimate expression.

If we wish to begin to explore the *manner* in which the complexities of personality might materialize, we shall need to create both an astrological *theory* of the personality and develop techniques for exploring the astro-dynamics of these ideas in action. Two techniques which *do* offer some scope here are those of harmonics and midpoints.[1]

This is not to suggest that these two techniques provide some miraculous 'answer' to our problems: they do not. But traditional astrology has clearly failed to go very far towards developing a coherent approach to the creation of a genuine astro-psychology, and these techniques, by their very nature, allow both a far greater flexibility and a far greater precision than the conventional approaches. Through applying them, we can very often see the myriad, but quite specific ways in which planets are interacting when the orthodox procedures deny any connection whatsoever. We shall start with the 5th harmonic chart.

The 5th Harmonic and the Function of Language

It is beyond the scope of this book to give a comprehensive survey of the theory and practice of harmonics, but we can remind ourselves here of some key ideas of the 5th harmonic chart itself.

John Addey and Charles Harvey connect the 5th harmonic with the Platonic concept of Mind and the products of Mind. In other words, planets which come together in the 5th harmonic will symbolize those energies which an individual will instinctively 'know' about, and will probably be able to give conscious expression to, or have power over in the form of a specific skill. It is this latter aspect which David Hamblin particularly stresses in relating the 5th harmonic to 'the creation of order out of chaos' and 'the search for order and form'. In this respect Hamblin allies it to the idea of an individual's particular 'style' or method; the manner in which someone goes about imposing a manner of order on the external world.

This is particularly pertinent when we recall that Roman families named only the first four of their children. Those which followed after were called Quintus, Sextus, Septimus, Octavius and so on. It was the same with the Roman calendar. The first four months took the names the Gods whose festivals they included; after that the months became numerical. Thass-Thienemann[2] states that, for the Roman mind, numbering really begins with 'five'. Indeed, there seems something peculiarly human about this figure, as if something idiosyncratic is being added to the four corners of the Earth, the four limbs, the four seasons and so on; something which seeks in some way to go beyond our natural boundaries.

There is a very strong case for suggesting that the number five, and thus the 5th harmonic, refers specifically to the ordering and empowering function of *language* and the way in which it might create a specific form of *consciousness* in the individual. It is this consciousness which then becomes impressed on the world in the form of art, style or some such similar external expression.

As we have already seen, there is very considerable evidence that both our consciousness and our personal unconscious are structured on linguistic lines, and that language is the medium by which order comes out of the chaos of our primal instincts. If this is so, then seeing the 5th harmonic in this light should indicate what our linguistic processes might be, what *other* energies are involved in our Mercury functions and, more importantly, the 5th harmonic may give us clues as to *how* specific mechanisms or concerns may operate in structuring the nature of consciousness.

In considering the manner in which the mind may function, and the possible role played by aspects in the 5th harmonic series, we must recognize that in many ways the distinction between 'conscious' and 'unconscious' is somewhat arbitrary. The boundary moves constantly, and we are permeated both by our knowledge and our 'un-knowledge'. It would almost certainly be unwise to consider that the conscious mind functions radically differently from the unconscious mind, that it uses quite different rules and language. Rather, in both areas there are expressed different facets of the same language, different aspects of the same principles.

We know from our own experience that the conscious mind can recognize and take over that which was previously unconscious, and can come to accept that which was previously unacceptable. In many respects the boundary between known and unknown is more like a net than a wall; a net whose mesh gets larger or smaller depending on our moods. There are moments when we are prepared to admit into consciousness thoughts and feelings that at other times we might deny entirely. It is often possible for some partially recognized sensation to move in and out of awareness, shifting its domain moment by moment as we wrestle with the implications of admitting its existence, like some Government minister juggling with an embarrassing statistic in front of the Opposition.

It is our capacity for denial as much as anything else which makes us strangers to our inner world, and it may be useful to think of the planetary instincts as patterns of energy continually linking the domains of consciousness and unconsciousness. In this light, the instincts that the planets represent become more focused and acceptable to us as they surface, more alien or alarming as we sense the age and remoteness of their source. It is possible that the 5th harmonic offers powerful clues as to the operation of this process, and how the universality of the linguistic process becomes individualized in each separate case.

If the 5th harmonic is in part a map of our linguistic functions, if it is intimately connected to the nature of language and the part it plays in structuring the dual worlds of the conscious and the unconscious, then it is reasonable to conjecture that those people whose primary concern *is* language should have particularly powerful or significant 5th harmonic charts. This would indeed seem to be the case, and it is these charts that we shall now examine.

Jacques Lacan is undoubtedly an individual who comes within this category, as is evidenced at once from his natal chart (Figure 8.1). His close NE square ME in the 8th house portrays linguistic concerns that might include psychoanalysis and the nature of dreams. What is most striking about his chart, however, is not seen at once owing to the manner in which convention demands

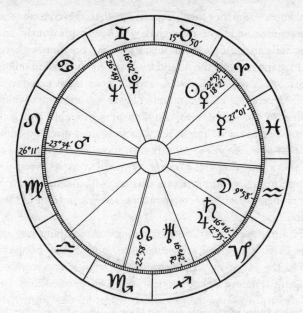

Figure 8.1 The natal chart of Jacques Lacan.

that it is laid out. If we omit some of the factors and all of the houses we see immediately just how important the almost exact Uranus opposition Pluto actually is. In Figure 8.2 we see that what is normally considered as a generational factor actually ties the Sun and the Moon to both Saturn and the MC – the whole career/ego structure in fact. Note that the Sun and the Moon are a quintile apart, and will of course form a conjunction in the 5th harmonic.

This pattern depicts someone who might identify (MC) with the role of the teacher (Saturn) and bring his 'heart and soul' (Sun and Moon) to that cause, a point resonating to the outer planets Uranus and Pluto, with all three pairs sharing the same midpoint. When Uranus and Pluto became conjunct during 1965–6 they were on the degree of that common midpoint – and this, not surprisingly, was the time that Lacan came to international prominence.

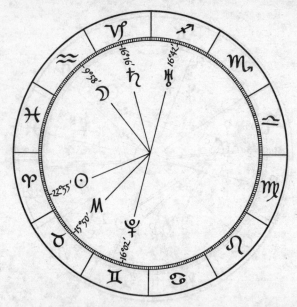

Figure 8.2 In looking at the Sun and Moon in Jacques Lacan's chart, we see how it is strongly configured with the Uranus/Pluto opposition as well as Saturn and the MC. The Uranus/Pluto conjunctions of the 1960s at 16° Virgo fell exactly on his Sun/Moon midpoint, when his revolutionary views achieved maximum public recognition.

While this gives us a nice image of how he functioned as a professional revolutionary in the world of politics and psychoanalysis, we can learn even more from looking at Lacan's 5th harmonic chart. Note, however, that Saturn is trine the MC and recall Lacan's well-known pun *Je père sévère*, which translates as both 'I am a strict father', and 'I persevere' – very apt for Saturn and the Midheaven.

In Lacan's 5th harmonic chart (Figure 8.3) we see much of the same pattern from another perspective. Here the Sun and the Moon come together square to the Uranus/Pluto opposition. The harmonic in which the Lights join is an important one. If the 5th harmonic does say something about the nature of our inner lan-

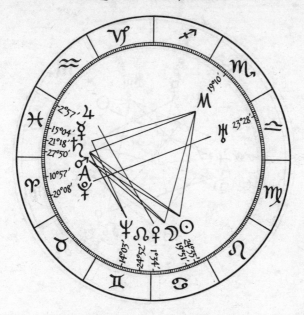

Figure 8.3 Jacques Lacan's 5th harmonic chart.

guage, then here is someone who will use it in a dramatic and revolutionary manner. The Sun and Moon also come together in the 5th harmonic charts of **Alfred Adler, Fritz Perls** and **Stanislav Grof.** Note that in Lacan's chart Mars and Saturn are also forming a conjunction. We shall see that pair again in the chart of Lacan's mentor, Sigmund Freud.

The Venus trine Jupiter that also exists in Lacan's 5th harmonic chart may refer in part to his noted capacity to attract female followers, and for giving a new psychological framework to one aspect of the growing cause of women's liberation. Lacan was, for many intellectual French feminists at that time, something of a god-hero. In the 5th harmonic we see an almost literal spelling out of a mind whose personal philosophy brought an optimistic message of freedom for women, if only those who could afford to inhabit the circles in which he held court.

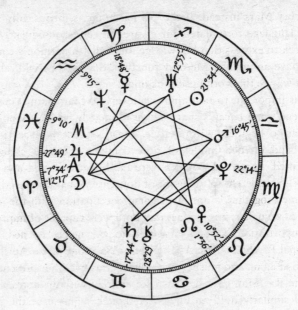

Figure 8.4 Sigmund Freud's 5th harmonic chart.

In the 5th harmonic chart of **Sigmund Freud** (Figure 8.4), Mars and Saturn are in a very close trine, with Mars square to Mercury and opposing the Moon. A Mars/Saturn contact in the 5th harmonic might suggest a language which seeks the control or mastery of sexuality. In Freud's case with Mercury and the Moon also involved, perhaps the specific issue of a sexual response to the maternal image may also be present; the 'control' aspect being amplified by Saturn's square to both Jupiter and Pluto. Though, as Hamblin points out, Moon/Mars contacts in the 5th harmonic can also associate with *humour*. Freud's preoccupation with the underlying meaning of jokes and his capacity for relating them is well attested to.

I can confirm Hamblin's observation of the frequent humorous expression of Moon/Mars contacts, although many may find this one hard to grasp at first, expecting perhaps a Moon/Mercury or

Mercury/Mars instead. If the 5th harmonic is intrinsically about how language formulates our awareness, and consequently how we seek to express that knowledge, then all 5th harmonic contacts will have an implicit Mercury function; that is, they will relate in some way to the workings of the mind.

It is important to note that whatever the Mars/Saturn contacts in Freud's and Lacan's charts might ultimately mean, it would not appear to be their writing *style*. Freud's prose is exceptionally clear and often a model of how complex thoughts should be presented. Lacan's discourses were rambling, confused and – for many – incoherent to the point of nonsense. What *does* bind these two men together is not just their preoccupation with the 'structure' of sexuality, it is the fact that both were capable of impressive extemporization. Freud's first talk to the newly formed International Psychoanalytic Association in Salzburg on 26 April 1908 began at 8a.m. and finished at 1. During this five-hour presentation on the Rat Man case Freud spoke entirely without notes. Lacan could similarly hold an audience, though in his case the actual presentation was more of a free-association than a formal lecture.

What connects both men here is not just the 'enduring' quality of Mars and Saturn, but the need to *justify* and prove, the need to cover every point; Freud through careful annotation and reference, Lacan by expounding complex, seemingly all-embracing linguistic theories. The 5th harmonic gives a specific edge to a Mars/Saturn contact, providing us with images of 'dedicated mental work', a 'great need to understand' or a 'desire to overcome inner doubts by hard work' which could easily apply to both men. It might also suggest that there may have been something like a need to justify everything – particularly one's inner urges or libido – to an internalized father-image by talking him down, hiding him behind words or trying to bury him deep within the constructs of the mind. It may be significant that both Freud's father and mother had Mars/Saturn contacts in their own 5th harmonic charts, Jakob a conjunction and Amalie a close square, and that Freud's wife, Martha Bernays, echoed Freud himself in having an almost exact 5th harmonic trine.

Another image which comes to us is that of a mind which has to wrestle with the certainty of its own extinction, that may see death as part of the creative process of life, as much a human instinct as the sexual urge. The Freudian 'morbido' is, on a number of counts, an unusual drive to postulate and must in part refer to very specific inner concerns. Saturn in its role as 'the professional' speaks of someone who seeks to be professionally concerned with sexuality, of a mind that needs to control and order basic human appetites. **Havelock Ellis**, in many respects the father of modern sexology, has a Mars/Saturn square in the 5th harmonic, the analyst **Wilfred Bion** had them in trine, as did **Anton Mesmer**, and **Ira Progoff** (see below) has a Mars/Saturn square in the 5th.

Whatever views we may have on specific Freudian theories, there can be no doubt that much of what we colloquially call the Self emerges from very primitive beginnings, where issues of pleasure and non-pleasure predominate in a world full of violent and urgent physical demands. It may be that a component of that something we call Mind grows out of a need to comprehend and master this raw landscape, that we come to use language as a tool to make our senses coherent, and to comprehend our surroundings. This would be our first creative, and thus, to the Freudian, sexual act.

In bringing together linguistically the conflicting urges or demands, so that we may make sense of them, we are starting a primary creative process that echoes human sexuality. As we shall see in the Wolf Man analysis on page 246, sexuality has been connected with the number five since the time of Pythagoras. By ordering, structuring and 'making' our world comprehensible in this way, we are drawing on some very primitive drives.

The 5th Harmonic Series

If the quintile series says something about how our mind is structured, and by implication how our – uniquely human – capacity for language plays a part in this, then those concerned with the nature of language should have strong quintile charts. This would seem to be the case.

In the twenty-five charts of linguists and translators that Paul Wright[3] has collated, aspects in the 5th harmonic series predominate: that is, the 5th, 10th, 15th and 25th harmonics.

Using the major aspects of conjunction, square and trine with 8° orbs, 52 per cent of the sample had Sun/Moon contacts in the 15th harmonic, 52 per cent had Sun/Mercury in the 5th harmonic, and 52 per cent had Sun/Jupiter in the 25th harmonic. Particularly significant is the fact of the Sun/Moon contacts. The harmonic series in which these two primary bodies come together is clearly of fundamental importance. While this is obviously a small sample, it gives us another pointer to the possible connection between the quintile series and the nature of language.

Returning to our previous sample of analysts, and exploring the 10th harmonic, we find **Jung** with a Mars/Saturn square of 91°, **Otto Rank** with another square, and both **Breuer** and **Adler** with a trine. Adler, who brought forward the notion of 'organ inferiority', seems here to have expressed his mental concerns most aptly, picking up on the demanding and judging facet of Saturn when confronted with the raw enthusiasm of youth.

If, for a moment, we take the view that the 5th harmonic is *purely* about the way in which language structures consciousness, and all of its other attributes proceed solely from this primary act of 'self-creation', then we shall need to examine the relationship between language and sexuality.

The 5th Harmonic and Procreation

Sexuality is indisputably the manner in which we create other human beings, and seen with this in mind the various Mars/Saturn aspects in the charts of psychoanalysts become a little clearer. It is a pattern which concretizes the sexual act and makes it part of our internal language, part of the real world. This language can be seen as having a phallic (pro)creative nature which echoes the potency which we ascribe to a God.

The Latin word *semen* refers to the seed of a plant as well as to human seminal fluid. Biblically, 'word' and 'seed' are interchangeable, as in St Luke's 'The seed is the word of God.' This interchangeability is echoed in the Orphic concept of *logos spermatikos*, the 'word-seed', the beginning of all things. In turn this reflects both in the opening sentence of Genesis – 'In the beginning was the Word' – and in St John's 'In the beginning was *logos*, and the *logos* was with God.' Thass-Thienemann reminds us that the second sentence of Genesis records how 'God moved upon the face of the waters'. The Hebrew word used for 'waters' in this sentence is *mayim*, which also meant *urine* or *semen*. Such a phallic/creative relationship between heaven and earth is also the linguistic root of the planet Uranus.

The Greek *ouranos* (heaven) is related by some authorities to *ouren*, urine, which connects also to the Latin *urina*. The idea that there is a heavenly God who fertilizes the earth with semen in the form of rain is fantasy constantly re-invented by children, whose own creation myths commonly demand that the father urinates into the mother to impregnate her.

In such myths 'word' and 'seed' come together; something grows from language, or is created by the act of speech. We create ourselves and our world through the process of language. What our parents and others *say* about us in early years contributes much to how we perceive ourselves to be, and our self-perceptions in turn contribute to how we actually behave. Psychologists talk about 'interior scripts', hypnotists often attempt to modify behaviour by suggesting new linguistic assumptions to be internalized. In the early part of this century there was a fad for attempting to change one's state of health and fortune by the repetition of self-serving phrases, an approach being re-adopted by some therapies today. Thus in speech, as in sexual reproduction, we mimic in a minor key the procreative power of the Gods.

The organ of speech, the tongue, is similarly charged with celestial and erotic powers. Besides being itself a metaphor for 'speech', the act of speaking in 'tongues' implies a direct contact with God. The language which is created then is utterly mysterious; no one understands it. As was implied earlier by linguistic philosophers, any language that *could* be understood was not divine, and could only be human. The language of 'tongues' is presumed to be God's alone.

God is recorded as speaking with a 'tongue of fire'. Fire, the primary phallic/creative energy, links naturally to the divine. All its visible expressions, too, are divine. The stars that twinkle and burn in the sky are the words of God being expressed in the heavens. The Old English *tungol-spraece* translates literally as 'little tongue speech', but its *meaning* is something else.

Tungol-spraece means 'astrology'. The stars were seen as the literal expression of the Gods speaking to the world in the language of fire, continuously creating the moment, burning their words into the cosmos, letting them rain down 'like fire'.

The biblical world was created by *language*; the world emerged from the *word*. The *naming* of a thing brings it into being, just as the initial Egyptian deity first created himself by calling out his own name. Until something is given a name it remains unknown; it cannot be given a place or a purpose. As we name, so we create, and in our creation we echo the power of the Gods.

As the Gods named and created us, so we name and create our own children. The major religions of the world are imbued with sexuality, most of them having incorporated the innumerable fertility rites which were the probable precursors of all organized beliefs. The phallic God, inseminating the earth with rain, is a primary icon reflected again and again in modern worship with the scattering of holy water or by anointments. The procession of priests into church or temple mimics the act of intercourse, where the secret miracle of conception takes place in its dark interior. The fact that sexuality is *constantly* called into being when a creative God is addressed is reflected in the enormous problems religions have in accepting the overt expression of sexuality itself.

Except for very few cults, such as some obscure Gnostic Christians, who echoed Indian Tantric sexual practices as a form of a sacrament or search for enlightenment, Christianity has continued to react to the individual expression of sexual passion as some form of challenge to its image of the unique Creator, as if it were some form of quasi-blasphemy.

Sexuality is to be denied totally by monks and nuns – as it is in those who are called to many other, non-Christian religions. The irony is, of course, that the very act of religion calls upon its ancient antecedents in all of us. In fact, this relationship between phallic creative power and the nature of God is very precise, and even stated quite clearly in the Bible.

In Genesis 24, verses 2–9, we read that 'Abraham said unto his servant, "Put, I pray thee, thy hand under my thigh: And I will make thee swear by the Lord" . . . And the servant put his hand under the thigh of Abraham his master, and swore to him concerning that matter.' Knowing that the Bible tends to be a little coy on matters of thighs and loins, we are right to be curious as to what is actually being described here.

The Bible is in fact telling us of the common practice in those times of a man swearing an oath to another by placing his hand on that man's penis, the organ seen as being synonymous with a God, as it shares some of a God's visible creative powers. It may come as something of a surprise to know that we still carry out this act today, whenever we wish to behave like a God and exercise our own *will*.

If we swear or make out a will we shall need two witnesses, or, to use their Latin name, *testis*, from which, of course, come both testicles and testament. In a literal sense, the testicles 'witnessed' the act of oath-taking and were thus party to it. The image of the phallic as being a creative energy is possibly one of psycho-analysis's most misunderstood concepts, especially by some feminist critics. In fact, many modern psychoanalysts use the concept of the phallus in what can only be described (except by them!) as a Jungian archetypal image. This is particularly true of those followers of Jacques Lacan. Astrologers unfamiliar with Lacan's concept of the phallus can perhaps think of it as an energy or drive which empowers us – another 5th harmonic signature – with a combination of the creative/assertive qualities of the three Fire signs. As with all principles or transpersonal energies, it has the potential to be signified by both sexes.

It has been suggested so far that language contains its own

history within itself. If this is so then the linguistic nature of the 5th harmonic may show the manner in which the 'self-creative' or phallic life-energy is wedded to linguistic processes. We can see, therefore, that there can be a strong case for suggesting that those whose lives are concerned with sexuality have such prominent Mars/Saturn contacts in this wave-form.

The Mars/Saturn midpoint is, of course, also known by the Ebertin school as the 'death axis', for the frequency with which the conflict between these principles is implicated in cases of illness, accident and death. In the case of Freud's family, no fewer than ten members had Mars/Saturn contacts in the 5th harmonic; we must not forget that his family was virtually wiped out in the camps of Auschwitz, Treblinka and Theresienstadt. If there was one thing it knew about, it was death.

The 5th Harmonic in Action

It would seem, in the charts that we have explored so far, that the inhibiting aspect of Saturn has given way to that planet's ability to make sexuality concrete. In the case of Freud and his fellow analysts, it is a map of the mind, something that justifies and explains, something that seeks to give substance to the threat of chaos. We see a similar theme in the 5th harmonic chart of **Marcel Proust**.

In Proust's 5th harmonic chart (Figure 8.5) we find a very close opposition of Saturn and Neptune, a wide Venus/Uranus opposition, Mars square to Jupiter, and Mercury bringing together the Sun and the Moon. This last aspect speaks of a mind that might need language to bind male and female together, set against a backdrop of the Saturn/Neptune preoccupation of a search for the sublime. Looking at this aspect, it is worth recalling that the title of his life's work is not *A Remembrance of Things Past* – that is the English publisher's title. Proust's original title translates more accurately as *In Search of Lost Time* . . .

Like Freud and the other analysts, Proust was obsessively concerned with the 'real' nature of his past and the source of his

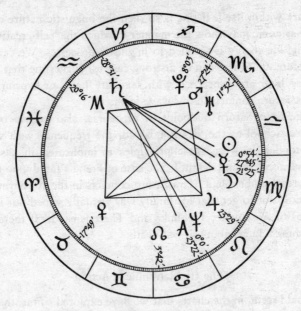

Figure 8.5 Marcel Proust's 5th harmonic chart.

motives. In his 15th harmonic chart (Figure 8.6), which John Addey would associate with all that gives intellectual enjoyment, we find once again a Mars/Saturn contact. Here Saturn closely conjoins Mercury and opposes Mars, which widely conjuncts Neptune.

Such a Mercury/Mars/Saturn/Neptune combination is an eloquent image of a mind that works by dipping into itself, trying to catch hold of the ineffable while living in the cloistered world of dreams. Its language lies stretched across the polarity of duty and abandonment, caught between the demands of the world and the needs of the spirit. It is a pattern which also expressed itself through his chronic ill-health – a classic Mars/Saturn/Neptune manifestation – and his need to isolate himself from the world. He lived for many years in the realm of night, sleeping during the day and waking only during the hours of darkness. His room was

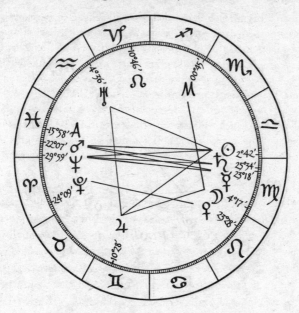

Figure 8.6 Marcel Proust's 15th harmonic chart.

cork-lined and insulated against sound and smell. It was a literal womb-symbol, which will be explored more fully in a moment, with a remarkable manifestation of an identical Mercury/Mars/Saturn/Neptune Complex Symbol.

An analyst taking quite a different approach to those discussed earlier is **Rollo May**. Rollo May is an existentialist, and his approach to clients is primarily philosophical. Existential analysts endeavour to explore issues of freedom, personal meaning and authenticity, and focus primarily on the client's sense of 'self in the world'. They may well use specific therapeutic techniques, or subscribe to some of the ideas of the more deterministic practitioners such as Freud and Jung, but ultimately their vision of the human being goes beyond a psychodynamic description, towards a philosophical reality.

A fundamental issue for all existentialists is that of *freedom*.

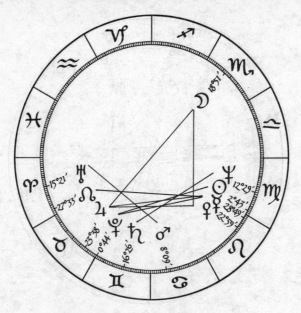

Figure 8.7 Rollo May's 5th harmonic chart.

Thus it comes as no surprise to see a powerful Moon/Jupiter opposition lying across Rollo May's 5th harmonic chart (Figure 8.7). Here is someone who *knows* about freedom, whose inner language strives to liberate his personal feelings through philosophical knowledge. He also has a very powerful Sun/Mercury/Venus conjunction, all square to Pluto. Rollo May's main concern in therapy is that his clients find a sense of their personal *power*. Again, here is a man who *knows* about power, and who speaks of power. One of his most popular books is called *Power and Innocence* and concerns itself with the experience of power and powerlessness. In this book Rollo May explores ways in which a sense of individuals' identity and meaning (Sun square Pluto) can emerge when individuals have the courage to liberate their own power and activate their true potential. He also writes of the violence (Mars square to Uranus) that often erupts when someone is made

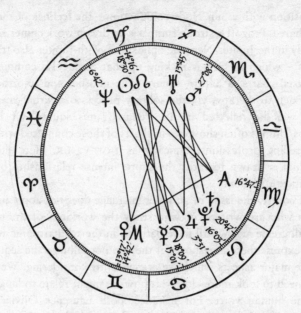

Figure 8.8 Ira Progoff's 5th harmonic chart.

powerless and impotent by their upbringing, or by the economic and racial divisions of modern society.

There is another very important pattern in this chart, one which often associates with sickness, or issues which emerge out of an experience of helplessness, and that is the Saturn/Neptune square. This particular aspect will be returned to in some detail during the course of this chapter, but in Rollo May's case it has a very specific meaning: he came close to dying from tuberculosis. It was in fact the manner in which he experienced this disease, and how he recognized the 'victim role' that conventional medicine encouraged him to play, which initiated his quest for self-affirmation.

In Figure 8.8 we see the 5th harmonic chart of **Ira Progoff**, who developed the idea of a therapeutic journal. Here, his close Moon/Mercury conjunction – writing about feelings – falls in a powerful opposition with a Sun/Node conjunction – the feelings of the self are shared. Progoff's strong emphasis on dream work comes across clearly in the Jupiter/Neptune opposition, with Jupiter also trining Mars – which in turn is picking up that contact so common in analysts' charts, a Saturn square. The unusual and unorthodox approach to therapy, via the solitary process of journal-keeping, may well be reflected in his Venus/Uranus square. Of itself, Venus/Uranus often shows up in charts of those connected with the counselling professions, typically as NO = VE/UR. Here the individual is drawn towards the short, intense relationship of the therapeutic session.

Of course, the issue of an inner language does not apply just to those who are writers, or who study the workings of the mind. We all create and we all have patterns in the 5th harmonic which may express these urges, even if they do not fall into the sequence of the major aspects which we are currently considering. We may also need to look more closely at how we might relate to language or the human voice. For instance, both **Laurence Olivier** and **Marlon Brando** are actors whose technique includes the need to find the essence of the character they are playing in a particular *voice*. Brando's much-publicized use of cotton-wool placed in his cheeks when playing the title role in *The Godfather* was not done to alter his appearance, but to produce the voice desired, and thus the character. Olivier has a close Sun/Moon opposition in his 5th harmonic chart with Mercury squaring the Ascendant, Brando has a Moon/Mercury trine. It may be that in both cases this chart is locating the centrality of language in their creative approach.

David Hamblin has commented on the apparent frequency of 5th harmonic contacts between Jupiter and the Sun in the charts of actors. Experience seems to bear this out – along with a prevalence of Moon/Jupiter aspects as well – and this is particularly important in the light of what has been discussed earlier. If the 5th harmonic contains within itself some echo of primal, godlike language, then the fact that Jupiter contact within the 5th harmonic charts of actors is a denominator of their *profession* is profoundly important. In both the East and the West, acting grew

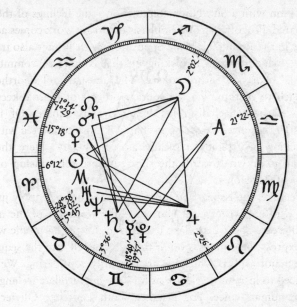

Figure 8.9 Autistic child: 5th harmonic chart.

out of the religious rites of the *priesthood*. Actors were initially 'acting out' truths on behalf of the Gods, often speaking for them in trance, like oracles, conveying their message to the populace. It would seem there is some echo of their original calling in the charts of those who take on the role of speaking for today.

If we choose charts of those who *cannot* communicate, this too can reflect in the 5th harmonic. In Lois Rodden's *Astrodata 2* are the charts of two autistic children (Figures 8.9 and 8.10). In the first case Saturn opposes the Moon, closely squared by Mars/ Node (a deep inhibition of the life-force expressed linguistically?) and Mercury is conjunct Pluto. These are powerful significators of silence. In the second example Mars and Saturn are again impli- cated. This time Saturn squares the Moon/Mercury conjunction and Mars very closely sextiles Saturn while opposing the MC. Not having a case history, it is not really possible to conjecture what

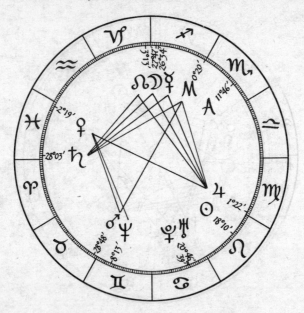

Figure 8.10 Autistic child: 5th harmonic chart.

part the Venus/Jupiter opposition in the second example might play. Interestingly, it picks out the identical degree of the Virgo/ Pisces axis that Mars/Node occupies in the first chart. This might well be a coincidence, and only more examples would indicate if this were so.

Quite another example of a deeply puzzling language- and communication-related condition is Tourette's Syndrome. Tourette's Syndrome expresses itself in the sufferer involuntarily swearing, grimacing, spitting or indulging in other similarly anti-social activities. In all other respects the victim may be quite normal, and this only reinforces the erroneous idea that he or she is acting in such a manner quite deliberately. Those afflicted exhibit abnormal brain-wave patterns and are usually left-handed. The onset of symptoms is when the 'left brain/right brain' dominance within the individual is being established. The fact that this typically

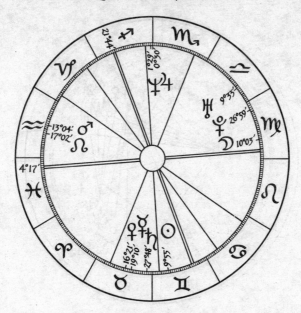

Figure 8.10a John Davidson's natal chart.

takes place at the age of five may or may not be significant in the light of the number under discussion.

Figure 8.10a is the natal chart of a Tourette's victim, **John Davidson**, who was the subject of a BBC television documentary during 1989, and whose symptoms included both swearing and spitting. Such 'angry language' may be hinted at by the chart's Mercury/Mars square, but overall it is not a map which points unambiguously to one of the central issues of John's life. It is most unlikely that any astrologer, knowing nothing of John's case, would think of according such overwhelming significance to that square. That 'square', however, is an almost exact 5th harmonic aspect and underlines much more precisely what the Mercury/Mars message is really saying.

In John's 5th harmonic (Figure 8.10b), we see that the Mercury/ Mars is in fact an almost exact trine. What's more, it's a trine

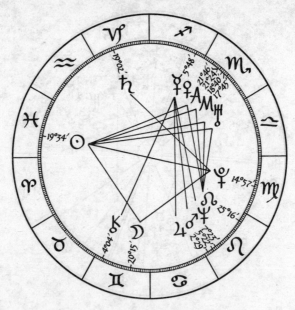

Figure 8.10b John Davidson's 5th harmonic chart.

which also includes Jupiter and Neptune, and picks up Chiron in an extremely close opposition. The Sun/Moon contact joins up with Pluto, which itself acts as a focal point for Venus, Saturn, Uranus, the Ascendant and the Midheaven. This is an impressively powerful chart, and here one would be hard-pressed *not* to see the importance of linguistic processes at work at this level.

John Addey considered that sub-harmonics of the 5th may also tell us something about health issues, and he extended this idea with examples which also included those in the 125th harmonic. Even if we do not go so far up the scale, there are obviously some sound reasons for assuming that issues in some way to do with the way an individual's mind works may also have correlations with the body. **Clare Francis**, the lone yachtswoman who also contracted the viral infection ME, has an exceptionally close Saturn/Neptune square in her 15th harmonic, with Mercury

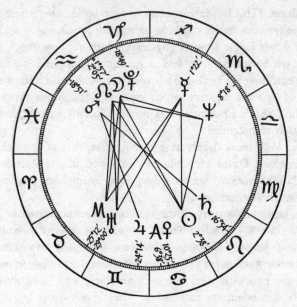

Figure 8.11 Helen Keller's 5th harmonic chart.

opposing Saturn and Uranus within 2′ of trining Neptune. Saturn/Uranus/Neptune contacts have been seen to correlate with cases of paralysis in midpoint work; here we may see the principle operating in another dimension, as well as also representing a woman who 'knows about' being alone at sea and lives out the language of that isolation.

The case of **Helen Keller** is also particularly appropriate here. At the age of nineteen months Helen Keller lost her sight and hearing. Yet, with the aid of a devoted teacher, she overcame her enormous difficulties and ultimately emerged as a noted lecturer and campaigner, with an impressive academic record. In her 5th harmonic chart (Figure 8.11), the radical Uranus/MC conjunction opposes Mercury, the Sun and Moon are in opposition, square to Neptune, and Mars closely opposes Saturn. Of particular importance is the Sun/Moon/Neptune T-square and the Mercury/Uranus opposition. (This last factor seems to crop up in cases where there is some fracture in the speaking or reading processes, as with the racing driver **Jackie Stewart**'s dyslexia – Mercury opposing Uranus in his 5th harmonic – or with a particularly original method of communicating.) The T-square with Neptune must indicate the sense of loss and mystery which surrounds the whole process of language, that its potential was initially lost to an infection, yet ultimately transcended.

If we look more deeply at a specific case, that of the **Gibbons twins**, which David Hamblin has explored in the Astrological Association *Journal*,[4] we see a very clear example of language at work in the 5th harmonic.

The remarkable story of the Gibbons twins is related in Marjorie Wallace's *The Silent Twins*.[5] It is a true story of two sisters, June and Jennifer Gibbons, who were ultimately committed to Broadmoor Asylum for various acts of arson. Until their imprisonment, the two girls were utterly inseparable and intensely emotionally dependent on each other. They spent virtually all their time locked in their bedroom, where they invented elaborate stories, wrote comics, collaborated on a novel and developed an idiosyncratic language of their own, which was coupled with bizarre signs and gestures. Their writings are a mixture of pulp romantic fiction and genuinely original and occasionally chillingly accurate observations on life. The chart which most succinctly depicts this activity, their 5th harmonic, was described by Hamblin as being one of the strongest and most integrated he had ever encountered. In Figure 8.12, which is Jennifer's 5th harmonic, we see exactly what he means.

Jennifer was the dominant twin, occasionally brutally so, but from childhood their relationship went through periods of great ambivalence, often punctuated with physical and emotional violence. In this respect the 5th harmonic association with 'power' is particularly apt; the twins seem to have been locked in a power battle from birth – perhaps even before. In their late teens they went through periods of writing *obsessively* – another 5th harmonic attribute amplified by the Sun/Pluto square – about every

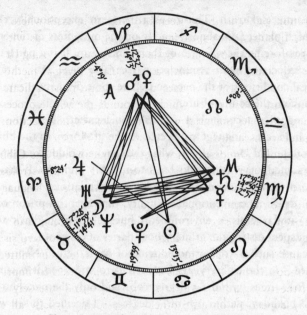

Figure 8.12 Jennifer Gibbons's 5th harmonic chart.

aspect of themselves and their relationship. Together and individually they analysed and explored every possible perspective of their tangled coalition, each struggling to find the other's weakest spot, yet ultimately each returning to the other for comfort and understanding.

In Figure 8.12 the close natal Moon/Neptune becomes part of a dramatic grand trine with Mercury, Venus, Mars, Saturn, Uranus and the MC; a trine that also locks in to the Sun, the Ascendant, the Node and Pluto. Only Jupiter is isolated (growth and wisdom locked out?), but is actually in a close 25th harmonic conjunction with Pluto.

If we examine the closest aspect first, the Mars/Saturn/Neptune trine, we see someone whose mind could delight both in disciplined mental activity, requiring much work and dedication, and also revel in the abandonment of personal will in favour of a collective, more universal truth. The grand trine is so exceptionally close that each planet falls almost exactly on the midpoints of the other two, reinforcing the strength of their symbolism. It is a pattern so often associated with renunciation (see also page 230), strange medical conditions or the need to pursue some permanent mystery throughout the course of life.

In many respects such a 5th harmonic pattern hints at some deep and secret language connected to the life force, to the libido. What the mind *knows* about, what the tongue would like to speak of, is something which harks back to mystery and loss. It may be overlaid with more common astrological correlations, such as the use of drugs, unconventional sexuality, time spent in prison or in some similar cloister environment, but its roots go back to a season spent testing the primary boundaries of existence.

Because such a 5th harmonic trine of Mars/Saturn/Neptune is so rare – in the eighty years between 1910 and 1990 it occurred only four times within 1.5 degree orbs and only the once, on the twins' birthday, within orb of .5 degrees – I decided to see what actually *happened* on such days.

On 25 August 1943 – the first example – the *Daily Express* reported that 18,000 German civilians had been *drowned* when RAF bombs had breached a 500-yard-long tunnel under the river Elbe, totally flooding it, together with its approach roads. This must surely rank as the largest single loss by drowning ever caused by an act of war, and is horrifically appropriate for a Mars/Saturn/Neptune contact. Mars/Saturn, the 'death axis', the factor coincidentally so prominent in the 5th harmonic charts of the top Nazis,[6] is momentarily touched by Neptune. Mars/Saturn, the traditional significators of tunnels and mining, is dissolved and flooded, breached by a higher power, and joins with Saturn/Neptune, the significators of 'shared suffering' and common bereavement. But what can all of this mean for the birth of the Gibbons twins?

Only a few hours before the twins were born, which was the next occurrence of a Mars/Saturn/Neptune grand trine in the 5th harmonic, the American submarine USS *Thresher* sank mysteriously in the Atlantic, with the loss of all hands. It was, and remains, the world's worst submarine disaster. Thus the girls were born when once more an exact 5th harmonic trine of Mars, Saturn and Neptune took its victims to the deep, betrayed by the failure of their trusted boundaries. What might this mean?

The peculiarly close, almost symbiotic relationship between the two girls probably started before birth. Specific behaviour patterns *can* be developed by the foetus prior to birth which continue on in life. For example, Dr Alessandra Piontelli has reported[7] on how a foetus licking its own umbilical cord, a prolonged activity witnessed with the aid of an ultrasound scanner, was the precursor of a subsequent feeding disorder which appeared to develop after birth. Such observations reinforce the need for astrologers to reconsider the relative importance of the actual birth moment, just as psychoanalysts will have to re-evaluate concepts of primary feeding symbolism in the light of such inter-uterine observations.

What often characterizes such strong Saturn/Neptune issues is the sense that personal energy is draining away; there is often a feeling of paralysis, a *failure* to establish an important boundary within the psyche, exposing mind and body to the ebb and flow of external events. The individual can often express a feeling of *powerlessness* to cope with even simple things, and by an unwillingness to act sets up a 'victim' situation where, by default, everything that life hands out is meekly accepted.

If we meet Saturn and Neptune for the first time in the inter-uterine state, if they mirror in some way an awareness of our boundaries and mortality in the midst of a previously untroubled ocean, then this primary experience might leave its mark in the form of an inability to act, a reluctance to explore. In such a situation we might have become aware of a finite boundary too early, and sense too soon Saturn's cold finality.

It is possible that the early recognition of ourself as being utterly weak, or having only the barest identity for our protection, which surrounds us like the transparent membrane of an uncalcified egg, continues to resonate with all later images of being helpless in the face of life. Thus we recognize too well the victim in the machine, the soul lost to life. We may become acutely aware of the frailty of the body, become drawn to seek that experience again and again within the hospice and the clinic, where the reality of Saturn and the world beyond is always hovering close by. This – and other facets of the Saturn/Neptune combination – are explored in more depth on pages 207–23.

If we were also to have Mars configured with the elements of such a Saturn/Neptune situation, we might also be very *angry* at what we perceive in such circumstances; an anger that may be hard to direct at its true target.

It seems almost inevitable that we return again and again to those situations which confuse or confound us, which are inextricably bound in to the tangled misunderstanding of our feelings. What we *know* about, if we have such a quintile trine of Mars, Saturn and Neptune, is precisely that which laid the web of our interior language; an anger locked into helplessness, a drowned rage against the limits of reality.

It is possible that the twins returned again and again to that angry womb and to some early, obsessive battle. The Moon, Mercury and Venus are all similarly implicated in the trine. Mercury's close conjunction with Saturn suggests a structured, formal language. They taught themselves writing with great care, analysing the structure of novels, buying dictionary and thesaurus, joining a writing college. They communicated with their parents by notes and messages. They manipulated and controlled their siblings and relatives with ritualized behaviour. There was not a childhood of give and take, there were no playground exchanges, no sharing. Their relationships with others were all formal, obsessive and ritualized. Only in the interior of their life together did some semblance of normal human intimacy begin to flower.

The sexuality embedded in the quintile, which is explored more fully on page 250, shows itself in this example with dramatic clarity. Jennifer lost her virginity in a *church*. The punning, Lacanian quality of the 5th harmonic ensured that she was, literally, laid upon the altar while her sister watched. Here the language of Mars, Saturn and Neptune becomes fact as it reconnects its symbolic energy with the world, a symbol first emerging as a word, then emerging from the word as an event.

Furious at being the one *not* chosen in the church, June tried to kill Jennifer two days later; she attempted to *drown* her in a river. It was an act that ended with the two girls wrestling with each other under water, coming to their senses just in time; an unmistakable echo of a much earlier encounter.

In prison June was to write of herself:

> ... I do not lead my life at all. It is pulled along by an invisible string. By whom? By what? A circumstance of the past. A force. I am just an onlooker. Yet I suffer as an onlooker would not. For if I came up to two people quarrelling bitterly, I would be suddenly glad of my own being; yet as an onlooker, I would still pick out one of the quarrellers and have deep pity in my heart. For one would lose. Looking at oneself, a character in a story. Born to lose. A character who deserves all sympathy; yet what sympathy there is in the reader is all doled out on to the characters. Who will ever guess she suffered? Perhaps her eyes, dark and brooding. Perhaps a discontented look upon her brow. Perhaps a twist of sadness lingering on her face. Only a sensitive person would know. This person would be intrigued. Compare the sadness of himself to hers; be puzzled. Finally he would delve into her past. She will hesitate to pronounce her past; feel afraid yet terribly anxious to reveal her pain. She will be somewhat like a martyr, special. She will feel chosen. Ah! she will sigh. Sympathy at last. There is understanding in this world after all. So I and she will weep uncontrollably: only for herself. Like as though we were watching a sad film in the movies. And she will weep for the character, only because she recognizes this character to be herself. She will cry partly out of relief to know that somebody in the world understands her; like the man she met at the party, like the time she laughed and out-laughed her friends. Why was she laughing? Partly out of anxiety, out of grief. No, she was not really laughing. She was laughing like a disturbed child who goes to a Punch and Judy and laughs; only for that split second does the child laugh, forgetting all his troubles. All this intense hate.

Again and again the prose circles the Mars/Saturn/Neptune trine; a language of loss, limitation, anger and abandonment. Except for brief moments, it is as if the anger and libido that is within her is sunk and lost like the submarine which vanished only hours before her birth. All the other planets anchored to this triangle only reinforce the permanence of its symbolism within her, and her life returns to its tale again and again. Even the Punch and Judy show reiterates it. Under the guise of Mercurial tricks and funny voices, Punch and Judy are wedded in violence to each other, unable to exist apart.

On the same day as the USS *Thresher* was lost in the Atlantic, an enormous security scandal broke in England when CND demonstrators started to hand out a highly classified list of the Regional Seats of Government: the exact locations of all the secret Government fall-out shelters throughout the whole of England. Carried out by self-styled 'spies for peace', this was probably one of the most elegant acts of subversion ever, redolent of the challenge to established power that such a 5th harmonic combination embodies.

During this period of exactitude, there were also scurrilous stories beginning to emerge in the press about a certain high-ranking Tory's connection with the *demi-monde*, but it was two months before the full story of Christine Keeler began to emerge.

The next occurrence of such a Mars/Saturn/Neptune trine in the 5th harmonic, during 26–28 June 1965, produced no dramatic headlines, though it certainly did not pass without expression. The London *Evening Standard* reported that on 27 June a man had been found drowned in a bath in less than *one inch of water*. Foul play had been ruled out, but the police admitted to being completely baffled. On the same day the Labour Party picked Jack Ashley as their candidate in a forthcoming by-election. Jack Ashley was later to fall victim to a mysterious virus which destroyed his hearing overnight, and subsequently dedicated his efforts to representing the plight of those disadvantaged by disease or illness. These are all classic expressions of such a planetary combination and remind us again – particularly in Ashley's case – that the birth chart does not contain the full or final code of our life; it is added to and amended by the events we incorporate.

While there seems to be more than just an echo of death, drowning and loss in such a grand trine, the air of mystery and confusion is expressed just as much in the lives of the Silent Twins. The repetition of such *themes* in such diverse circumstances, with such precision, is indeed remarkable. It would suggest that a close analysis of how each day reflects the hidden language of astrology may ultimately offer a coherent understanding of what might be taking place.

The final occurrence of a 5th harmonic Mars/Saturn/Neptune grand trine took place on 14 December 1966. It would seem that the theme of drowning, which began so violently in 1943, and diminished in the two following occurrences, has faded out completely, to be replaced by more familiar images. Just a day before the grand trine's exactitude, Iraq had to shut down the whole of her northern oil field's production to avoid what the *Daily Telegraph* reported was a 'flood of oil' which posed an enormous fire hazard. On the same day Harry Roberts was jailed for thirty years for killing three policemen, and a British company made a dramatic oil find in the North Sea. With oil and prisons we are on more familiar Saturn/Neptune territory, but not completely free from a slight echo of 1943. In New York, two men and a woman were arrested exactly on the 14th for a much publicized fraud. It was alleged that the woman had conspired with the two men to fake her own death for an insurance fraud. The method? Drowning.

It has to be recognized that one manifestation of the 5th harmonic chart does seem to be connected with the expression of *power*, perhaps for the reasons given earlier. **Adolf Hitler** had a particularly strong 5th harmonic chart[8] which included a massive Moon, Jupiter, Saturn, Neptune and Ascendant conjunction closely opposing Mercury – apt for a man whose 'voice' was found in prison, writing *Mein Kampf*, and who had the ability of a born performer to seduce and captivate the crowd. (See also page 275.)

One of Hitler's main themes was the unification of Germany. The Jupiter/Saturn cycle is very much connected with the building up and breaking down of 'generational' issues, its synodic period being twenty years, and this also applies to its literal expression in the form of buildings and boundaries. In fact, Germany was unified under Hitler for a twelve-year period, the first time in its history that this had happened. Interestingly, Jupiter/Saturn/Neptune were again closely configured at the end of 1989 when the Berlin Wall fell apart in the wake of change and the two countries were unified emotionally, if not legally.

The 5th harmonic connection with power is also very evident in the charts for murderers **Ian Brady** and **Myra Hindley**, who were responsible for the sadistic sex-killings of several young children. Besides being particularly powerful charts, there is also a striking 5th harmonic synastry between them which points clearly to the compulsive nature of their relationship.

In Brady's 5th harmonic chart (Figure 8.13) the Pluto/Ascendant conjunction is closely square to a Sun/Node opposition, while the Moon is in a similar T-square to Mars/Jupiter, and Uranus is square to both Mercury and Venus. It is a language of power and action; the action stemming from deep emotional roots and seeking physical expression in the world. It has often been noted that Moon/Jupiter contacts appear in the charts of murderers more often than might be expected. This pattern does not reflect a desire to kill, but more probably indicates that such individuals are prone to believing in their own 'divine right' to do whatever they feel like. It is an emotional and 'philosophical' arrogance that becomes dangerous only when coupled to other factors, perhaps amplified here by Jupiter's own trine to Uranus, which stresses individualistic expression.

Furthermore, in Brady's case the exceptionally close Saturn/Pluto trine ties into his T-square, and this seems to have resonated to the sadistic activities of the Nazis, for which he had a deep fascination. A trine in the 5th harmonic often indicates that which gives us great mental pleasure. It is certainly worth noting also that the square from Uranus picks up two clear significators for the sexual killing of young children, Mercury and Venus – a factor amplified by the Mars/Neptune trine. The 'language' of this facet of Brady's 5th harmonic is deceptive, erratic and drawn to the sexually unusual. It is a language constructed in fantasy and idiosyncrasy, probably emerging out of very early physical needs

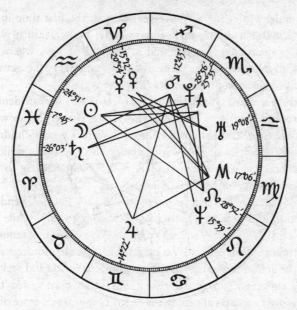

Figure 8.13 Ian Brady's 5th harmonic chart.

(Moon/Mars/Jupiter), and rooted in the emotional and physical discrepancy between the insignificant individual and its overwhelming devouring needs – Sun/Pluto/Node. Some aspects of this possibility are discussed more fully in Chapter 12.

Myra Hindley (Figure 8.14) has the identical Sun/Node opposition, with Pluto opposing her Moon, Venus and MC conjunction. Again, early issues of emotional power tug at her roots and again, like Brady, there is a close Jupiter/Uranus aspect. In Hindley's case there is an almost exact opposition, tying in to Pluto. The significators of children and their language are also there – a Mercury/Mars opposition – so is that factor explored already in the case of long-term imprisonment – a Saturn/Neptune opposition. Thus at the centre of her 5th harmonic chart is a Grand Cross of Mercury, Venus, Mars and Pluto, creating a powerful, sexually charged pattern of language. If the 5th harmonic does in some

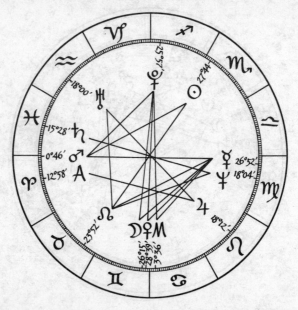

Figure 8.14 Myra Hindley's 5th harmonic chart. Note how both Brady and Hindley have Sun/Node oppositions picking up similar degrees in the fixed signs.

way describe how language develops within us, and which directions it pulls us towards, then the sexual, procreative aspects of its derivation – discussed above – may well be specifically amplified in patterns such as these.

What is really remarkable, however, is the manner in which Myra Hindley's Sun/Node axis lies almost *exactly* on the Pluto 'handle' of Brady's T-square, while her Neptune conjuncts his MC and her Moon is within minutes of squaring his Saturn. The basic dynamics of their unconscious language clearly emerge from these few patterns.

Turning to quite a different chart, we can see a most dramatic example of the quintile series's capacity to illustrate linguistic structures, as in the case of **Gottfried Leibniz**, whose 5th harmonic chart is depicted in Figure 8.15. Leibniz was close to being a

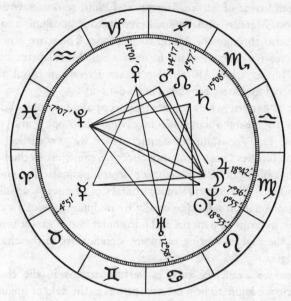

Figure 8.15 Gottfried Leibniz's 5th harmonic chart.

universal genius. He was a lawyer, physicist, counsellor, diplomat, mathematician, philosopher and librarian. The Elector of Hanover, George I, for whom Leibniz at one time worked, referred to him as a 'living encyclopedia'. Leibniz's contribution to Western philosophy has been considerable, and it is probable that he was the first person to suggest the idea of the unconscious. He also wished to create a *perfect language*.

Leibniz was particularly interested in how language 'worked' and sought to create a language which would reflect the full logical complexity of what we say, with a construction blending mathematics and philosophy. In his 5th harmonic chart, which is strikingly appropriate for such a task, we see something of the major themes of his creative life.

Leibniz's 5th harmonic chart is a remarkable example of how the creative energy of social forces is wedded to personal direction.

The grand trine of Saturn, Uranus and Pluto resonates with that of Moon, Mercury and Venus, keyed in to it via Pluto and connected also through the Moon to Neptune. There are powerful, direct creative energies in the form of a Sun/Mars square and the Venus/Jupiter trine. All the planets are actively involved and in some way integrated into the quintile dynamic.

It is a pattern which is most appropriate for someone who wished to create a language involving philosophy and mathematics. The Venus/Jupiter contact which we saw earlier in the chart of Jacques Lacan probably refers here not just to the beauty of philosophy, but also to Leibniz's great diplomatic and counselling abilities. The Saturn/Uranus contact is a frequent significator of a mathematical mind (especially by midpoint), or of an ability to think in terms of patterns and harmonics. MO = SA/UR is in fact one of the highest-scoring midpoint significators in the charts of astrologers.

When we again see such powerful patterns in the chart of someone we *know* to be a creative genius in the field of linguistics, then we must again consider the possibility that the 5th harmonic may be a primary significator of that process. Not just in the chart of Leibniz, or only in the 5th harmonic charts that we have explored so far, but perhaps for us all.

9.

A Degree of Meaning:
A Case Study of Saturn and Neptune

✩ ✩ ✩ ✩ ✩ ✩ ✩ ✩ ✩ ✩

One idea put forward so far is that all events may in some way imprint themselves upon a primal zodiac and thus we have, at some level, access to everything that has ever happened. This knowledge can also be thought of as being the unconscious memory of everything that has happened to the human race, which in turn becomes overlaid with the residues of our own, more personal unconscious.

This process of imprinting would occur at the degrees touched by planets at the time the events take place. Hence certain degrees may tend to re-occur in charts set for similar events, or transits to the same point may result in the repetition of familiar phenomena. Such ideas would lie behind observations made about degree areas, for example.

Little has been done to explore degree areas in detail – apart from the tradition of noting subsequent transits to eclipse points or noting correlations with fixed stars. This traditional approach would tend to support the idea of a primal zodiac and its attendant concept of 'planetary memory', in that it suggests a repetition of phenomena occurring when subsequent transits trigger the same point. However, there is another view of the possible creation of degree areas which should also be considered; this approach stems from the use of harmonics.

In his *Harmonic Anthology* John Addey makes some very pertinent observations on the possible nature of degree areas. His pioneering research work tends to support the idea that if there is a certain degree associated with a particular trait, then there should also be a degree which is *not* associated with that trait. Using the model of harmonics, if the peak points of the wave-form all mark positive correlations with a characteristic, then the troughs mark points where that characteristic is absent. The simplest example of this is the concept of positive and negative signs in the zodiac. If *positive* is a quality we associate only with certain signs, then it is not found in *negative* signs; these two possibilities always alternate, as in a wave-form.

Not surprisingly, if this idea is extended into looking at different wave-forms, then some anomalies begin to creep in via the actual wavelength itself, and how it may become subdivided by odd rather than even numbers. This need not concern us here; what is important to note is that basic harmonic theory tells us that positive and negative qualities resonate around the circle of the zodiac, and Addey suggests that degree meanings may manifest in the same way. As this might seem to imply that the zodiac comes with all its degree meanings already built in, so to speak – which is actually the reverse of what is being suggested here – it is necessary to examine this apparent contradiction.

It has already been proposed that the zodiac is a numeric process, that the way it 'works' is based on number – on harmonics, in fact – but that these numbers need not be external, divine ideas, but may simply be an integral part of the zodiac; in short, the way it 'is'. What is being suggested here is that an *event* – the end result of an interaction between the zodiac and the instigator of the event – becomes fixed or imprinted in the zodiac at the degrees sensitive at the moment of its manifestation. Once an event or a sensation becomes embedded in this way it must inevitably interact with the process of the zodiac itself; it cannot exist in isolation from it.

This would strongly suggest that the natural process of the zodiac would be to create harmonics or 'traces' of that memory as a resonant effect of its own being, just as the Aries point is reflected in the major quarters of the astrological year and in the twelvefold division of the signs.

This process of dividing and subdividing is an expression of the zodiac's own being; it is how the zodiac 'works' and is reflected in all the cycles of astrology. The *nature* of that which is thus divided and expanded – in other words, the 'meaning' of a particular degree – is not inherent within the zodiac itself, but once embedded within the zodiac it might then interact with the basic harmonic rhythms of the circle, appearing as a polarity, for instance, rather than as a single point.

If it were possible to deduce *when* a certain degree became associated with a specific meaning then this would suggest that whatever took place at that time *imprinted* its nature upon the zodiac, and not the other way about. Such degrees as were active for the event in question would then continue to resonate to the nature of that event. In turn, these degrees might *then* influence events or characteristics when they were themselves stimulated by transiting planets, and become integrated into the charts for such moments. Thus they would tend to reinforce the association for which they then become known. This would be another example of the 'recursive loop' described on page 65.

To explore some of the possibilities of this idea we should see how the process might operate both collectively and individually. If we start at the collective level we can focus on major conjunctions and note what occurred when the planets involved came together in the zodiac, and how this point may subsequently have become sensitive in some specific manner.

Figure 9.1 shows the degrees of the zodiac that have contained a Saturn/Neptune conjunction from 900 to 2000 AD. In the event of such a meeting being a *triple* conjunction, the *middle* degree of the three has been used. In all cases, the conjunction has been indicated on the zodiac with the date of its occurrence.

If we look at Figure 9.1 for a moment we will see that these dates are not spread around the chart randomly. Indeed, they seem to be placed with extreme and consistent precision. In virtually all cases it will be noticed that what we see is a complex series of interlocking cruciform patterns. Each conjunction point is exactly square to a conjunction that took place 288 years ahead or in front of it (two examples are indicated), and a Grand Cross spanning nearly 900 years is erected within the zodiac. Figure 9.2 depicts three such crosses involving the 1667, 1846 and 1989 series of Saturn/Neptune conjunctions.

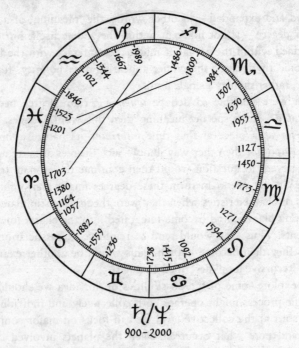

Figure 9.1 Dates of Saturn/Neptune conjunctions since 900 AD. The dates are indicated against the degrees at which the conjunctions took place. In the event of there being a *triple* conjunction, then the middle degree position has been indicated. Note that conjunctions every 288 years are *square* to one another, as indicated by three examples.

In 1989 the major theme of world events was unquestionably the re-assessment of world Communism and the collapse of the traditional East European boundaries. As has often been pointed out, the Berlin Wall crumbled within days of the final Saturn/Neptune conjunction. This theme of 'political boundaries' flows through the four 'arms' of the 1989 Grand Cross.

In 1127 the marriage of Henry I's daughter, Matilda, to Geoffrey Plantagenet of Anjou maintained the substantial British base in France, following the abortive 1123 attempt by a coalition of French barons to oust Britain from Normandy. In 1127 the French

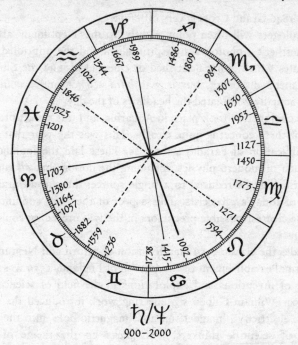

Figure 9.2 Three Grand Crosses created over long periods of time by successive Saturn/Neptune conjunctions. See the text to note how similar themes recur as events at each arm of the cross.

also recognized Matilda as Henry's heir. This theme was picked up again during the Saturn/Neptune conjunction of 1415, when the Battle of Agincourt in that year ensured the English domination of France, which then became part of Henry V's kingdom.

Two years after the 1703 conjunction, England and Scotland united under James I. This act finally bridged, in constitutional terms at any rate, the historic divide that had separated the two nations, and laid the constitutional foundations for the modern British monarchy. Thus a major theme of the Grand Cross which was completed with the Saturn/Neptune conjunction of 1989 is the 'bridging of boundaries' and the creation of a practical and enduring vision of unity.

The 1846 Grand Cross is very different.

Astrologers will often point, rightly, to the 'Neptunian' affairs of anaesthetics, photography, spiritualism and the unbridled use of opiates which either flourished or emerged around the time of the planet's discovery, but it was *hard science* and *revolution* which actually dominated the headlines of the day.

The conjunction took place in Aquarius, and this sign expresses both of these concerns quite clearly. This was the year that saw the publication of Faraday's theories. These laid the foundation for much of modern physics, including the notion that *all* energy can ultimately be reduced to a single source: the current grail of many of today's physicists. This aspect of the 1846 conjunction had the clearest possible precursors in the two preceding conjunctions.

Besides the classic 1559 manifestation of Saturn and Neptune in the formal establishment of the Church of England, 1559 was also a year of inventions and explorations in the field of science. In that year William Gilbert's pioneering work introduced the very words 'electricity', 'magnetism' and 'magnetic pole' into the language of scientific thinkers. This picks up the theme of the Saturn/Neptune conjunction Grand Cross which was laid down in 1271.

1271 saw the publication of Thomas Aquinas's *Summa Theologica*; a revolutionary work which in part attempted to heal the rift between religion and science, particularly the thought and philosophy of Aristotle. Just three years prior to the 1271 conjunction the first true magnetic compass was invented in the West. While its principles were not understood, it did allow reliable navigation for the first time.

Thus the 1846 conjunction of Saturn/Neptune seems both to be picking up the 'scientific' theme by virtue of its exact aspect to previous conjunction points (transits to past events, in fact), and adding more to the 'revolutionary thinker' theme with the publication in 1848 of Marx and Engels's *Communist Manifesto*, in the so-called 'year of revolutions' which shook the whole of Europe. While we could expect the 'revolutionary' aspect of this major event to re-surface when 26° Aquarius is transited in the future, there are several other facets to this period which will be explored shortly.

If we look at events which took place during the 1667 Grand Cross, we see yet another theme appearing. The first date coincides with Walcher of Malvern observing an eclipse of the Moon. This is the first recorded Western astronomical observation. In 1380, there is no record of any particular astronomical event, but a report on the building of the world's largest gun, a 25-inch calibre mortar, known as the Great Gun of Ghent.

In 1667 the 'telescope' theme is picked up with Newton's invention of a new type of refractor lens and the development by the Navy of a navigational quadrant with a sighting telescope attachment – a revolutionary invention. Within a year of the 1953 conjunction the world sees both themes come together with the detonation of the hydrogen bomb and the building of the world's largest optical *and* the world's largest radio telescopes.

What begins to emerge here is a picture of how the events which take place at these major conjunction points imprint on their zodiac degrees the nature of what has come into being, to be triggered by later aspects, *and* lay down a sort of 'sub-rhythm' theme which is sometimes called into being during other, less related conjunctions. 'Magnetism' is a theme which seems to re-occur when certain phases of the total Saturn/Neptune cycle are touched, stimulating previous occurrences by aspect, and one which can be traced back to an initial occurrence.

In another case the 'telescope' theme appears clearly in 1846 with the actual discovery of Neptune (and the foundation a year later of the Carl Zeiss optical works), as does the 'explosive' theme of the 1953 Grand Cross. 1846 is also the year nitroglycerine was invented. The following conjunction, in 1882, brought the invention of the brass cartridge, and the conjunction after that, in 1917, saw the invention of the explosive amatol. Though without doubt the biggest single explosion of 1917 was the Russian Revolution – started as the battleship *Aurora* opened fire on the Winter Palace.

It is hardly surprising that discoveries in chemistry are made during a Saturn/Neptune conjunction. As these planets rule research into chemistry, we could almost expect this to happen with every occurrence. Yet it is the specific area of application, in this case *explosives*, which seems to be the result of a pattern laid down as far back as 1381 by the makers of the Great Gun of Ghent. We must remember that this was a major discovery, for it effectively made castles obsolete. We must also remember that the discovery of nitro-glycerine in 1846 was hailed as a move for *peace*. Many genuinely believed that with such destructive power now loose in the world no country would risk going to war. 1952 brought a similar 'deterrent' argument with the detonation of the hydrogen bomb. It is most unlikely that astrologers would associate 'explosives' with Saturn/Neptune, yet as we have seen it is a theme which has followed one phase of their conjunctions for over 600 years.

If we look more closely at events which took place during Saturn/Neptune periods we can see how these particular themes, which appear to resonate to the degrees of the conjunction, are overlaid with more familiar Saturn/Neptune imagery. Religious issues, church buildings, diseases and matters of social justice appear again and again with striking similarity.

Saturn/Neptune Conjunctions

734

734 Image worship condemned by the Greek Christian church.

735 Archbishopric of York established.

984

984 Pope John XVI murdered (20 August).
     Earliest dated astrolabe made.

1021

1020 Chinese use floating magnet for navigation.
      Chartres Cathedral burns down.

1057 —

1092

1091   Walcher of Malvern observes eclipse of the Moon. First Western astronomical observation.

1092   Su Sung's *Astronomical Treatise* printed.

1093   Shen Ku'a *Essays from the Torrent of Dreams* printed; contains first literary reference to magnetic navigation, and describes movable type.

1127

1127   Marriage of Matilda to Geoffrey of Anjou.

1128   Adelard of Bath translates Al-Shahrastani's *Book of Religions and Sects*. First comprehensive history of religion.

1164

1163   Construction of Notre-Dame Cathedral commenced.

1164   Foundation of Malmesbury Abbey.

Constitution of Clarendon limits ecclesiastical jurisdiction, and defines the roles of Church and State.

Becket exiled.

1201

1200   Rouen Cathedral burns down.

1201   Development of Samurai dwelling in Japan. Houses enclosed by ditch and wall.

Work finished on façade of Notre-Dame.

Work begun on Siena Cathedral.

1202   Leonardo Fibonacci writes *Liber Abaci*. Earliest Latin account of Hindu number theory.

1236

1235   Notre-Dame finished.

1236   Work starts on Strasbourg Cathedral.

1237   Pope Gregory IX reforms the Benedictine Order.

Henry III and Alexandra II agree on the Anglo-Scottish border at Treaty of York (23 September).

1271

1269   First true magnetic compass invented.

1270   River Maas dammed and diverted into Rhine. Land reclaimed is called 'Holland'.

1272   Thomas Aquinas publishes *Summa Theologica*.

1272   Regensburg Cathedral begun.

1307

1306   Scots revolt of Robert Bruce put down by British.

1307   Lincoln Cathedral completed.

       Divine Comedy begun: 'Abandon hope, all ye who enter here'.

       Master Jacob of Florence writes *Treatise on Mathematics*.

       Dietrich of Freiburg writes *Treatise on Optical Meteorology*.

1344

1343   First European Commission on Public Health set up, in Venice.

       Levi ben Gerson writes *De Harmonicis Numeris*, a treatise on arithmetic and music.

       Jean de Meur completes *Treatise on Mathematics, Mechanics and Music*.

1344   Work commenced on Prague Cathedral.

1380

1379   The Great Schism.

1380   Wycliffe Bible available.

1381   Wat Tyler rebellion over the poverty of peasants and farm labourers. Also against Poll Tax, which was set in November.

       Archbishop of Canterbury killed.

       Black Death in Egypt.

       'Great Gun of Ghent' manufactured, with 25-inch calibre.

       Printing by movable type in Limoges.

1415

1414   Lollards plot against the throne. Many hanged.

1415   Pope John XIII deposed.

       Agincourt.

       Wycliffe's work condemned and burned.

       Giovanni de Fontana publishes first Treatise on Military Technology.

1416   Dutch fishermen use drift nets for the first time.

1450

1450   English nobility enclose land to raise sheep; leads to extreme poverty on the land.

       John Cade leads a Peasants' Revolt against taxes.

1486

1485   'Navigation Act' passed by Henry VII.
        Battle of Bosworth.

1523

1522   Circumnavigation of the globe.
        Mennonite Order established – agrarian- and poverty-based.
        Martin Luther's *New Testament* published.

1523   First English manual of agriculture published.
        First Marine Insurance issued (in Florence).
        Act of Parliament creates corporate body for physicians.

1559

1558   British lose Calais.

1559   Church of England formally established.
        Puritanism starts.
        Cortez's *Art of Navigation* published.
        William Gilbert's researches introduce the concepts of 'electricity'
            and 'magnetic pole' into the scientific language.

1594

1593   Absence from church on a Sunday, in England, is made a criminal
            offence.

1595   Widespread revolts in Ireland.
        First appearance of heels on boots.

1630

1629   500,000 die of plague in Venice.
        First steam turbine built.

1630   Huron tribes decimated through diseases.
        1,000 pilgrims leave for America, and will found Boston.
        Pope dissolves Congregation of Female Jesuits.

1631   London Clockmaking Company founded.

1667

1665/6   Great Plague.

1666   Great Schism with Russian Church.
        Newton establishes the laws of gravity.
        Newton publishes his theory of colour.

1667   Discovery that respiration needs fresh air.
        Newton invents new type of reflecting telescope.

1667   Navigation quadrant is modified to include telescope sight.
        Mexico Cathedral completed after ninety-four years.

1668   Merk & Co. established as chemists.

1703

1703   London's first daily paper started.
        Three-mile territorial claim by Holland.
        Yellow fever in New York.

1704   Newton's *Theory of Optics* published.
        British capture Gibraltar.

1738

1737   Theatre censorship introduced in England.

1738   John Wesley converted; was to found Methodism in 1739.
        Hydronamica published, laying the foundations of hydro-
           dynamics.
        First cuckoo clock!

1739   Potato harvest fails in Ireland.

1773

1772   Old age pensions first proposed.

1773   The Jesuit Order is dissolved by the Pope.
        First iron bridge built.
        Boston revolt over taxes on tea.

1774   Discovery that plants produce oxygen.
        Publication of *Experiments and Observations of Different Kinds
           of Air*.

1809

1809   Dalton publishes *A New System of Chemical Philosophy*.
        Iron anchor chains patented.
        Discovery of light polarization.
        De Saussure determines the chemistry of alcohol.
        Nicotine discovered.

1809   Samuel Hahnemann formulates theory of homoeopathy.

1846

1845   USA found the Naval Academy at Annapolis.
        Royal College of Chemistry founded.
        First submarine cable laid across the Channel.

1845   First Oxford and Cambridge Boat Race at Putney.

1846   Neptune discovered.
        Smithsonian Institution founded in Washington.
        Faraday lays foundation of modern physics.
        Mormon migration to Great Salt Lakes.
        Famine in Ireland following potato harvest failure.
        First popular newspaper (*Daily News*) published in England.
        Nitro-glycerine invented.
        Anaesthetics used in operations.
        Act of Parliament regulates steam-ships.
1847   Carl Zeiss opens his optical works at Jena.
        Financial crisis in Britain.

1882
1881   Freedom of the Press established in France.
1882   Kynoch invents brass cartridge case.
        First hydroelectric plant designed.
        Society for Psychical Research founded.
        Eddystone Lighthouse built.
        First reinforced concrete bridge built.
        Work on Channel tunnel stops.
        Three-mile territorial limit agreed at Hague Convention.
        Tuberculosis bacillus discovered.
1883   Anthrax inoculation developed.
        Introduction of liquid compass.
        Sickness insurance introduced in Germany.
        Brooklyn Bridge opened.
        GMT time zones established.

1917
1916   Roche-Lima isolates the typhus bacillus.
        Invention of the explosive amatol.
1917   100-inch reflector telescope built at Mount Wilson, USA.
        Prohibition proposed in USA.
        Munitions ship explodes in Halifax Harbour 6 December – 2,000
            killed, much of town destroyed.
        Russian Revolution.
1918   Quebec Bridge opens.
        Worldwide influenza epidemic starts. Will kill 20 million.

1953

1952 First H-Bomb.
England disputes fishing rights with Iceland.
Coelacanth caught – believed extinct for 50 million years.
Contraceptive pill invented.
Mass immunization against polio.
Construction of USS *Nautilus* begins.
120-inch telescope built on Mount Hamilton.

1953 Submarine crosses Atlantic without surfacing.
Gas Council begins exploration for natural gas.
Myxomatosis spread to rabbits.
Smog in London.
Disastrous floods kill 1,800 in Holland, 300 in England.
First major research projects into industrial pollution.
World's largest radio telescope at Jodrell Bank.

1954 Second largest solar telescope opens in Oxford.
Worldwide concern over atomic testing and radioactive pollution.
St Lawrence Seaway opens.

1989

1988 Channel Tunnel project.

1989 Floods in England and Wales.
False claim by American scientists, claiming to generate energy from 'heavy water'.
Food infections.
Major environmental concerns recognized by governments.
Collapse of Communism in Eastern Europe.
Demolition of Berlin Wall.

1990 Launch of Hubble space telescope.
BSE.
First moves to create common EC currency.

While this list is far from complete, it does demonstrate how both the individual and the recurring themes overlap, or how one theme emerges out of another. For instance, Neptune traditionally rules *fashion*, *disease* and *drugs*. While the second two more readily associate, we may have some doubts as to how *fashion* can also be fitted in. In fact all the major drug companies of the modern world, the Saturnine manifestation of Neptune, began life making aniline dyes for the fashion industry. When it was discovered that aniline dyes had a vital role to play in medical research (their ability to stain tissue samples allowed unprecedented observation of disease processes), the dye companies dominated the field and used their knowledge of chemistry to enter the drugs market. Thus fashion blurred almost imperceptibly into medicine.

Many of such major turning points took place during the 1846 conjunction – during which time Neptune itself was discovered – and some major patterns were laid down which show up quite specifically in certain degrees only *after* the 1846 conjunction. It is this conjunction – and the discovery of Neptune – that we should look at more closely.

The 1846 conjunction of Saturn and Neptune – which was a *triple* conjunction – took place at 25°, 26° and 27° Aquarius. In fact this was the last major conjunction at these degrees since Saturn and Uranus met at 25° and 27° Aquarius in 1081 AD. We should also note that Saturn and Uranus met again at 25°, 26° and 27° Scorpio in 1897, picking up the other fixed polarity.

The major astrological event coinciding with the Saturn/Neptune conjunction of 1848 was the discovery of Neptune itself. The discovery took place at around midnight CET on the night of 23 September. As this time is accurate to within twenty minutes or so, we can confidently use all the planetary positions, including the Moon, even if an exact chart is not possible. The planetary positions for the discovery of Neptune are shown in Figure 9.3.

When we start to look at the actual chart for the discovery of Neptune, we see that it does indeed contain elements which are far removed from the passivity we normally associate with the ninth planet. There are some ruthless urges here, which were later to manifest through that most Neptunian of states: the dream.

We see at once that the discovery of Neptune took place on an important day. The Sun is at a Cardinal point; in other words, the event is anchored directly into the main astrological calendar. Saturn and Neptune are less than a degree apart and Mercury is at the midpoint of the next upcoming conjunction pair, Saturn and

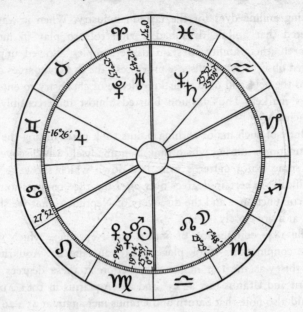

Figure 9.3. The discovery of Neptune.

Uranus. In fact there are some very powerful midpoints. Mars is on both NE/PL and SA/NE, Saturn and Neptune are both on MA/PL and both Venus and Pluto are on MA/SA – the so-called 'death axis' of the Ebertin school.

The energy that is coming into the world at the moment of discovery contains much that is most un-Neptunian. It is a message also full of Mars, Saturn and Pluto, as befits the year which also saw the invention of nitro-glycerine. Furthermore, the discovery point is in the technological sign of Aquarius, recalling, as we have seen, major scientific discoveries of earlier centuries.

Before leaving the Discovery chart we should look at the 5th harmonic of that moment, which is shown in Figure 9.4. Here the Moon is almost exactly configured with Neptune, in an extremely close opposition, and is in the 'full moon' phase of its relationship with the Sun. Mercury and Pluto are on the same degree, also

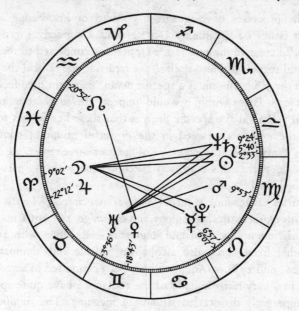

Figure 9.4 The discovery of Neptune: the 5th harmonic chart.

aspecting the Moon, and Mars is in a wide trine to Uranus. If we believe that some new 'language' is coming into the world at this moment, the language of Neptune, then what type of language will it be, what kind of universal mind will it express?

For a start, it will be very much concerned with the nature of 'mind' itself. Both the Sun and the Moon pick up the major conjunction and thus reinforce the central importance of the whole 5th harmonic theme. We have seen in Chapter 6 how such 5th harmonic Sun/Moon contacts relate to a powerful expression of its basic principles in the life of the native. Could this moment say something about *how* this language will be expressed, *where* it might be applied or *what kind* of experiences will bring its knowledge into manifestation?

If this was the chart of an individual we might suggest that the overall strength of the chart could incline towards a natural facility for the processes of language, a concern or knowledge about health issues or spirituality (SA/NE) and a capacity for deeply powerful creative thought (ME/PL), perhaps connected to the process and regions of Pluto itself. If we return to the radical chart, of which the 5th harmonic is a specific detail, we might then feel that whatever is latent within it would 'imprint' this message on to the primal zodiac at the specific degrees that these key bodies touch, with the *energy* contained in the powerful midpoint configurations. Drawing on the examples of the previous chapter, we could also suggest that this map may be concerned with the nature of language itself.

Charles Carter and Maurice Wemyss associate 25° Leo/Aquarius with mathematics, ethnology and *language*, 26° Aquarius with neurosis, communication and linguistics and, along with 26° of the other fixed signs, also alcoholism, suicide and 'immorality'. Both 26° and 27° Leo/Aquarius have been connected to astrology. Thus in a very narrow band of the zodiac we have quite specific but apparently dissociated strands of meaning. The significance of the association with *language* will be returned to more fully in a moment, but we also need to see how such other, varied meanings may cluster together.

First we must recognize that it would be unwise to put a blind faith in degree meanings, treating all suggestions equally, for there are some real problems here. Lists of degree meanings tend to be distilled from a variety of sources, generally never given, and to some extent collated randomly over the years. It was not always recognized that the time a planet spent in different degrees could vary enormously.

Over a ten-year period, for instance, it is possible for Mars to spend 400 per cent more time in one degree than another (see Figure 9.5). This has profound implications for data claiming to represent the essence of specific degrees, as certain degrees may be common for *each* event and *every* birth for a period of weeks, or even months. Such disparity of time spent at specific zodiacal locations is common to *all* bodies – obviously more so for the outer planets – and results from the complex nature of the planetary orbits plus the more obvious effects of retrogradation.

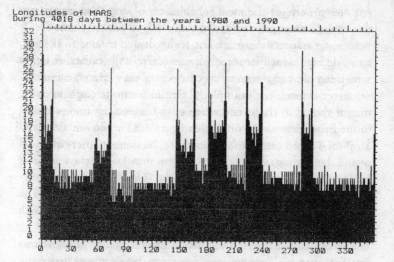

Figure 9.5 The distribution of Mars through the 360° of the zodiac during the ten years between 1980 and 1990. The scale on the left shows the number of days Mars spent at each of the degrees indicated by the scale at the bottom. We can see that, at a rough average, Mars spent about eight days at each degree but that certain points around 5° Aries, 10° Gemini, 5° Virgo, 5° Libra, 15° Scorpio and 0° Capricorn were occupied up to *four times* as often. Any research of Mars by sign or degree must take such extreme fluctuations into consideration for each time period being investigated. (Graph produced by Mark Pottenger's FAR program.)

Meanings which are based on associations with the fixed stars can be similarly suspect when the matter of precession is taken into account. With no knowledge of *when* the degree association was arrived at, we are unable to determine where it is located *now*. The rate by which the degrees of the zodiac precess against the backdrop of the fixed stars is approximately 1° every seventy-two years. This *is* significant in exploring degree areas, as many examples are given which are several hundred years old.

Finally, those degrees whose meanings are arrived at psychically risk being the most arbitrary of all, and are often the hardest to pin down. Perhaps the most reliable sets of degree meanings are those which emerge from the detailed study of related charts.

In some respects these are not really degree *meanings* as such, more degrees which in some way associate with events or imply something akin to the contacts of synastry on a more generalized or universal level. For example, 9° Gemini seems to show up more than it should in charts connected with London. Issues associated to the British monarchy often pick up 27°/28° of the mutables and 4°/5° of Gemini/Sagittarius appear to be connected to flight. It would be wrong, however, to claim that 9° Gemini 'means' London or 5° Sagittarius 'means' flight. These degrees obviously occur in charts which have nothing to do with these subjects. The most we can suggest is that *at one level* there is a resonance with some underlying experience.

The fact that it is inappropriate to suggest that 27° Leo/Aquarius, for example, 'means' astrology can be demonstrated quite simply. Using the charts of 286 astrologers and doing a simple degree count of the planets out to Jupiter, plus both angles, quickly revealed that this polarity has no particular significance. Using an orb of 1°, a total of twenty-four 'hits' is registered at 27° Leo/Aquarius, which is in fact average. As a matter of interest the lowest-scoring polarity was 2° Taurus/Scorpio and the highest was 2° Virgo/Pisces. 2° of the other polarities do not score significantly. The highest single degree counts were 20° Leo/Aquarius (Sun), 23° Gemini/Sagittarius (Moon), 12° Taurus/Scorpio (Mercury), 22° Taurus/Scorpio (Venus), 9° Leo/Aquarius (Mars), 17° Taurus/Scorpio (Jupiter), 0° Gemini/Sagittarius, 24° Virgo/Pisces (Ascendant) and 23° Gemini/Sagittarius (Midheaven).

We also have to recognize that *how* we count the degrees is most important. We can consider that everything from 26°0' up to 26°59' is to be regarded as '26°' or we can round everything up or down to 26°. In the latter case we would then capture everything which falls between 25°31' and 26°30'. At first glance this might seem to have only a slight effect, perhaps shifting one or two counts forwards or backwards by a point or two. In practice, with a reasonable number of charts, it can make a considerable difference.

Using the same 286 charts and 'rounding' to 26°, there are some very significant changes. 2° Virgo/Pisces remains the highest with an increased score, but 22° and 23° Gemini/Sagittarius score the highest on *both* Moon and Midheaven counts. Mercury is highest at both 7° and 8° Taurus/Scorpio (the previous 12° score is now no longer significant) and Venus now scores highest at 21° Taurus/Scorpio and 27° Aries/Libra. The lowest-scoring point of all is now 18° Aries/Libra, but the highest-scoring Solar position remains 20° Leo/Aquarius. Thus neither method indicates that 26°/27° Leo/Aquarius placements have any significance in the charts of astrologers.

Counting degrees in this manner is rough and ready research, but it is exactly the approach which has generated the degree lists to which we refer today. If we take the highest-scoring sets of degrees we find them associated with faith, the spine and painting. The highest-scoring single group (2° Virgo/Pisces) is associated by Wemyss with 'resignation', although from what he does not say. Possibly statistics!

This brings us to the most important point we need to consider before leaving the mechanics of degree areas: just how much evidence *really* is there for such traditional meanings?

As we have seen, Wemyss quotes both 25° and 26° Leo/Aquarius as being connected with language, and in *The Wheel of Life* amplifies this by stating that philologists (those who study the science of language) have planets in 25° of the fixed signs and 25°/26° Virgo/Pisces. He then gives nine sets of birth data, presumably to back up his claim.

When calculated, and using an orb of one degree, not *one* of the noted philologists has planets in either 25° of the fixed signs or 25°/26° Virgo/Pisces.

Yet there undoubtedly is something to these degrees. For when we subject Paul Wright's collection of twenty-five timed charts of language specialists[1] to the same analysis, some 20 *per cent* have planets in 26° Leo/Aquarius. While this might suggest that Wemyss drew his conclusions from charts other than those he quoted, the real implications are far more important.

Wemyss's data *is* of language specialists, the charts he investigated were of noted philologists; yet there is *no* correlation with 'language' degrees. Paul Wright's data *is* of language specialists; and there *is* a significant correlation with the 'language' degrees. What is happening here?

All of the Wemyss data is *prior* to 1846; all of Wright's data is *post* 1900. In 1846, not only was Neptune discovered at 26° Aquarius, but on that same degree was a Saturn/Neptune conjunction, and, as we have already observed, there is some evidence that aspects created at the time relate to the nature of language itself. Furthermore, in 1897 a Saturn/Uranus conjunction at 25°/26° Scorpio emphasizes the other fixed axis. Within weeks of this conjunction Freud formally began his own self-analysis, which ultimately had the most profound effect on our understanding of the nature of *language* and its relationship to the unconscious.

If we start to look at these results in the light of what has been suggested so far, they would tend to confirm the idea that the zodiac is in some way *alive* with all that has taken place, and responds in some appropriate manner when the specific degrees are transited. The events which created such affinities with specific locations have become embedded upon the zodiac as the result of human action and endeavour. Once established, such energy points continue to resonate until the issues that brought them into being are resolved. Furthermore, it offers us another glimpse of the way in which the actions of one person, or the after-shock of one event, may affect us all. Those born as such degrees are underlined in this way by the cosmos may well be better able to assimilate such new knowledge or experience on behalf of their generation. At an individual level, such events and experiences contained within the zodiac would equate to the Freudian concept of archaic memory. They are the astrological parallel of what he described; the residue of events that actually took place, and to which we have unconscious access.

While the 'language' aspect of 26° Aquarius may be relatively clear, the other assumed meanings – alcoholism, mathematics, ethnology and 'immorality' – may not so readily fall into place, although mathematics can frequently be seen as a language of its own. 'Immorality' is a highly subjective assessment, and it remains to be seen whether this degree really *does* show up in the charts of alcoholics and ethnologists. As we have already discovered, the 'language' degree was *not* present in the charts of noted philologists born prior to the 1846 conjunction. As Saturn/Neptune itself has much to do with the symbolism of alcoholism, it may be that their conjunction points may have something of that relevance for the following generation.

As suggested earlier, one of the implications of using an image of something like a primal zodiac is that specific degrees will wax and wane in importance – or even occasionally switch on and off as they are either reinforced or denied by the activities of each new generation. This obviously has considerable implications for large-scale research. What may be very potent for one generation may have very little to say for the following one.

Why it is that only some will pick up on key points throughout the zodiac is obviously open to endless speculation. It could be that we may only respond to a particular message if our genetic structure, personality, emotional state or social circumstances are of a certain wavelength, and capable of being stimulated by the intricacies of planetary alignments at specific moments. For some, the meaning of certain degrees may emerge quite naturally in life; others might connect with such messages only obliquely, if at all. Yet some degrees contain powerful messages which affect us deeply, even if we do not recognize the fact. Similarly, mass movements within society will shift the course of our lives even if we do not, at a personal level, share any affinity with the ideas being expressed.

The pioneering work that Freud began in August 1897, as the Saturn/Uranus conjunction of that year exactly squared the previous Saturn/Neptune conjunction, resulted both in a practical method of 'working with dreams' and laid the foundations for our understanding of the psychological significance of language. As such, it has touched something in all of us, perhaps because it also resonated with our most fundamental Saturn/Neptune issue: how we experience and define our primary boundaries.

Saturn/Neptune aspects so often correlate with some form of loss or sacrifice, or the abandonment of earthly prizes for the sake of a higher ideal. In this respect the two planets more accurately parallel the Christian myth than does Neptune on its own. The typical Christian cathedral, cold, grey and cheerless with a high, vaulted roof that is lost in darkness, but filled with plainchant, is an almost literal outworking of the planets' combined symbolism. Nothing can more clearly demarcate the boundaries of the real world than the stone walls of a church, but inside, it invites union with the sublime.

It is as if the 'edge' between Saturn and Neptune represents the mystery that moves matter to transcend itself. The issues which surround it constantly return to the boundaries between 'real' and 'unreal'. In illness, the SA/NE midpoint is frequently an indicator of diseases which are hard to define and diagnose, or arise mysteriously within the body. Baldur Ebertin associates it with trauma from previous lives, and often suggests that hypnotic regression be part of the therapeutic process.

At a more universal level, André Barbault connects Saturn and Neptune to political movements such as Socialism and Communism, for they more accurately depict the need to express common purpose, and build a society of high ideals. Many have commented on the fact that Communism seems to be as much a religion as Christianity, and both have shown Saturn's dictatorial ruthlessness in dealing with heretics. Certainly, the Saturn/Neptune cycle has marked major phases in the development of Communism – such as its virtual abandonment with the 1989 triple conjunction – although it was equally in evidence in 1953 with the death of Stalin. Perhaps what parallels Communism and Christianity most closely is their attraction to people who seek martyrdom for a common cause, who wish to confess to real or imagined sins, or to die for a greater cause. This has never been more graphically portrayed than during the 'show trials' of Stalin's imagined enemies.

Shortly before Stalin's death there were a large number of such farcical trials, both in Russia and in the Eastern bloc countries.

A Degree of Meaning: A Case Study of Saturn and Neptune

Writing at the time – during the time of Saturn/Neptune conjunction – psychoanalyst Augusta Bonnard commented on how the metapsychology of the trials reminded her of the sudden influx of cases of children with school phobias that she was then seeing.

She noted that the common denominator in the children's background was the fact that their parents all lived in isolation within the community. For religious, social or pathological reasons, the families had cut themselves off from all ordinary social contact. Bonnard came to believe that the children's phobias of school came about because of the child's perceived threat to the internalized image of the parent. That is, ordinary school life was beginning to force the children to question how they were being brought up, consequently to question the nature of their parents. This was too frightening a task, and the anxiety it generated became attached to the immediate source – the school.

The fact that the children were ready, at some level, to undertake such questioning, is a strong indication that unconsciously they recognized the unnaturalness of their situation. No doubt the hostility that this latent awareness produced only served to exacerbate the phobia. Thus, paradoxically, the children sought to achieve freedom from their situation by remaining at home – where the situation would not be questioned and brought out into the open.

The image of rigid conformity hiding within the stream of ordinary life is a powerful Saturn/Neptune icon. It is the image of an internalized authority figure, both feared and revered, about which nebulous fears begin to emerge as a direct result of its isolation within the community. It is remarkable that the analyst was presented with so many cases at such a time, and she drew immediate parallel with what was taking place in Russia.

There, loyal communists were confessing to a variety of totally implausible charges. The confessions were apparently being given freely, and were often coupled with the victims demanding their own execution. To quote Augusta Bonnard:

The plight of these apparently phobic children suggests a comparison between their psychic reality and the external reality of an intelligent and sane Soviet citizen. It is against his background of paranoia as a State system of mass indoctrination ... and his real inability to escape from behind the Iron Curtain, that these show trials should be regarded. They should be viewed in this light not only from the angle of the victim, but also from that of the expectant public. It can be seen that the Soviet citizen who possesses critical judgement (reality sense) is firstly in danger of conflict (from which will arise guilt feelings similar in quality to those which properly relate to disowned id impulses), and next of his life, since uncensorious awareness of a differing reality is equated by the State with potential disloyalty.[2]

In other words, Bonnard is suggesting that the guilt feelings created by an inner awareness of the highly unrealistic nature of Stalin's Russia are probably identical with those normally felt when encountering frightening unconscious urges ('disowned id impulses'). The urge to protect the ego against its loss at the hands of total fantasy forces a *collusion* with the reality of the State, just as the children colluded with the unreality of their home circumstances rather than expose themselves to alternative views by attending school.

It would seem very clear that during the early 1950s the Russian people were experiencing Saturn/Neptune as the 'illusory reality of the State', and that this was directly echoed by the phobic children, whose *personal* ego-identities were being threatened by what was beginning to emerge in the unconscious as a result of their encounters at school. In the case of the show trials, many victims apparently co-operated in their own destruction because if they did not *they would have nothing left*. The belief that Stalin's Communism was right and just was the only thing that sustained them. To question that belief would be to question their own existence. This is exactly the same behaviour as witnessed by innumerable Christian martyrs – another Saturn/Neptune occupation – who would face the flames as heretics in the cause of a loving Christ rather than admit that the whole thing might just be a charade. In both cases, the alternative to acquiescence would be the ultimate Saturn/Neptune experience: to die for an illusion.

A Degree of Meaning: A Case Study of Saturn and Neptune

There can be little doubt that the image of the ascetic can be very appropriate for those with strong Saturn/Neptune contacts, particularly when their midpoint is configured with the personal planets or the angles. Such contacts can often correlate with a need to suffer, to renounce a way of life or give up something; often something that might be quite valuable in the eyes of the world. What often characterizes strong Saturn/Neptune issues is the sense that personal energy drains away, that there is a *failure* to establish an important boundary within the psyche, exposing mind and body to the ebb and flow of external events. The individual can often express a feeling of *helplessness*, an inability to cope with even simple things. By such an unwillingness to act, there is so often set up a 'victim' situation where, by default, personal authority seems to drain away and control is given over to circumstance.

A correlation with alcohol and drug abuse is another common aspect of Saturn/Neptune which reinforces what is often an ambivalent attitude towards life. There is a possibility that there are echoes here of very early inter-uterine experience, as if the Saturn side of the equation – almost certainly a main contributor towards the later process of ego-formation – begins to recognize that there are limits to the amniotic universe, our primary boundary.

As an aside here, it is probably of interest to note that of nineteen timed charts for men whose hobby is cave diving – that is, using an aqualung to swim in total darkness through submerged caves – 26 per cent had the pattern MC = SA/NE! If the Midheaven refers to those aspects of ourself we may be more conscious of, then here the goal may be to repeat a very early experience!

With regard to Stalinism and Russia, however, there is one final observation we can make which once more underlines the poverty of a psychology in which astrology plays no part.

Those psychoanalysts who attempt to interpret history on Freudian lines have put forward the basic proposition that the general method of child-rearing adopted by a country will in some way dictate its later political nature. For them, political changes can come about *only* after there has been a change in parenting attitudes towards the generation which actually brings about social change. As the changes that took place in Europe during 1990 all originated in Russia, this theory would demand that there were dramatic changes in child-rearing some fifty years previously. This in fact *was* the case; the Revolution swept away many primitive customs, some of them quite barbaric. What particularly concerns us here are those practices which were *forbidden* by the Communists, for it was these which may well have contributed to the psychological climate in which Stalinism could flourish.

The generation that experienced Stalinism would have been brought up with methods that other parts of the world had not used for centuries – if ever. Swaddling – bandaging a baby up for months at a time – was a universal fact of life. Infants could be so used to being tightly bound that they would scream if left *unbound*; the parallels with boundaries and a later capacity to feel secure *only* when rigidly controlled are obvious. Also universal was the brutal custom of baptism in ice-cold water.

There is abundant evidence[3] that new-born babies were immersed in freezing water, rolled in the snow, and left to dry off by themselves. In summer, baptismal water was deliberately left to cool before being used; the infants typically being left submerged in the stone font for an hour. The childhood mortality rate in pre-Revolution Russia was 50 per cent.

Both the swaddling and the baptism in ice-water are redolent of Saturn/Neptune; the infant in the font is repeating its inter-uterine life, and the service celebrating this act is a concretization of a Neptunian mythology which glamorizes sacrifice and denial. If all such early experiences open us to *quite specific* aspects of planetary energy, then 'Saturn/Neptune' will have been powerfully embedded within the Russian psyche. This may have made Russians particularly open to that *other* Saturn/Neptune manifestation: Communism. It is not that Communism is directly related to swaddling or ice-water baptism in a *causal* or linear sense – this would be an example of the naïve pathologizing that dominates much deterministic psychology. What *is* being suggested here is that, in being powerfully opened up to a very *specific* astrological principle in childhood, a deep susceptibility is being created to *all* aspects of that principle throughout life, and that such a planetary memory becomes embedded within the psyche of a nation.

We have seen that it may be possible for the major planetary cycles to lay down specific patterns within whole groups of people, some of which may focus around precise degrees. In the following chapter we shall take this idea further by exploring in greater detail examples in the charts of individuals.

10.

Case Studies:
Triggering Our Memories

* * * * * * * * *

In the previous chapters we have considered ways in which we may wish to re-evaluate the processes of astrology, concentrating on the idea of a succession of experiences and events becoming embedded within a collective zodiac, to which we might all have access. We have also suggested that an individual's experience might pre-date the actual birth chart, and that this birth chart itself may become overlaid with the events of life, with each degree continuing to hold the memory of all that has taken place as it has been transited. In this chapter we shall start to look at examples of these processes in action.

As we have just seen, specific degrees such as those occupied at the moments of major conjunctions continue to be 'active' with an apparent disregard to the passage of time. These degrees are relatively easy to locate precisely *because* they mark significant meeting points on the zodiac. If we wish to look at events which are *not* related to the major phases of the planets then we are going to have to pay much greater attention to recording what actually takes place at each zodiacal degree; in other words, to explore what memories may be embedded in each moment of the chart and how they may later be activated as their degrees are again transited.

In order to illustrate just how precisely such points in the birth chart can respond to a sequence of transits, the examples quoted will focus primarily on the use of midpoints. This technique has been available to the astrologer since the 1920s, though it is only in more recent years that it is beginning to be more widely used. Readers unfamiliar with the use of midpoints should refer to Appendix 1 on page 342, which outlines the basic theory and gives some brief examples of its application.

The Use of Sequence

We can start our investigations in a more general way by noticing how transits of the planets and angles can trigger the nature of basic planetary patterns. Such transits often reveal how events or sensations within our lives follow familiar sequences as the transiting bodies trigger a succession of planetary energies in an identical order. For example, someone may have JU/UR followed by SA/NN and complain that every time they experience some burst of enthusiasm for a new project (JU/UR) it always ends in disappointment (SA/NN). Such an experience would suggest that the individual in question has never really confronted the 'hard realities' needed to put their enthusiasms into practice, and thus with no practical back-up they would tend to fail. Being aware of this, they can begin to recognize that 'serious relationships' or 'business connections' (SA/NN) may be needed to ground their enthusiasm and allow it to take root in something real.

In another example, we can note that the writer **Graham Greene** has the natal pattern AS = SO = MO/NE = MA/SA = NE. Two personal points, the Sun and the Ascendant, lock these midpoint combinations together with Neptune and they find potent expression within Greene's work. Time and time again he writes of idealized love that is followed by death, or love that becomes in some manner a sacrifice. This aspect of a *religious* sacrifice is also marked by his Jupiter, which is on the SA/NE midpoint.

In fact Greene's Jupiter brings together MA/PL, SA/NE, SO/SA and MA/UR. This gives us a picture of something to do with death or violence (MA/PL), something which may be spiritual or connected with drugs (SA/NE), issues to do with control and authority (SO/SA) and finally something which ends abruptly, and perhaps violently, MA/UR.

We could also see this as the story of someone going to Vienna to attend the funeral of a friend who was killed by a truck, only to discover that there was some deception going on over a matter of stolen drugs, which got him involved in problems with the occupying authorities, which ended with him witnessing a death under the streets of the city. In other words, Greene's Jupiter (success) tree carries in its branches the plot for *The Third Man*.

In fact, the issues of death and sacrifice, of alcoholism and suicide, of deception and spying, and of lost faith against a background of violence, all dominate much of Greene's work. We see here how events and themes repeat within life as an echo of the transits that stimulated their occurrences. At a practical level this can offer us a lot, if we know how to look for them.

The Pattern of Events

Figure 10.1 is part of a graphic ephemeris for 1987. The curved lines depict the positions of the planets during that year, and drawn in over these from left to right are 'William's' natal positions. These are always straight lines, and every time there is crossing between the natal lines and the planet lines this indicates a transit that is one multiple of 45°. It may be a conjunction, an opposition, a square, a sesquiquadrate or a semisquare. In other words, we can see at a glance *all* the hard aspects for the year.

William came for a consultation in November 1987, following a personal disaster on the stock market. He had been trading Options and had expected the market to rise; as we know now, it fell dramatically on Monday 19 October. We can see that the New Moon for that month is exactly hitting William's AS/MC midpoint and that Saturn is crossing both his Moon and his Pluto. William has Neptune on his Sun/Moon midpoint natally, which actually form a T-square in his 5th harmonic chart. Thus we might suggest that he has a mind which knows about Neptune, that he can speak its language. Gambling and speculation is very

Figure 10.1(*opposite*) 'William's' transits for 1987 on a 45° graphic ephemeris. For clarity and confidentiality only the Moon, Pluto and the AS/MC midpoint have been drawn in. Note the New Moon falling on William's AS/MC midpoint in October, and how the final Saturn crossing of his Pluto coincided with the Stock Market crash on 19 October. The previous two such crossings had marked periods of near-disaster in William's financial trading.

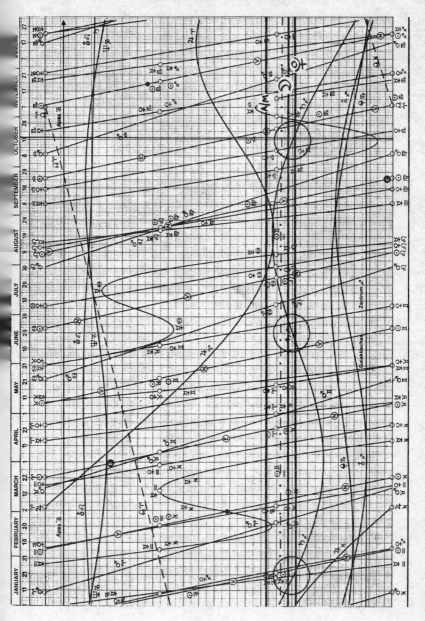

much a Neptune matter, and Neptune certainly took control during 1987. Despite having a very good understanding of how to buy and sell Options – a notoriously tricky undertaking – William somehow or other allowed himself to get into a position which at one level he knew was most unrealistic. He had committed far more money to the market than he should have done, and in doing so had broken some of the basic rules of Options trading. When the crash came, the underlying weakness of his trading philosophy was exposed.

Initially, the first few days after the Crash brought losses; while these were excessive, William's personal financial position could still sustain them. However, to make matters worse, the brokerage house handling William's account took certain steps to protect their own losses, which effectively allowed their clients to be further exposed by almost quadruple their original stakes. William got caught up in this, and when the market fell even further the following week he potentially owed his broker far more than he possessed, including his house and his car.

We can see that Saturn *also* crossed his Moon/Pluto lines in January and June, and William was asked what had happened then. He replied that he had very nearly lost his money on the market on both occasions; in fact Saturn to such a Moon/Pluto combination frequently correlates with some great emotional up-heaval where loss or hardship predominate. In this case it was the *third* passage of Saturn which triggered the actual event, perhaps highlighted by the New Moon on his AS/MC.

If William had been able to discuss his plans with an astrologer prior to October 1987, it is quite possible that these two 'near miss' experiences would have emerged and he might well have decided to stay out of the market until after the aspect had completely passed.

If we explore our own charts, looking for patterns such as these, we will frequently find that similar occurrences take place within our own lives, that a repetition of a transit corresponds with the return of a particular state of mind or correlates with familiar experiences. While such personal observations will obviously help us to understand the dynamics of our own life more fully, there is still much more we can learn from such precise observations.

Laying Out Our Information

To take this idea further we need to construct a simple diagram which shows how each midpoint falls in the Cardinal, Fixed and Mutable signs. As each grouping of four signs are all in hard angles to the other, it is sufficient to note only the midpoints in *one* of each quarternity to know the midpoint placings in *all* of that group. Obviously, this task is made most simple by the use of a suitable computer program.[1]

When we have set up the Cardinal, Fixed and Mutable sort we can use it to note transits and lunations to midpoints and see how patterns begin to emerge. We can also add the positions of planets for synastry purposes, and see how these two groups *also* interact: as has been often pointed out, we often act as a *transit* to another person, as they do to us.

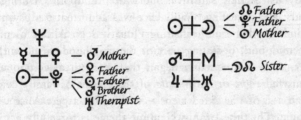

Figure 10.2 Part of the Cardinal/Fixed/Mutable sort for 'Alice', showing synastry contacts with family and therapist.

In Figure 10.2, we see part of the C/F/M sort for 'Alice', to which have been added the planetary positions for her father, mother, brother and sister. We see immediately that this is not a random grouping. Certain parts of her chart are touched again and again by the synastry contacts with her immediate family. We would thus expect transits to those points to activate issues connected to the dynamics of her family. This was indeed the case.

Alice was the youngest of three children, each born approximately seven years apart. Her father was a Christian minister, with whom Alice was never able to relate. She used to have an image of him as a vampire-like creature who might swoop down on her from the pulpit. Note how the father's Pluto is conjunct Alice's Sun/Moon midpoint. Issues of *feeding* also revolved around her father, rather than her mother, and as a child Alice used to steal and eat her father's favourite cakes. Once, her father forced Alice to eat a plate of ice-cream as a punishment for being greedy.

Despite being the youngest child, Alice felt she was far from the favourite; her elder sister was seen as more attractive and the recipient of greater attention. She experienced childhood as an isolating experience, where her needs and wishes were ignored by the family as a whole. As an adult she easily recognized that her tendency towards compensatory eating, plus a ferocious temper and fits of blind jealousy, were reactions against this early environment.

During 1971, Neptune and Uranus were 135° apart and both exactly on Alice's sensitive Sun/Moon midpoint. During this period, after an eating binge, Alice was admitted to a psychiatric hospital. At that time transiting Pluto was on Alice's own Sun/Pluto midpoint, re-stating part of the childhood theme with her father. Alice subsequently began therapy with a woman whose Uranus fell *right in the middle* of the cluster of family contacts around 12° of the Fixed signs – which also aspect Alice's natal Neptune. Thus the Uranus/Neptune theme is forcefully activated once again.

We can see in Figure 10.2 that both the Moon and Node of Alice's sister fall on her MA/MC and JU/UR midpoints at around 12° of the Mutables. During one session Alice began shaking with fury at the subject of her sister – at the *precise moment* when both the Moon and the transiting MC were conjunct these two midpoints. The emotional affect which had been there since childhood was, quite literally, triggered by the astrology of the moment.

An even more graphic example can be seen in Figure 10.3,

which is part of **Adolf Hitler's** Cardinal/Fixed and Mutable sort.
The synastry between Hitler and his mother includes his mother's
Pluto falling exactly on his SA/MC and PL/NN midpoints, the
latter configuration often described as indicating 'fated or brutal
relationships'. We know from biography that Hitler worshipped
his mother, although she could do little to protect him from her
husband, who could be described with clinical accuracy as a sadist.
In fact, Hitler's father died as the Sun crossed the PL/NN midpoint
– and Hitler himself committed suicide at an identical configuration.

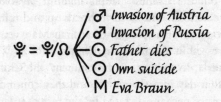

Figure 10.3 Transits and synastry with Hitler's Pluto/Node midpoint.
This midpoint of 'fated contacts' is conjunct his mother's Pluto (left),
and also received transits on days of major importance in Hitler's life –
including his own suicide.

We can also see that Mars was exactly on the PL/NN midpoint
as Hitler invaded Austria, and again when he invaded Russia.
This point also marks the MC of his mistress, Eva Braun. We may
wish to conjecture what it might mean if a man attacks a country
as Mars transits the synastry point between himself and his
mother, and this will be returned to in the following chapter when
we shall see how planetary cycles are *also* involved.

We can see another example of the 'fated' or universal quality of
Pluto and the Node if we examine a very important event in the
history of modern China – the Cultural Revolution of 1966. We shall
also see how it is reflected in the massacre of students on 4 June 1989.

The Cultural Revolution

The events of 4 June 1989, when units of the People's Army

massacred students in Tiananmen Square, are reflected not in the
chart for China itself nor in the declaration of the People's Republic. They register *precisely* in the chart for Mao's call for a
Cultural Revolution, made on 13 August 1966, when the Chinese
people 'absorbed' into their psyche the prevailing astrological climate; the climate of a social revolution symbolized by Uranus and
Pluto, and subsequently acted out with a fury throughout the
land.

During 1965 and 1966 Uranus and Pluto formed triple conjunctions around 16° Virgo. This major cultural cycle affected us all to
some degree, but the Chinese people made it *personal* by their
own, collective actions. The need to break up and reform society
on the revolutionary principles of Chairman Mao was most dramatically expressed in China by the Chinese; not in Westminster,
Berlin or Bulgaria. In 'taking on the moment' the Chinese people
incorporated that day into their lives, and they continue to resonate to it, its nature perhaps dictated by the fact that Uranus/Pluto
for the Cultural Revolution fell on China's PL/NN midpoint.

At the time of the 1989 student demonstrations for democracy
Uranus and Pluto were exactly one-seventh of the circle apart.
This septile aspect is one of inspiration; a nation that had begun,
in 1966, to resonate to this cycle now was awakened again by the
need for large-scale social reforms, 'turned on' by the image of
freedom through social change. China expressed this need most
strongly because China had incorporated the seed moment of the
current Uranus/Pluto cycle into its collective during 1966. It was
now effectively part of the national chart, locked into the PL/NN
midpoint. The demand of the masses was for freedom and massive
social change, for an end to the corrupt use of power and for far-
reaching economic reforms.

As we can see in Figure 10.4, Jupiter *precisely* squared the
Uranus/Pluto conjunction point as the students began to gather in
Beijing during the end of May 1989. Mars returned *precisely* to its
position on 13 August 1966, when it was also exactly conjunct
Jupiter on that day. As the massacre took place Venus in the sky
was exactly *to the minute* square to the Saturn of the announce-

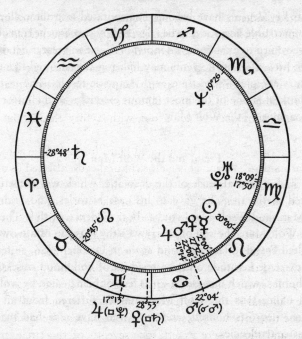

Figure 10.4 Transits on 4 June 1989 to the planetary positions of 13 August 1966 (Moon omitted), when Chairman Mao made his call for a Cultural Revolution. Note that transiting Venus is *exactly* square to Saturn during the Tiananmen Square massacre of 4 June, and that Mars on that day had returned to within minutes of its original position.

ment of the Cultural Revolution, touching the symbol of authority itself, and Pluto similarly marking the Saturn with a sesqui-quadrate to within a degree. If the time of the massacre, 3:14 a.m. CCT, is correct, then this multiple Venus/Saturn/Pluto aspect would be picked out by the Ascendant for the moment with a similar precision.

As we know from more traditional astrology, we find that a chart set for the start of something, for an historical event, for the invention of a new product, for the primary moment of a scientific discovery, echoes through the following centuries. Here we see how its key degrees have become incorporated into the collective with remarkable accuracy, to be triggered by subsequent transits.

If we return to examining an individual case in greater detail we can see how a series of events may link together around identical planetary energies – sometimes with dramatic results. The case we shall look at is one of the most famous examples in the history of psychoanalysis – the Wolf Man.

Freud and the Wolf Man

Freud had a natural sense of the dramatic, which was sometimes reflected in the titles he gave to his case histories, and both his 'Rat Man' and 'Wolf Man' studies bear evidence of this. The so-called Wolf Man, the son of a very wealthy Russian estate owner, consulted Freud in late 1907 and again in October 1926, suffering from extreme lassitude and the residues of childhood obsessions and phobias, which included a great fear of being eaten by wolves. By all indications the Wolf Man's father suffered from an obsessional neurosis himself, and may well have also had manic/depressive tendencies.

Freud analysed the Wolf Man twice, and he was later also analysed by Ruth Mack. Despite claims often made by the Freudian camp, he was never completely cured of his condition, but his case allowed Freud to explore theories about the development of infantile sexuality and dream symbolism. His case continues to be studied in psychoanalytic circles, and also has much to offer astrologers; not just in how it is reflected in the Wolf Man's birth chart, but in the actual *process* of that reflection.

The Wolf Man was born on Christmas Day in the Gregorian calendar (6 January 1887 NS) and experienced his major dream the day before his fourth birthday. This key date, and subsequent research by Freud and the Wolf Man with regard to the timing of traumatic events, allows us to explore the case history from an astrological perspective with a far greater confidence than is usually possible with childhood occurrences. The Wolf Man case is fully recorded in Freud's *Complete Psychological Works*, Vol. 17.

What follows is a highly condensed extract compiled from memories which returned to the Wolf Man during the course of his analysis.

The Wolf Man: The Case History

The Wolf Man was brought up in a small family, having only one sister, who was two years older than he. Both children were looked after by an old nurse and a succession of governesses. His mother suffered from a variety of abdominal complaints which considerably weakened her, and his father had periodic bouts of depression, during which time he was sent to a sanatorium. Thus the two children were frequently thrown back on to their own resources, or into the company of the servants.

At the age of eighteen months, an event clearly placed by its season and precise location, the infant awoke from his afternoon's sleep to witness his parents having sex. His mother was on her hands and knees and his father was entering her from the rear.

Almost exactly a year later he came upon one of the servants, a girl called Grusha, on her hands and knees washing the floor and experienced intense excitement at viewing her in the same position in which he had seen his mother. He attempted to relieve this excitement by urinating on the floor. Grusha scolded him with the warning that she would cut off his penis if he behaved in that way again.

His next clear sexual experience took place at the age of three and a quarter. It began with his sister suggesting that they should show their genitals to each other, which they did. His sister then took hold of his penis and stimulated him, telling him incomprehensible stories about his nurse doing similar things with the other servants. He subsequently attempted to inveigle his nurse also to play with his penis; she replied with a warning of the injury that could result. Following his nurse's rejection he began to develop temper tantrums and sadistic behaviour. Concurrent with this episode he recalled being told the story of a fox who attempted to catch fish during the winter by dangling its tail through the ice; the tail froze and broke off.

During this period he was particularly aggressive to one governess, so much so that she ultimately left. He recalled, however, one disturbing event when she had pulled the back of her long dress up, bunching it together to mimic a tail and had pranced about pretending to be a pony to amuse him. The 'tail', of course, ceased to exist the moment she released her dress. Similar castration themes were also recalled: watching his father kill a snake and being told told that a certain sweet was 'a chopped up snake'.

Among childhood fairy stories that had left an impression on him was one in which a wolf had its tail cut off, and another in which a wolf covers itself in white flour, to disguise its grey fur, and thus succeeds in eating six goats; a seventh escaped.

Immediately before his fourth birthday he dreamed that he was in his bedroom. Suddenly the windows flew open and he looked out at the big walnut tree that grew outside. In its branches were 'six or seven' white wolves, all staring in at him. The wolves had big bushy tails, like foxes, and fur like the fleece of sheep. Each wolf had his ears pricked up like that of a listening dog. The boy awoke screaming, convinced he was about to be eaten.

After the dream, his wolf phobia developed and he also began to have sado-masochistic fantasies. His sister used to tease him by showing him a picture book of a wolf striding along, which would reduce him to hysterics. In the years that followed, these phobias were succeeded by a pious period of religious prayer and devotion, which was also obsessional in nature, and then by the age of ten he had begun to suffer from intense depressions which occurred around 5 p.m. each day. Later he was to go through a phase of deliberately linking religious themes to obscene words and having a compulsion to relate religion with excrement. This religious facet was exacerbated by the fact of his own birth on Christmas Day.

Other, more temporary, neurotic symptoms included a phobia of yellow butterflies, obsessional forms of breathing in and out and – when much older – highly erratic behaviour over issues of money. At the age of eighteen the Wolf Man contracted gonorrhoea from a brief though very emotional affair with a peasant girl. It was the effect of contracting this disease that precipitated the apathetic illness that resulted in his treatment by Freud. While Freud's specific interpretations of this case are beyond the purpose of this book, some of his main observations are well worth recording as they demonstrate a way in which unconscious images might work which will be explored from an astrological perspective later.

Obviously, the issue of castration is paramount. The little boy witnesses his parents' sexual activity and when he attempts to mimic it with Grusha he is threatened with losing his penis. This is repeated when his nurse warns of 'injuries' should he offer his penis to her following seduction at his sister's hands, and reinforced by scenes such as witnessing his father killing a snake.

Sexual energy thus regresses back to its earlier, anal stage; hence the sadistic behaviour and attendant obsessions with their excremental component. Freud's reasons for this fact are given fully in his *Complete Psychological Works*, but any astrologer who has difficulty linking these images together should consider the two sides of Pluto. The neurotic reactions to money can be similarly related to this early fixation. It was Freud's conclusion that, for a number of reasons, the Wolf Man identified primarily with the passive role of his mother, psychically and sexually. Overt sexuality, for him, ran the certain risk of castration. Ultimately, this passivity reached such neurotic proportions that the Wolf Man was unable to take any personal decisions whatsoever, and relied totally on others.

The peasant girl from whom the Wolf Man contracted a venereal infection was called Matrona. Initially, he was highly reluctant to impart her name to Freud, probably because of its 'motherly' overtones and the implications of being genitally 'wounded' through an act of sex with someone so named.

Further analysis on the linkage between the peasant girl of his affair, the servant girl Grusha from his childhood and his early phobia of yellow butterflies revealed an interesting series of images. He recalled, as a child, following a yellow butterfly until it settled on a flower; as he watched, it opened its wings and he became terrified and fled. He recalled that the colour of the butterfly was the same as a particular pear that he liked, which was known locally as a 'grusha'. Freud suggested that the butterfly opening its wings into a 'V' stimulated the memory of his mother's intercourse and his sister's genital display. He also regarded it as particularly significant that the boyhood depressions became most intense at five o'clock – when the hands reached the Roman figure V.

Parenthetically, in the *Journal of the American Psychoanalytic Association* Dr Austin Silber reports a case of an acute panic attack that a patient experienced while travelling on a bus.[2] The panic attack was experienced at 11.15 a.m. On association the patient remembered that many years before she had been told of her father's death at that time, and had suffered a panic reaction. The subsequent panic attack took place as the bus passed New York's 56th Street: her father had died in his fifty-sixth year.

This modern case example directly parallels Freud's observations on the formation of idea associations, on how an outline shape can come to represent the female legs spread apart, the wings of a butterfly opening, the Roman numeral on a clock and the pricked-up ears on a dream wolf. In the modern example, street numbers and a clock dial echo the residue of parental loss, triggering a repetition of the original reaction when the two symbols come together again. Freud's actual analysis of the dream's latent content points to other ways in which the unconscious seems to handle such visual metaphors.

Such associations may also possess even deeper levels than the purely personal. Neo-Platonic number symbolism links the number five to the concept of marriage – the joining of the 'male' number two with the 'female' number three to create the number five, which John Addey has described as the number of sexual penetration[3] – thus the strictly 'numerical' aspect of the clock face 'V' may reinforce an internal image of sexual union. Its other aspect, the symbolic *shape* of the letter 'V', may also have a more universal sexual meaning than Freud was aware of. Thass-Thienemann records that 'the two lines forming an angle are called in Greek *skelos*, in Latin *femur* and in German *Schenkel* – all denoting the same segment of the leg which is between the trunk and the knee, in other words, the genital area. For this reason the angle is charged with a repressed sexual meaning. The Latin *femur* also means the genital parts.'[4]

Returning to the symbolism of the dream itself, the six or seven wolves refer to the fairy story in which the goats are eaten. The wolves have white fur like sheep, again an echo of that same story. The wolf has come to represent the dangers of sexual (animal) desire – it can lead to castration. The wolf lost his tail, and so did the fox. This is doubly underlined in the dream by giving the wolves foxes' tails. In the dream the windows suddenly open: this mimics the recollections of an eighteen-month-old baby who suddenly wakes up to witness frightening, animal-like behaviour by his parents.

The Wolf Man's Chart

If we look at the Wolf Man's natal chart (Figure 10.5), we see three clear correlations with what we know so far: the Sun/Saturn opposition speaks of the depressed, authoritarian father, the Capricorn Sun-135-Pluto suggests a pattern that might encourage obsessive tendencies whenever attempts are made to actualize the Self, and the Mars in Aquarius trine Uranus suggests the possibility of erratic and unusual sexual experiences in its contact with the 'castrated' planet.

The Sun, Node and Pluto are on the SA/UR midpoint, a symbol of extreme inner restlessness with a further obvious reference to castration anxiety, but it is MA = VE/NE = SA/PL which speaks most eloquently of sexual fantasy that becomes so deeply repressed as to be totally denied in the form of the apathy experienced by the patient.

This actual midpoint sequence needs to be explored more closely, and Figure 10.6 shows the full structure, although the Moon and angle contacts are omitted as no birth time is available.

If we follow the sequence through in the way it will have been

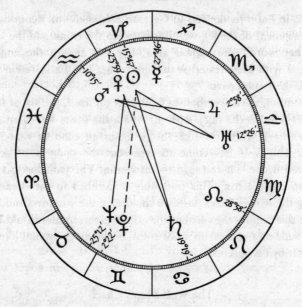

Figure 10.5 Noon positions for the Wolf Man's natal chart (Moon omitted).

Figure 10.6 The Wolf Man's Mars midpoint tree.

triggered by innumerable transits, we note first of all the MA = SO/PL: a powerful image of sexual awakening. The Sun-135-Pluto aspect connects up with the Wolf Man's Mars. Ebertin gives for this combination 'The desire to perform record achievements . . . the tendency to work to the point of physical breakdown.' The fact that this is the one thing the Wolf Man *can't* do, and indeed experiences total apathy and a complete inability to take any decisions about his life, almost certainly relates to the fact that SA/NN follows immediately afterwards. Energy becomes blocked, there is a sense of physical loss, the Mars diffuses to a shared depression. Next comes MA = VE/NE, for which Ebertin suggests 'A strong wishing power on an amorous basis, the state of being unsatisfied, misdirected energy, sexual aberration. Love longings without fulfilment.' Again comes Saturn in the guise of MA = SA/PL and Ebertin's 'Brutality, assault or violence, ruthlessness ... maltreatment.' Finally MA = VE/NN gives 'Awareness of one's personal charms, the ability to utilize one's charms to advantage. An impulsive attachment, the desire for love.'

Thus we see in this a sequence of Energy – Denial – Fantasy – Denial – Fantasy. The most powerful of these are those midpoints closest to Mars, VE/NE followed by SA/PL: the sexual fantasy is followed by a ruthless denial of sexual feeling, in effect a castration.

The other midpoints we would associate with the double issue of sexual energy and fantasy followed by denial or loss are those midpoints involving Mars, Jupiter, Saturn and Neptune in their various relationships. In fact these play a very large part in the actual sequence of events as experienced in the Wolf Man's earliest childhood.

At the time of witnessing his parents' intercourse significant midpoints were being contacted (Figure 10.7). The Nodal contacts – which, by their Lunar nature, have much to do with family relationships – awakened or stimulated his thoughts about Plutonic issues (ME/PL), which might become obsessive or deep-seated, and may have linked them to the basic midpoint of emotional/sexual relationships, VE/MA. On the other side of ME/PL, less than 17' away, is MA/SA – the one midpoint that most succinctly describes the potential battle between father and son over the issue of sex and self-assertion.

Simultaneously, transiting Saturn is being experienced on the midpoint so often expressing basic physical energy and enjoyment, MA/JU, and the midpoint frequently activated in cases where mental or physical conditions can be their hardest to treat, SA/NE. Saturn there can only reinforce its own side of the equation, emphasizing the sense of self-denial and renunciation.

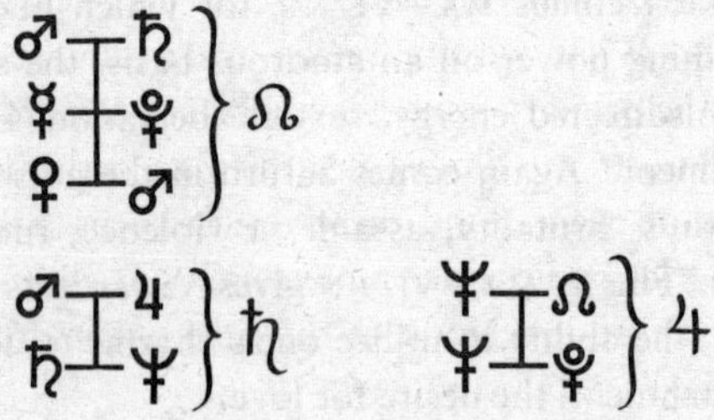

Figure 10.7 Embedding the trauma: major transits operating at the time of the Wolf Man witnessing parental intercourse.

Jupiter crossing the natal Sun on the NE/PL midpoint seems to have exaggerated the worst side of this combination, 'peculiar states of soul-experience, the pursuit of fantastic ideas, self-torment, mania, obsession, confusion, a grievous loss' as Ebertin describes it. It is a midpoint frequently associated with those who, one way or another, are attracted towards depth psychology, probably by its association with the image of seeking profound emotional truth through dreams or altered states. Freud himself had ME = NE/PL – a pattern repeated in the sky the day he met Jung. His daughter Anna had MC = NE/PL, William Fliess had MA = NE/PL, Stanislav Grof, a leading exponent of LSD therapy, has AS = VE = NE/PL and Fritz Perls – another one-time advocate of LSD – has a similar AS = NE/PL.

This sensitive NE/PL midpoint had been transited by Saturn when his sister's 'seduction' had resulted in the nurse's threat of genital injury for such sex games. Furthermore, transiting Neptune was to cross this midpoint exactly during the autumn of 1907 when the Wolf Man experienced such lassitude and inner confusion as to require hospitalization.

More importantly, *at the time of the wolf dream, the identical triplicity of MA/SA, ME/PL and VE/MA were being transited by Mars and Saturn, and the Node.*

In other words, the Mars/Saturn 'message' that had been in-stilled while witnessing the primal scene is now activated. Not only this, it is activated when those planets which best symbolize the castration theme are themselves transiting their own natal positions together with the other factor previously present, the Moon's Node. What we are seeing is an almost complete re-statement of the primary issue heavily biased towards the energies of Mars and Saturn. It is almost as if the planets themselves contain the memories of events, and these return to us again and again when the relevant bodies once more touch our charts. In the Wolf Man's case, the Moon's Node, at the time of the dream, was also exactly on Freud's natal Moon!

In recalling the significance of the number five in the Wolf Man's case, we have to consider the possibility that in this specific example the Wolf Man's 5th harmonic chart may also be signifi-cant. We note that here Sun and Jupiter are conjunct, exactly square to Mercury: images of the child and the god-like father come together with tension, as do both Venus/Node and Mars. Most striking, however, is the almost exact square of Saturn and Neptune. We have already seen how aspects between these two planets so often indicate an area of ill-health or point towards an indefinable mental condition. Here they are located in the number that, as a child, triggered acute depressions when touched by a clock's hand.

It would seem that, as an image of the *mind,* the 5th harmonic chart shows the language out of which this mind has constructed its environment, as was suggested in Chapter 6. This subsequently reflected itself, for obvious reasons, in a 'style' of behaviour that included bringing together the weak and ineffective (Saturn/Nep-tune), the powerful father (Sun/Jupiter) and the twin planets of sexuality (Venus/Mars).

As a child, the Wolf Man had attempted a number of musical and artistic pursuits, and from this had emerged a joy in painting, a possibility deducible from his natal NE = ME/VE. The image of Mercury/Venus as the 'creative child' is a strong one. In being brought together by Neptune, these artistic sensibilities are refined by the contact, which as well perhaps alludes to the loss and unreality which characterized much of his early years. But there is clearly more than this to the Neptune. Both his sister *and* his wife committed suicide, one with poison and the other by gas. In the months following his wife's suicide he began painting again, recognizing only afterwards that this had started on the anniversary of his sister's death. Another expression of this Neptune contact emerged when, as a young man, he was excessively concerned about his appearance, particularly his complexion. He developed obsessions about getting spots, and resorted to wearing make-up from time to time to improve his appearance, although there was no evidence that such measures were in any way necessary.

Other Cases

The examples that we have looked at so far begin to illustrate how the chart may become overlaid with separate moments, and how this content may emerge at subsequent transits. We might want to consider the possibility that the concept of a *traumatic event* is one such moment. Something may take place in childhood which 'freezes' aspects of the chart in a particular way, literally embedding the trauma within it, to be released into partial consciousness at some later date.

Such an image would certainly have something to offer the psychotherapist. Despite all the theories about the workings of the psyche, there is no real explanation as to why the traumas of childhood may lie dormant for a decade or more before emerging within the life of the individual. It is conceivable that a transit to the original point re-activates the memory of the day in question and may precipitate a neurotic reaction, or some form of repetition. Here, such an embedded chart, with its various symbols and messages, may be contained within the individual like the screen memory or complex symbol outlined on page 92, to be later lived out in a variety of ways, perhaps picking up different, literal aspects of the embedded moment and its chart.

For example, a fourteen-year-old boy, James, answered the

phone at around three o'clock in the morning to be told that his mother was about to die and that he should immediately attend the hospital where she was being treated. The nurse making the phone call had thought she was talking to the boy's father, and blurted out the news quite unaware that she was talking to James. Now an adult, James still, understandably, regards the childhood house where all this took place as being a depressing place. It was apparently a very large Victorian building, rather forbidding in appearance, with very thick, ivy-covered walls.

At the age of forty-four James attended a residential study course which was held at a university. The room which he was allocated was in a very old building, with thick, ivy-covered walls and was of a rather forbidding appearance. Although James found the course he was attending quite fascinating, he felt a growing sense of foreboding and had problems sleeping. On the second night he was virtually unable to sleep, and was inexplicably depressed, to the extent of entertaining suicidal thoughts.

It was subsequently discovered that during that night Saturn had returned, *to the very second*, to the degree it occupied on the night of the childhood phone call.

The psychologist would suggest that the image of ivy-covered walls and old buildings triggered submerged memories and tugged at half-forgotten feelings. But for the astrologer this simply will not do. For a start, this was hardly the first time James had been inside an old, ivy-covered building. Furthermore, 'old buildings' and 'ivy-covered walls' are *not* just part of the incidental background; they are as much a part of Saturn's symbolism as the imminent death the phone call announced – for, at that time, Saturn literally *called*. What's more, Saturn was there *again*, repeating its precise statement, when the environment of the past was partially re-created. Its energy also manifested as *depression* – a classic defensive reaction to pain and anger. The astrological evidence suggests that the initial event was in some way embedded within the chart, to be subsequently activated when Saturn made a precise return. The more charts are examined with this process in mind, the more such event repetitions are revealed.

About two years after this event, James received a phone call from a hospital to inform him that his elderly aunt had been admitted and was seriously ill. At that moment the Sun was triggering the *same* midpoint that Saturn had marked at the time of his mother's death. The parallels between these two events are so obvious that no further comment would be needed were it not for one final fact. The condition of James's aunt continued to deteriorate, and within a few days she was dead. James was with her at the end and she died at the moment the Midheaven touched that precise midpoint one final time.

The midpoint in question was Jupiter/Neptune, the focal point of those planets which, by transit one to the other, so often correlate with death in more traditional astrology. If one aspect of Jupiter/Neptune *is* death, in its guise as a 'happy release', then with James it had come far too early. For some reason he had been 'burdened' with Saturn when his mother died, and this had set up a pattern which is far more complex than the ones previously explored – after all, it involves the lives and deaths of *others*, those quite beyond James's control. Finally, the moment at which his aunt died shows in *James's* chart with absolute precision. Given this case history, and knowing that his aunt was seriously ill, any astrologer might have predicted – to within a minute or so – those eight points during the day when James's aunt was most likely to die.

If we can register our own experiences so precisely in *another's* chart, then we are moving towards realms of astrological interaction which are beginning to mirror the complexities which we so often associate with the collective unconscious.

Transits of the Midheaven

In many respects we can think of the turning earth as an image of our conscious and unconscious processes. As the earth revolves, as each degree rises and falls in the sky, echoing the progress of the sun, so might material surface and then sink within us. It is notable that time and time again memories and sensations come into consciousness that parallel those midpoints activated by the transiting angles – particularly the MC. A woman reported a sudden memory of being a little girl during the war, and running into a room just after a bomb had gone off. She recalled running across a red carpet that was covered in broken glass: at that moment the MC was crossing her Mars/Uranus midpoint!

During a consultation a man announces that he is suddenly feeling weak – just as the MC is crossing his Mars/Neptune midpoint. Another suddenly introduces an anecdote about his rather severe upbringing as the MC transits his Saturn. Several clients have attended consultations where issues of parental loss have emerged at the MC crossed points in their chart which marked either their synastry with the deceased parent, or had been transited at the time of death and were now being re-activated.

Many such examples are relatively trivial, and do not always throw much light on our situation, but this is not the real issue. In noting what is actually taking place within us, moment by moment, we see how we are interacting with real time transits, and how embedded and forgotten charts are being stimulated within us. In other words, we begin to get some idea of our interaction with the inner and outer world which goes way beyond conventional synastry. We begin to get glimpses of the actual process of life, as it is happening, and we see some of its hidden dynamics while they are actually taking place – this is something that several former residents of Vienna would have given their couches for!

In practical terms we may choose to meditate when the MC is due to cross areas of our chart we know to hold problems for us, to see what may emerge as images within us, and what we may learn from them. We may even choose to set the time of a consultation to ensure that certain degrees of a client's chart will be activated during the session. In this way we can explore the possible expression of past experiences, including synastry with parents and families, as events within the world; do we behave in different ways when the parental charts within us are activated, as with the case of Hitler? (See Chapter 11, page 243.) Do particularly dramatic moments live on within us, and repeat in some small degree when they are touched by a transiting body? It is relatively easy to find out.

During a simple meditation exercise, 'Grace' describes just such an experience. Grace had transiting Uranus over her Venus/Jupiter midpoint and did a meditation during the few minutes that the MC aligned with Uranus and crossed Venus/Jupiter, Uranus/Neptune, Saturn/Pluto and Uranus/Ascendant. These four pairs are all within 48' of arc in Grace's chart and would thus all be crossed by the MC in just over three minutes.

Grace described experiencing a series of images which included seeing two factions about to engage in a fight: 'There was a painful feeling of not belonging to either camp, yet identifying with both. There was a great schism between them that seemed unbridgeable. Suddenly there was a terrific explosion right between them both. It was a volcano which shot up red hot lava which obliterated both sides with a thick smooth hard crust. I felt devastated. It was such a grief that could almost not be borne, and yet couldn't be escaped. Such beauty on both sides was gone for ever, and could never, ever, return.'

The exercise left a very powerful impression on Grace and she subsequently researched what had taken place on these points, although even without any further information we can see that the volcano that suddenly erupted, leaving a thick, hard crust over everything, could well have been the Saturn/Pluto conjunct Uranus/Ascendant.

Grace subsequently discovered that within the orb of these midpoints lay the following factors: the Sun was there together with Pluto on the day Grace married her first husband, and was there again when she left him quite suddenly; in fact, the Node was there when they divorced. Her first son was conceived when the Sun was there, so was Jupiter when her second son was conceived, as was Saturn when a later conception ended in a miscarriage. Uranus was there when she divorced her second husband – having married him when both Jupiter and the Node were also on that degree. A very important relationship had ended with the Sun at that position, and it had also been there when her *parents* married.

With such a powerful emphasis on the making and breaking of relationships in Grace's life it is hardly surprising that the theme of two factions, both of which she could identify with, are central images. We also see how parental patterns can be repeated in the life of their offspring, as common degrees are subsequently activated with similar results or themes – in this case with the symbolism of marriage.

It was obviously an emotionally painful area, and a lot of powerful feelings lay under the surface, ready to erupt, as the volcano symbolized. It was also an area of inner union – of inner partnerships as well as outer ones – made sensitive by the accumulation of events at that point. In fact Grace's meditation continued with 'the lava cooled and then a large daisy grew in the centre of the place . . . then, with the flower between them, the Lovers from the tarot pack appeared and I felt that something had been resolved'.

With this moving image we get a glimpse of how we may in some way heal those events which we hold within us, either those resulting from our own early experiences or, in some more complex manner, those we might carry for family or society.

This capacity for similar or identical themes to span generations or cross cultures is particularly baffling, for here there can be no doubt that the original issue does *not* lie in our own chart, and that we are responding to events or situations which pre-exist our birth, and yet are part of us also. In the following chapter we shall see how, when using astrology in quite a specific way, this phenomenon can be described in a manner that has yet to be confronted, and has the most profound implications.

II.

Case Studies:
Patterns in Family Charts

* * * * * * * * * *

We have seen a number of examples of how major events in life may become embedded within the natal chart, only to be activated as an experience or a memory when the points of contact are subsequently transited. We have also seen, in the case of both James and Grace, how events in the lives of those *other* than the native can repeat within the native's own life when common degrees are activated. Such occurrences can be seen as possible evidence for the concept of a shared or collective zodiac, to which all charts are resonating and responding.

The idea that charts may link up across generations is, of course, hardly new – after all, it forms the basis of all conventional synastry. However, what may *not* be so apparent from the conventional perspective is just how precise such contacts might be, nor how certain aspects of an individual's behaviour or personality may precisely match attributes of those close to that individual. There are techniques for exploring groups of charts which may reveal how individuals and events are actually connected across time with remarkable accuracy, which may force us to reconsider again what we mean by such expressions as 'personality' and 'events': both may emerge equally from the same underlying factors.

Whereas previously we have considered the individual's chart and asked, in effect, 'What has happened to him or her?' and noted the repetitions of previous events, we shall now explore a series of charts and observe how they appear to be all different phases of common, underlying cycles. We shall start with a simple series of aspects within a family.

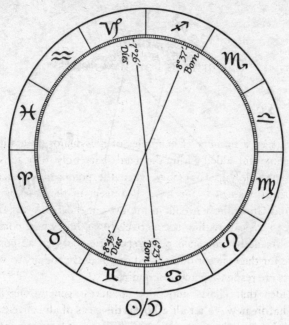

Figure 11.1 The Sun/Moon midpoint at birth and death of a married couple.

Patterns in a Family

The charts we shall be looking at all come from one family, from which the times of births and deaths are known for at least three generations; again, we shall be focusing on the use of midpoints. In *every* case quoted in this chapter only the actual, *direct* midpoint is being used. Even though using the other seven possible points produces further, dramatic synastry, these are omitted here for clarity.

Figure 11.1 shows the Sun/Moon midpoint for the birth and death of the mother and father. We see that in both cases the midpoint for death is exactly opposite the midpoint at birth – in one case to within eleven minutes. Whereas there *do* seem to be

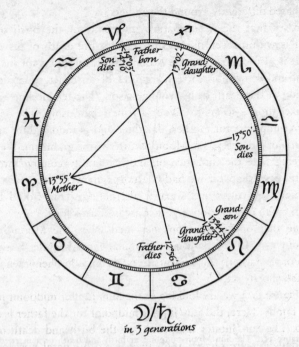

Figure 11.2 The Moon/Saturn midpoint in three generations of the same family. Note that the female line tends to trine aspects, the male towards square aspects.

repeating patterns of birth and death which are common in quite different sets of families, as we shall see during the course of this chapter, it would be wrong to say that people tend to die when their Sun/Moon midpoint is opposed by the transiting Sun/Moon; many other factors would appear to be involved.

To get some idea of how such cycles might interlock at the moments of birth and death we should look at Figure 11.2, which shows the Moon/Saturn midpoint in one family for three generations. Here we note that there are two, quite clear, patterns taking place. The Moon/Saturn midpoints for birth and death in the *male* line pick up the same *degrees* as that in the female line, but are phased differently around the zodiac.

We see that the Moon/Saturn midpoint for the birth of the father is within seven minutes of that for the death of his eldest son. It is also opposed to the Moon/Saturn midpoint for his own death, and to within thirteen minutes of an exact square to its position at the death of his youngest son. The female line – with one exception – seems to favour a trine relationship. The Moon/Saturn midpoints for mother, daughter and granddaughter are all within half a degree, as is Moon/Saturn for the grandson. We may be seeing here the influence of another family coming into the picture, or perhaps, if we had charts for many more generations, we might see trines and squares alternating. This would be in keeping with observations in other areas of astrology.

Note that one of the sons has died when the Moon/Saturn midpoint is half-way between a dominant family cycle (birth and death of the father); this appears to be a common phenomenon, as we shall shortly see.

In Figure 11.3 we are looking at the Sun/Jupiter midpoint in the same family. Here, the Sun/Jupiter midpoint for the father is at 18 SG 20. The Sun/Jupiter midpoints for the birth and death of his only daughter are phased 166° away from his natal position. In other words, he exists at the midpoint of his daughter's total Sun/Jupiter cycle. The son's natal Sun/Jupiter midpoint does not come into the picture, but at the son's *death* the Sun/Jupiter is 83° from the father's: another example of a family member dying when a major cycle is exactly half-way through its rhythm; at the midpoint in fact.

If we look at Saturn rather than Jupiter we see a similar pattern of phasing. In Figure 11.4 the Sun/Saturn midpoints for the grandson and great-grandson are within a degree (within a day) of being at the midpoint of the great-*grandfather's* own Sun/Saturn midpoint. This synastry spans more than 100 years and is quite precise.

Finally, in Figure 11.5a, we see the Mars/Saturn midpoint across three generations. The grandfather's Mars/Saturn is at 5 CP 50, and when he dies it is conjunct its position at the birth of his

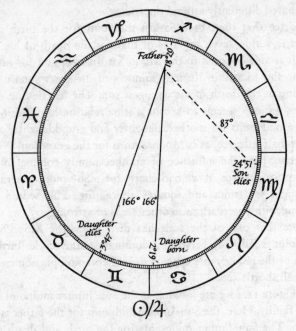

Figure 11.3 The Sun/Jupiter midpoint in the charts of a father and his children. Note that the SO/JU midpoint for the death of the son falls exactly midway between SO/JU of father and daughter.

daughter. This does not exactly mirror the Mars/Saturn position for the birth of his own father, but the Mars/Saturn midpoints for the birth of his son and his grandson *do* mirror each other to within a degree.

Figure 11.5b shows the sequence when viewed from the position of the *father* in the previous example. Now the Mars/Saturn midpoint for *his* grandson's birth and death mirror precisely across his *own* Mars/Saturn, showing the continuation of an interlocking theme. We shall see in the next series of charts that this 'mirroring' effect is by no means uncommon.

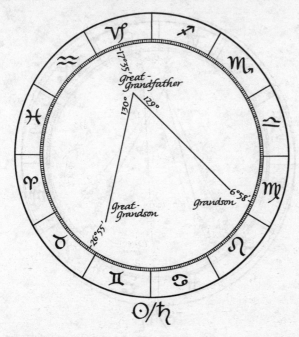

Figure 11.4 The Sun/Saturn midpoint in the charts of a grandfather, his grandson and his great-grandson.

The Freud Family

In the family Bible, Jakob Freud recorded two dates that were vital to *him*, the place and time of his *own* father's death (21 February 1856 at 4.00 p.m. LMT, 49 N 50, 24 E 00) and the place and time of birth of his first-born son, named Schlomo after his grandfather, later to be called Sigismund, then Sigmund. No details of any other family member were entered in Jakob's Bible, either before or after the birth of his first son.

We know from extensive documentation that Freud both idealized his father and saw him also as a rather weak man, occasionally even as a cowardly one. Jakob Freud's gift to his son of a large illustrated Bible, full of pictures of the Egyptian gods, had the

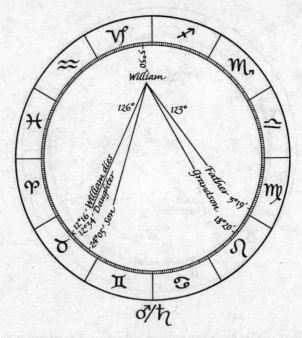

Figure 11.5a The Mars/Saturn midpoints of a family.

most profound effect on the young Freud. The history of Egypt fascinated him, and he became an avid and highly knowledgeable collector of Egyptian antiquities, re-creating on his desk and in his house the illustrations he had pored over in childhood. He mythologized his relationship with Jakob as a re-working of the Biblical legends of Joseph and Moses, and the psychic meaning of religion was an issue that dominated his life; in some respects even more so than for Jung.

Recognizing so much Neptune in all of the above we may choose to plot 'writing in a Bible' in the form of the Mercury/Neptune midpoint for the three men, to see what this may tell us. When we lay out the Mercury/Neptune midpoints for Freud and the dates for both his father's and grandfather's deaths (Figure

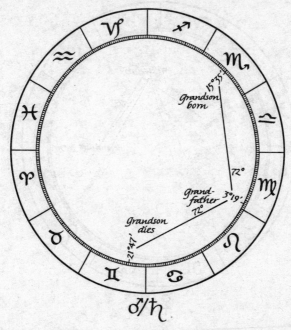

Figure 11.5b The Mars/Saturn midpoint for the birth and death of a grandson, phased from the grandfather's Mars/Saturn position.

11.6) – in other words we begin to explore the continuation of what may be a family theme – we see that Jakob Freud's Mercury/Neptune midpoint falls *exactly* midway between the Mercury/Neptune midpoints for his father's death and his son's death. Thus Jakob's own birthday lies at the midpoint of these two identical events. Note that this is on the *exact* day, not the day before or the day after.

If we pursue one aspect of death and turn to the Chiron theme, which also encompasses some of the issues of healing, being isolated and 'un-owned' by society, and the confrontation of personal human mortality (a major Freudian theme), we see it is strikingly picked up by the female line. Figure 11.7 shows Freud's Sun/Chiron midpoint to within a degree – in other words, to

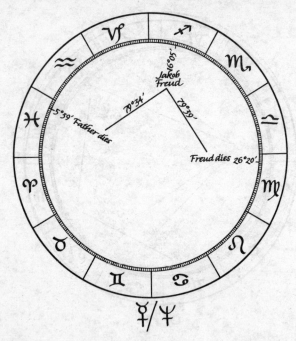

Figure 11.6 The Mercury/Neptune position in the chart of Freud's father (Jakob), and its position at the birth and death of Jakob's own father and the death of his son Sigmund.

within *a day* – of being exactly at the midpoint of both his mother's and his wife's death dates *and* his daughter's birth and death dates. We can also see that his mother was actually born with her Sun/Chiron midpoint just two degrees away from its placement at her death. As a matter of fact, on the day Freud himself died his Sun/Chiron midpoint was just *one day* away from the position it held when his father Jakob died.

Examples of this continuous process of symbolic expression come at us from many quarters. The Mars/Neptune theme – central to Freud's work on the sexual revelations of dreams – is graphically portrayed in Figure 11.8. Here we see that Freud was born when his Mars/Neptune midpoint was half-way between its

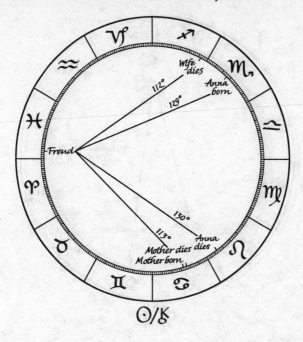

Figure 11.7 The Sun/Chiron midpoint for Freud, together with that for his mother's birth, his wife's death, and the birth and death of Anna Freud.

position at the birth of his wife and its position at the birth of his daughter, who was, of course, also to become a psychoanalyst. Both mother and daughter were to die within days of an identical Mars/Neptune placement. Note especially how his daughter Anna died with Mars/Neptune *exactly* midway between her father's natal Mars/Neptune position and her own natal Mars/Neptune placement. This again strongly implies some specific resonance to a particular degree or aspect within the genetic unfoldment of a whole family.

What we are seeing here goes way beyond conventional synastry in both its precision and its implication. Portrayed in these charts are examples of interlocking patterns of symbolic geometry,

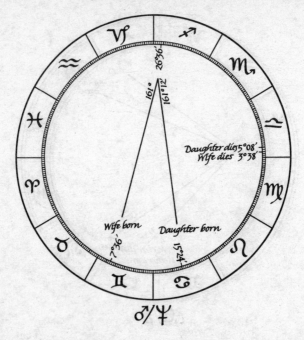

Figure 11.8 Mars/Neptune in the charts of Freud (at 26 SG 36), his wife and his daughter. Note that the Mars/Neptune position for the death of his daughter falls half-way between his birth and her birth.

spanning generations with remarkable internal consistency. The theme of one incarnation flows into another, and it would seem that as the partners alternate in Shiva's dance so the moments of life and death mark the boundaries of their exchange.

If we lay out the Mars/Saturn theme for the Freud family (Figure 11.9), which we have already commented on in another context in Chapter 8, we can see at a glance how non-random its distribution actually is. As we have observed in a previous case above, one pattern here is an exact trine spanning generations, and in another, that of Anna Freud herself, we can note how Mars/Saturn at her death has returned *exactly* to its natal position. Such repetition of family themes in the form of transits or

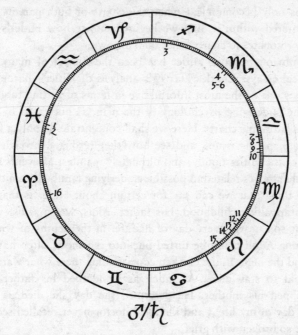

Figure 11.9 The Mars/Saturn midpoints in the charts of some of the Freud family. (1) Birth of Freud's father. (2) Death of Sigmund Freud. (3) Lucian Freud born. (4) Ernst Freud born. (5) and (6) Birth and death of Anna Freud. (7) Freud's mother born. (8) Freud's mother dies. (9) Freud's daughter Sophie dies. (10) Freud's father dies. (11) Freud's wife born. (12) Freud's grandfather dies. (13) Freud's daughter Mathilde born. (14) Freud born. (15) Mathilde dies. (16) Freud's brother dies.

contacts which symbolize them – in this case the 'death instinct' – can be dramatic enough within the history of the individual family. But sometimes, when patterns in the sky repeat the patterns in a parent's charts, the effect is catastrophic.

Adolf Hitler

While many of the events in Hitler's life can be plotted by using conventional transits, the full implication of some of the chart patterns only become clear when the charts of both parents are incorporated within it, and we begin to notice how Hitler's astrology resonates to charts other than his own.

For obvious reasons Hitler has been the subject of many astrological essays. Charles Harvey's analysis of Hitler's harmonic charts[1] is one of the most informative in terms of getting to grips with the underlying psychology of the man, as portrayed by the various harmonic charts. Here we shall concentrate on only a few, but quite specific issues, and see how they resonate through the charts of the Hitler family, and ultimately manifest as events that are in themselves related to possible underlying family dynamics.

One thing that we can say for certain about Hitler is that he had an appalling childhood. His father, Alois, was a sadist who beat his son nearly every day of his life. In the depths of winter the young Adolf could be turfed out into the snow, often having to spend the night in the chicken coop, finding there what warmth he could to stay alive. As much as he loathed his father, he worshipped his mother. He described the day she died as the 'worst day of my life',[2] and the local doctor never recalled seeing anyone so broken with grief.

In the years which followed his mother's death, during which time Alois also passed on, Hitler pursued an erratic art education and served with distinction during the whole of the First World War. Despite conspicuous bravery he remained a Corporal throughout the entire war, his superior officers noting that he 'lacked leadership potential'. This observation would appear to confirm the suggestion that during the First World War superior officers were much the same on both sides of the trenches.

After the war, and a long period of extreme poverty and aimless drifting, Hitler became involved with the German Workers' Party. He spoke on its behalf on many occasions and became actively involved in its administration. In due course he was able to disband the organization and on 20 February 1920 set up in its stead the National Socialist German Workers' Party – the Nazi Party.

Shortly after first becoming aware of the original German Workers' Party, Hitler spoke on its behalf. It was a day that

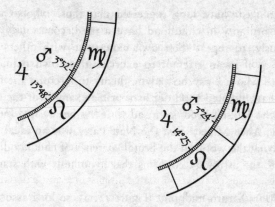

Figure 11.10 The Mars/Jupiter midpoint in the chart of Hitler's father (left) and its repetition on the day of Hitler's first speech for the DAP (right). This is the only time this century that this repetition happens.

changed his life; in *Mein Kampf* he records joyfully 'I can speak!' Not only could he speak, he captivated his audience from the start and even extracted 300 Marks from them for Party funds. From that moment on his political life took an almost fated course.

We can see in Figure 11.10 that on the day of Hitler's first speech Mars and Jupiter stood in the sky almost *exactly* as they did in his *father's* chart. Planets which must have been experienced in their bluntest and most brutal all through his childhood repeated an exact pattern – *for the only time this century* – as one of the world's most brutal political careers began. As the parental pattern re-formed in the sky, so was the brutality of its original expression given a hard voice in the world.

In both cases Jupiter falls on Hitler's Mars/Saturn midpoint and Mars on Hitler's Sun/Moon midpoint. The Mars/Saturn theme dominates the history of the Hitler years, perhaps as the active expression of the parental anger that was also experienced by the young Hitler at the centre of his being – Sun/Moon. This repetition of Mars and Jupiter in the sky also underlines the basic cornerstone of Hitler's policy for a reborn Germany – *military expansion*.

Psychologists have long suggested that those who experience extreme brutality in childhood have a need, consciously or unconsciously, to repeat their own experience with others as the victims, as if in an attempt to exorcize their own pain. Those historians who use psychoanalytic theory to interpret the facts of history have pointed to Hitler as a prime example of the sadist's victim who himself becomes a sadist. It has been noted by many, including Alice Miller,[3] that the Nazi Party was an ideal vehicle for repaying the world in the brutal currency of childhood. As we shall see, the astrology confirms this hypothesis with staggering accuracy.

The Mars/Saturn midpoint (Figure 11.11), so long associated – in its negative form – with death, cruelty and the 'war machine', plays a central role: on the very day Hitler formed the Nazi Party, the Mars/Saturn midpoint was *precisely* the same as it was in his *father's* chart – to the very minute. Again, Hitler's life appears to be resonating to a pattern which pre-exists his own life. It was as if the Party were a living tribute to Alois, one which somehow resuscitated him or reinforced the synastry that had existed in life between father and son. Whatever had been embedded in childhood became permanently alive in the Party apparatus.

Alois's Mars/Saturn midpoint falls exactly on Hitler's close natal Moon/Jupiter conjunction, and picks up both his Moon/Jupiter and Saturn/Neptune midpoints. Again, at a central Lunar and feeling level, this is a graphic image of how Hitler's formative years were corrupted and blighted by his father's brutality. It is worth noting that when the Sun crossed that *exact* point on 30 June 1934, Hitler gave the order for the systematic murder of his former brownshirt colleagues during the Night of the Long Knives.

Even more dramatic synastry between Hitler, his parents and the major events of his life can be found when we observe the very precise patterns which exist when specific midpoints are plotted in on a single chart form.

In Figure 11.12 we see the Mars/Saturn midpoint at work again in the Hitler family. On the date Hitler declared the Nazi Party to

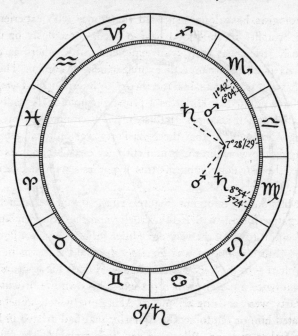

Figure 11.11 The Mars/Saturn midpoint in the chart of Hitler's father (dotted line) and Mars/Saturn for the founding of the Nazi party. The noon positions are only 1 minute apart and thus would be exact during the course of the day.

be the only legal party in Germany – the beginning of his absolute dictatorship – Mars/Saturn in the sky is *exactly* as far from his Mother's Mars/Saturn as his father's was at birth. In other words, viewed from *his mother's perspective*, she is at the midpoint of his father's and his dictatorship's Mars/Saturn midpoints. Similarly, the Mars/Saturn midpoint on the day she died lies *exactly* the same distance away from Hitler's own Mars/Saturn midpoint; thus issues of the relationship between Hitler, his father, the life and death of his mother and the formalization of his tyranny are *more precisely linked by astrology* than any possible psychological theory could hope to match.

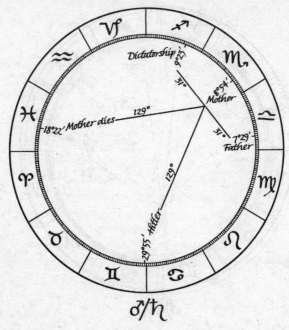

Figure 11.12 Mars/Saturn in the charts of Hitler, his parents and on the day of his assuming total dictatorial control of Germany.

In harmonics, such a relationship which focuses on how several bodies relate to a single point is called *phasing*. It may be necessary now to use the term *phased midpoints* to indicate when we are exploring such a dynamic.

Staying with Mars/Saturn, we see that when it is phased from Hitler's own Mars/Saturn midpoint (Figure 11.13) it picks up a major mirror-image of individuals and events.

Goering, Speer and Hess all have their Mars/Saturn midpoints 169° from Hitler's own Mars/Saturn. We have already noted that the Nazi Party came into being when Mars/Saturn repeated its placement in the chart of Hitler's father; here Rommel's Mars/Saturn is only a degree away and both mirror Mars/Saturn on the day a bomb nearly killed Hitler in 1939 at an attempted assassina-

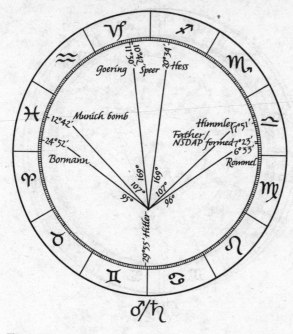

Figure 11.13 Mars/Saturn in the charts of Hitler, his staff and two major events.

tion. It is important to remember here that his father also nearly killed Hitler on many occasions and Rommel, too, was actively involved in the July 1944 plot to assassinate the Führer. Thus these zodiacal points pick up *content* as well as *contact*, and the themes actively link and mirror across Hitler's own Mars/Saturn axis.

Figure 11.14 shows another example of phased midpoints. Here the Sun/Uranus midpoint (self-will) is phased from Hitler's father. Alois's Sun/Uranus midpoint lies at the centre of the beginning of Hitler's dictatorship and the date of the foundation of the Third Reich. Similarly Sun/Uranus for his mother is equally phased from the Sun/Uranus of his mistress, Eva Braun. If we look at the same Sun/Uranus midpoint from the 'point of view' of the

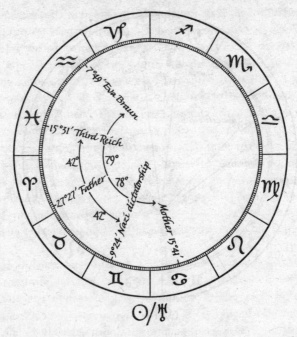

Figure 11.14 Sun/Uranus in the charts of Hitler's father, mother, wife, the foundation of the Third Reich and the declaration of Hitler's dictatorship.

foundation of the Third Reich (Figure 11.15), we see that its position on that day is on the midpoint of Hitler's suicide (perhaps the ultimate act of 'self-will') and its position on the day his mother died.

If we look at this from another perspective, that of the Sun and Saturn, we see the same theme almost identically re-stated.

In Figure 11.16 the Sun/Saturn midpoint for his mother's death is exactly conjunct its position at the foundation of the Third Reich, prompting us to question if some of its mausoleum-like architecture is in some way a tomb to his own buried feelings. This point is 160° from the Sun/Saturn midpoint in his father's chart, which itself might have no particular significance were it not for the Sun/Saturn position at Hitler's suicide – half-way, and on the midpoint, between the two.

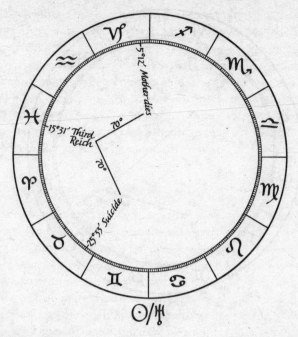

Figure 11.15 Sun/Uranus midpoints phased from the foundation of the Third Reich.

Finally, Mars/Neptune in Figure 11.17 shows what might be a key underlying dynamic in Hitler's life. If Mars/Neptune indicates a point of deception, something sexually ambiguous, a misdirected libido, a confused intention or one of the many similar possibilities astrologers have given to it over the years, then this figure gives us a graphic picture of the Mars/Neptune energy at work.

Here the Mars/Neptune midpoints for Hitler, his mother, his father's death and his attack on Poland all form a virtually perfect Grand Cross. The force that began with his first speech, when the Mars/Neptune of that day *also* marked the point of his father's death, can be seen as the resonant expression of one of the most basic psychic dynamics, the Oedipus complex. Here the Mars/Neptune axis of the son bisects that of his mother's birth and his

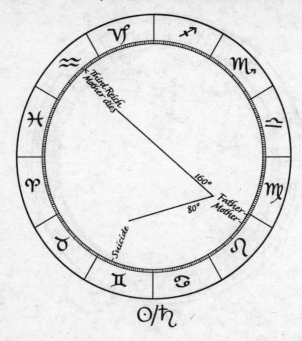

Figure 11.16 Sun/Saturn midpoints for births and deaths in the Hitler family. Note again the tendency for an event to take place at the midpoint of two others.

father's death, and links directly to what many would see as its symbolic expression – the rape of a country. Again, we are seeing an event that has been enacted by an individual emerging in part out of patterns which pre-existed that individual's life, and described by astrology with absolute precision.

Group Charts

If we take the trouble to dig beneath the more obvious layers of the birth chart we can see that astrology must function as some form of process or continuum, and that it will never be understood in terms of a static birth chart alone.

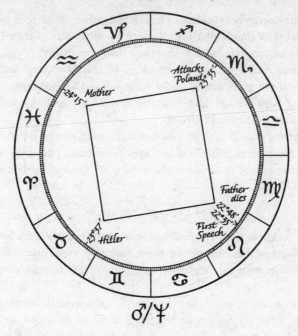

Figure 11.17 The Mars/Neptune midpoints for Hitler, his mother's birth, his father's death and his invasion of Poland which, of course, started the Second World War. The Mars/Neptune for Hitler's first speech for the DAP is conjunct its position on the day of his father's death, as was Mars/Jupiter (see Figure 11.10).

In the few examples we have explored we see that events and individuals are intermixed in the flow of time, that actions and their consequences blur together, first one appearing to influence the other, then in turn appearing to fall under the sway of what has gone before. Again and again we are forced to reconsider how we may be interacting with our own past, and with the past of others, as we move within the matrix of time. The concept of a primal or collective zodiac may help to focus on some aspects of this bewildering situation, as it suggests that there are key, common points to which we connect, and which we, in our own turn, may actively influence. Thus individuals may be seen to act out, and thus alter, collective issues, or by the nature of their birth actually incorporate them within their own personality.

Viewing the processes of astrology in this way may demand that we think more deeply about what – if any – boundaries exist between who we are and what we do. This possibility will be returned to in the final chapter.

What we should look at now are some examples of individuals being brought together around specific events, and how such events can mirror in all of them around quite specific degrees.

The Challenger Explosion

In this example, given Figure 11.18, we have the Mercury/Saturn midpoint for the moment of the *Challenger* explosion, and its relationship with the Mercury/Saturn midpoints for the crew of seven.

We can see at once that they form a dramatically consistent pattern. Mercury/Saturn itself may give us an image of a 'final journey' or 'death through travel', but equally reflects the highly disciplined nervous system and controlled mental processes that are prerequisites for astronauts. As we are so often reminded, major aspects of the personality may become reflected again and again in life as events. Here we see that only the astronaut McNair is left out of the mirror-image synastry that emerges when we lay out all the Mercury/Saturn placements.

Assessing the statistical probability of all this is extremely complex, but as a step towards this, a modified version of Mark Pottenger's excellent aspect-counting program, FAR, was created by the author to handle midpoints. During the eleven years from 1939 to 1950, which covered the period during which all the astronauts were born, only some 43° of the zodiac, from 15° Sagittarius to 28° Capricorn, could *not* have been occupied by the Mercury/Saturn midpoint, leaving the vast majority of the chart open to potential Mercury/Saturn occurrences – which, as we can see, did *not* happen. In fact, the Mercury/Saturn midpoint

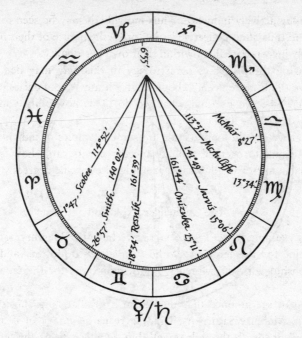

Figure 11.18 The Mercury/Saturn midpoints in the charts of the *Challenger* crew, phased from the Mercury/Saturn position on the day the *Challenger* was lost.

occupied each possible degree for between one and fifty-three days during these eleven years, giving a mean of 26.5. None of the astronauts' birth dates fell during a peak, but Smith and Jarvis were born on days when the total contacts were twenty-six and twenty-seven days respectively. The others were Scobie (eight days), Resnik (twenty-four days), Onizuka (twenty-four days), McCauliffe (eleven days) and McNair (twenty-five days). Thus all the astronauts were born on low to average days for Mercury/Saturn degree placements.

The main point, however, which does have to be considered is the remarkable consistency of pattern, or phasing. No attempt has been made to quantify this statistically, but seven further charts

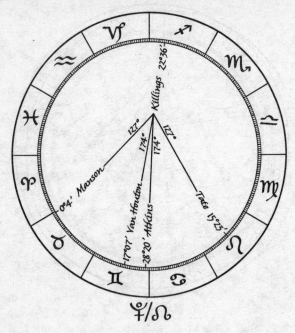

Figure 11.19 The Pluto/Node midpoints for the Sharon Tate killings.

calculated for random dates between 1939 and 1950 showed no such consistencies whatsoever; readers are encouraged to try further such samples for themselves.

Other Group Events

Particularly dramatic events which, in one way or another, pull people into participating within their expression have often been explored astrologically. One such event was the Los Angeles killing of the actress Sharon Tate, on 9 August 1969, by members of the so-called Manson Family.

Figure 11.19 shows the Pluto/Node midpoints for the night of the murder, and we see how Sharon Tate's Pluto/Node midpoint is phased with Charles Manson's, as are those of two of her

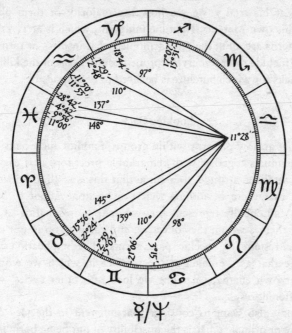

Figure 11.20 The Mercury/Neptune midpoints in the 7th harmonic for Peter Sutcliffe (whose 7th harmonic ME/NE is at 11 Libra 28) and for its position on seventeen dates for attacks and murders believed to have been carried out as a result of 'voices from God'.

killers, Susan Atkins and Leslie Van Houton. This midpoint is often associated with 'fated' or deeply powerful events, as we have seen in the previous chapter with Adolf Hitler's Pluto/Node midpoint.

In England, a man who became known as the Yorkshire Ripper confessed to the murder of thirteen female victims, although there may have been further attacks not dealt with at his trial. The man, Peter Sutcliffe, was a paranoid schizophrenic who believed he was acting under God's orders to kill prostitutes, the occupation of many of his victims. If we look (Figure 11.20) at the Mercury/ Neptune midpoint – the voices from Heaven to which Sutcliffe referred at his trial – we see how the majority of them phase around his own Mercury/Neptune midpoint, which is at 11 LI 28. The patterns are all in the 7th harmonic (what inspires or turns us on) and include the Mercury/Neptune positions for all the killings and attacks for which Sutcliffe is believed to be responsible.

Looking Back

In looking at how patterns within groups, families and events can link individuals together with remarkable precision, it is easy to adopt a fatalistic attitude, to assume that this was all 'destined to be' and that there is nothing that can be done about it. Such patterns can equally represent how we may be resonating to underlying themes within the collective, and carrying on in our own lives the residue of specific past events. The implication here might be that as we changed the manner in which we worked with our own energy, so might we lock into other cycles, with quite different results.

We may also want to consider that inherent in the idea of a collective or primal zodiac is the possibility of our being born 'into' the process of events and subsequently adding to them by our own actions. Such happenings would not be fated or pre-destined by past lives or the laws of karma, but would naturally emerge from the core material contained in those degrees which are activated at the moment of our birth, and our reactions to this material.

In this respect we are all born into the *history* of something which pre-exists our own individual consciousness, and is active in its own way without the participation of that consciousness. Indeed, even the body into which we are born has a genetic history of its own which resonates, as we have seen with the 'red-hair' example, to quite specific planetary cycles, regardless of whatever else might be happening.

Such possibilities also demand that we may need to look again at how Mind and Body might co-exist – or how they might *not*, as the case may be. For there is no doubt, as in the case of many transvestites, all transsexuals and certain schizophrenics (and in many less dramatic examples such as eating disorders), that a significant proportion of people do not feel at home in their bodies at all. This may not be all due to socially acquired values. Events which are already in operation, which are under way at the time of our birth, remind us that we are each born, to use R. D. Laing's analogy, as a 'stone-age baby into a civilized world', and have to make the best of what we may find there.

An image we might get from the concept of a primal zodiac is of life as a process which knits together all that which is buried within the degrees of our birth date, and that which is subsequently liberated through the act of Being. It is as if all which exists, timeless and simultaneous, as memories and symbols, is suddenly accessible to our Being at the moment of birth, to set down within the track of time, and to make of it what we will in the course of life.

The ways in which we might confront what we are, and how we might accept or reject certain aspects of that which we find within ourself, are often related to the workings of one of astrology's more secret domains: the eighth house. In the following chapter we shall see to what extent this might be justified.

12.

The House of Ill-repute

☆ ☆ ☆ ☆ ☆ ☆ ☆ ☆ ☆

It is ironic that from the *solar* point of view the 8th house corresponds to that part of the day when, for most of us, the sun is at its warmest and most comforting. During the late part of long summer afternoons, when we might ideally choose to do nothing more demanding than sit in a deckchair and stare into space, the sun is crossing the darkest corner of the sky, touching the point that echoes the year's end and winter's encroachment. This part of the sky, which in the birth chart becomes the 8th house, symbolizes the deepest and most profound area of our psychological development, and perhaps because of this fact has the worst reputation of any sector of the diurnal circle.

Up to now we have used a number of quite precise examples to explore the idea of events or sensations being repeated as specific degrees of the zodiac are triggered; we should not forget that major *themes* also repeat, sometimes in a more general manner. In some respects the relationship between an overall theme and its specific expression bears comparison with the symbolism of the houses and the midpoints contained within. The major themes of life are common to all of us, but their particular expression is more focused, and consequently individually experienced and interpreted.

In Chapter 4 we considered if it is really correct to think of there being an ultimate 'truth' to a situation or a person. It may well be that what we perceive as being 'true' owes more to the manner in which we interpret something than to the thing itself, if indeed it were ever possible to see it. However, whether or not this view is acceptable, there seems no doubt that we are constantly drawn to re-experiencing or re-discovering certain aspects of ourself. These are generally connected with experiences which continue to disturb our own perceptions, as if something is constantly tugging at our sleeve, telling us that all is *not* well.

The process we go through to search for what we believe may at last be the truth is associated in astrology with the eighth house. In some cases, of course, we shall be looking not at the literal 8th house, but at other manifestations of its basic principles expressed through strong Pluto aspects or in Scorpio themes; these parallel possibilities are always to be assumed.

The 8th House

Traditional astrologers seem to have had few problems in describing the inhabitants of the 8th house. Its natives were a bad lot, much given to fornication and general debauchery on a fairly basic level, interspersed with the odd power-struggle and a little light murder. It was a style of life no doubt paid for by inheritances gained through nefarious means and, what was worse, actively *enjoyed* by the participants. Conspicuous villainy is one thing, but to be seen so brazenly enjoying the fruits of the labour of others was a hard cross for the ancient moralists to bear. Threats of an early or violent death, losses through marriage or unwise speculation, betrayal through partnerships, and affliction by that old standby, the Pox, were to be heaped upon this house like divine refuse on what has come to be the zodiac's finest dumping ground.

One way or another there can be little doubt that this particular corner of the birth chart has assumed the role of celestial compost heap. While lip-service may be paid to the need and value of good quality mulch in the great scheme of things, the actual heap itself is seen primarily as a place to *dispose* of life's little disasters. All the psychic equivalents of those alien growths, found to be sprouting green fur at the back of the refrigerator one morning, which resemble nothing we ever recognize as having bought, are similarly disposed of at arm's length just in case we might suddenly realize what they once were. Metaphorically or in reality we consign them to the bowels of the earth, hoping they will ultimately turn into something more fragrant and socially useful, but preferring on the whole not to be kept closely informed of the actual mechanisms of their transformation.

Mystically orientated astrologers, shovelling through this detritus in search of the process that can reduce all it touches to the basic elements of life, for re-assembly on a better plane, came to re-interpret these primary descriptions in terms of death and rebirth. Viewed in this way the 8th house can now rise to the heights of the eagle, where before it could only hide under the rocks along with scorpions, toads, slugs and the nether end of the arachnid kingdom.

It *is* truly a house of extremes, capable of quite diverse expression, generally in those areas of life of which we are most unaware and which we often actively deny. Thus we ensure that it is a guarded area, frequently blank and seemingly impenetrable, giving the impression that nothing is really going on behind its walls. It can lie as if in a winter landscape, inert and unresponsive, quietly deflecting all attention towards the more exuberant abodes on either side. If you knock and inquire you will be directed to the wild philosophy parties taking place at number nine or the gatherings of open enemies frantically socializing at number seven.

It may appear as solid and aloof as a merchant bank. Cold, formal and efficient; sitting on cellars of hard currencies and bearer bonds, disdaining all but the very wealthy and even then receiving only by prior appointment. It is a place where deals are made and bargains struck. Bargains that one day will have to be honoured in full, when those things which are now said with a polite smile will take on quite a different meaning as the fine print is examined and the true cost assessed. Those who have not recognized that money is only the outward manifestation of power will neither receive nor survive a second appointment.

In the popular mythology of Hollywood it can also be the Old Dark House that Hides a Secret. It is that familiar gothic building set far from the road, obscured by trees and darkened by scudding clouds; a fatal attraction for the unwary traveller – generally depicted as female – whose dangerous curiosity will not sustain her through the night. For whatever is hiding there, whatever secret defied interment with the last of the family, still exerts a magnetic pull on anyone who passes by, as if some inner compass suddenly dips in recognition of a hidden mystery that lies just out of sight. However oblique or unknown, its reality stirs something in us that we all recognize, something from long ago that we thought had gone away with childhood.

It is this growing awareness of our continual connectedness to past events that begins to alert us to the true nature of the 8th house. It personifies the process of analysis for us, perpetually returning to question itself, to indulge in an unremitting re-assessment of its emotional roots, as if needing to know how to protect itself against the excesses of its own reactions. The timeless quality it embodies is an echo of Freud's depiction of the timeless *id*; where all that ever happened to us that we cannot assimilate still bides within, awaiting our silent acknowledgement as its incorporation into life.

Within the 8th house we recognize that what has happened to us emotionally is open to many interpretations which could never have been made at the moment of their experience. The material may have been too raw, too violent and too all-consuming to confront and re-direct; even to *touch* it, to acknowledge its existence with just a glance might have swept us away. It may also have been too subtle, too full of things felt deeply but incoherently, as a child confronts the overwhelming complexities of adult life, of its violence and betrayals, of love that manipulates and bludgeons, of affection and physicality that slides towards a dark intent.

Each unspoken event marks us and in some manner directs us to circle its memory, continuously re-tracing its pattern and repeating an echo of the original discord. There is within us the need to return and repeat the most primal of moments; to cut the cord that ties us to the dark side of our fate.

The 8th house resonates with these images of death and rebirth because they mark the place where the circle joins, where it can be cut, re-drawn and taken back into life. The 8th house strives to express the ultimate truth of this act and liberates the reservoir of healing power that crisis makes available to the psyche.

The fact that it is *crisis* rather than calm reflection or inner meditation that releases such potential hints at why the 8th house seems to come alive only when there is a threat of death. The death may be literal or symbolic, but in either event will almost certainly revolve around the issue of profound emotional change; a change that leaves the individual irrevocably altered in some way, dead to their previous life. It is as if the 8th house *can* only act in this manner, and continues to pull towards itself all the material that we have ignored for too long. As in a nuclear reactor, there is a need for a sufficient quantity to be present before anything can happen, before the critical mass is reached and a chain reaction can begin.

This issue of crisis and killing, of seeking the hidden forces or hunting something out, is a major theme of the 8th house and seems to take two clear forms. It can be 'killing' by the simple act of denial; a complete blocking out of early memories and their attendant energies, with the probable consequence of adopting a parallel attitude towards the external world. We might then take a controlling position with others, seeking to repress in them whatever echoes we detect of the themes held in abeyance within. But it is not something that can be left alone; the energies are too persistent and the need to seek them out is too strong. Life will conspire to create constant scenarios in which the potential for confrontation contains the sub-text of our original denials.

From the outside these will generally look like simple power struggles. We may ask ourselves why it is that we are continually getting embroiled with people who are trying to manipulate us, forcing us in all innocence to respond in similar style. We might feel continually threatened in some manner, finally needing to pre-empt our fears by taking the initiative and manipulating others from the start, rationalizing this by claiming that we seek only to secure our basic rights.

In extreme cases we might develop paranoid delusions which stem from our concealed confusions and are expressed in classic

8th house style. In such cases people are believed to know something about us, they seek to control us, to spy on our every move or endeavour to discover some guilty secret. We cannot trust anyone; even the most ordinary actions betray a sinister motive. The postman is really working for the government and is reading our mail, our boss is on the phone to our parents every day reporting our behaviour, strangers on buses are trying to entrap us by making sexual suggestions through a secret sign language.

While the list of clinically observed symptoms of paranoid behaviour is obviously extensive, they frequently revolve around issues of sex and power, control and domination, in which secret messages and hidden codes abound. People who symbolize power and authority in some form – policemen, social security staff, government workers, older members of the family and so on – are most likely to be the subject of paranoid projections and the issues are often those of revealing secrets, knowing something that others do not, or involve the existence of huge plots and conspiracies with manifest Plutonian themes.

In these extremities the 8th house is concerned with manipulation and power from the point of view of the victim. *Someone else* always seems to have the upper hand, *someone else* is calling the shots and making the running; there is nothing we can do but cover our tracks as best we can. This is perhaps because there is still too much trapped and locked away in childhood rooms, too strong an identification with the powerlessness of early years. Once familiar with what it is like to be powerless and afraid, this facet of the 8th house has the knowledge of a hunter's ways known only to the prey.

Such early experiences often embodied raw Pluto energy in some form of rape or emotional assault, which at the time had to be endured because there was no possible avenue of escape. The theme of incest, of the massive discrepancy in size and power between adult and child, is one that constantly recurs in 8th house issues. The individual may return again and again to this theme in the form of an involvement with huge organizations or a compulsive attraction to projects of massive cost or scale, which seem to echo the early proportions of childhood encounters with their sense of enormity and inevitability. The sensation of 'fate' that so often surrounds 8th house or Pluto issues mimics the child's perception of its role within the context of the parental world, and may also bring up other specific power issues which will be examined shortly.

The 'incest' motif may of course not be a literal sexual assault, but some form of coercion which inveigles the child into acting against its own desires, making it the guilty party in a secret complicity. This might take the form of crude emotional manipulation by which the adult dominates the child, or indeed even *gives* the child unasked-for power by suggesting that it is the sole purpose of the parents' staying together or the recipient of endless sacrifices which were paid in blood and suffering, now due in fealty to the parents.

As in the case of sexual incest, however, this coercion will almost certainly force the child into a collusion against his or her own real feelings, having to deny and negate them in order to avoid destroying the framework of the family by either expressing its own demands or its outrage. In such a situation the child is often given a terrible power; it has a *secret*. It knows what crimes have been committed, what power games are being played and whom to accuse, but to do so would be to destroy itself. It can only endure and wait. It is a classic 8th house posture and explains why those with such a placement can so often sense duplicity in others with a shark's acuity for blood, and then respond to it with the compressed rage of years.

The other side of the 8th house comes into play when the issue of 'killing' is not one of denial. Something is not obliterated from consciousness because it is too painful. It is 'killed' because it is no longer necessary or has to be got rid of as it blocks future development. In practice, however, these two sides are often hinged in a polar response; first controlling, then eliminating. Often this is played out within the 8th house as a constant battle, with first one side and then the other gaining dominance. It is as if it is forever seeking a way to become the mirror image of itself, to reverse the initial untenable position. To this end it can assail the barriers of sex and death, pursuing a union of perfection and timelessness which obliterates all perceived duality.

Fusing the masculine and feminine elements within us in an attempt to achieve some form of rebirth or transcendent state recalls the alchemical writings of Jung. It is in these works that he elaborated on the nature of individuation, the key process of human integration which he believed could grow out of the mystery of this inner conjunction.

Jung had the Sun and Moon lying in opposition in his 7th harmonic chart, which would suggest that he was inspired or turned on by the concept of bringing together opposing polarities. In fact virtually all of his work as a healer and thinker rests on the concept of bringing together and reconciling *opposites*. His theory of the workings of the unconscious *demands* that oppositions exist, that they are actually created through the process of adopting a specific stance towards life and that a major purpose of our existence is to try to bring together within ourselves these opposing forces which we, in part, bring into being.

We can see at once that his own Sun/Moon contact in this harmonic is of primary importance, and to miss it is to miss the main thrust of his whole life. In evaluating Jung's contribution to psychological thought we must also recognize his own probable need to see things in terms of basic polarities, and how these would tend to constellate around the issues of masculine and feminine. This may not be the only way of exploring our inner divisions, and in choosing to view things from a different perspective we might recognize that some apportionments are not archetypally pre-programmed as may first appear. The divisions that occur within us may not all be laid at the door of a universal cosmic sexuality; we might simply be doing the splitting ourselves.

In Chapter 6 we noted what appeared to be a strong Uranian symbolism attending the actual moment of the infant's separation from the mother, the cutting of the umbilical cord. The sense of shock or alienation that can accompany this experience is, as we have seen, well attested. A major component of the Uranus principle in the course of life revolves around the issues of individuality and identity. Much of what comprises 'identity', our sense of who we are, is that which we accept or do not accept of ourselves.

Certain characteristics or feelings we are happy to acknowledge; others we deny. What we might split off from ourselves will tend to become repressed or projected – classic 8th house phenomena – though the actual process of 'splitting' is more complex and might involve what we consciously and unconsciously believe ourself to be. In other words, a probable contradictory 'truth' of ourselves which the 8th house will re-work again and again in the course of life.

In this respect each of the outer planets has its own version of the Truth. While Neptune and Pluto have room for some very contradictory concepts – Neptune in particular! – the Uranian approach is extremely one-sided. This accords in the world with the well-known image of Uranus as the fanatic. It often surfaces in fascist guise as a political theory or way of life that is supposedly universal and must be believed by everyone simply because it is true. In this frame of mind there is *no* opposition allowed, as those so possessed by this way of thinking cannot conceive that an opposing view is even possible. In the terminology of neo-Trotskyism it is simply the result of 'false consciousness'. Counter-argument can only be built on 'false consciousness' and thus every counter-argument is wrong by definition. This is not only very convenient for the hard of thinking, it is also very Uranian.

On a purely psychological level, much of this need for a perfect and uncontradictable vision of the world probably stems from issues evolving out of our initial interpretation of early separation experiences such as birth. Here the infant becomes aware of there being an Other for the first time, and is dethroned from its position in the centre of the universe. There is something outside of and independent of its experience which is perceived as threatening. Existentialist philosophers, putting Uranus to work in another of its natural environments, have explored the possible threat of the Other to the Self in many of its guises. At his most extreme, Jean-Paul Sartre described the Other as being a threat to the Self by its very existence; the Self can have no certainties in a world where the Other lives. Here we get another clear sight of Uranus in action, of the fear that *being separate and different* actually engenders, and of the awful void that this separation creates. In the silence of that emptiness the Self may become defined by the Other, and annihilated by that contradictory definition. All too often this fear results in the compensatory claim of Uranus that we are all the same with the same needs, same hopes and same wishes. At a more personal level we often try to maintain an inner equilibrium by splitting situations or feelings into two halves; that which we can cope with and that which we cannot.

While poets and lovers have known from the time of the Gods that humans can love and hate the same person at the same time, it was not until Sigmund Freud made it part of his official policy for the human race that the process came to be more fully understood. For Freud it became axiomatic that for there to be a powerful *hate* stemming from early experiences there also has to be a powerful, unconscious *love* of equivalent proportion. Similarly, overwhelming protestations of perfect filial or conjugal affection were to him a clear indication that something *very different* was cooking on the back burner.

Freud was the first to describe the processes whereby individuals tended to act out one part of an inner polarity while denying or projecting its opposite component, generally responding to it only in others. He did *not* see such ruptures as indicative of a cosmic process, dependent on ideas of Yin and Yang or archetypal oppositions, but solely as the mechanism by which humans tended to deal with their inner conflicts.

While this certainly oversimplifies some issues it also demystifies many others and makes them accessible to understanding and change. In having to confront the possibility that we are, at one level, simply *choosing* not to see an important side of ourself, we can guard against the common astrological tendency towards convenient esoteric rationalizations. We may have to recognize that not everything we do is a literal mirror of the imagined macrocosm. Some of our astrological processes may be more instinctual than symbolic, and the people who join the League Against Cruelty to Cats and then demand hanging, flogging and castration for all moggie-bashers might simply have found a socially acceptable way to keep in touch with their latent sadism.

Where the 8th house really starts to incorporate such issues is in the dynamics of its own polarity with the 2nd. Together, they are often seen as describing in some way the balance of our resources. The Taurean, 2nd house marks the more external world of money, property and practical everyday possessions. The 8th house can describe our inner, more complex reserves. These reserves tend to be our emotional values, the more intricate financial matters arising from the complexities of marriage or intimate partnerships, and consequently our sexual attitudes and attachments. In effect, how we have invested – a very 8th house word – our energy in the world.

The 8th house forces us to ask how we use this inner energy and to question to what symbols, situations or individuals it is primarily attached. In other words, it functions here as the process which helps us uncover the truth of ourselves, in part by bringing to the surface all that we identify with.

The Resources of the Other

As we have seen, of key importance here is how well we are in touch with our emotional roots. These early attachments and experiences go a long way in defining what we are prepared to accept of ourselves, and in turn what our admitted and unadmitted 'resources' are. What we see as 'inside' and 'outside' of ourselves – us or the Other – and our subsequent reactions to any denied material starts very early. While most of the issues are, in fact, very much of the 8th house, the process of denial, of cutting off, may be in part more Uranian. It is as if the Pluto/8th house energy describes the latent content of what is repressed and the manner in which it is dealt with – the process of the 8th house already described – and Uranus has been used at an instinctual level to maintain the equilibrium of the ego by cutting off what is unacceptable, allowing only the good to be incorporated.

The first object the infant has to incorporate is its mother, and it is at the breast that the first 'splitting' process begins.

The work of psychoanalyst Melanie Klein on the early months of life focuses on the procedure of how the baby appears to deal with its primary relationship with the world. The images of 'good' and 'bad' mothers referred to in Chapter 2 are built in the first weeks of life as the baby's rage and devouring needs are projected on to its relationship with the breast, or emerge in the issues of feeding and holding.

Klein maintained that the infant experiences its mother in two main ways. The 'good' mother, the 'good breast', is the mother who provides milk on demand, who comforts and changes the baby, who always holds it when it cries – in short, is perfect and fulfils the baby's every need. The 'bad' mother, the 'bad breast', is of course the opposite; but the bad breast receives its energy from the *baby*.

In effect, the baby manufactures the experience of the bad breast out of its own rage and frustration and its inability to transfer these on to the good, comforting breast, on to the mother when she is doing everything the baby wants. The baby cannot accept that it feels such rage against the good breast, so it creates another one, another image of the mother, which might become as dangerous and devouring as the baby perceives its own demands to be. Later this projection will seem to take on a life of its own, as all good projections do, and probably come back in many guises. Again, we might want to compare this approach to the formation of alternative 'mother images' with the archetypal concept proposed by Jung.

The relevance of the Freud/Klein theory for astrologers is in its relationship with the primary power issues of the 8th house. The patterns are laid down there and may also indicate how we may subsequently deal with rage; are we eaten up by it? We also get some powerful images of the 'either/or' nature of how we tend to deal with powerful unconscious and *conscious* feelings. Through the process described by Freud and Klein we can both deny and express our 'forbidden' urges at the same time. We deny that *we* are doing anything, but we can liberate enough of the energy to release the inner tension and make it bearable. It is just that, from our point of view, it is not *us* who is actively expressing these urges, it is someone else. Thus we can see that the questions raised by this approach, such as 'who *really* has the power, who *really* is doing what to whom' are central to our understanding of the 8th house. It may indeed be part of the 8th house function to endeavour to recapture the lost power and energy split off in infancy.

The other major issue of feeding similarly brings us back into the 2nd/8th polarity; the baby quickly learns to manipulate its mother by refusing to eat. This direct 'denial of food = denial of love' message can drive even the most placid of parents into paroxysms of rage: guess whose rage it *really* might be. This is the control of resources at a most primitive level. It is an attempted dictatorship over what is to be incorporated into the body/psyche, and intertwined with issues of love, aggression and survival. Parents can react to their baby's refusal to take food as if it is in imminent danger of dying – one of the central motifs of the 8th house – it is the battle of wills which follows such episodes that often tests out major aspects of the parent/child relationship to the limit.

Having Your Friends for Dinner

The 8th house deals with the whole process of incorporation; from what is acceptable to take in, right through the process of its inner transformation to its ultimate elimination. As has been pointed out, we identify with what we are prepared to take into ourselves, we reject what we refuse to assimilate. Food that is the recipient of negative group projections looks revolting to us: slugs, snakes, weasels, rats and so on are abhorrent to the vast majority of Westerners and form no part of their diet for that reason alone.

Just how powerfully we can react to physical substances if they are, or are not, part of ourselves is quite remarkable. Those substances connected with the functions of life are intimately associated with the 8th house and consequently heavily overlaid with projections. Most people feel queasy at the sight of blood; some actually become hysterical when witnessing no more than a mild injury where scarcely any is shed. Blood is traditionally the medium that holds our life essence. In colloquial terms, it is through our blood that we inherit all our qualities and our fate. Its history is *our* history and in many societies 'blood-feuds' can be carried on for generations, even when there is no clear idea as to how the initial conflict started.

The declaration of a blood-feud or the signing of a pact in blood traditionally bind the participants to their respective destinies. From that moment on, all involved are held to their word and can never go back. Their previous existence has 'died' and now an obsessive purpose consumes their life. They can take on the burden of the family's guilt or rage and do whatever is required, for however long it takes to achieve the necessary goal or extract the required vengeance.

Such a pact can also be seen as a formal declaration of what takes place covertly in many families, where the 8th house holds the ancestral ghosts in thrall and remorselessly plucks at the weakest of each succeeding generation until finally its secret is exorcized by sacrifice or insight.

Blood is also one of the most powerful of human symbols and its shedding is a core 8th house image. The ritual spilling or drinking of human blood forms the basis of many cannibalistic religions, including Christianity. In drinking blood, some of the virtue of the deceased is absorbed by those who remain, ensuring that a vital part of the victim is now re-incorporated into the world of the living. This can be seen as an act of revenge, of worship, of incest or as a way of exorcizing guilt, depending on the manner of the victim's death and the purpose of the ritual.

It is very rare in societies that practised cannibalism for human meat or blood to be seen purely as an alternative food source. Many taboos surrounded what could or could not be eaten, and many of them mirror the incest taboos. One Polynesian tribal poet writes:

Your own mother,
Your own sister,
Your own pigs,
Your own yams that you have piled up,
You may not eat.

Other people's mothers,
Other people's sisters,
Other people's pigs,
Other people's yams that they have piled up,
You may eat.[1]

Pigs were, in effect, other people's *money*, and this poem is an indication of the powerful emotional undertow in the 2nd/8th polarity of possessions and their latent, psychic content: the taboo against consuming females of the same family extends to the property and money of that family as well. As the psycho-historian Eli Sagan puts it: 'The cannibal eats those who are *other* – who are *not me*. Civilized society enslaves or exploits or makes war on those who are not me – those who are not human.'[2] This 2nd/8th house division between that with which we can identify and that which has to be denied is expressed in human warfare with monotonous regularity. The different forms of aggression and rage are traditionally related to both houses and their correlation with the underlying motives of most wars – possession of property as a symbol of emotional power or the need to destroy one's own projections – is equally a part of classical astrological symbolism.

Cannibalism and the drinking of blood can also be an attempt to reconcile the victor with the vanquished and merge the aggressive urge with the need to possess and retain, healing an inner split that these instinctive drives can create. In such a way we finally own what we have killed. To make a victim part of our own body is the ultimate act of possession, and it is one that can be played out on many levels, depending on the needs of the society in which it takes place. It can be a simple act of revenge or it can achieve religious status, giving a literal rebirth to those who have died and the complete physical fusing of identities so often sought in 8th house sexuality.

The need to re-incorporate something of the gods that were presumed to have lived once on earth as mortals lies behind ceremonies where an individual or a substance is first made godlike through ritual and then consumed. Many sacrificial victims are first treated *as if* they were gods before being killed and eaten, as in many Aztec ceremonies, or the basic themes of eating human meat and drinking blood are paralleled in symbolism, as in the Christian mass. Some early forms of Christianity attempted to go further, to re-incorporate the 'forbidden' side of human nature that is so often held within the 8th house, as witnessed by Gnostic rituals involving the drinking of menstrual blood and semen.

It is almost certainly because of our unconscious identification with blood as our 'essential self' that we can become so distressed when we actually *see* it. The fear is, perhaps, at having to confront something that we know is inside us. While it is inside it is safe, but outside it is quite different: we can no longer control it. Like rage or feelings of hurt, it just spills out. We similarly do not object to having saliva in our mouth, but the moment it leaves our lips as spittle it becomes disgusting and supposedly disease-ridden, another recipient of group projections.

Groups themselves operate on similar lines. Those inside the group, held together by emotional or financial bonds, can regard themselves as being quite different from other mortals. Someone may be a vital member of a group for many years but on leaving there can be a profound change of attitude towards them. This is very common when people retire from work. They receive their cheques and gold watches, are told to 'come round any time for a chat', but rapidly discover that if they take up this offer they are treated with aloofness. After a while their colleagues react to the memory of their former workmates as if they were dead. Interestingly, it is *very* common for recently retired men to suffer a fatal illness, which might be regarded in part as taking the acting-out of a group projection to an extreme degree!

Blood and death also come together in their most basic and

ordinary form with the fact of women's menstruation. Here the flowing of blood indicates the loss of a potential life, and traditionally the woman becomes unclean and guilty until she has in some way atoned for the 'sin' of losing that life, of allowing it to bleed away unmourned. There are innumerable taboos surrounding the alleged uncleanliness of the menstruating woman – the woman who is actively in touch with the fearsome process of life and death, holding within her its flowing magic – and these are most succinctly formalized in the Western world with the Jewish ceremony of *mikvah*, the cleansing bath.

While many Jewish women may experience the *mikvah* as being more than a simple act of purifying the body after their period or the birth of a child, the fact remains that it is a ceremony imposed upon them by men and focuses exclusively around the issue of their spilling blood. Jewish men, in common with other Semitic races, also focus on the issue of *their* ritual bleeding: circumcision. Depending on the culture, circumcision must take place either in the first few days of life, or during early adolescence. In the Jewish faith it is a blood pact that seals a covenant with the God of Abraham, in other sects it marks the transition from boy to man. It is the one male period, as irrevocable a statement as the girl child's first bleeding, and like all rites of passage it marks the death of a former existence and reinforces the finality of that change.

It may also be that much of the obsessional neurosis which manifests as a phobia of touching that which is perceived as being unclean gets its compulsive energy from an unconscious identification with this aspect of the 8th house: of blood and death as being one. The image of blood as somehow unclean or contaminated is a peculiarly potent one, now revived via AIDS. That we may carry death within us is a possibility not easy to confront. That we may somehow get something inside us which poisons our 'life blood' and turns us into agents of our own destruction is an obvious outworking of the Plutonic theme.

Nowhere is the 8th house energy more powerfully expressed at a somatic level than over the issue of what happens to that which leaves us, that which we can no longer control, that which is no longer a part of our body. It is at this point, over the matter of early toilet training, that Pluto emerges with a vengeance from the royal drains.

Psychoanalysts maintain that urination and defecation are some of the earliest sexual experiences, not least because they make the infant aware of its genitals. This awareness follows after the oral stage – the baby's pleasure in sucking at the breast and taking milk – and it is termed, not unnaturally, the anal stage. Here the baby's pleasurable sensation focuses libido in a generalized manner around the genitals and broaches the issues of holding in and letting go. With the advent of toilet training the power issues these actions symbolize take on considerable proportions, which can lay down major patterns of behaviour in life. To see the significance of this it may be necessary first to explore some of Freud's concepts on the oral and anal stages, and see how they may be reflected in the polarity of the 2nd and 8th houses.

Stages of Sexual Development

In psychoanalytic terms everything that we take into ourselves is some form of oral gratification; it gives us pleasure which somehow or other mimics our very early feeding experiences. It is a pleasure not just in food, but in everything that we assimilate. Art and music are thus also oral pleasures; music comes in through our ears and visual images come in through our eyes. The connection of Taurus to music, art and food should not be missed at this point! Nor should the not too uncommon 2nd house problem of *over*-acquiring be ignored.

Unsatisfactory feeding experiences can lead to what has been termed *oral fixation*. Part of the libido, part of our essential driving force, becomes fixated or stuck over the issue of things coming in to us, an issue we may constantly return to. This might be through some overt eating problem, but is more likely to be connected to a neurotic inability to be satisfied, to become defined by *things*, to identify only with our property. We may need *more* pictures on our walls, *more* books on our shelves, *more* of every-thing in general to fill up some inner emptiness, and our language constantly reminds us of the underlying issues.

We talk about our *taste* in art, of whether or not something is *too sweet*, if a sentimental film has a *sickly* ending, if a novel leaves a *bitter* taste, or makes us feel *sick*. Our worst insult might be to call a painting pure *chocolate-box*. It is interesting that this Venus-ruled confection mirrors its interior sweetness on its exterior packaging so consistently. This has proved to be a fatal attraction to those with 2nd house or Venus problems, especially as a substi-tute for the other Venus function, relationships.

If the 2nd house symbolizes issues to do with acquiring material possessions or taking things or sensations *into* us, then the 8th house focuses on their eventual elimination. As we have seen, much of how we get rid of things, what we identify with or what we reject falls in the 8th domain along with such seemingly con-tradictory matters as sex, death and money. It is here that as-trology was one jump ahead of Freud. Indeed, we see once again that astrology is the only coherent body of knowledge that can make sense of this seemingly bizarre jumble of attributes. But we should not ignore what Freud has to offer us; his own understand-ing of these issues can shed some additional light on the underlying dynamics of the 2nd/8th polarity.

Traditional German legend contains a character called *Dukaten Scheisser*, an elflike creature who embodied two specifically Pluto-nian themes by excreting gold coins for fortunate peasants to find. The painter Rembrandt was much taken by this image and produced some semi-pornographic etchings of the elf engaged upon his task. This legend is perhaps the earliest non-astrological linkage of two classic 8th house themes: money and excrement. A duality that does not come together again until we meet them in the work of Freud.

Freud recognized early on that we tend to have a very ambiva-lent attitude towards money; we prize it and work for it, but claim that the pursuit of it is the root of all evil: another clear example of the splitting process at work. In his self-styled *drekkologikal* notebooks, in which he gathered observations while developing his ideas on anally related phenomena, Freud came to connect money with excrement in the sense that children come to recognize it as connected to something produced out of their own efforts for their parents' pleasure. Books advising parents on toilet training often underline this theme of 'baby's first gift to the world', though infants generally realize early on that it can also be less of a gift and more a source of emotional blackmail. It can gain its mother's praise and love by what it holds in or what it lets out; in this way the child's performance on the toilet is frequently a barometer of the shifting emotional relationship with the mother. Something that may well get played out on a much larger scale in adult life.

The anally fixated individual is often very concerned with praise and achievement, of doing things methodically, of seeing them through to the end and producing something tangible. The fixation can produce a very down-to-earth character, unwilling to let go of anything until it is 'done properly'. But however much such values may be appreciated by the world at large, its ambivalence towards the end-product of such efforts – money – is shown all too clearly in the language used to describe this 'filthy lucre'.

The successful businessman is *stinking rich* or *filthy rich*, even if he is considered to be as *common as muck* and *rolling in it*. And why shouldn't he be? After all, *where there's muck there's brass*. Even *doing his business* is itself a common euphemism for defecating. He has *made his pile* and is now *cock of the dung heap*. American army slang has it that 'on pay-day the Eagle shits'; in Hollywood it is said that 'Money is like manure: neither one of them is any use until it's spread around.'

We are psychically no nearer to reconciling the conflict symbolized by the activities of the little *Dukaten Scheisser* than were the German peasants of the Middle Ages, and in many ways this is unsurprising. We attach a tremendous importance to money and it comes to symbolize many conscious and unconscious desires which are, in many respects, quite unconnected to the substance itself. We hope that it will bring us happiness, even though Freud warns us quite categorically that it will *not*.

For him, all our later happinesses reflect aspects of childhood's primary needs which have been 'deferred' to adulthood. But children are completely and utterly indifferent to money; it means nothing to them, and its subsequent pursuit can never fill any of our fundamental desires. A quest for money alone is psychologically doomed to failure, and can only be viewed as a displaced attempt to heal some other ill or quell some hidden guilt.

Ironically, someone caught on this particular wheel probably revives all the early associations which surround a need to produce something out of the self, something that produces pleasure or wins praise. The circle becomes complete, for however well the infant performed on the toilet, however much praise was received, the final outcome is still something that is seen to be unwanted and disgusting, redolent of a guilt that still persists.

It is worth recalling here that some authorities claim that the German word for money – *Geld* – comes from the same root as the English *guilt*. Particularly significant, from a Plutonic point of view, is the fact that the Old German usage of *Geld* meant 'sacrifice' and has the same source – *Vergeltung* – as 'revenge'; the main Plutonic themes are thus unmistakably linked by language.

Those historians who take a psychological perspective of history claim that the traditional Christian penchant for persecuting Jews stems not so much from the allegation that Jews 'killed Christ' but from the fact that Christians were forbidden to be money-lenders. Usury was exclusively a Jewish profession and thus attracted all the unconscious guilt-feelings associated with its symbolic association with excrement. The Jews became a convenient vehicle for the Christian community's 8th house projections, necessitating regular 'purges' which frequently entailed their wholesale eviction from towns and the seizure of Jewish property: the projection was thus reclaimed in a symbolic and highly profitable form. This connection between money, death and guilt even emerges in the rituals of the Aztecs, where it also incorporates cannibalism and human sacrifice: most definitely a full 8th house!

The Kingdom of the Sin

The Aztec zodiacal system contains two central cycles, one of 365 days and one of 260 days. Every fifty-two years these two cycles came together and these were marked by periods of intense sacrificial activity, carried out to ensure that the Sun would be successfully reborn to start another cosmic period.

Lloyd deMause, one of the founders of modern psycho-history, describes[3] how the Sun came to be identified with the collective guilt of the Aztec peoples – who also referred to their gold as 'the shit of the Gods', which is similar to the Babylonian description of *their* gold as 'the shit of Hell'.[4] Along with receiving the offerings of sacrificed prisoners, the Sun was also seen by the Aztecs as the recipient of the blood that every citizen was obliged to shed by regularly cutting their limbs or genitals to ensure a plentiful supply of Solar food. As the Aztec culture thrived and became richer and more successful, its guilt grew, and with it the need to feed the Sun, from which all bounty and life was believed to come.

Every fifty-two years the Sun was seen as so polluted with the blood of the people – in reality, according to deMause, their guilt-projections – that it had to be cleansed and born anew to start a further cycle. A special fire ceremony accompanied the death and rebirth of the Sun – a period when all *economic activity* within the land would cease. Once again the tie-in with the 8th house issues of money and guilt is unmistakable, allied here to a literal death through sacrifice.

The fire ceremony entailed a human sacrifice in which the victim's heart was ripped out and a fire kindled in the chest cavity, symbolically re-lighting the Sun in the heart of the people. From this fire, torches would carry the flame to all portions of the kingdom, heralding the start of a new Solar cycle. The fire was also seen as a cleansing of sins and guilt, and the creation of a new, though temporary innocence. The Plutonic theme comes back again and it is particularly interesting to recall here the observations of Stanislav Grof, quoted on page 120, with regard to the cleansing fire at the time of birth and the hallucinated encounters with the Aztec god Tlacoltentl, the devourer of filth.

As far as the 8th house is concerned, we are constantly reminded that there is a dark side to all our endeavours. Everything has a price in basic human terms and we delude ourselves if we think we can forever escape facing the inner, hidden component of that outer achievement we so proudly offer the world. That we may seek to *control* so much of our instinctual life points strongly to there also being an association of Saturn with the 8th house processes.

Saturn and the 8th House

Saturn was the traditional Lord of Death, both in the passing and in the carrying out of its sentence, drawing the boundary that marks the ultimate limits of our earthly life. This need to contain and control, to school our desires in the ways of the world, to apply the absorbed values of our society upon us and to embody the stern and the just in every aspect of our being, inevitably sets it upon a collision course with the 8th house. This duality of purpose may give us another image of *why* the 8th house processes are so frequently associated both with holding on *and* with letting go. Our 8th house 'issues' and problems emerge not so much from our experience of the natural course of Plutonic energy, but from its disturbance or its repression.

We have seen how Uranus plays a significant role here, functioning through denial and separation, through splitting off and 'castrating' our desires with an action that seems to parallel our separation from the primal Pluto energies we experienced at birth. Such energies as these are often too tough for Uranus, too vibrant and much too primitive; they get stripped from us, leaving Saturn to build its estate upon this early divide.

Saturn is possibly at its most negative when it tries to raise itself up on top of such a fracture, to institutionalize and maintain it. At such a time it becomes not a wall but a façade, built not to keep something *out*, but to keep it *in*. Saturn then imposes the demands and strictures of the world on top of what might be a primal trauma. In doing so it brings the values of the world to bear on something that pre-existed the condition of the world, giving worldly shape and form to the early wound, or hiding it from sight under a pattern of denial.

If we do actively involve Saturn in this way, by relegating to the 8th house all those feelings and impulses that Saturn dictates not to admit into consciousness, then we would need to explore the possible roles the relationship between these two particular instincts might play in the dynamics of the psyche.

They are a powerful combination, with tremendous creative potential. Saturn has the capacity to 'concretize' some of Pluto's emotional substance as well as to wall it from sight. In bringing together these two energies we are simultaneously joining together our capacity for emotional and physical endurance. The potential for dedicated work, ruthless self-denial, the will and ability to reach the furthest extremes of human experience and to break down all resistance are all inherent in this pair. So, too, is the darkest side of human nature; what is created with them can also perpetuate the blind, hidden reasons of the mind.

One creation myth of the Aztecs has a Mercury-like figure, Xolotl, stealing the dry bones of a former race of men from the realms of the underworld. In making good his escape the bones are shattered, thus losing the perfection endowed them by their previous owners. The gods revive the bones by spilling their own blood on them and create the Aztecs, now bound to perpetuate bloody sacrifice in memory of their own creation.

Another myth has Quetzalcoatl creating Man and Woman from figures of dust, into which he mixed sacrificial blood taken from his genitals. Again, Saturn and Pluto are brought together in a sacrifice, which is obviously linked with sexuality.

For the Aztecs, sex was inextricably intertwined with sin and guilt, and seen as an offence against the Gods. Priests frequently mutilated their own genitals, and only sacrifice could completely atone for the sins of the human condition, sins which were frequently depicted as being a form of excrement, linking again these two aspects of the Plutonic.

From the start the Aztec midwife greeted new-born infants with a dirge to their unworthiness, singing to them:

Perhaps he comes laden with evil; who knows the manner in which he comes laden with the evil burdens of his mother, his father? With what blotch, what filth, what evil of the mother, of the father, does the baby come laden?[5]

With a greeting like that the infant was being reminded that, all in all, life for an Aztec was going to be about as cheerful as Ebertin's description of the Saturn/Pluto midpoint! For this particular intersection Ebertin gives 'hard labour' and 'cruelty', though there is also the aspect of the dedicated researcher in this combination, as in Freud's 8th house Saturn.

Strong Saturn contacts with the 8th house and its rulers frequently suggest an especially strong linkage of sexuality with guilt, coupled with great inflexibility and a difficulty of 'letting go' in all its forms. The ruthless denial that Saturn and Pluto can combine to create can at times be turned outwards, resulting in overtly sadistic behaviour and the need to destroy continuously the external objects of inner projections, as if at some level trying to kill fear itself.

In many respects the huge stone pyramids that the Aztecs created, built block upon Saturnine block and culminating in the sacrificial slab, might be viewed in part as concretizations of their sexual guilt, in which death by sacrifice is seen both as an honour and the only escape from the primal sin of being human. There is a horrible irony that this culture was so emotionally similar to the Catholicism of the day, and was ultimately to fall victim to it under the heel of the *conquistadores*.

If there *is* a component of Saturn in the 8th house, as far as human experience is concerned, then it has to be faced and the fears that might congeal around it have to be brought out. Saturn's potential for denial of the instinctual inner life often results in powerful barriers being created during our formative years. When these are eventually broken through, the natural energy of the 8th house so often reverses our actions to show us their shadow side, revealing the underlying motives or our own unspoken thoughts. Freud's remark that the truth is merely a lie stood on its head is a classic 8th house observation; likewise his comment that fear conceals a hidden wish.

Coming Together

Behind astrology's carnival symbolism there lurk some hard realities which we are adroit at ignoring. We may have to recognize that many of the polarity conflicts which we observe within ourself and others are less to do with the inner expression of archetypal dualities than the outward expression of our own unresolved emotions. The possibility that we might be elevating the path of least resistance to the function of a deity may appear less uplifting than claiming an affinity with the infinite, but it is one that has to be confronted. The wealth of symbolism that astrology offers us as a path for self-understanding is not best utilized as the rationalized source of our ills. All the more so, as in the 8th house we have the natural catalyst for pursuing their exploration and resolution.

A major part of the 8th house function is to identify within us that which has been denied, split off or repressed. It constantly seeks to make us aware of our unrecognized drives and fuse together opposing forces. The well-publicized 8th house association with sexuality is a direct expression of this drive at work. In fact James Hillman associates bisexuality with this Dionysian drive towards total liberation: 'approximation to the hermaphrodite is a death experience, the movement into death proceeds through bisexuality. Death and bisexual consciousness are what Dionysus involves.'[6] Even if we are not completely happy with this blending of Pluto and Dionysus into one astrological motif, there can be little doubt that in confronting the sexual nature of our being we have also to recognize its bisexual component, and the part that it has played in our inner development.

Its association with power and manipulation, as we have seen, may well come about in part through an attempt to redress the imbalance of very early experiences; to liberate the energy still lying trapped and unrecognized in childhood.

Much of what takes place in the 8th house can be seen as an attempt to create circumstances whereby such hidden material can be brought to our attention, to be united with consciousness and made whole. The anecdotes of self-destruction often told about Scorpio energy probably arise from witnessing this phenomenon in action. Like the inhabitants of a city straddling a fault line but searching for a way to make earthquakes, there can be within the 8th house an obsessive need to dig away at its own foundations, continually testing their strength and validity. This is clearly not a rational process; the truths of the 8th house are not those of the intellect but those of *life*. Far from being formal and conservative, the 8th house is at heart emotional, primitive and full of un-reason. If it bears the persona of control it is because of its inner tumult, of a secret need to transmute its destiny by changing its past.

To this end the 8th house can almost be thought of as a circular process. It returns everything to itself until some form of trans-formation and rebirth releases us from this inner ritual. The *experience* of the 8th house is frequently that of returning again and again to those things within us which need liberation from our own controls. Much of what we experience as upheaval is the direct result of our resisting the natural outworking of what is essentially a healing process. In many respects the 8th house is the embodiment of the analytic paradigm. Through it we find that the one place we continually return to is the one from which we are trying to escape. If we do not recognize the implications of this, it often becomes a surreal nightmare, where the doorway out of the room we dread leads into the room itself.

For many this room is a frame of mind or a state of being that might only be brought on when it is finally recognized that there is a need to lose all that which must be lost, no matter what the cost to self or others. In this respect the 8th house can be a place where people go when they no longer believe the explanations, can no longer stomach the excuses, can no longer pretend that it isn't happening. It is a room where all that was held on to is now let go. A place filled with sloughed skin and sour sweat and the recognition that whatever cannot be carried out has to be left behind forever.

What finally survives this process is recognized as the emotional truth of the situation, the existential reality of what we are and who we are. It is here that the 8th house comes closest to the traditional image of the Phoenix arising anew out of its own destruction, or of the sacred Salamander surviving the fire unscathed. Again we meet the analytic paradigm. The experience itself is the catalyst of transformation, the wordless agent of change. Once all that was denied is assimilated and understood, there is no longer the need to protect the self against the projections of its own hidden desires, and a true fusion is reached. What is being suggested here is that the 8th house, with its attendant Scorpio and Pluto symbolism, has a *specific* psychic function which lies underneath any symbolic associations we may connect it to. It is a process we activate instinctively to compensate for the Uranian propensity for splitting-off and denying parts of ourselves. It could be in this way that Pluto has become often confusingly identified with both repression and release; closer examination of the actual sequence of trauma may reveal more complex dynamics, and subsequently a clearer lineage of events. The actual *content* or nature of the trauma may or may not be shown in the literal 8th house or through the relevant Pluto aspects; these could equally be to do with the nature of its *release*.

The anger/depressive reaction to denied libido, for instance, is often depicted by Mars/Saturn aspects, which might be elsewhere in the chart and at first glance seem to have no connections to any Plutonic themes that may exist as well. But we all have an 8th house and we all have a Pluto, however benignly lit by its compatriot planets. As an instinctual energy it will *always* function when it is appropriate for it to do so. We may have nothing in our birth chart that suggests we might kill someone for a loaf of bread. Two weeks without food might dramatically change that, and it is most unlikely that we would learn about such a potential by looking for the significators of food.

Those whose lives *are* dominated by the 8th house are often compelled by their own inner needs to uncover the primary secrets of their existence, however painful these might be and no matter what upheavals have to be endured in the process. For many this need for inner completeness is such that there can be no real security until this process is undertaken; it is too close to their emotional centre to ignore. If the 8th house becomes the house of extremes along the way then it is because, for some, no cost is too high to achieve this end.

While we become most aware of this process in action when there is some dramatic component to its expression, it would be wrong to suggest that upheavals and earthquakes are the inevitable fate for those with strong 8th house energies, or those undergoing transits of Pluto. For many, the Plutonic process is something which takes place in the solitude of their inner life. The change is that which comes from years of quiet experience rather than months of high drama. Nor is it necessarily deeply *unconscious*. Many are acutely aware of their need to transform and deepen their lives, choosing to take specific spiritual paths or externalizing this urge by embarking on a career which clearly embodies mechanisms for changing society.

This balance between what is conscious and unconscious within us is an acutely subtle one, with boundaries that seem to shift with our moods and awareness. This is never more true than with the residues of childhood; events and feelings that we might now instinctively claim are 'unconscious' were once brilliantly illuminated by experience and might have remained so for some time.

So much of what we claim we 'are' is really only that which we recognize or admit to, which may partly be dependent on what we can recall or remember. Can we really claim that we 'are' only what we can accept of ourselves, or is there the 'truth' of ourselves waiting to be discovered? In the final chapter we shall look again at one of the tasks an astrologer is so often asked to undertake: to describe this truth for others.

13.

Life, the Universe and Everything

* * * * * * * * * *

Whatever approaches or techniques we may use as astrologers, their effectiveness – or otherwise – is partly determined by the skill with which we are able to work with our clients. Much of our success or failure here will depend on how well we can see and hear what our clients are telling us, and how well we can convey to them what their charts appear to be confirming. To a very large extent this will depend on what our own needs are, and on what we actually believe is taking place within the consultation. Our unspoken assumptions about the nature of our work will hijack the session at every turn, no matter how straightforward the client's situation may appear to be.

A client might come to an astrologer with a relatively simple request. For example, he or she may require a date on which to launch a new business venture and ask that we select something auspicious. Assuming – and this is very rarely the case – that we are given a relatively free hand with regard to the time frame, we can go about our task in a reasonably methodical manner.

After having decided which astrological significators best fit the project's symbolism, we shall select a day when the relevant planets receive beneficial aspects. We shall check how these aspects relate to the client's own chart, and we may well have gone over their life with them to locate particularly successful periods to see what was happening astrologically at such times. If possible, we would try to incorporate such significators of past successes into the current venture, by noting their transits to the client's own chart on the day, as well as checking the other major up-coming transits and stations.

This may mean having to look at a number of possible days, and we may even decide to favour the client's own personal astrology over the actual inception map. This will depend a lot on how favourable the previous aspects have actually been and how many *other* people are to be involved in the day-to-day running of the new business. Our attitude to the inception map will vary depending on whether the client is the *sole* manager, or just one of many. At any rate, we shall employ a number of techniques and come down to a final day. We shall then look at this day in greater detail and select a specific time. It will be this date and time that we then suggest to our client.

At this level the way in which we offer our services as astrologers is fairly straightforward, and is much like that of an accountant or a lawyer – and might parallel an even older profession. Our client obviously shares our belief in the usefulness of astrology and asks us to 'act it out' on their behalf. Undertaking the task is a clear indication that we believe we have something to offer, and that it is bound up with the truth of astrology.

Even if we are not entirely happy with our chosen moment, we can comfort ourselves with the thought that it surely must be better than nothing. But even if we have truly cocked it up and given our client an Ascendant conjunct the Degree of Woe, a Void of Course Earth and a retrograde Part of Fortune, was this not Meant to Happen? After all, it just has, hasn't it? And isn't astrology the Ultimate Truth? Aren't we all Players in Some Greater Reality and shall we ever stop asking Rhetorical Questions?

Those familiar with Douglas Adams's *The Hitch-hiker's Guide to the Galaxy* will know that the answer to Life, the Universe and Everything is 42. This observation – provided by *Deep Thought*, a malfunctioning computer – is most unlikely to make much impression on those who daily tout in the marketplace their own claims to know Ultimate Reality, generally as a prelude to offering you a share in it for a small fee. Sometimes such groups unconsciously parody themselves, as in the case of one organization which uses as its slogan *Perceive Reality as it really is*. Presumably money is refunded should Reality ever be perceived as it really isn't.

The New Age deluges us with paperback Reality at every turn. Bookshops abound with True Purposes, Spiritual Meanings, Unshakeable Facts, Arcane Knowledge, Mystic Awarenesses, Karmic Destinies and Ultimate Truths of every shape, colour and size. In the racks and carousels of such literature we learn that Reality can be reached by thought or by non-thought, by singing and dancing or by sitting silent and still, by Tantric sex or by non-Tantric celibacy, by Being or by Not Being, by group discussion or by individual silence, by thought or by massage, by the application of unguents and oils or by meditation on colour, by drugs or by wholefood, by acceptance or by rejection, by belief in rationality or by submission to any number of religions, creeds, cults, gurus, masters, sages, mystics, enlightened ones, in this life or in past lives, on this planet or in some distant galaxy and – of course – by astrology.

The quest for reality and meaning in life would seem to be a basic human drive, and to some extent essential for our well-being. The fact that this need may propel us down some dubious or even ludicrous routes from time to time in no way diminishes its central importance. Such diversions, however, should serve to warn us of how our own desires can sidetrack us, sometimes with disastrous consequences. This is particularly true in the practice of astrology, as not only is the actual *role* of the astrologer fraught with social projections, but the very nature of astrology encourages a belief that we – as astrologers – know what is Really Going On. The possibility that one day it might at least point the way there only increases the dangers, and underlines our need to explore whatever 'truth' we are able to offer, and our own reasons for choosing to dispense it.

At the 1989 Astrological Association conference Babs Kirby presented an important paper on some of the issues faced by the counselling astrologer. Part of her paper was concerned with some practical aspects of counselling, which lie beyond the scope of this book, but she also identified some specific issues which need to be addressed by all astrologers. To quote from Kirby's paper:

Astrologers frequently state that they don't have all the answers. Why this need to state this if they're not also considering that perhaps they do? ... As astrologers doing counselling work with clients we are particularly prone to our clients thinking that we have this secret knowledge of them, and that they are there to elicit this [knowledge] from us ... that we have the magic answer to all their problems, and if we don't produce it, it's because we're withholding.

Babs Kirby continues by pointing out that this 'knowing/not knowing' dynamic frequently results in the astrologer/client relationship falling into one of a number of traps, in which both parties start to act out specific scenarios. These scenarios include the astrologer as Saviour and the client as some form of Victim, or the client testing out the truth of astrology by manoeuvring the astrologer into a Prophet/Charlatan role.

While the reasons that clients and astrologers can get themselves caught up in such complications are obviously as numerous as there are clients and astrologers, there is probably one overriding factor: the need in both parties for the astrologer to have an 'answer'. For the answer to be of any value, it must, of course, be True.

In other words – be they spoken or unspoken – there is the need and belief that the astrologer has the Truth, and ought to give it to the client. Behind *this* assumption lies the belief that there must actually be a Truth to give in the first place. But is this really so?

A Time for Truth

We saw in Chapter 4 that any claims to have objective knowledge of non-tangible 'truths' are always built on philosophically shaky ground, but as this issue emerges so often within the practice of astrology it is well worth exploring a little further.

The writer Roland Barthes described life as being like a *floating opera* in his novel of that title. In this book he gives us an image of a man sitting on the bank of a river – the river of time – while downstream floats a brightly-decked barge on which an opera is being performed; this performance is Life, and the man on the bank has to make sense of it.

The opera started way downstream; the man on the bank cannot have known the beginning of the plot, nor can he ever know how it will turn out, for the barge will have long floated out of sight and sound. He has to try and make sense of what he sees during the short time the performance is visible.

This is a poetic version of how Time is often described, as a linear process with Tomorrow at one end and Yesterday at the other. In the middle is Now, and events are seen as emerging from the future, becoming concrete in the present and then disappearing into the past, which is traditionally described as 'misty', as befits such a river environment.

It would seem that all attempts at portraying Time via such diagrams are to some extent doomed to failure. We can be fairly certain that whatever Time may turn out to be, it is most unlikely to be accurately portrayed in such a simplistic manner. What is more interesting about such sketches is what they reveal of the sketcher.

Linguistically orientated philosophers remind us that the very nature of having a language that includes *was*, *is*, and *will be* predisposes us to experience life in these stages. There are a number of tribal cultures which simply do not have such tenses, and their members experience life in quite a different way, making no distinction whatsoever between what is going on and what – from our linguistic point of view – has ceased to take place, has 'happened'. In such cultures the idea that a thing has stopped 'happening' just because a specific event is in some way no longer visible would be regarded as absurd. Events do not cease to be, but continue on seamlessly, in different forms; there is no 'past' for it to go to.

Simply to state that an event 'is' in the past – as we invariably do in all Western cultures – creates a fundamental contradiction in language. 'Is' can only refer to the present, it describes the nature of the present; only the present *is*. Some philosophers, such as McTaggart and his followers, have postulated a series of time referentials which concentrate on the relative sequence of events. They suggest that events can be described as coming before or after other events, without any tense-related words such as *was*, *is*, or *will be*, in an endeavour to get round this linguistic problem.

It is an area that is as much a minefield for all philosophers today as it was in Plato's time, when he tried to circumvent the whole thing by suggesting that behind this changing, time-dependent world of fleeting thoughts and flickering shadows lay a True Reality where all could be explained.

If we insist in portraying Time as a linear process, moving in a straight line from Tomorrow to Yesterday, on which events float like the barges of Barthes's novel, we are obviously implying that events are in some way pre-formed in the future. In other words, that they have actually 'happened' before they happen; for how else could they have come into being? Furthermore, this passive view of events suggests that their subsequent 'happening' in the present has nothing to do with the nature of the present itself, as the event in some way pre-dates the moment of its appearance in the 'now'.

This is the reverse of what astrology traditionally suggests takes place.

It is the contention of traditional astrology that events come into being which are the precise mirror of that which is going on in the *now*; the 'now' as measured by the Earth's relationship to the Solar System. The event cannot pre-date the 'now', because it is *defined* by the nature of 'now', and until the 'now' happens that nature cannot be defined. Every so often traditional astrology has to skip a beat, so to speak, by allowing events to be defined by eclipses which haven't quite yet taken place.

We have seen in the ideas put forward so far that we cannot really think of an event as just being an expression of the present planetary configuration, as if it has passively absorbed it. There is something of the event which pre-dates it; it is built on its own history and it resonates to the harmonics of its own past. If we try to place this approach in the context of our simple river diagram, we would have to see the barge as representing the result of an interactive relationship with the observers on the bank. The barge is not destined to 'be' any one thing; it constantly evolves and re-evolves according to its relationship with the cycles of the planets as they express their principles or instincts within the frame of time.

Thus we should perhaps cease to think that there is a fixed event, waiting to emerge when it reaches the present, and instead envision a constant blur of possibilities held within the matrix of the initiating moment. We might think of these possibilities as constantly responding to the modulation of their own initial symbolism. If this were to be the more correct picture, then we would be quite wrong in thinking that the barge is any one 'thing', or that there is a single outcome to anything.

In other words, we can never be sure what will actually emerge in the present, what the barge will be like when it passes us. In fact, it would be wrong to think of the barge 'passing' us at all, as if we were somehow static in time. It may be more accurate to think of us going through a period of interaction with whatever is taking place on board the barge, during which time all our responses may become part of the equation too. It is almost as if the watchers on the bank had suddenly been spirited aboard the barge, like metaphysical pirates, to take their part in the production. This would certainly parallel some of the ideas currently being expressed in modern physics, although it is not being presented here for this reason.

Adopting such an astrological paradigm to describe the nature of an event also offers philosophers insight into how Time might be more properly considered. If we were to accept that an event was in some way the property of the moment, in that the *moment* brings it into being no matter how much it may then reflect or reveal its own past, we would see that it is quite erroneous to even consider where an event 'was' before it happened, or what it gets up to later on.

As we saw in Chapter 4, when looking at how existentialism views the concept of Truth, we had to question whether there ever could be an objective, ultimate Truth, lying quite outside our experience and understanding. We saw that there are some basic contradictions in claiming an ability to assess the nature of a thing of which we are quite ignorant, and for which task Reason – if such a beast actually exists – seems quite inadequate. More importantly, we may also recognize that the boat and the shore and the river co-exist, and are quite inseparable. For the existentialist, Truth is similarly wedded to the nature of Being; it is the subjective experience of our existence in Time, not something apart from it, pre-formed and waiting to happen. Those events which participate in our experience shift and change *within* the matrix of time, not beyond it, and such truths as we encounter arise from this. Like the ancient Gods met on the highway, dressed in the guise of mortals, they may initiate the unexpected at any moment.

As we have seen, the most profound experiences can emerge as the modest tick of the Midheaven crosses the degree that is tense with meaning, a degree it has crossed countless times before; but *this time*, now, inexplicably, it is different. As in the case of the 'strange attractor' that pulls the grey conventions of mathematics into wild loops, like party streamers strewn over a sober gathering, an inner truth unravels from its own surroundings, dazzling us in sudden recognition of ourselves.

This awareness, emerging out of the nature of the experience itself, out of our Being, forces us to confront whether we can really think of there ever being an 'answer' to any of the intractable problems of life. The belief that there is such an answer, or truth, *before* the event – which is what so many clients wish to hear from us – not only makes the event existentially irrelevant, and thus the 'truth' quite pointless, it also represents a doomed attempt to remove the nature of truth from the only experience which could bring it into being – the experience of confronting the issue for which an answer is being sought.

In her conference paper Babs Kirby reminded us that it is very easy for astrologers to collude with their clients' anxieties about the future while inflating their own image of the detached guru. She comments: 'it could be argued that there is no true understanding that's devoid of experience . . . and we are in danger of losing our humility to life, and its joys and sufferings, by becoming over-detached'.

While it is perfectly understandable that someone experiencing a particularly heavy transit will want to know what is the most sensible thing to do to be free of it, this similarly misses the point, and the astrologer can unwittingly collude with this attitude by trying to 'help'.

Babs Kirby described the typical confusion that can accompany a Neptune transit, and how astrologers will often try to assist their clients 'out' of the transit instead of through it via appropriate routes. The message that is then being given in such circumstances can only serve to underline the client's own anxieties about their sensations (and perhaps also the astrologer's), as well as reinforcing the client's belief that something is 'wrong' with them, something that the astrologer is trying to 'cure'.

In recognizing that the truth of a situation lies within the experience of it, and that its importance lies in the choices that it will inevitably bring – the very choices that so many clients seek to place in the hands of their astrologer – it follows that we cannot talk about there being a 'right' choice prior to the situation being experienced. This idea of the 'right' choice is an obvious variant of the fallacy of there being an 'objective truth' that needs uncovering by the consultant. What we perceive as being 'right' can emerge only from our subjective sensation of the circumstances in which we are immersed. To some extent it is erroneous to think even then in the finite terminology of right and wrong.

While we would obviously wish to act in a manner appropriate to our situation, the core issue is one of *choice*, rather than correctness *per se*. This theme dominates the works of philosophical writers such as Sartre and de Beauvoir. For them, and for other existentialists, the key issue is that of our need to confront the nature of our life and accept responsibility for making our own choices. These decisions are often taken *without* any clear understanding of their ultimate outcome; in other words, of whether they are right or wrong. If we knew – absolutely – that only one direction was the correct path to take, then there would be no real choice; the path would then be obvious, and to take any other could only indicate perversity.

This attitude contrasts starkly with the assumption of much astrology that there is a 'true' path awaiting discovery, and that the astrologer is there to reveal it. Here, astrology is often used in a manner quite divorced from the life and experience of the individuals concerned, making them almost redundant within their own existence, as if they play no part in it whatsoever beyond being the passive recipients of their fate. To what extent this attitude exists to bolster the self-importance of the astrologer as the one to reveal this 'fate' is open to question.

Fated Attractions

Much of current astrology appears to rest on precisely those assumptions that we have been questioning. It is frequently used to explain the world as we assume it to be, or to back up our prejudices and beliefs, as archetypes have been used to confirm the superiority of a race or culture, or the inevitability of specific occurrences. Astrology is frequently used to support the creation-myths of analytical psychology or naïve New Age spirituality, most of which assumes that the Universe Provides in much the same manner as did the middle-class families from which its adherents first emerged, flexing their chargecards, as Aquarius dawned.

The assumption that something only happens if it is *meant* to happen is the ego's ultimate rationalization, and all can be subsumed to it. It is a breathtaking solipsism to assume that what is taking place in the heavens, or what exists within our birth chart, refers only to *us*, as if we are being singled out for special favour. Again and again we have to note that the major cycles of the planets seem to resonate with patterns in a shared or collective zodiac, and that key degrees triggered there pull us in and out of events in a manner which simply does not allow for individual meaning and discrimination.

The success or failure of ventures would seem so often to echo the rise or fall of their relevant cycles, or result from an individual's ability to harness the particular tide, rather than the expression of something that was 'meant to be' and was given the cosmic wink. Ironically, many would appear to prefer a cosmos which knowingly engineers Dachau, rather than consider the suggestion that *knowing* may not be there at all, that it may fall to us to provide whatever meaning there might be.

At an ordinary, human level we seem to connect to the past of all things. Issues arise out of that collective that may affect us profoundly, but over which we have no real control. We may lose our job, not because we have failed in any way at work, but because our company goes bankrupt. What is taking place in its nativity, or within the general ebb and flow of business cycles, effortlessly eclipses the activity in our own chart. As in the case of William (page 238), who lost everything in the Stock Market crash of 1987, the cosmos was in no way conspiring against *him*. Whichever way he may have chosen to speculate would have made no difference to the outcome of the market; the wave swept him away as it swept away a thousand others.

William could obviously have avoided his loss by never playing the market at all, but thousands of non-speculators have also lost their homes in the years which followed the crash, simply through being unable to pay mortgage rates that climbed as a result of the world's financial re-adjustments. Such events fall like a blind Fate on the guilty and the innocent alike, and there would appear to be no individual reason or meaning.

The general astrological response towards the possibility that an important event within the life of an individual may have no intrinsic meaning, in that it has not in any way arisen out of the life of that individual nor has any inherent significance, is one of *denial*. Desperate calls are made to past lives, to karma, to destiny or to the God that works in mysterious ways; anything to ward off the possibility that the universe may just be unwinding, and that we occasionally get in its way. Often these fantasies of errant destiny are imposed upon the client under the guise of counselling to explain how astrology 'works' and to reassure the *astrologer* that, contrary to what the client is actually saying, all is still well, all is unfolding as it should.

Paradoxically, one of the most pervasive methods of such denial would seem to be through using the concept of the unconscious. Somehow – perverse and mysterious as any ancient deity – our unconscious inveigles us into disaster with infinite cunning. Such patterns of unconscious behaviour that we may see within the framework of our relationships are often wildly inflated to blot out the encroaching cosmos, lest it appear indifferent to our secret endeavours. Observations which may be quite correct within the context of our own lives are applied to the workings of the universe, workings which we are now presumed to order and direct.

To put this into context we could use a true story which appeared in a national newspaper during the writing of this book, a story carried, no doubt, because it encapsulated so much of post-Thatcher England.

The story was of a woman who was dying from cervical cancer. She was a single parent living in a partially derelict council estate on the fringes of a decaying northern industrial town. The estate was run down and graffiti-ridden; it was virtually without amenities and its only industries were drug-dealing and prostitution.

The local Social Services had effectively abandoned the estate altogether, along with the lives of its inhabitants, owing to government restrictions on their funding. The woman's cervical cancer was beyond treatment because a test result had been lost, or mislaid, or mistaken or otherwise misrouted to limbo by a wholly underfunded, overstretched diagnostic service. Thus the woman sat and waited, and smoked her cigarette in a landscape of unremitting gloom.

Presumably her unconscious was somehow responsible for all of this.

Whatever natal aspects she may have had, if these, too, had not been mislaid, cut back or withheld, were no doubt 'challenging'. Perhaps her astrologer would help her confront why she had unconsciously got herself into this situation, why she had created the slump, cut her benefits, arranged for the Social Services to lose her medical diagnosis and given herself cancer. Like the Jews, the socialists and the homosexuals, who must also have colluded with the Third Reich's desire to exterminate them – how else could it have happened? – she had effortlessly ingratiated herself into the environment and waited for death while the tower blocks decayed around her; no doubt her fault too.

Here, a simplified version of the unconscious has become the core of a mystical philosophy, which one day may well be its true role, but in the hands of many astrologers, and no small number of psychologists, is frequently used with breathtaking arrogance and more than a hint of sadism.

The assumptions of 'cause' appended to this woman's story have all been made by astrologers and therapists over the years, in a wide variety of cases, and this attitude towards pathologizing human nature may well need to be questioned.

In assuming that a psycho-pathology – in other words, a sickness – lies at the root of all human experience we make two important claims: we imply that human nature is essentially diseased, and we suggest that there exists a science to cure it. We have seen that the major attempts of Freud, Jung and others to create a psychological science have failed in this respect, and that this failure was inevitable.

We may learn a lot about the periphery of our own experience from science, particularly such aspects of our behaviour as emerge in part from physical or chemical characteristics, but the essence of human nature, the act of 'being human', is utterly inaccessible to scientific endeavour. The nature of our Being can only be approached from philosophical and metaphilosophical directions.

The question here is: what *language* should such metaphilosophers use to conduct their investigations?

We have seen that it is within the nature of language itself to contribute to the situation it describes – out of the mystery of its own nature – and that it can *only* describe that which its words allow it to reveal.

Astrology offers to language a unique set of concepts; words which may describe not only the essential energy of things, but the manner in which they might link together. From a psychological perspective it is neither hierarchical nor reductive. Something is not dismissed or reduced by being seen as just 'symbolic' of something else; all contain the same shared essence, and all existents emerge from the nature of their own being, potentially true to it.

The language of astrology allows us a far greater flexibility to explore the nature of our lives and the way in which we confront the problems it may bring, and this language is perhaps not assisted by attempts to redefine in terms which have emerged from medical science. This does *not* mean, however, that we might feel free to completely ignore all the observations that the psycho-diagnostical approach has so far offered.

Psychoanalysis has given the world an invaluable technique for approaching the nature of the psyche and for exploring its symbols. The issue here is how they might best be interpreted by astrologers without imposing upon the client some rather suspect theories of 'cause' – psychological *and* astrological.

This issue is not whether our unrecognized and unresolved urges can impel us towards personal disaster in some area of life; this possibility is so well recorded that it is probably not really in doubt. Neither is it denied that illness, for example, may well be a manifestation of some underlying, unresolved conflict or a convenient excuse to avoid facing some of life's issues. Many clear examples of such a situation could be given, though the genetic component of innumerable diseases precludes simplistic theorizing. The question is directed more to the underlying assumption that such behaviour is somehow a cosmic principle, that this is how things always are, that this is the essential, explicable nature of our being.

We have seen that from the start concepts of archetypes have been used to reinforce social structures and prejudices, all of which have tended to benefit the world-view of those who proposed such ideas in the first place. We may want to question the claims that are made for their existence as objective realities.

Far from uncovering an underlying form expressing its purpose in the world, we may instead be witnessing the manner in which we explain and interpret experience to our own advantage. Archetypes may be no more than the way in which *we* choose to link together different aspects of the psyche, to create patterns which are recognizable to us precisely because they *are* recognizable to us. As we have seen in Chapter 4, phenomenologists have long suggested that we are in a continual process of *interpreting* the world around us, often investing it with values which we then claim are actually 'out there'. In reality we may be participating in a highly complex maze of social and psychic forces which are in a state of constant flux, and in which we constantly re-define and re-interpret the nature of our experience.

Alternative Realities

Where depth psychologists use the concept of the unconscious as the container for all that which we do not consciously recognize as a part of our own being, phenomenologists use the idea of the Other. These two words are *not* interchangeable, as they emerge from quite different disciplines and serve quite contrary purposes. We have seen how depth psychology assumes the existence of an unknown realm, called the unconscious, as a catch-all for the collection of psychic forces believed to underpin the personality, and also existing as a repository for memories, forgotten experiences and repressed desires. In searching the unconscious we may liberate our energies, integrate our personality and locate the source of our experience. The Other is very different.

For phenomenologists, the Other describes all that which is 'not I'. More importantly, the existence of the Other is an essential prerequisite for an understanding of what that 'I' might mean (or what the 'truth' may be). The Other plays an integral part in defining what each of us means by 'I' by offering us a constant vista of all that is 'not I'. As we saw with the example of Sartre in Chapter 4, we are thus in some part inevitably defined by the Other, and our individuality is demarcated as much by what we experience ourself to be as by what we believe ourself *not* to be. Sartre has even suggested that such concepts as 'nothingness' must inevitably exist so that a sense of *being* is possible at all.

The 'I/Other' axis is the polarity along which we constantly struggle to make sense of our own being in the world. This essentially Uranian process of clarifying and splitting experience to create that which is unique to ourself almost certainly underpins much of Melanie Klein's theories, which were touched on in the previous chapter. We also see how this basic phenomenological approach may throw light on Jung's constant preoccupation with dualities, as well as illuminating the polar oppositions built in to the signs of the zodiac. We may similarly see why the two-series of aspects (2, 4, 8, 16, etc.) constantly recur when things come into being and achieve their own identities.*

This constant definitional process, in which both I and Other are in a continual state of re-interpretation (as new information comes into awareness or familiar experiences are re-assessed) is, as we have previously seen, in marked contrast to the idea of timeless archetypes and pre-existing patterns. The occultist's 'as above, so below' may be more properly explored in terms of the interaction between what is defined as Self and what is experienced as not-Self, and the manner in which we choose to select and present our perceptions of that initial divide.

In choosing to say that what is 'above' controls what is 'below', for example, we must first select sets of corresponding character-istics for the two realms – and why are there always just *two* such domains? Having chosen them because they correspond that way *for us*, we then act as if this correspondence is somehow divorced from the very perceptions and value-judgements that have just distinguished them. Very often such connections are also invested with cosmic significance and are seen as defining the truth of a situation or its assumed underlying realities.

---

* It is almost axiomatic in phenomenology that consciousness is always conscious-ness of *something*. In whatever state we are, we are in some way engaged in 'reaching out' or being conscious of some specific feeling, object, sensation or mental process. It would seem that this form of continual engagement with 'some-thing' is integral to the experience of existing. Those wishing to explore these ideas further are referred to Ernesto Spinelli's *The Interpreted World*, Sage Publications, London, 1989.

This is a trap we may all easily fall into, and we see abundant evidence of such a process at work when we investigate prejudices about sex, race or nationality. In such examples a group is identified only by those characteristics we choose to perceive as being different from those characteristics we acknowledge as 'ours', and which are subsequently interpreted as expressing an underlying meaning – almost invariably a negative one (and one which the identifying group does not wish to own).

The suggestion that *all* which befalls us is what we want may also emerge from similar processes, and be equally self-serving. After all, why provide expensive hospitals to cure people if they really want to be ill in the first place; don't the poor just *choose* to have no money? Here an individual theology, generally revolving around how a conceptual process is believed to operate, is now decked out with cosmic authority and applied wholesale to the world.

It would be interesting to explore what the starving and the dispossessed of our planet have to say about the underlying dynamics of their poverty – and who they feel might benefit the most from maintaining such causal mythologies about it. They may well consider that consulting rooms set in privileged European suburbs are not necessarily the best points of departure for investigating such matters.

In our search for 'causes' we should be aware that those philosophers who adopt what is termed a 'structuralist' attitude towards language (and they would see *all* that can be discussed as coming under the heading of language) constantly return to what they perceive as the contradictory and opposing forces present within language itself, and claim that it is *these* forces which are reflected in social behaviour and attitudes.

Thus structuralists tend to confine their analysis to tensions inherent in the *present* of a situation (what we have referred to as the synchronic axis) and insist that an analysis of any situation can always be explained by its own internal dynamics, without reference to temporal externals – if, indeed, anything truly external to the present can be considered to exist at all. This is in stark contradiction to those who explore the present/past axis – the diachronous plane – and prefer the more conventional procedure of explaining the present in terms of what has happened in the past.

The ideas presented so far suggest that astrology is ideally placed to explore, both mathematically and symbolically, the twin axes of the synchronous and the diachronous, seeing them not as opposing or alternative frameworks, but as complementary, and inevitably so. The birth or event chart graphically depicts the synchronous axis of the 'now' of that moment, and can be interpreted within its own dynamics; it will have much to tell us.

We can then place this chart within the context of all that has gone before, comparing a child with its parents and grandparents, a town with its county, shire and country, a score of events with the individuals who participated in them. Here we explore in the diachronic axis the evolutionary process, not of a remote or archetypal Idea working through us, but of the Being in which we all participate interactively.

Astrology is a method of description and analysis with a uniquely objective component. It may be the ideal medium in which a true metaphysic of Being may evolve. Astrology is ideally suited to describing, both mathematically and symbolically, how we might experience or interpret what may be external (or Other) to ourselves, and how we might interact with that process.

It is precisely because of this great potential that astrologers should not continue to ignore either the language or the findings of this century's challenging philosophies. What they often reveal is something of the manner in which we make sense of our Being, and how we might confront our own nature.

Facing Ourselves

In working with clients, astrologers have to be constantly aware of their capacity to impose 'realities' on the lives of others – especially when it is so often done with the active approval of the client, who may actually attend the consultation with such a purpose in mind.

We have seen that the search for a 'truth' in such a way is probably doomed to failure, and astrology may well be at its most useful in attempting to explore the patterns that have played their part in bringing us to the point at which we are *now*, so that we may be better able to understand the processes of our lives. This, of course, may emerge for us as the 'truth' of our situation, and we will be fortunate if this is so. However, such an awareness would have emerged out of ourselves, and would not have been imposed upon us.

We might think of the manner in which we make such assessments, indeed, in which we make *all* interpretations of our world, as reflecting the unique planetary constellation that we hold within ourselves.

The dynamics of our chart disclose the nature of our being in the world, a being that Heidegger claims is itself 'primordially determined' by the nature of Time. Not in a fixed or finite sense, but as a point of departure, as a stance or orientation towards Being. It is the point from which we are capable of making infinite re-assessments of what we are, and the meaning of our participation and experience of life.

We may also recognize, as we re-evaluate the nature of our experiences, just how much previous certainties or self-assessments – our former 'truths', in other words – have been altered by the passage of time. Passionately held convictions may now seem quite unrealistic, particular memories may now be viewed in a totally different light; yet were we wrong at the time; indeed, are we really the same person?

The slow shift from child to adult blurs the world of childhood emotions, where everything was larger than life, and every issue immediate and overwhelming. We have built upon this, layer upon layer, changing our sensation of the world with the passage of time, slowly reclaiming the landscape of our early years, and we should be wary of pathologizing the intricacies of this process. It may also be unwise to assume that the adult, with unconscious connivance, can do everything that the child could not, or now to use denial to dispel any sense of adult insignificance; the universe still remains larger than us, its powers much greater.

Where once all our woes were due to evil eyes, magic rays and malefic bodies aligned against us – in other words, we were once all victims of *someone else* – we have now shifted our stance 180° and declared ourselves to be as Gods, the secret perpetrators of all unspoken intent, conspiring with the cosmos against our own stated purpose, manipulating its unseen landscape towards personal catastrophe.

You secretly *wanted* this, didn't you? Cancer, rape, abandonment, a spouse's death, a child hit by a truck; all your fault, your chart, your unconscious. We reel, sandbagged by appalling possibilities; guilt leaks in easily through childhood channels. We remember times when *yes*, we *had* once wanted this thing, and *yes*, we *did* once wish for that thing, and *yes* it happened, didn't it? Wasn't it always *our* fault that our parents argued, weren't *we* responsible for the shouts, the cries, the slammed doors? The darkness was always our doing and the echo of childhood omnipotence, that first denial of our paralysing helplessness, creates a need for *something* to be there, and makes it easy for us to admit to anything now.

Psychoanalysis has opened us to recognition of ourselves, with enormous benefits. It has also shown us our capacity for lies and deception, for engaging in a myriad evasions wrought out of inner confusion. We have seen disgust masking desire or love covered with a patina of hate. We have walked through landscapes we would not acknowledge to another, woken from dreams we would not reveal to ourselves. We have shuttled symptoms from mind to body and back again, we have emptied ourselves of recollections and rearranged our histories to impress the neighbours. Like apparatniks of the ego we have airbrushed out our unrecognized desires, blending them into anything acceptable, anything that was prepared to tell us that everything was still all right.

Aware of ourselves in this way, we may face the cosmos as petty criminals, and like most petty criminals assume that such is the state of all. If we do this, then we invest the cosmos with the metaphysics of an infantile conspiracy, one which places us at its centre and one which has the same desires, urges and motives that we may find within, and effortlessly colludes with us at every turn. Here we are in danger of behaving like Jung, of claiming that astrology is nothing more than our unconscious lifted to the stars so that we may see it better.

We would also be making the most elementary mistake of all, of believing that how *we* react is how the cosmos *is*, and finding within it only a knowing conspirator with our unrecognized desires.

Such a universe shifts easily into the embodiment of paternalism. It shares with the Freudian myth a strict but just father, continually dishing out rewards and punishments commensurate to our supposed spiritual requirements. Such-and-such happens to us because we 'need' to experience it; we have a Lesson to be Learned. Somewhere along the line we have blotted our cosmic copybook and now must set to our task again until all is to the teacher's satisfaction.

From such an approach we have created a simplistic fiction of assumed Realities; the 'real' reason that we have met so-and-so, the 'true' purpose for such-and-such, the 'cause' of this and the 'reason' for that. We have given ourselves the airs and graces of the Gods, to know their desires and purposes.

To an extent this is inevitable, we cannot help projecting some of the nature of our being on to the world around us, but we might also explore what need we have for the reality we claim to find there. The Kantian philosopher Ernst Cassirer describes this attitude towards 'reasons' in his *Philosophy of Symbolic Forms*:

A conspicuous trait of nature, a striking characteristic of a thing or a species is 'explained' as soon as it is linked with a unique event in the past, which discloses its mythical generation ... Here a stage has been reached at which man's thinking no longer contents itself with the mere giveness of things, customs and ordinances, with their simple existence and simple presence; it is not satisfied until it succeeds in somehow transposing this presence into the forms of the past. The past itself has no 'why'; it *is* the why of things. What distinguishes mythical time from historical time is that for mythical time there is an absolute past, which neither requires nor is susceptible of any further explanation. History dissolves being into the never-ending sequence of becoming, in which no point is singled out but every point becomes a *regression in infinitum*.[2]

We can recognize in astrology's expression Cassirer's description of *being* as a 'never-ending sequence of becoming'. In this profound phrase we see that the 'truth' of something, what it 'is', can only be temporarily knowable. If we somehow interrupt the process of its 'becoming' we probably know only what it *was* the moment before we intervened; again we hear an echo of contemporary physics, the *regression in infinitum* is also the recursive loop playing endlessly in silicon.

If, momentarily, we stop the process, we can say that what we see is caused by that which has previously occurred; we have the 'thing' and its cause. But what we see, that which we have disconnected from time for our inspection – as in a birth chart that is caught and frozen – would have become something else had we not halted its expression. Again and again we come back to recognizing that we cannot separate what we perceive as Truth from the nature of our Being; they are indivisible, existing without limit in the flow of time.

The flow is sequential and unidirectional, and it gives us the astrological axis with which we are most familiar. This is the diachronic axis – from present to past – on which we can plot a clear sequence of events. On this axis A follows B, and not the other way about. The ideas of planetary memories, of events becoming embedded within the zodiac, individually or collectively, all emerge naturally from this sense of linear time, where one thing may be layered upon the other as a succession of moments.

It may be that each such moment keys us into the primal zodiac, and connects us to the memories and possibilities held within the degrees that we have touched. It is as if a stone sent skipping across the lake remains forever bound to the ripples left in its wake. When a wave lifts the water and disturbs the spreading circles, so something shifts within the stone, an echo from the point of its departure, and in some small way its flight moves in sympathy with the patterns of its past.

These instants, when stone and water meet, can join us to those symbols that were brought to the same point by some act of life. Their memories and happenings flow out across the water, co-existing timelessly in the synchronic plane – the 'now' of each event – spreading out their possibilities like the ripples; neither one before the other, neither caused nor causing.

As the ripples meet and cross, so do their nodes link endless possibilities. Like the processes of thought and dreams, their symbols join and unravel beneath the surface of events. As we meet on their degree, so might we engage in their expression. If passively, then we may move with them as if along a line of fate, predictable and destined as they unfold themselves, unwittingly repeating their designs within the substance of our lives.

At each such point we may also make some new departure or addition. With each such act we shift and transmute our circumstances, impress some fresh possibility, some new design upon the nature of the moment, and the hidden message shared within it through the world.

In being *there*, with each moment, we may learn what truth it has for us, what truth it *is* of us. Within the language of each moment we may hear all things, for the desires and drives that have brought us to that point are as gifts from the ancient Gods; they spiral backwards through the light of stars, and link us all into the roots of time.

Appendix 1

A Brief Introduction to Midpoints

☆ ☆ ☆ ☆ ☆ ☆ ☆ ☆ ☆

The basic theory of midpoints, or planetary pictures as it is also referred to, was developed in Germany during the First World War by Alfred Witte and his followers. One of Witte's pupils, Reinhold Ebertin, went on to formalize the system which is used today by the majority of those interested in midpoint work. Ebertin's approach discards some of Witte's more complex ideas, and his use of hypothetical planets. Ebertin's findings are brought together in his master work, *The Combination of Stellar Influences*, known by the acronym COSI. This book is recommended to all those who intend to make a study of midpoints, and is also regularly consulted by astrologers practising quite different techniques, for the wealth of information it contains.

It may well be that in the future some of Witte's ingenious analysis of intricate planetary patterns will become incorporated again within the main body of the work; indeed, some of the 'mirror' examples given here in Chapter 11 would be recognized at once by Witte. For our purposes, however, we shall concentrate on the basic outline of midpoint theory and practice as developed by Reinhold Ebertin.

In working with midpoints astrologers focus on the simplest and most basic astrological relationships – those of the planets themselves. The planets are seen as holding the core energies of astrology, and the patterns they form one with the other are seen as central to an understanding of what may be taking place within the birth chart.

Midpoint users interpret the planets in exactly the same way as other astrologers, but they also consider the points in the chart that lie exactly *half-way* between each pair of planets. These points, known as *midpoints*, are seen as holding the combined energy of both planets, in exactly the same manner as if they were mini-conjunctions.

To non-midpoint users this idea may seem strange. For a start, it means that a point in space is designated as important, and is actually interpreted. However, we do this all the time. The Ascendant, the Midheaven, the Moon's Nodes, and of course the all-important Aries point itself, are all points in space; so are the signs and all the house cusps. They are all intersections or divisions of different circles; there is nothing actually 'there'. The midpoints of planets may be viewed in precisely the same manner, as a point in space where energies change or meet.

In the case of midpoints, the actual point half-way between two planets is seen as bringing together the qualities of the two planets involved. As with a conjunction, the aspect does not seem to have any specific quality of its own; it is described best by the nature of the two bodies which are actually coming together and fusing their combined meanings. Whether this meeting will be easy or difficult, tense or relaxed, depends almost entirely on *which* two planets are in contact.

For example, the Mars/Jupiter midpoint would hold an assertive, extrovert energy, full of fire and enthusiasm for life. The Moon/Venus midpoint, on the other hand, is far more reflective and sensitive. It speaks of a need for emotional harmony, and presents a picture of the need to acknowledge feelings, to allow space for the shifts and subtleties of inner life. All of us, of course, have both Mars/Jupiter and Moon/Venus midpoints in our charts, but how they will express themselves in the individual life depends extensively on what planet is actually *on* the midpoint in any specific case. It is here that we need to look at a diagram.

Figure A.1 shows the Moon and Saturn positions in a chart, and we see the Moon/Saturn midpoint lying between both bodies. If a *third* planet happened to be on the actual midpoint itself, we would say that it was 'on the midpoint' of Moon and Saturn and begin to interpret the three bodies together. Experience has taught us that a planet in *any hard aspect to the actual midpoint* can be regarded as being 'on the midpoint' of the planetary pair, just as powerfully as if it were lying on the actual, midway position. The hard aspects we would use are 0°, 45°, 90°, 135° and 180°, and all these possible positions are indicated in the diagram. In Figure A.1 we see that the Moon's Node is lying 135° from the Moon/Saturn midpoint and is thus interpreted as being 'on the midpoint'. This is written Node = Moon/Saturn or NN = MO/SA where '=' means 'on the midpoint of'. To interpret this we would first start with the Moon and Saturn, and see what their combined energies suggest.

The Moon and Saturn represent, among other things, two different kinds of rhythms at work within us. The Lunar function is related in part to our emotional responses, to images of the feminine, to issues of early caring and to our emotional well-being; it also regulates some of the

Figure A.1 The Moon/Saturn midpoint lies midway between the Moon and Saturn, and is activated by a body at *any* multiple of 45° to it. Here the Node is 135° to MO/SA and thus is described as being 'on the Moon/Saturn midpoint'.

fluid-related functions of the body. In this respect Saturn refers to rhythms which may become imposed on us from *without*; things which are learned and studied, habits which we may adopt out of duty or fear, or which reflect the needs of society. Put together, the Moon/Saturn midpoint is often a point of emotional self-control.

People with a 'strong Moon/Saturn' often have a reserved disposition, a well-developed sense of emotional duty, a need to serve others – often the public – and may experience considerable emotional inhibitions in earlier years. A planet actually *on* or in any 45° aspect to the Moon/Saturn midpoint will say a lot about how the combined energies may manifest in the individual case.

Mercury at that midpoint suggests someone who is mentally attuned to their sense of self-discipline; perhaps they actually encourage this aspect of themselves through study or by following a particular way of thinking. They could also have a natural ability to write about feelings, to control and shape them through language. A Jupiter there as well may impart the ability to philosophize about the nature of human emotion, to accept difficulties willingly and to recognize when things have to be left behind.

A Uranus on the Moon/Saturn midpoint, on the other hand, may appear in the chart of someone who is much more restless in the face of perceived emotional demands. Any emotional pull may be seen as restrictive and frightening; the individual may constantly be getting out of situations that threaten them, or demand from them a feeling-response, or some similar commitment. There could be considerable fear around the issue of separation, perhaps going back very early; consequently, separation tends to be a significant issue in life.

The Moon's Node on the Moon/Saturn midpoint, as in the diagram, may relate to an individual whose contacts and associations bring them into areas of life in which Moon/Saturn principles dominate. In fact, the example given is from the chart of a nurse. Here, the energies of Moon and Saturn refer to the nurse's need to keep personal feelings in check, to be a 'professional carer', to have a disciplined approach to the needs and patterns of the body; inevitably, issues of loss and separation will have to be faced routinely.

Not all our midpoints are activated by having a planet making an aspect to them in the way described. Many midpoints are unoccupied, but may be triggered by transits or progressions. Many people begin using midpoints when they realize that transits to such major midpoints as the Sun/Moon and Ascendant/Midheaven can correlate with profound changes in life, which are otherwise unexplained in terms of conventional transit lore. Similarly, the moment-by-moment transits of the Ascendant and Midheaven themselves can activate areas of chart to very profound effect, as we see from examples given here in Chapter 10.

In all cases the orbs used in midpoint work are very close: a maximum of 2° where the Sun, Moon, Ascendant and Midheaven are being considered, and 1.5° when looking at the planets and the node. In transit work, often an orb of 20 or 30 *minutes* is routinely used; rarely would one look beyond a degree.

One can start working with midpoints at a very simple level, just looking at one or two pairs which may have particular interest for us, or focusing on the main ones such as Sun/Moon and AS/MC (if the time of birth is accurate). When experience has been gained, we can work with all of them and also explore the way in which the actual *sequence* of midpoints around the chart may say something about the manner in which experiences come to us, and may also describe our own habitual responses to life.

In practice, midpoint users tend to concentrate on exploring the possibilities inherent in three-factor combinations (Neptune = Sun/Moon, etc.) and a very considerable amount of quite precise information can be obtained from viewing chart factors in this way. For instance, NE = SO/

MO is found in the charts of Mick Jagger, Jimi Hendrix, Jacques Cousteau, Henry Miller and Israel Regardie. While each has used it in his own way, it is a very obvious part of them and we lose something if we ignore it. In all cases we would suggest that it is the central factor, the planet which is on the midpoint of the other two (in this case, Neptune) which brings together or focuses the energy of that particular pair.

Looking to see what each one of the three factors might bring to a situation is integral to working with midpoints, though it is something virtually *all* astrologers already do. When we look at a planet by *sign*, by *house* and by *aspect* we are putting three different pictures or stories together, and trying to see what images emerge. Using midpoints in such a manner allows us to explore in considerable detail how the planets within us are continually interacting, what each might be bringing to the other and how each is contributing to the whole.

In looking at three-factor combinations, such as NE = SO/MO or NN = MO/SA, we would first treat each one as a separate picture or story and ask: *what might each have to say?* When we have examined the first pair of midpoints brought together by the central factor we will then move on to exploring the *second* pair brought together and so on, for planets typically bring together quite a few midpoint pairs, and each one has something to contribute to the overall story.

When we have explored what each has brought to our understanding of how the central planet might 'work' in an individual's life we can begin to get a far more comprehensive picture of how a particular planet is implicated in many different areas of an individual's life. We might observe how, in certain circumstances, Mars might be configured with Saturn only when Neptune issues are involved – if the three were brought together in the pattern NE = MA/SA, for example – yet there might be few Mars/Saturn issues in *other* areas of life. In all cases we are seeking to explore the intricacies of planetary dynamics, and how they might mirror our experiences.

A full description of these interpretative techniques, together with ways in which the sequences of experience and behaviour patterns might be explored, is to be found in *Working with Astrology* by Michael Harding and Charles Harvey, published by Arkana, 1990.

Appendix 2

Chart Data

✩ ✩ ✩ ✩ ✩ ✩ ✩ ✩ ✩

(Used or referred to in the text)

Adler, Alfred	7 February 1870	04:18 GMT	48 N 13	16 E 20
Autistic child 1	9 January 1962	11:23 GMT	21 N 19	157 W 52
Autistic child 2	1 July 1966	23:02 GMT	40 N 45	73 W 57
Bormann, Martin	17 June 1900	10:43 LMT	51 N 33	11 E 2
Brady, Ian	2 January 1938	00.40 GMT	55 N 51	4 W 16
Brando, Marlon	3 April 1924	05:00 GMT	41 N 17	96 W 1
Braun, Eva	5 February 1912	11:05 GMT	48 N 9	11 E 33
Cassirer, Ernst	28 July 1874	(birth time not known)		
Davidson, John	1 July 1971	01.00 GMT	55 N 37	2 W 52
Eichmann, Adolf	19 March 1906	08:00 GMT	51 N 10	7 E 4
Ellis, Havelock	2 February 1859	08:30 GMT	51 N 22	0 W 6
Fliess, Wilhelm	24 October 1858	(birth time not known)		
Francis, Clare	17 April 1946	11:45 GMT	51 N 24	0 W 19
Freud, Sigmund	6 May 1856	18:30 LMT	49 N 38	18 E 9
Freud dies	23 September 1939	02:00 GMT	51 N 32	0 W 10
Freud, Anna	3 December 1895	15:15 CET	48 N 12	16 E 23
Anna Freud dies	9 October 1982	(time not known)		
Freud's mother	18 August 1835	(birth time not known)		
Mother dies	12 September 1930	(time not known)		
Freud's father	18 December 1815	(birth time not known)		
Father dies	23 October 1896	(time not known)		
*Martha Bernays (wife)	26 July 1861	(time not known)		
Martha Bernays dies	2 November 1951	(time not known)		
Gibbons, Jennifer	11 April 1963	05:20 GMT	12 N 45	45 E 12
Grof, Stanislav	1 January 1931	05:50 GMT	50 N 05	14 E 25

* Note: Freud's wife was born on the same day of the year as Jung.

Hess, Rudolf	26 April 1894	08:00 GMT	31 N 12	29 E 54
Hindley, Myra	23 July 1942	00:45 GMT	53 N 31	2 W 16
Himmler, Heinrich	7 October 1900	14:30 GMT	48 N 8	11 E 35
Hitler, Adolf	20 April 1889	05:38 GMT	48 N 15	13 E 3
Hitler, suicide of	30 April 1945	14:30 CET	52 N 32	13 E 25
Hitler, July bomb	20 July 1944	11:42 CET	54 N 5	21 E 24
Hitler, Munich bomb	8 November 1939	21:20 CET	48 N 8	11 E 35
Hitler, attacks Poland	31 August 1939	11:40 CET	52 N 32	13 E 25
Hitler, attacks Russia	22 June 1941	14:15 CET	52 N 32	13 E 25
Hitler's mother	8 December 1860	(birth time not known)		
Mother dies	21 December 1907	(time not known)		
Hitler's father	7 June 1837	(birth time not known)		
Father dies	30 January 1903	(time not known)		
NAZI Party formed	20 February 1920	(time not known)		
Janet, Pierre	30 May 1859	(birth time not known)		
Jung, Carl	26 July 1875	19:30 LMT	47 N 36	9 E 19
Keller, Helen	27 June 1880	16:02 LMT	34 N 44	87 W 42
Lacan, Jacques	13 April 1901	14:20 CET	48 N 52	2 E 20
Leibniz, Gottfried	1 July 1646	18:12 LMT	51 N 19	12 E 20
May, Rollo	21 March 1909	07:20 GMT	40 N 46	83 W 49
Mesmer, Anton	23 May 1734	(birth time not known)		
Neptune, discovery of	23 September 1846	24:00 MET	52 N 32	13 E 25
Olivier, Laurence	22 May 1907	05:00 GMT	51 N 14	0 W 20
Perles, Fritz	8 July 1893	05:00 CET	52 N 30	13 E 25
Progoff, Ira	2 August 1921	14:00 GMT	40 N 45	73 W 57
Proust, Marcel	10 July 1871	23:30 LMT	48 N 50	2 E 20
Rolf, Ira	19 May 1896	16:30 GMT	40 N 45	73 W 57
Rank, Otto	22 April 1884	(birth time not known)		
Speer, Albert	19 March 1905	11:00 GMT	49 N 39	8 E 28
Stewart, Jackie	11 June 1939	13:50 GMT	55 N 34	5 W 12
Tausk, Victor	12 March 1879	(birth time not known)		

Use was also made of the Scottish data assembled by Paul Wright, see Appendix 3, and of data collected by Steve Eddy, quoted in Chapter 9.

Appendix 3

Addresses for Further Information

✫ ✫ ✫ ✫ ✫ ✫ ✫ ✫ ✫

The central address for information on every aspect of astrology is:

The Urania Trust
Centre for Astrological Studies
396 Caledonian Road, London NI IDN
(Tel: 071-700-0639)
(Fax: 071-700-6479)

The UT will send you on request a free copy of their latest annual *Calendar of Events and Directory* and updates. Please enclose a stamped and addressed envelope when writing for information, or two International Reply Coupons when writing from overseas.

The Centre has one of the most comprehensive collections of material on astrology anywhere in the world and can supply information about all the main schools and organizations in the UK and internationally.

This is also the central address for:

The Astrological Association of Great Britain and its **Book Service**. The AA is the outstanding international astrological organization and the main coordinating body in British astrology. Its membership is open to all levels of interest from students to professionals. Its bi-monthly *Journal* is considered to be one of the finest in the world and carries a regular section on midpoints and articles and studies which take account of the latest work and ideas in the field.

The Faculty of Astrological Studies, which is generally acknowledged to be the most outstanding teaching body in astrology anywhere in the world. Its patrons are Dr Baldur Ebertin, Dr Liz Greene, and Robert Hand. It runs regular courses and summer schools on midpoints and harmonics, and these methods form an integral part of their Diploma training programme.

The Centre can also supply you with the latest information on computer programs for harmonics, midpoints and ACG. There is a growing range of software available. The Astrological Association issues a regularly updated booklet with addresses and information about all the main suppliers both in the UK and overseas. A copy of the latest edition is obtainable directly from the address above. There is a small charge for this and other AA information leaflets.

The Association of Professional Astrologers. This is the professional body for Astrologers in the UK. For information about the requirements of membership, or for a list of consultants, contact the Secretary, 49 Nassau Road, Barnes, London SW13 9QG.

UK *Suppliers of Astrological Software*

Astrocalc, 67 Peascroft Road, Hemel Hempstead, Hertfordshire HP3 8ER (Tel: 0442-51809). Can supply a whole range of software for many systems, including research modules, graphic transits, astro-geography and for the generation of midpoint trees.

Electric Ephemeris, 396 Caledonian Road, London N1 1DN (Tel: 071-700-0666/0999, fax: 071-700-0666). Provides a constantly updated integrated program which includes a wide range of options, including midpoints and harmonics.

Matrix Software UK, contact Martin Davis, PO Box 9, Pitlochry, Perthshire PH9 0YD (Tel: 0796-3910). Their wide range of software includes Blue Star, which has comprehensive midpoint and harmonic features.

Roy Gillett Consultants, 32 Glynswood, Camberley, Surrey GU15 1HU (Tel: 0276-683898). Supplies Rob Hand's *Astrolabe* software for IBM and Macintosh machines, plus horary, electional and research software. Also available is Mark Pottenger's CCRS program, with extensive natal and research facilities.

Computer Services Offering Calculations

The UT Centre can supply an up-to-date listing. A few of the main international services are:

Astro-Computing Services, PO Box 34487, San Diego, California 92103-0802, USA (Tel: 619-297-9203). This is Neil Michelsen's pioneering service which is probably the finest of its kind. Write for a copy of their latest comprehensive catalogue. Within the USA use Freephone 1-800-826-1085.

Addresses for Further Information

Astro*Carto*Graphy, Box 959, El Cerrito, California 94530, USA (Tel: 415-232-2525). Jim Lewis's original service. His ACG maps come complete with a listing of Latitude crossings and a valuable interpretation booklet. He can also provide personal reports regarding specific areas in the world. For supplies of Lewis's *Mundane Source Book* contact Astro-Numeric Services below.

Astro-Dienst Zürich, Scheuchzerstrasse 19, CH-8033 Zürich, Switzerland (Tel: 010-41-1-361-6464). This is the most sophisticated European computer service and has a very comprehensive catalogue of services including some very beautiful Astro*Carto*Graphy options.

Astro-Numeric Services, 11163, San Pablo Avenue, PO Box 1020, El Cerrito, California 94530, USA (Tel: 415-232-5572). One of the oldest services, with a wide range of options including Astro*Carto*Graphy. Write or phone for catalogue. They are the agent for Jim Lewis's *Mundane Source Book* of ACGs for all ingresses and lunations. Issues are available from 1979 on. The following year is usually available from March of the preceding year.

Starwaves Chart Calculation Service. Chart calculations using Electric Ephemeris software, and interpretations using Robert Hand's *Astrolabe* programs. Catalogue from Starwaves, 89a Honor Oak Park, London SE23 3LB (Tel: 081-699-6732).

Publications

Polarity Newsletter. A regular publication covering all aspects of astrology, especially strong on techniques such as midpoints and harmonics. For further information contact the Editor, Archie Dunlop, c/o the Urania Trust at the address above.

Forthcoming Books on Midpoints and Cycles. Two books, *The Sun and Moon in Astrology* and *Astrology – Individual and Collective*, both by Charles Harvey, will be available from the publisher, Consider, 20 Paul Street, Frome, Somerset BA11 1DX from May 1992. The first is an in-depth study of the Sun/Moon midpoint in all its combinations, natal and transiting. The second explores the birth chart in relation to pre-natal planetary aspects.

References

* * * * * * * * *

1. Shrinking the World: Astrology and Psychotherapy

1. Henri Ellenburger, *The Discovery of the Unconscious*, Basic Books, New York, 1970, p. 57.
2. C. G. Jung, *The Collected Works*, ed. H. Read, M. Fordham, G. Adler and W. McGuire, Routledge & Kegan Paul, London, 1957, Vol. 7, para. 305f.
3. H. Eysenck and G. Wilson, *The Experimental Study of Freudian Theories*, Methuen, London, 1973.
4. Ernest Gellner, *The Psychoanalytic Movement*, Paladin, London, 1985.
5. Michael Fordham (ed.), *Analytical Psychology: A Modern Science*, Academic Press, London, 1973.
6. Rough Times Collective, *The Radical Therapist*, Pelican, London, 1974, p. 215.
7. R. D. Laing interviewed on *Didn't You Used to be R. D. Laing?*, video tape produced by Third Mind Productions, Vancouver, 1989.
8. See Ernst Kraft, *Modern Astrology*, Vol. XXVI, No. 11, 1929.
9. Hector Hoppins, *Spring*, 1950.

2. Time and Time Again: Re-thinking Synchronicity

1. C. G. Jung, *The Collected Works*, ed. H. Read, M. Fordham, G. Adler and W. McGuire, Routledge & Kegan Paul, London, 1957, Vol. 8, para. 962.
2. ibid., para. 960.
3. ibid., paras. 439–40.
4. ibid., para. 1187.
5. ibid.
6. ibid., para. 1186.

7. Marie-Louise von Franz, *The Voices of Time*, ed. J. T. Fraser, Allen Lane, London, 1968, p. 223.
8. Jung, *Collected Works*, Vol. 8, para. 961.
9. ibid., para 962.
10. ibid., Vol. 15, para. 82.
11. ibid., Vol. 8, para. 325.
12. ibid., Vol. 9, para. 7.
13. ibid., Vol. 15, para. 82.
14. ibid., Vol. 8, para. 927.
15. ibid., Vol. 13, para. 49.
16. ibid., Vol. 8, para. 988.
17. ibid., para. 993.
18. ibid.
19. ibid., para. 994.
20. ibid., para. 1174.
21. ibid., Vol. 18, para. 1198.
22. ibid., Vol. 8, para. 1186.
23. ibid., para. 995.
24. Peter Roberts, *Astrology – The New Vitalism*, Aquarius Books, London, 1989.
25. Jung, *Collected Works*, Vol. 8, para. 1180.
26. Ira Progoff, *Jung, Synchronicity and Human Destiny*, Delta, New York, 1973, p. 163.
27. See Nick Kollerstrom, *Astro-Chemistry*, Urania Trust, 1990.
28. *Psychological Perspectives*, Vol. 3, No. 2, 1972.
29. Astrological Association *Journal*, Vol. xxx, No. 5.

3. The Selective Unconscious: Archetype, Race and Illusion

1. C. G. Jung, *The Collected Works*, ed. H. Read, M. Fordham, G. Adler and W. McGuire, Routledge & Kegan Paul, London, 1957, Vol. 8, para. 339.
2. ibid., para. 277.
3. C. G. Jung, 'Mind and Earth', in *Contributions*, Routledge & Kegan Paul, London, 1928, p. 118.
4. Jung, *Collected Works*, Vol. 8, para. 273.
5. ibid., para. 280.
6. ibid., Vol. 9 (i), para. 15.
7. ibid., Vol. 8, para. 414.

8. ibid., Vol. 9 (i), paras. 89–465.
9. Michael Fordham (ed.), *Analytical Psychology – A Modern Science*, Academic Press, London, 1980.
10. Jolande Jacobi, *Complex, Archetype and Symbol*, Princeton University Press, n.d.
11. S. Freud, *The Standard Edition of the Complete Psychological Works of Sigmund Freud*, ed. J. Strachey, Hogarth Press, London, 1971, Vol. 23, pp. 99–100.
12. ibid., p. 98.
13. Ernst Jones, *Sigmund Freud*, Hogarth Press, London, 1957, Vol. 3, p. 334.
14. S. Freud, *New Introductory Lectures on Psychology*, Penguin, Harmondsworth, 1983, Vol. 2, p. 106.
15. Jung, *Collected Works*, Vol. 8, para. 738.
16. Freud, *Standard Edition*, Vol. 17, p. 97.
17. Jung, *Collected Works*, Vol. 10, paras. 353–4.
18. ibid., para. 19.
19. ibid.
20. ibid., Vol. 11, para. 770.
21. ibid., Vol. 10, para. 416.
22. Anneliese Aumuller, lecture delivered 17 February 1950, New York; published in *Spring*, 1950, p. 12.
23. Max Schur, *Freud: Living and Dying*, Hogarth Press, London, 1972, p. 446.
24. Jung, *Collected Works*, Vol. 10, paras. 966–7.
25. ibid., para. 962.
26. ibid., para. 97.
27. ibid., Vol. 18, para. 674.
28. Told to Jacques Lacan by Jung. Quoted in *Écrites – A Selection by Lacan*, Tavistock Press, London, 1977, p. 116.

4. Alternative Archetypes

1. Gottlob Frege, *The Foundations of Arithmetic*, Blackwell, Oxford, 1974.
2. Rupert Sheldrake, *The Presence of the Past*, Fontana, London, 1988.
3. Richard Tarnas, 'Uranus and Prometheus', Astrological Association *Journal*, Vol. XXXI, Nos. 4 and 5.

4. Julian Jaynes, *The Origins of Consciousness in the Breakdown of the Bicameral Mind*, Houghton Mifflin, Boston, 1982.

5. Medard Boss, *Psychoanalysis and Daseinsanalysis*, Basic Books, New York, 1963, p. 54.

6. Philip Mairet, introducing Jean-Paul Sartre's *Existentialism and Humanism*, Methuen, London, 1985, p. 14.

5. Interpreting the Unconscious: Astrology and the Primal Zodiac

1. *The Freud/Jung Letters*, ed. William McGuire, Hogarth Press/ RKP, London, 1974, p. 25.

2. C. G. Jung, *Memories, Dreams and Reflections*, Vintage Books, New York, 1963, pp. 208–9.

3. ibid., pp. 161–2.

4. C. G. Jung, *The Collected Works*, ed. H. Read, M. Fordham, G. Adler and W. McGuire, Routledge & Kegan Paul, London, 1957, Vol. 10, para. 491.

5. ibid., Vol. 5, para. 508.

6. For a full description of the number theories of Wilhelm Fliess, see Frank Sulloway, *Freud, Biologist of the Mind*, Fontana, London, 1980.

7. Reported by Freud's doctor, Max Schur, in his *Freud: Living and Dying*, Hogarth Press, London, 1972, p. 94.

8. *The Complete Letters of Sigmund Freud*, ed. J. Masson, Harvard Press, 1985.

6. The Cosmic Womb

1. Otto Rank, *The Trauma of Birth*, Harper & Row, New York, 1973, p. 117.

2. Stanislav Grof, *Realms of the Human Unconscious*, Souvenir Press, London, 1979, p. 98.

3. ibid., p. 151.

4. ibid., pp. 151–2.

5. ibid., p. 139.

6. *Observer*, 10 June 1989.

7. Grof, *Realms of the Human Unconscious*, p. 131.

8. S. Freud, *The Standard Edition of the Complete Psychological Works of Sigmund Freud*, ed. J. Strachey, Hogarth Press, London, 1971, Vol. 22, pp. 20 ff.

9. Michael Harding and Charles Harvey, *Working with Astrology*, Arkana, London, 1990.

7. Life Sentences: Symbol, Cycle and Language

1. Sigmund Freud, *The Psychopathology of Everyday Life*, Ernest Benn, London, 1954, Ch. 1.
2. Ernst Cassirer, *Language and Myth*, Dover, New York, 1953, p. 54.
3. Milton Sirota, *The Psychoanalysis of the Child*, XXIV, pp. 252 ff.
4. C. G. Jung, *The Collected Works*, ed. H. Read, M. Fordham, G. Adler and W. McGuire, Routledge & Kegan Paul, London, 1957, Vol. 2.
5. ibid., paras. 999 ff.
6. Paul Kugler, *The Alchemy of Discourse*, Bucknell University Press, London and New York, 1982, p. 23.
7. Theodore Thass-Thienemann, *The Interpretation of Language*, Jason Aronson, New York, 1973, Vol. I, p. 180.
8. Kugler, *Alchemy of Discourse*, p. 55.
9. ibid., p. 59.
10. Cassirer, *Language and Myth*, p. 11.
11. Thass-Thienemann, *Interpretation of Language*, Vol. II, p. 124.
12. Dubrov and Pushkin, *Parapsychology and Contemporary Science*, Consultants' Bureau, New York, 1982, p. 43.
13. ibid., pp. 49 ff.
14. Percy Seymour, *Astrology: The Evidence of Science*, Arkana, London, 1990.

8. The Quintessence of Creation: Sex, Language and the 5th Harmonic

1. See Michael Harding and Charles Harvey, *Working with Astrology*, Arkana, London, 1990.
2. Theodore Thass-Thienemann, *The Interpretation of Language*, Jason Aronson, New York, 1973, Vol. 2, p. 143.
3. The timed data researched from Scottish Birth Certificates is available from Astrocalc Ltd (see Appendix 3).
4. See David Hamblin's analysis of the harmonic charts of the twins in the Astrological Association *Journal*, Vol. XXIX, No. 4, 1987.

5. Marjorie Wallace, *The Silent Twins*, Penguin, Harmondsworth, 1987.
6. See Harding and Harvey, *Working with Astrology*, p. 162.
7. Alessandra Piontelli, *International Journal of Psycho-analysis*, 1987.
8. See Harding and Harvey, *Working with Astrology*, p. 222.

9. A Degree of Meaning: A Case Study of Saturn and Neptune

1. Paul Wright's Scottish data is available from Astrocalc Ltd (see Appendix 3).
2. Augusta Bonnard, *International Journal of Psycho-analysis*, Vol. xxv, 1954.
3. Lloyd deMause, 'Childhood Origins of Soviet and Eastern European Democratic Movements', *Journal of Psychohistory*, Vol. 17, No. 4.

10. Case Studies: Triggering Our Memories

1. Available from Astrocalc Ltd (see Appendix 3).
2. Austin Silber, *Journal of the American Psychoanalytic Association*, Vol. 37, 1989, pp. 337 ff.
3. John Addey, *Harmonics in Astrology*, Fowlers, London, 1976, p. 118.
4. Theodore Thass-Thienemann, *The Interpretation of Language*, Jason Aronson, New York, 1973, Vol. i, p. 278.

11. Case Studies: Patterns in Family Charts

1. Charles Harvey, 'Harmonic Charts', *Astrological Association Journal*, Vol. xx, Nos. 1 and 2.
2. All references to events in Hitler's life quoted here come from Milan Hauner, *Hitler: A Chronology of His Life and Times*, Macmillan, London, 1983.
3. See also Alice Miller, *For Your Own Good: The Roots of Violence in Child-rearing*, Virago, London, 1987.

12. The House of Ill-repute

1. Margaret Mead, *Sex and Temperament in Three Primitive Societies*, Mentor Books, New York, 1950, p. 73.

2. Eli Sagan, *Cannibalism*, Psychohistory Press, Harper & Row, New York, 1974, pp. 73 ff.
3. Lloyd deMause, *Reagan's America*, Creative Roots, New York, 1984.
4. Lloyd deMause, *Journal of Psychohistory*, Vol. 16, No. 2, p. 3.
5. Burr Cartwright Brundage, *The Fifth Sun: Aztec Gods, Aztec World*, University of Texas Press, 1979, p. 186.
6. James Hillman, *The Myth of Analysis*, Northwestern University Press, 1972, pp. 280–81.

13. Life, the Universe and Everything

1. Martin Heidegger, *Being and Time*, Blackwell, London, 1990, para. 19 ff.
2. Ernst Cassirer, *Language and Myth*, Dover, New York, 1953.

Index

✫ ✫ ✫ ✫ ✫ ✫ ✫ ✫ ✫

General Index

Adams, Douglas, 320
Addey, John, 3, 39, 61, 100 ff., 170, 191, 207, 250
Adler, Alfred, 55, 175
  Mars/Saturn in 10th harmonic chart of, 179
American Institute of Psychoanalysis, 12
American Journal of Psychiatry, 5
Anima, 10
Animus, 75
Archetype
  astrology and, 6, 84, 165
  Boss, Medard, and, 74 ff.
  chaos theory and, 64 ff.
  dreams and, 90 ff.
  failure of, 75 ff.
  Frege, Gottlob, and, 62
  Freud, Sigmund, and, 48 ff.
  harmonics and, 63
  hypertext and, 69
  Jolande Jacobi's definition of, 45
  Jung's definition of, 37, 42 ff., 44 ff., 45
  Lacan, Jacques, and, 182
  Greek gods and, 72
  meaning and, 37
  number and, 61 ff.
  philosophy and, 78 ff.
  Plato and, 42 ff., 60 ff., 72, 77 ff.
  Popper, Karl, and, 47
  process and, 63
  Progoff's definition of, 36
  Prometheus and, 72

  race and, 51 ff.
  Self and, 84
  Sheldrake, Rupert, and, 48, 67 ff.
  social attitudes and, 54, 59, 322
  Tarnas, Richard, and, 71 ff.
  types of, 43, 44, 45, 58
  unconscious and, 47
Astro*Carto*Graphy, 136, 138
Astrologers, charts of, 226 ff.
Autism, 189 ff.
Aztecs, 311 ff.

Barbault, Andre, 230
Barthes, Roland, 322
de Beauvoir, Simone, 327
Binswanger, Ludwig, 14
Bion, Wilfred, 178
Birth trauma, 115 ff.
  Grof, Stanislav, and, 115 ff.
  Rank, Otto, and, 114
Bonnard, Augusta, 231
Boole, George, 61
Boss, Medard, 74 ff.
Brady, Ian, 202 ff.
Brando, Marlon, 188
Breuer, Joseph
  Mars/Saturn in 10th harmonic chart of, 179

Cannibalism, 302 ff.
Cardinal/Fixed/Mutable sort, 241 ff.
Carter, Charles, 19, 224
Cassirer, Ernest, 146, 156, 339 ff.
Cave divers, charts of, 233

Challenger
  explosion of, 284
  ME/SA in charts of crew, 285 ff.
Character traits, research into,
  35
Chaos theory, 64, 109
Circumcision, 306
Complex symbols, 136 ff.
Cooper, David, 15
COSI, 342
CoEx, 115 ff.
Cycles, 95, 100, 162, 166, 328
  conjunction of Saturn/Neptune,
    210 ff.
  Jupiter/Saturn, 201

Daseinanalysis, 14
  Heidegger, Martin, and, 82
Davidson, John, 189
  charts of, 192
Death axis, 183
Degree areas, 200 ff.
  Mars distribution in, 224 ff.
  Saturn/Neptune conjunctions of,
    210 ff.
Diachrony, 41
  language and, 154, 156
  synchrony and, 340
Dionysus, 315
Dreams, 74 ff., 91 ff.

Ebertin, Reinhold, 20, 342
Eddy, Steve, vi
Ellenburger, Henri, 9
Ellis, Havelock, 178
Empiricism, theory of, 79 ff.
Esterson, Aaron, 15
Eysenck and Wilson, 12
Existentialism, 13, 85
  Boss, Medard and, 74
  May, Rollo, and, 185 ff.
  Plato and, 86
  psychology and, 18
  Sartre, Jean-Paul, and, 298 ff.

Feedback, *see* Loop
Fierz, Professor, 33
Fliess, Wilhelm, 96 ff.
Francis, Clare, 191
Franz, Marie-Louise von, 26
Frege, Gottlob, 62 ff.
Free association, 92, 126 ff.
French Institute of Psychoanalysis, 123
Freud, Anna, 271 ff.
Freud, Jakob, 177, 268
Freud, Sigmund
  America and, 57
  anti-Semitism and, 53
  archaic memory and, 49, 93 ff.
  astrology and, 68, 84, 96 ff.
  Bernays, Martha, and, 177
  books burned, 51
  claim for cure, 12, 14
  cycles and, 96, 162
  death and, 183
  description of unconscious, 6, 48,
    299
  dreams and, 89 ff., 229
  drekkological diaries of, 308
  8th house and, 314
  family charts of, 267 ff.
  Ferenczi, Sandor, and, 95
  5th harmonic chart of, 176
  Fliess, Wilhelm, and, 96 ff.
  free association and, 126 ff.
  history and, 51
  id., 50, 293
  instincts and, 98
  Jung, C. G., and, 89 ff.
  Klein, Melanie, and, 301
  Lacan, Jacques, and, 122, 177
  language and, 112, 127, 140, 143 ff.,
    147, 155
  libido, theory of, 98
  Mars/Neptune and, 145, 270
  Mars/Saturn and, 177 ff., 268 ff., 272
  Mercury/Saturn and,
    268 ff.
  money and, 308 ff.

Moses, identification with, 268
Moses and Monotheism, 50
  paternalism and, 338
  projection and, 299
  psychosexual theories of, 98, 307
  repression and, 144 ff.
  screen memories, theory of, 110
  Sun and, 97
  Sun/Chiron and, 271
  theory of evolution, 95
  Thoth myth and, 167
  Totem and Taboo, 50
  Wolf Man and, 177, 267 ff.

Gauquelin, Michel, 35 ff., 99
Gassner, Johann, 7, 8
Gibbons twins, 193 ff.
Gnostics, 181, 305
Goebbels, Joseph, 55
Goering, 52
Graphic emphemeris, 238 ff.
Greene, Graham, 237 ff.
Grof, Stanislav, 40, 105, 311
  and LSD, 100

Hamblin, David, 61, 176, 188, 193
Harmonics, 63 ff., 207
  sexuality and, 250
Harvey, Charles, 2, 3, 61, 170, 201, 346
Hermes, 167
Heidegger, Martin
  Other and, 83
  phenomenology and, 81
  Plato and, 82
  Time and, 337
Hill, Judith, 39
Hillman, James, 315
Hindley, Myra, 203 ff.
Hitler, Adolf, 201
  PL/NN aspects, 243
  phased midpoints in charts of, 275 ff.
Hitler, Alois, 274 ff.

Hoppins, Hector, 20
Hubers, the, 168
Humanistic psychology, 13
Hume, David, 80 ff.
Hypertext, 69 ff.

I Ching, 30
Id, 50, 293
Incest, 296 ff.
Instincts, 98
  and archetypes, 41, 42
  and astrology, 100

Jacobi, Jolande, 45, 47
Jaynes, Julian, 72
Joyce, James, 85
Jung, C. G.
  Africa and, 56
  Africans and, 55 ff.
  alchemy and, 14, 30
  anima and, 10
  astrology and, 23 ff., 27 ff., 31 ff., 40, 74, 338
  Boss, Medard, and, 74
  chance and, 33
  claim for cure, 12
  dreams and, 89 ff.
  dualities and, 297, 334
  Fierz, Professor, and, 33
  four functions of, 9 ff.
  Freud, Sigmund, and, 51, 89 ff.
  Germans and, 51 ff.
  I Ching and, 30
  Jews and 51 ff.
  Kugler, Paul, and, 149 ff.
  language and, 148 ff.
  libido and, 10
  Mars/Saturn and, 179
  meaning and, 25
  Memories, Dreams and Reflections, 89
  Mercury and, 31
  Nazi party and, 51 ff.
  Pauli, Wolfgang, and, 24

Jung – *contd*
  precession and, 29 ff.
  Ptolemy and, 33
  regression and, 94
  Rudyhar, Dane, and, 20
  7th harmonic chart of, 297
  Sun/Moon and, 267
  synchronicity and, 24 ff.

Kant, Immanuel, 79
  existentialism and, 80
  Hume, David, and, 79
  Leibniz, Gottfried, and, 79

Keller, Helen, 192, 194
Kingsley Hall, 15
Kirby, Babs, 321 ff., 326 ff.
Klein, Melanie, 301 ff.
Kollerstrom and Drummond, 38
Kolisko experiment, 38
Kugler, Paul, 149 ff., 151 ff., 155
Kraft, Ernst, 19

Laing, R. D., 15 ff., 289
Lacan, Jacques, 14, 112, 140, 143 ff.,
    146, 182
  5th harmonic chart of, 174 ff.
  natal chart of 173
Lamarck, Jean-Baptiste de, 51
Language, 123 ff., 127, 142 ff., 155
  astrology and, 136 ff., 153, 157, 161,
    321
  Aemenko and Nikolaiva's research
    into, 159 ff.
  Bible and, 179 ff., 182
  5th harmonic and, 170 ff.
  Freud, Sigmund, and, 112, 140,
    147
  Jung, C. G., and, 148 ff., 155
  Kugler, Paul, and, 149 ff., 151
  Lacan, Jacques, and, 112, 140, 143 ff.,
    146, 205
  Lévi-Strauss, Claude, and, 151
  Leibniz, Gottfried, and, 205

Mercury and, 128 ff.
  sexuality and, 179 ff., 204, 250
  Thass-Thienemann, Theodore, and,
    150 ff.
  time and, 232
  unconscious and, 125
  wave-forms and, 160
Leibniz, Gottfried, 79
  5th harmonic chart of, 205
Lévi-Strauss, Claude, 151
Libido, 98
Lockerbie, 136 ff.
Loop, *see* Feedback
LSD, experience of 115 ff.
  therapeutic use of 117 ff.

Maid of the Seas, 136 ff., 160
Manson, Charles, 286 ff.
Martin, Joyce, 40
deMause, Lloyd, 311 ff.
May, Rollo
  5th harmonic chart of, 185
McTaggart, J. E., 323 ff.
Meditation, with astrology, 37
Mercury, 128 ff.
Mesmer, Anton, 7, 8, 178
Metaphor, 154
Metonymy, 154
Miller, Alice, 276
Monads, theory of, 79
Morgan, Augustus de, 61

Nazi party
  charts of leaders, 278 ff.
  formed, 274
  Freud's theories and, 54
  Jung and, 51 ff.
  Mars/Saturn and, 277 ff.
  Third Reich and, 280
Neptune, discovery charts of,
    222 ff.
Number
  as Idea, 61
  as process, 63

Index

Olivier, Laurence, 188
Other, the, 298, 333 ff.

Pauli, Wolfgang, 24
Phenomenology, 333
  Heidegger, Martin, and, 81 ff.
  Plato and, 78
Philosophy
  Daseinanalysis and, 14
  humanistic psychology and, 13
  Laing, R. D., and, 16
  language and, 140
  therapy and, 18
Piontelli, Alessandra, 197
Plato, 42 ff., 48
  forms and, 60 ff., 64ff., 72, 77 ff.
  Kant, Immanuel, and, 80 ff.
  number and, 250
  Other and, 83
  phenomenology and, 82 ff.
  Self and 86 ff.
Popper, Karl, 47
Pottenger, Mark, 225
Primal zodiac, 107 ff., 164, 289
Progoff, Ira, 36
  5th harmonic chart of, 187 ff.
Prometheus, myth of, 72
Proust, Marcel, 183
Psychoanalysis
  research into, 12
  training in, 11
Psychological astrology, 19
  Anima and, 10
  Jungian interest in, 20
Psychosexual phases, 98

Quetzalcoatl, 313

Rank, Otto, 40
  and astrology, 114
  Mars/Saturn in 10th harmonic chart
    of, 179
Redheads, research into, 39
Recursion, 64, 164, 209
Rudyhar, Dane, 20

Sagan, Eli, 304
Sartre, Jean-Paul, 327, 333
Scorpio, 291 ff.
Screen memories, 110
Seymour, Percy, 160
Sheldrake, Rupert, 48, 61
  and morphogenetic fields, 67 ff.
Sidereal zodiac, 29
Silber, Dr Austin, 250
Sirota, Milton, 147
Spinelli, Ernesto, 334
Spring, 20
Stalin, Joseph, 232
Structuralism, 335
Sutcliffe, Peter, 287 ff.
Synchronicity
  astrology and, 29, 35 ff.
  causality and, 25, 32
  correspondences and, 34
  definitions of, 24 ff., 31, 36
  example of, 26
  failure of 35 ff., 37, 103
  Franz, Marie-Louise von, and, 26
  meaning and, 25 ff.
  Roberts, Professor, and, 35 ff.
  Progoff, Ira, and, 36 ff.
  synchrony and, 83, 88
  testing of, 25, 27 ff.
Synchrony, 38 ff., 41, 113
  diachrony and, 154, 340
  language and, 154, 156

Tarnas, Dr Richard, 71, 107
  research of, 72 ff.
Thass-Thienemann, Theodore, 150,
    171, 180
Time, 322
  astrology and, 108 ff.
  chaos theory and, 109
  language and, 323
  Plato and, 324
  McTaggart, J. E., and, 323 ff.
Thompson, Jacalyn, 39
Thoth, 167

Tiananmen Square, 244 ff.
Tlacoltentl, 120, 311

Unconscious
  Africans and, 55 ff.
  analysis of, 17
  archaic memories and, 49 ff.
  archetypes and, 47
  astrology and, 6, 27 ff., 111, 257,
    258 ff.
  complex symbols and, 92
  discovery of, 9
  ego analysis and, 122
  experience of, 16
  free association and, 92, 127
  Freud's definition of, 6
  Jews and, 51 ff.
  history and, 51
  Lacan, Jacques, and, 122, 125
  language and, 123 ff., 127, 140,
    143 ff., 147, 149 ff.
  latent content of, 93

Mercury and, 128 ff.
Midheaven and, 258 ff.
Neptune and, 129 ff.
Uranus and, 131 ff.
planets and, 134
Pluto and, 132 ff.
recursion and, 109
use of, 330 ff.
USS *Thresher*, 196, 200

Vico, Giambattista, 7, 85

Whitehead, A. E., 60
Weimar Republic, 102
Wittgenstein, Ludwig, 139
Witte, Alfred, 20
Wolf Man, 246 ff.
  chart of, 252
Wright, Paul, 227
Wemyss, Maurice, 224 ff.

Xolotl, 313

Index of Main Aspects

Sun/Moon, 166, 173, 174 ff., 179, 183,
    188, 190, 192, 223, 238
Sun/Mercury, 183, 255
Sun/Venus, 195
Sun/Mars, 195
Sun/Jupiter, 188, 195, 255
Sun/Chiron, 271
Sun/Neptune, 192
Sun/Pluto, 186, 194

Moon/Mercury, 183, 188, 188, 195
Moon/Venus, 202
Moon/Mars, 202
Moon/Jupiter, 186, 202
Moon/Saturn, 168, 189, 195
Moon/Uranus, 195
Moon/Neptune, 192, 195, 237
Moon/Pluto, 202, 238

Mercury/Venus, 195, 202
Mercury/Mars, 190, 203
Mercury/Jupiter, 255
Mercury/Saturn, 168, 191, 195, 244
Mercury/Chiron, 190
Mercury/Uranus, 132, 183, 191, 192,
    203
Mercury/Neptune, 132, 172
Mercury/Pluto, 132, 253
Mercury/Midheaven, 195, 202

Venus/Mars, 253
Venus/Jupiter, 175 ff., 189, 260
Venus/Saturn, 153, 195
Venus/Uranus, 188, 195
Venus/Neptune, 195, 251 ff.
Venus/Pluto, 186, 202
Venus/Midheaven, 202

Mars/Jupiter, 183, 202, 253, 275
Mars/Saturn, 175, 179, 192, 196 ff., 222, 237, 253, 277
Mars/Uranus, 186, 195, 237, 259
Mars/Neptune, 145, 202, 259
Mars/Pluto, 237
Mars/Node, 189
Mars/Midheaven, 242

Jupiter/Uranus, 202 ff., 242
Jupiter/Neptune, 188, 190, 258
Jupiter/Pluto, 244
Jupiter/Midheaven, 202

Saturn/Uranus, 195, 206, 229
Saturn/Neptune, 183, 187, 191, 195 ff., 203, 207–25, 237, 255
Saturn/Pluto, 202, 206, 251, 253, 260
Saturn/Ascendant, 200
Saturn/Midheaven, 173, 195, 243

Uranus/Neptune, 260
Uranus/Pluto, 173, 206

Pluto/Node, 243, 244
Pluto/Ascendant, 202

Ascendant/Midheaven, 240

Phased Midpoints
  Sun/Moon, 263
  Sun/Jupiter, 266
  Sun/Saturn, 267, 282
  Sun/Chiron, 271
  Sun/Uranus, 280, 281
  Mercury/Saturn, 285
  Mercury/Neptune, 270
  Mars/Saturn, 268, 269, 273, 278, 279
  Mars/Neptune, 272, 283
  Pluto/Node, 286

ARKANA – NEW-AGE BOOKS FOR MIND, BODY AND SPIRIT

A selection of titles

With over 200 titles currently in print, Arkana is the leading name in quality new-age books for mind, body and spirit. Arkana encompasses the spirituality of both East and West, ancient and new, in fiction and non-fiction. A vast range of interests is covered, including Psychology and Transformation, Health, Science and Mysticism, Women's Spirituality and Astrology.

If you would like a catalogue of Arkana books, please write to:

Arkana Marketing Department
Penguin Books Ltd
27 Wright's Lane
London W8 5TZ

ARKANA – NEW-AGE BOOKS FOR MIND, BODY AND SPIRIT

A selection of titles

The Child and the Serpent: Reflections on Popular Indian Symbols Jyoti Sahi

Within the religious structure of the Indian village, Jyoti Sahi discovered a contact with symbolism reaching beyond what is specifically Hindu. Using the central figures of Hindu popular religion, *The Child and the Serpent* demonstrates that the myths of folk culture are living . . . and have a power beyond the merely rational.

The Second Ring of Power Carlos Castaneda

Carlos Castaneda's journey into the world of sorcery has captivated millions. In this fifth book, he introduces the reader to doña Soledad, whose mission is to test Castaneda by a series of terrifying tricks. Thus Castaneda is initiated into experiences so intense, so profoundly disturbing, as to be an assault on reason and on every preconceived notion of life...

Dialogues with Scientists and Sages: The Search for Unity
Renée Weber

In their own words, contemporary scientists and mystics – from the Dalai Lama to Stephen Hawking – share with us their richly diverse views on space, time, matter, energy, life, consciousness, creation and our place in the scheme of things. Through the immediacy of verbatim dialogue, we encounter scientists who endorse mysticism, and those who oppose it; mystics who dismiss science, and those who embrace it.

Zen and the Art of Calligraphy
Omōri Sōgen and Terayama Katsujo

Exploring every element of the relationship between Zen thought and the artistic expression of calligraphy, two long-time practitioners of Zen, calligraphy and swordsmanship show how Zen training provides a proper balance of body and mind, enabling the calligrapher to write more profoundly, freed from distraction or hesitation.

ARKANA – NEW-AGE BOOKS FOR MIND, BODY AND SPIRIT

A selection of titles

A History of Magic Richard Cavendish

'Richard Cavendish can claim to have discovered the very spirit of magic' – *The Times Literary Supplement*. Magic has long enjoyed spiritual and cultural affiliations – Christ was regarded by many as a magician, and Mozart dabbled – as well as its share of darkness. Richard Cavendish traces this underground stream running through Western civilization.

One Arrow, One Life: Zen, Archery and Daily Life
Kenneth Kushner

When he first read Eugen Herrigel's classic *Zen in the Art of Archery* at college, Kenneth Kushner dismissed it as 'vague mysticism'; ten years later, he followed in Herrigel's footsteps along the 'Way of the Bow'. *One Arrow, One Life* provides a frank description of his training; while his struggles to overcome pain and develop spiritually, and the *koans* (or riddles) of his masters, illustrate vividly the central concepts of Zen.

City Shadows Arnold Mindell

'The shadow destroys cultures if it is not valued and its meaning not understood.' The city shadows are the repressed and unrealized aspects of us all, lived openly by the 'mentally ill'. In this compassionate book Arnold Mindell, founder of process-oriented psychology, presents the professionals of the crisis-ridden mental health industry with a new and exciting challenge.

In Search of the Miraculous: Fragments of an Unknown Teaching P. D. Ouspensky

Ouspensky's renowned, vivid and characteristically honest account of his work with Gurdjieff from 1915–18.

'Undoubtedly a *tour de force*. To put entirely new and very complex cosmology and psychology into fewer than 400 pages, and to do this with a simplicity and vividness that makes the book accessible to any educated reader, is in itself something of an achievement' – *The Times Literary Supplement*

ARKANA – NEW-AGE BOOKS FOR MIND, BODY AND SPIRIT

A selection of titles

Head Off Stress: Beyond the Bottom Line D. E. Harding

Learning to head off stress takes no time at all and is impossible to forget – all it requires is that we dare take a fresh look at ourselves. This infallible and revolutionary guide from the author of *On Having No Head* – whose work C. S. Lewis described as 'highest genius' – shows how.

Shadows in the Cave Graham Dunstan Martin

We can all recognize our friends in a crowd, so why can't we describe in words what makes a particular face unique? The answer, says Graham Dunstan Martin, is that our minds are not just computers: drawing constantly on a fund of tacit knowledge, we always *know* more than we can ever *say*. Consciousness, in fact, is at the very heart of the universe, and – like the earth itself – we are all aspects of a single universal mind.

The Magus of Strovolos: The Extraordinary World of a Spiritual Healer Kyriacos C. Markides

This vivid account introduces us to the rich and intricate world of Daskalos, the Magus of Strovolos – a true healer who draws upon a seemingly limitless mixture of esoteric teachings, psychology, reincarnation, demonology, cosmology and mysticism, from both East and West.

'This is a really marvellous book . . . one of the most extraordinary accounts of a "magical" personality since Ouspensky's account of Gurdjieff' – Colin Wilson

Meetings With Remarkable Men G. I. Gurdjieff

All that we know of the early life of Gurdjieff – one of the great spiritual masters of this century – is contained within these colourful and profound tales of adventure. The men who influenced his formative years had no claim to fame in the conventional sense; what made them remarkable was the consuming desire they all shared to understand the deepest mysteries of life.

ARKANA – NEW-AGE BOOKS FOR MIND, BODY AND SPIRIT

A selection of titles

Weavers of Wisdom: Women Mystics of the Twentieth Century Anne Bancroft

Throughout history women have sought answers to eternal questions about existence and beyond – yet most gurus, philosophers and religious leaders have been men. Through exploring the teachings of fifteen women mystics – each with her own approach to what she calls 'the truth that goes beyond the ordinary' – Anne Bancroft gives a rare, cohesive and fascinating insight into the diversity of female approaches to mysticism.

Dynamics of the Unconscious: Seminars in Psychological Astrology Volume II Liz Greene and Howard Sasportas

The authors of *The Development of the Personality* team up again to show how the dynamics of depth psychology interact with your birth chart. They shed new light on the psychology and astrology of aggression and depression – the darker elements of the adult personality that we must confront if we are to grow to find the wisdom within.

The Myth of Eternal Return: Cosmos and History Mircea Eliade

'A luminous, profound, and extremely stimulating work . . . Eliade's thesis is that ancient man envisaged events not as constituting a linear, progressive history, but simply as so many creative repetitions of primordial archetypes . . . This is an essay which everyone interested in the history of religion and in the mentality of ancient man will have to read. It is difficult to speak too highly of it' – Theodore H. Gaster in *Review of Religion*

The Second Krishnamurti Reader Edited by Mary Lutyens

In this reader bringing together two of Krishnamurti's most popular works, *The Only Revolution* and *The Urgency of Change*, the spiritual teacher who rebelled against religion points to a new order arising when we have ceased to be envious and vicious. Krishnamurti says, simply: 'When you are not, love is.' 'Seeing,' he declares, 'is the greatest of all skills.' In these pages, gently, he helps us to open our hearts and eyes.

ARKANA – NEW-AGE BOOKS FOR MIND, BODY AND SPIRIT

A selection of titles

A Course in Miracles: The Course, Workbook for Students and Manual for Teachers

Hailed as 'one of the most remarkable systems of spiritual truth available today', *A Course in Miracles* is a self-study course designed to shift our perceptions, heal our minds and change our behaviour, teaching us to experience miracles – 'natural expressions of love' – rather than problems generated by fear in our lives.

Sorcerers Jacob Needleman

'An extraordinarily absorbing tale' – John Cleese.

'A fascinating story that merges the pains of growing up with the intrigue of magic . . . constantly engrossing' – *San Francisco Chronicle*

Arthur and the Sovereignty of Britain: Goddess and Tradition in the Mabinogion Caitlín Matthews

Rich in legend and the primitive magic of the Celtic Otherworld, the stories of the *Mabinogion* heralded the first flowering of European literature and became the source of Arthurian legend. Caitlín Matthews illuminates these stories, shedding light on Sovereignty, the Goddess of the Land and the spiritual principle of the Feminine.

Shamanism: Archaic Techniques of Ecstasy Mircea Eliade

Throughout Siberia and Central Asia, religious life traditionally centres around the figure of the shaman: magician and medicine man, healer and miracle-doer, priest and poet.

'Has become the standard work on the subject and justifies its claim to be the first book to study the phenomenon over a wide field and in a properly religious context' – *The Times Literary Supplement*

ARKANA – NEW-AGE BOOKS FOR MIND, BODY AND SPIRIT

A selection of titles

The Ghost in the Machine Arthur Koestler

Koestler's classic work – which can be read alone or as the conclusion of his trilogy on the human mind – is concerned not with human creativity but with human pathology.

'He has seldom been as impressive, as scientifically far-ranging, as lively-minded or as alarming as on the present occasion' – John Raymond in the *Financial Times*

T'ai Chi Ch'uan and Meditation Da Liu

Today T'ai Chi Ch'uan is known primarily as a martial art – but it was originally developed as a complement to meditation. Both disciplines involve alignment of the self with the Tao, the ultimate reality of the universe. Da Liu shows how to combine T'ai Chi Ch'uan and meditation, balancing the physical and spiritual aspects to attain good health and harmony with the universe.

Return of the Goddess Edward C. Whitmont

Amidst social upheaval and the questioning of traditional gender roles, a new myth is arising: the myth of the ancient Goddess who once ruled earth and heaven before the advent of patriarchy and patriachal religion. Here one of the world's leading Jungian analysts argues that our society, long dominated by male concepts of power and aggression, is today experiencing a resurgence of the feminine.

The Strange Life of Ivan Osokin P. D. Ouspensky

If you had the chance to live your life again, what would you do with it? Ouspensky's novel, set in Moscow, on a country estate and in Paris, tells what happens to Ivan Ososkin when he is sent back twelve years to his stormy schooldays, early manhood and early loves. First published in 1947, the *Manchester Guardian* praised it as 'a brilliant fantasy . . . written to illustrate the theme that we do not live life but that life lives us'.

ARKANA – NEW-AGE BOOKS FOR MIND, BODY AND SPIRIT

A selection of titles

The Epic of the Kings Shah-Nama by Ferdowsi

This lucid prose translation of Persia's national epic preserves the descriptive beauty and dramatic tension of the tenth-century original. Ferdowsi's sweeping account of the history, myth and legend of the Iranian Empire from birth to fall is a classic narrative in the tradition of Virgil and Homer.

Therapeutic Touch Janet Macrae

A universal vital energy – known in India as *prana* – underlies all living organisms. In 'therapeutic touch' its flow is channelled into healing: obstructions are cleared, energy is replenished, and balance and harmony are restored to the diseased system. This comprehensive and practical guide shows how we can all take advantage of this powerful yet gentle method.

Muslim Saints and Mystics Farid Al-Din Attar
Episodes from the Tadhkirat al-Auliya' (Memorial of the Saints)

'Glory be to me!' So cried Abu Yazid al-Bestami, founder of the ecstatic or 'drunken' school of Sufism, while rapt in union with his God. Mysticism, as testified to in these selections from the one prose work by the great twelfth- and thirteenth-century Persian poet Farid Al-Din Attar, is not always a respecter of conventional piety or dogma. Here, deeds, parables and miracles evoke the riches of the interior Sufi world.

Inner Work in the Wounded and Creative David Roomy

A number of psychiatric patients, four architects on a spiritual journey to Greece, and a poet afraid of his poetry – these are some of the contrasting characters whose inner dramas are entered into by therapist David Roomy in this quest for sanity in an insane world.

ARKANA – NEW-AGE BOOKS FOR MIND, BODY AND SPIRIT

CONTEMPORARY ASTROLOGY – A NEW SERIES IN ARKANA

Series Editor: Howard Sasportas

The ancient science of astrology, founded on the correlation between celestial movements and terrestrial events, recognizes the universe as an indivisible whole in which all parts are interconnected. Mirroring this perception of the unity of life, modern physics has revealed the web of relationship underlying everything in existence. Despite the inevitable backlash as old paradigms expire, we are now entering an age where scientific explanations and models of the cosmos are in accord with basic astrological principles and beliefs. In such a climate, astrology is poised to once again emerge as a serious tool for a greater understanding of our true nature. In readable books written by experts, Arkana's *Contemporary Astrology* series offers all the insight and practical wisdom of the newest vanguard of astrological thought.

Titles already published or in preparation

The Gods of Change: Pain, Crisis and the Transits of Uranus, Neptune and Pluto Howard Sasportas

A Handbook of Medical Astrology Jane Ridder-Patrick

Character and Fate: The Psychology of the Birthchart Katharine Merlin

Chiron and the Healing Journey: An Astrological and Psychological Perspective Melanie Reinhart

Working With Astrology Michael Harding and Charles Harvey

Saturn: A New Look at an Old Devil Liz Greene

The Karmic Journey Judy Hall

Saturn In Transit Erin Sullivan